WAR

ROAD TO THE BREAKING
BOOK 8

CHRIS BENNETT

War

Copyright © Christopher A. Bennett – 2023

ISBN: 978-1-955100-07-6 (Trade Paperback)
ISBN: 978-1-955100-08-3 (eBook)

Names: Bennett, Chris (Chris Arthur), 1959- author.
Title: War / Chris Bennett.
Description: [Spokane, Washington] : [CPB Publishing, LLC], [2023] |
Series: Road to the breaking ; book 8
Identifiers: ISBN: 978-1-955100-07-6 (trade paperback) | 978-1-955100-
08-3 (ebook)
Subjects: LCSH: United States. Army--Officers--History--19th century--Fiction. |
United States-- History--Civil War, 1861-1865--Fiction. | Confederate States of
America. Army--Fiction. | Women spies--Southern States--Fiction. | Freed
persons--United States--History--19th century--Fiction. | Gettysburg, Battle of,
Gettysburg, Pa., 1863--Fiction. | LCGFT: Historical fiction. | BISAC: FICTION /
Historical / Civil War Era. | FICTION / Sagas.
Classification: LCC: PS3602.E66446 W37 2023 | DDC: 813/.6--dc23

To sign up for a
no-spam newsletter
about
Road to the Breaking
and
exclusive free bonus material
visit my website:

http://www.ChrisABennett.com

War [wôr] noun:

1. A conflict carried on by force of arms, as between nations or between parties within a nation.

2. A state or period of armed hostility or active military operations.

3. Techniques and procedures of war; military science.

DEDICATION

To
Ericka McIntyre,
my most excellent editor,
who has been instrumental
in taking my books
from good to great.

And since this one is "your" book,
please ...
just go easy on me this time, Ericka!

*(**Authors note:** She didn't ...)*

Contents

Chapter 1. Under Attack 1

Chapter 2. Counterespionage 26

Chapter 3. A Hard Nut.. 43

Chapter 4. Beset and Besieged 75

Chapter 5. Cut Off 95

Chapter 6. The Road Less Traveled 130

Chapter 7. Many Paths and Errands...163

Chapter 8. The Hunt for Lee 196

Chapter 9. Gettysburg 217

Chapter 10. Race to the River..256

Chapter 11. Caught in the Act..278

Chapter 12. The Fight for Freedom..290

Chapter 13. Confederate Inferno 312

Chapter 14. Digging Out of Hell..358

Chapter 15. Dread of Disaster 403

Chapter 16. Death's Feast..418

Chapter 17. Reckoning 446

War – Facts vs. Fiction...465

Inaugural Address – First Governor of West Virginia.........473

Snowbound 478

Acknowledgments...479

Recommended Reading 479

Get Exclusive Free Content 480

"Easy for men to second guess the general in hindsight after the battle is lost. But they weren't there, forced to make the hard life-or-death choices in the heat of the moment, without the advantage of knowing the final outcome."

– Nathaniel Chambers

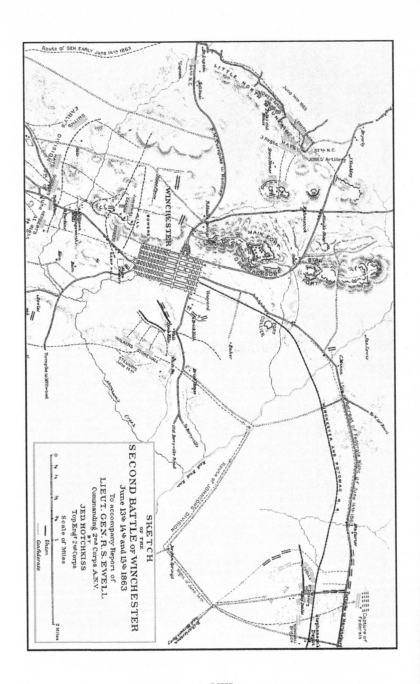

SKETCH
OF THE
SECOND BATTLE OF WINCHESTER
June 13th 14th and 15th 1863
To accompany Report of
LIEUT. GEN. R.S. EWELL.
Commanding 2nd Corps A.N.V.
BY
JED HOTCHKISS
Top Eng.r 2nd Corps
Scale of Miles

Union
Confederate

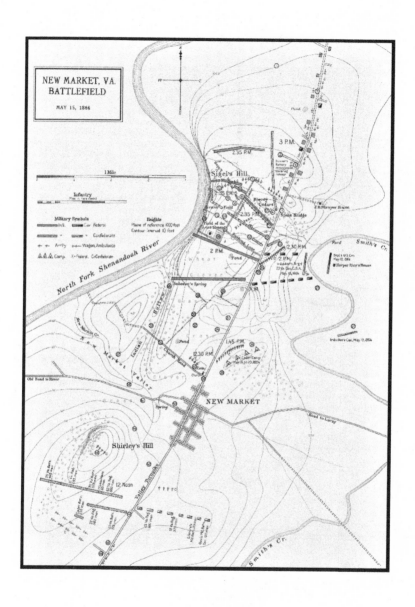

NEW MARKET, VA.
BATTLEFIELD

MAY 15, 1864

Chapter I. Under Attack

"There is not an enemy within forty miles of us,
as reported by our cavalry scouts ..."
- Sergeant Milton Campbell
12th West Virginia Regiment

Monday May 18, 1863 – Sherwood, Missouri:

Sergeant Ned Turner, First Kansas Colored Regiment, removed his blue Union kepi-style uniform cap to wipe the sweat from his forehead, before turning back toward the barn.

"Hey, Gib, how much more corn y'all got up there?" he shouted at the open hatch to the hayloft.

A moment later, another black man in a blue Union uniform, with a private's single stripe adorning his sleeve, gazed out at Ned. "Well, sir ... they's another goodly pile of it ... I'd say we's 'bout halfway done, Sarge," Private George Gibson answered, tossing another armload of fresh corn onto the growing pile of cobs in the wagon waiting below. The bed was beginning to fill up, and Ned was wondering how they'd fit the rest of the corn in. Other units were spread out around the farm, also filling wagons with the recently harvested bounty.

"All right ... just keep at it," Ned answered. "Ain't got all day," he added, knowing it was entirely unnecessary, and just his anxiety talking. He returned his attention to the road that led east toward the small village of Sherwood less than a mile off. His company had ridden in from the Union fort at Baxter Springs, Kansas, some seventeen miles in the other direction, off to the west. He knew they were now firmly in rebel bushwhacker country—though they'd seen no sign of them so far—so he continued to keep a keen watch.

Lieutenant Harris, their company commanding officer—a young man of hardly more than twenty years and a decent enough fellow for a white man, to Ned's thinking—had a half-dozen mounted scouts out patrolling the neighborhood. But Ned

1

liked to do his own watching and not count on someone else when his neck was at stake. Also, he'd had more than his fill of Missouri rebel bushwhackers and knew exactly what they were capable of … and it was always nothing good.

Ned figured they were pushing their luck with this raid, just to gather some supplies and to punish the locals for supporting the rebels—the very reason they'd picked this particular farm. Its owner, one Andrew Rader, was reportedly away fighting with the Confederate Army—at least that's what they were told by a local who claimed to be pro-Union. And though Rader was not at home, his wife and young daughter were. But they had fled the house and headed for town when the Union soldiers arrived.

Ned had wanted to call off the raid for fear Mrs. Rader would sound the alarm and summon the locals for a fight. But once someone noticed the freshly harvested corn, the lieutenant ordered them to load it into wagons and take it away with them. Others searched the farmhouse for other foodstuffs, weapons, or ammunition.

Ned looked back up toward the hayloft and saw another black soldier, Private Bell, lean out and dump another armload of corn into the wagon. But as Bell was brushing off his hands, he suddenly clutched at his chest with a pained look across his face. A red stain spread from under Bell's hand before he pitched forward into the wagon. In the same instant, Ned heard the distant report of a rifle.

Before he'd even turned to face the noise, Ned's revolver was clear of its holster. He crouched to the ground on one knee, pulled back the hammer, and squeezed off a shot. He'd aimed at a rising puff of smoke, drifting up from a hedgerow fifty or sixty yards off toward the town, but he assumed he'd not hit anything from that distance. "To arms! We's under attack!" he shouted. "Prepare to return fire!"

Then he reached over and grabbed his own rifle from where it rested against the wagon, already loaded. More rifle shots rang out and impacted against the wagon and the barn behind it. Ned immediately returned fire, then began reloading his rifle. He heard and felt several hard jolts, like heavy objects falling into the wagon. He glanced up and realized it was the privates who'd been up in the hay loft. They'd jumped down into the pile of corn in the wagon, and now were scrambling off to retrieve their rifles from where they'd been stacked just outside the barn door, all the while dodging incoming rifle rounds that kicked up turf and ripped through the barn walls in a flurry of splinters.

After another minute, three privates, rifles now in hand, plopped down next to Ned, where he lay prone on the ground. They began returning fire, even as the enemy could be seen moving closer toward a new hedgerow only thirty or so yards away.

Ned looked across the farmyard to another outbuilding and saw a dozen black Union soldiers, with Ned's old friend and fellow sergeant Caleb in the lead, streaming out into the yard, rifles at the ready. They took shelter behind a split rail fence and began firing on the rebels.

Then Ned looked over toward the farmhouse, where another dozen or so soldiers had been sent, and he groaned: their rifles could be plainly seen, neatly stacked out in the yard, leaving them completely exposed to the rebel gun fire. He saw one soldier peek out the front door of the house but immediately duck back inside as bullets peppered the doorway.

"Damn it!" Ned cursed even as six more of his men came scrambling up from where they'd been rummaging inside the lower level of the barn. "We need to cover for them that's stuck in the house. Fix bayonets, and prepare to charge."

The men gave him concerned looks, but obeyed. When all were ready, Ned looked over toward Caleb, still crouched behind the split rail fence, and caught his eye. Ned mimed his attack, signaling that Caleb and his men would provide covering fire. Caleb nodded his understanding.

"All right men … let's move," Ned called, jumping up obeying his own order. He charged straight at the rebel position with a shout, firing off a few rounds from his pistol before holstering it, and thrusting forward with his bayonet. His men followed, incoming rounds impacting around them. One man fell, but they reached the waist-high hedgerow that sheltered the rebels and

3

crashed through. Twenty or so rebels had been firing from behind the hedge, but now all was in chaos as the determined and desperate black Union soldiers were in their midst, stabbing with bayonets, firing off rifles, and clubbing with buttstocks. The rebels who survived this initial furious onslaught scrambled away in a panic.

But Ned's small victory was short lived, as more rebels could be seen streaming up from the town—dozens, all armed with rifles or pistols. Ned's men were now taking incoming fire from these new adversaries, so they took shelter in a shallow ditch, reloading and returning fire the best they could. Ned realized they were once again in a dire, untenable position, and called for his men to fall back. But even as they scrambled back toward the barn, more rebels surged forward and cut them off, so once again Ned and his men were reduced to hand-to-hand, tooth-and-nail fighting.

And then suddenly, Lieutenant Harris, mounted on his horse, was amongst them, shouting and slashing at the rebels with his saber. Two other mounted Union scouts accompanied him—one a white man and the other black—and these men emptied their revolvers into the enemy, driving them off.

"Come, Sergeant ... we are badly outmanned and beset!" the lieutenant shouted. "We must withdraw before we are entirely surrounded!"

They were now completely cut off from the farmhouse by the rebels pouring in, who were now taking up positions beside the barn where Ned and company had been unloading corn. The Union soldiers were forced to retreat back along the road toward the west. But Ned was gratified to see that their covering attack had not been in vain; he could no longer see any stacked rifles out on the lawn, and gunfire was now belching forth from the farmhouse windows, both on the lower and upper levels.

Ned's men met up with Caleb's and another company, and together they moved down the road at a fast trot, Lieutenant Harris and his scouts riding behind, covering their backs with their revolvers. They'd marched only a half mile or so when the lieutenant ordered a halt and had them form up in line of battle behind a dip in the road.

He was now down off his horse, leading it over to confer with Ned and Caleb. "Sergeants ... we left men back in the farmhouse. I'm of a mind to counterattack and drive off the enemy that we might rescue them. Thoughts?"

Caleb immediately agreed, and Ned was gratified to see that his old friend, who'd always been the least aggressive of the freemen fighters, now had a fierce determined fire in his eye and was ready to strike back hard at the enemy.

But Ned reluctantly disagreed, shaking his head sadly, "Can't do it, sir, bad as I want to. While we was movin', I counted somewheres 'round a hundred rebels, and more comin' in by the minute. By now they'll be thick as fleas on a hound. And also ... while we was hunkered down in the ditch, I seen one of the rebs was wearin' an officer's uniform—a major, I think."

"Oh! Well, yes, that *does* make a difference. It means they're not just a disorganized rabble. They'll likely be deployed effectively, and may not be easily driven off," the lieutenant concluded with a frown.

"Yes, sir, that was my thinkin' on it as well. We try to bust our men out now and we'll most likely just get ourselves kilt."

Lieutenant Harris paused and gazed back toward the farmhouse. Ned was surprised to see that the young lieutenant's eyes looked watery, and he spoke in a quiet tone, barely louder than a whisper, "But ... they're our men. We can't just abandon them..."

"It's a bitter pill, Lieutenant," Ned answered, "but best we can do is send a couple o' our scouts back to the fort at the gallop so's to bring back help, while we fall back a few miles 'til we can find a good defensible spot to hunker down for the night. Then we hope and pray our men can hold out long enough for us to come back in the morning and slaughter these devils.

"Speakin' of ... looks like we got more of our own troubles..." Ned nodded his head back toward where they'd come from. Rebels with rifles could be seen trotting up the road toward their position. As soon as they'd gathered enough men, an attack would no doubt be forthcoming.

The lieutenant gazed in the direction Ned was looking and nodded. "All right, let's move out, gentlemen. Sadly, there's nothing more we can do here for the moment."

Ned nodded, then shared a grim look with Caleb. They both knew the chances of the men left behind at the farmhouse still being alive come morning were next to zero.

ৡ৵ঙৣৱৡ৵ঙৣৱৡ৵ঙৣ

Tuesday May 19, 1863 – Sherwood, Missouri:

Ned gazed at the bodies, or what was left of them, laid out on the floor in the farmhouse. There had been fifteen men in the house, and three others that'd been killed in the fighting outside. All the bodies had been mutilated beyond recognition; many were missing heads or limbs. Several had been gutted, their entrails spilling onto the floor.

Ned seethed with a hatred and anger he'd not felt in years. *What kind of animals could do a thing like this?* he asked himself, shaking his head in disgust. But to that question he had no answer. As horrible as his life as a slave had at times been, he'd never witnessed anything like *this*.

He strode back out into the yard and exchanged a look with Captain Mathews, the black freeman officer who'd first welcomed Ned into the regiment. The captain, who held a dark scowl, nodded at Ned but said nothing.

The regiment's commanding officer, Colonel James Williams, a white man, had led the relief expedition himself, though it had now become a burial detail instead. The colonel stood a few yards away from Mathews, staring down at the grass in the yard. When Ned approached the colonel, he was surprised to see that Williams had an enraged look on his face, and appeared watery eyed. He glanced up at Ned, "This is a terrible, sad day, Sergeant."

"Yes, sir," Ned came to attention and snapped a salute, which the colonel returned in a half-hearted manner. But Ned could think of nothing else to say, so he went ahead and gave his report.

"All the dead are now laid out in the house as you ordered, sir. Along with their belongings and … various body parts that we could find…"

The colonel nodded, "Very good, Sergeant. Please, gather the men, if you would."

"Sir!" Ned snapped another salute, then both he and Captain Mathews trotted off to spread the word.

When the entire unit was assembled—some six hundred men, more than a dozen horses, and three mobile artillery guns they'd brought along—the colonel removed his hat and stood solemnly on the lawn in front of the farmhouse. The men followed his lead, coming to attention and removing their hats as well. Then the colonel took a small, dog-eared Bible from his coat pocket, flipped open to a page he'd marked, and read aloud a passage from it.

A sudden image of Captain Chambers quoting the Bible came into Ned's head. It had been on the day they'd left Belle Meade for Kansas, what now seemed like a lifetime ago, even though it had only been months.

"Amen," the colonel finished, replacing his hat. He strode directly to Captain Mathews, his face holding a dark frown, "Captain, burn this house to the ground."

While the fire yet raged, and before the farmhouse roof had completely collapsed, the column was formed up into companies, and they marched into the small village of Sherwood, which had been evacuated by its citizens at the arrival of the Union column earlier in the morning. Of the rebel bushwhackers and their Confederate officer, there was no sign.

Once the column had secured the village, Colonel Williams ordered his officers to torch every house, barn, shed, and outbuilding in Sherwood in retaliation for the murder and desecration of his eighteen brave men. And then he ordered that the name "Sherwood" should be stitched into the regimental flag next to "Island Mound," in recognition of the small but intense firefight here, and to forever honor the fallen.

ഉ൩ശ൝ഉ൩ശ൝ഉ൩ശ

"Major Wiggins, sir..." one of the privates called out as Jim Wiggins moved along the row, hunkered down to keep his head below the level of the stone wall they were hiding behind. Wiggins paused and leaned down, resting his hand on the private's back where the young soldier crouched next to the wall clutching his rifle, one of a long line of blue-clad men doing the same.

"What is it, Private?" Wiggins asked.

"Major ... we've been wondering about that strange whistling noise in the air above us. Joe here says it's bullets flying by overhead, but I think it must be bees."

Jim snorted a laugh and slapped the private on the back, "First gunfight is it, son?" he grinned, slowly shaking his head. "Yes ... yes, Private ... it's most certainly *bullets* ... courtesy o' them fellers over yonder in gray."

He chuckled again, and continued on his way, "You'll get used to it, Private," he called out as he moved on down the line, the distinctive shape of his Henry repeating rifle bouncing along, strapped to his back. *Bees!* he thought and snorted a laugh as he trotted along. *Guess I'd best keep my head down so's not to get myself stung!*

When Major Wiggins reached the center of the wall, he stopped and snapped a salute at his commanding officer, who returned it smartly. Wiggins was not surprised to see the familiar figure of a gigantic hound sitting next to his commander.

"Capt—uh, sorry ... I mean *Colonel*," Wiggins began and grinned, rolling his eyes and shaking his head, "Old habits, sir..."

"Never mind *that*, Mr. Wiggins. Thoughts?" Colonel Nathaniel Chambers asked.

Lieutenant Colonel Thomas Clark, standing next to the colonel, leaned in to hear as well. Both men wore serious, concerned looks, but no sign of fear or panic.

"Well, sir," Jim Wiggins reached up under his hat and wiped the sweat that was threatening to run down into his eyes. "Seems to me this here's more than the 'cavalry raid' we've been told to expect. For one, these fellers are acting like regular infantry, not horse soldiers afoot. And for another … seems to me there's a damn sight more o' these yahoos than there by rights ought to be. They drove in our skirmishers like a bunch o' schoolboys that done run into a hornets' nest. No sir, no kind o' cavalry raid that I ever heard of."

Nathan nodded, "Agreed, Mr. Wiggins. This is something more … something we've *not* been expecting. That being the case … prepare all companies to receive an enemy assault. I expect it'll be forthcoming, and I would give our *friends* a proper, Twelfth West Virginia greeting."

"Yes, sir!" Jim snapped another salute, then pivoted to return to his position down the left flank.

Nathan turned to his second in command, "Tom—"

"Already on it, sir," Tom turned to Tony, who stood next to him. "Corporal Anthony, please relay the colonel's orders to the captains on the right flank—all companies prepare to meet an assault by the enemy momentarily."

Tony snapped a salute, "Sir!" He pivoted and headed off down the wall to the right at a fast trot, keeping his head low. And though Tony was a black freeman—the only one in the regiment—and as such could only be given the rank of corporal, all the officers and men knew he was the colonel's unofficial aide de camp, and had served with him for years. This afforded Tony a status far beyond his rank. Everyone in the regiment knew when he spoke it was with the colonel's authority. And if anyone had a problem with that arrangement, they hadn't the nerve to say so out loud. Everyone knew Colonel Chambers was not a man to cross.

Nathan nodded as he watched Tony trot off, then pulled out his brass spyglass, removed his hat, and carefully leaned up onto the top of the wall to peer out. Harry the Dog gazed up at him and took a step toward the wall. But if the animal had a mind to join his master looking up over the wall, he was quickly disabused of the notion. "You just stay *down* now, Harry. There's a good boy…" Nathan commanded in low tones, "I'd rather you didn't get a bullet through that immense head of yours." Harry promptly plopped his backside down on the ground, and continued to gaze up at his master, seemingly unbothered by the sharp rebuke.

Nathan gazed out southward across a pasture to where another rock wall stood parallel to their own, slightly downhill and 150 yards away. The long stone wall now hid an unknown number of rebel combatants. Intermittent puffs of smoke, followed by the popping of rifles and bullets zipping past overhead, or pounding into the stone wall in front of them, were the only sign of the enemy's presence. But Nathan's instincts, honed by years of combat, told him that Jim Wiggins was right: this was no small-time raid. It was the beginning of something bigger … but *what?*

"What are you up to?" he whispered to his unseen enemy. A moment later, he dropped back down behind cover, then turned to the east and held up his spyglass again. He was gratified, but not surprised, to see the 110th Ohio Regiment in position to cover his left flank. The 110th Ohio's commander, Colonel Joseph Keifer, had impressed Nathan as an extremely capable and confident leader. And there was no better feeling in battle than to know that the officer guarding your flank was up to the task.

He lowered the spyglass and looked down the row of his own regiment at his men now facing the wall, ducking their heads below its four-foot-high top, prepared to raise up and fire at the enemy on command. And though he knew he and his men from Texas had trained them well, for many of them this would be their first real taste of serious combat. *Will you be up to the task?* he wondered. And then he answered his own question: *Yes … I know you will … you're my men, after all!*

And then he chuckled as he thought about Jim Wiggins' little slip of the lip, referring to him as "Captain," rather than "Colonel." *Old habits, indeed,* he thought. He recalled the moment when his title had changed, along with that of the rest of his men…

෴෨෬෬෭෨෴෨෬෬෭෨෴෨෬෭෨

(Six Months Earlier...)

Sunday January 18, 1863 – Wheeling, West Virginia:

Nathan had to admit to a certain amount of eager anticipation as he paced back in forth in Governor Pierpont's modest office, awaiting the arrival of his men from Texas: longtime farmhand-turned-soldier Zeke, and Phillipe, Tom's cousin by marriage and French Army veteran. Nathan had left church early to make the necessary arrangements, sending one of the governor's couriers with a message requesting that the men meet him at the Customs House in downtown Wheeling straightaway.

Governor Pierpont stood to one side, arms folded across his chest, with Harry the Dog sitting next to him, tongue hanging out. Pierpont gazed at Nathan with an amused look, but otherwise refrained from commenting on the latter's growing impatience.

Finally, there came a knock on the door, and the governor immediately answered in his bold, unmistakable voice, "Come in!"

The door opened, and Tom entered, followed closely by Jim, Stan, Billy, William, Jamie, Georgie, Phillipe, and Zeke. They had to squeeze close together for all to fit into the small office.

Nathan stood to attention in front of them and snapped a salute, dressed in a crisp blue Union Army officer's uniform, complete with gold trim and shiny brass buttons.

By instinct and long training, the men stood to attention and returned the salute, then immediately surrounded their Captain, shaking his hand, patting him on the back, and congratulating him with great enthusiasm and boisterous good will.

Governor Pierpont beamed.

Only Tom seemed unenthused. He held back, a frown knitting his brow.

Nathan looked over at him with curiosity, "What's the matter, Tom? Not happy to see me back in uniform?"

But Tom continued to scowl, "It's not *that*, sir. That's a thing I've wished for and dreamed about for ... years now, as you well know. It's just ... *sir*, that's a *colonel's* uniform! A *colonel?!* It's ...

11

it's a damned *insult*, sir. It ought to be a brigadier's uniform at the very least, preferably a major general's. I just can't believe it..." He shook his head.

Governor Pierpont nodded, and seemed ready to respond, but Nathan waved him off, "It's all right, Tom. I appreciate you saying so, and I can't say I disagree. But ... getting me a general officer's commission right now has proven to be extremely problematic. From what the governor tells me, McClellan still has many friends in Congress in the Democrat party—there's even talk of them putting him up as their next presidential candidate, if you can believe it. It seems they're prepared to do everything they can to prevent me from becoming a general, or at least to delay it so long it becomes a moot point. So, we've decided to take another tack, and avoid a showdown with Congress by settling for the rank of colonel."

"Well, I can understand it ... but it's still not *right*," Tom answered.

Nathan stepped up to Tom and put a hand on his shoulder, "It'll do for now, Tom. A colonel's rank is sufficient to command a regiment, and even a brigade if it comes to it. And the governor has persuaded the War Department to back date my commission to the beginning of the war on account of my previous service in Mexico and Texas, so I'll have seniority over very nearly every other colonel in the army.

"Once I've proven myself in the field, McClellan's friends will have no grounds for raising an objection, or at least they'll be shouted down by those who're more sensible, one can only hope," Nathan shrugged.

Tom nodded but was yet unconvinced, and his sour expression remained. But his demeanor brightened up a minute later when Nathan handed him a neat, new uniform on a hanger, and he saw the insignia on the shoulder patch.

"Welcome to the Twelfth, Lieutenant Colonel Clark," Nathan grinned, extending his hand.

Tom took the uniform and the proffered hand with enthusiasm, returning Nathan's grin, "Thank you, sir. I will do my best to live up to this honor."

Nathan clapped him on the shoulder, "Of that there can be no doubt, Mr. Clark!"

Then Tom had a sudden thought and chuckled, "*Oh!* Now I understand why you've been growing out your beard lately, sir ... so you'll look the part of a proper Union officer!"

Nathan grinned and rubbed at his chin, which now sported a neatly trimmed "goatee" beard, in addition to his usual mustache, "Well, I'm not all that concerned with *looking* the part, but I will confess I had noticed it was a new trend among the field officers, so I asked General Rosecrans about it. Turns out it's a thing more of a practical nature than of a fashionable one; it's a great bother to shave regularly when out campaigning, living out of a tent, etcetera. So, just letting the beard grow and occasionally giving it a trim with scissors is a logical solution."

"Ah ... makes sense. And I do think it looks good on you, sir. If you don't mind my saying so."

"Thanks, Tom. I'm still getting used to it myself."

Then Nathan approached Jim, but this time he held out two uniforms, one identical to Tom's with a lieutenant colonel's silver oak leaves on the shoulder patches, and the other bearing gold oak leaves, signifying the lower rank of major.

"Mr. Wiggins, I'm afraid you will have to make a choice," Nathan held up one of the uniforms. "The army will only allow us to have one lieutenant colonel in the regiment at this stage, but I believe you *deserve* the rank based on your years of service, your knowledge, and your capabilities—not to mention that you've already proven yourself bearing that rank temporarily during our recent action at Harpers Ferry. So, if you so choose, you can accept the lieutenant colonel's commission, and we will arrange for you to join one of the other West Virginia regiments. I know any one of them would be more than delighted to have your expertise and fighting spirit.

"Or ... you can accept the lesser rank of major, and join the Twelfth as third in command."

Without even a moment's hesitation Jim reached out and grabbed the major's uniform, "Hell, sir ... I'd be a damned private if it meant fighting with you and the other men. There's no choice to be made, sir. And I thank you."

"No ... thank *you*, *Major* Wiggins, and welcome to the Twelfth," the two men shook hands with great warmth and enthusiasm.

Nathan then handed out captain's uniforms to Stan, William, Jamie, Georgie, Phillipe, and Zeke, with William given the additional title of regimental head surgeon. Each man shook hands with Nathan in turn as he accepted his new uniform.

Then Nathan stepped up in front of Billy, looking him hard in the eye, "I am ashamed and embarrassed to tell you I was unsuccessful in my efforts to obtain an officer's commission for you. You certainly deserve it, and you can believe I tried everything I could think of, including appealing to the Secretary of War himself. But unfortunately, the War Department has record of you enlisting as an Indian Scout with the U.S. Eighth Infantry before the war, and they'll not allow an Indian to be an officer in the Army—the theory being we are technically in an ongoing state of belligerence out West against the Indian tribes in general, other than the so-called 'Civilized Tribes' in Indian Territory. Never mind the fact the Tonkawa are our *allies* in that conflict!" He shook his head and scowled.

"It made me downright furious, I can assure you—the governor can attest to that! But all my fussing and fuming has been to no avail.

"I did hear that some men have changed their names, and have lied about their race, which I am prepared to support you in doing, if you wish, though it galls me that it would be necessary."

But Billy just shrugged, "You know such things matter nothing to me, Captain. To the Tonkawa, a man is a leader because of his actions, not some stitching on his shirt, or a title another man gives him. I have fought for you all these years because you are my war chief, not because the Army calls you 'captain' and puts gold bars on your sleeve."

Nathan nodded, and extended his hand. Billy took it, and the two shook hands, locking eyes wordlessly for a moment before breaking it off. Then Nathan handed Billy a uniform with a sergeant's chevron on the sleeves, it being the best he could do under the circumstances.

Then to the everlasting delight of each of the newly recruited soldiers in the room, Nathan moved over to the corner of the room, pulled open the lid on a long, rectangular wooden crate sitting on the floor and pulled out something long, and metallic. He held it up to the awestruck men, and ratcheted the lever action on a shiny new Henry repeating rifle.

He handed the rifle to Jamie O'Brien, their resident gunsmith. Jamie's eyes went wide, and his mouth hung open. "Sweet mother of Jesus ... and all the saints..." he muttered.

"What do you think of *that*, Mr. O'Brien?" Nathan asked with a grin as Jamie gazed up and down the length of the rifle, examining it in detail, before working the lever action several times himself.

"Why, Captain ... it's ... it's the Holy Grail o' guns, is what it is, sir. An honest-to-God *repeating* rifle. Never thought I'd see one ... And what a beauty she is too, sir..."

"She's yours," Nathan grinned. He reached back into the crate and pulled out another, handing it over to Tom. Tom grinned, but wasn't taken by surprise like the others. Nathan hadn't been able to resist telling him about the wonderful new rifles after he'd returned from meeting with Benjamin Tyler Henry in Washington city. And he had already shown them to Tom when the crate had arrived on the train from New Haven, Connecticut a few days earlier.

Nathan proceeded to hand rifles out to each of the men in the room. And then, after giving them a moment to admire their new weapons, asked them to set the rifles aside, and line up to take the officer's oath, which was then administered by Governor Pierpont, who grinned broadly throughout, despite the solemnity of the ceremony.

ନ୍ଦ୍ରେ୧୫ଥ୍ୟ ଠ୍ୟର୍ଚ୫ଥ୍ୟ ଠ୍ୟରଏ

Later that day, back at Belle Meade Farm, Nathan's last order of business concerning the regiment was to meet with Tony. While he'd had a pretty good idea how the other men would react to his offer to join the Twelfth, he had no idea how this meeting with Tony was going to turn out.

The two men sat on the tiny deck at the back of the farmhouse gazing across the small table at each other. Nathan casually puffed on a cigar, and Tony waited patiently for him to begin the conversation.

"Tony, as you've no doubt heard, I've been given command of the Twelfth West Virginia Volunteer Infantry Regiment, and the men from Texas, plus Zeke and Phillipe, have joined as my officers.

"Yes, sir," Tony answered with a nod, "it's pert near all that's been talked about since y'all got back from town earlier. It sounds like good news for you, sir."

"Yes, I believe so. Thank you, Tony," Nathan nodded. "So, I'm sure you're wondering why I asked you to come speak with me..."

Tony just shrugged, "Reckon you don't need no reason, after all we been through."

Nathan smiled, "Thank you, but I do in fact have a reason, and that is that I'd like you to consider joining the Twelfth ... as my *unofficial* aide de camp."

"Aide de camp? What's that?"

"Well, the *standard* meaning in the army is an officer's personal assistant in the regiment: making sure the command tent is properly erected, the commander's personal items are properly cared for, stowed during travel, and unpacked when needed. Delivering messages, relaying orders, writing letters, and so on."

"Oh..." Tony looked down at the table.

"Sounds a lot like being a servant ... or even a *slave*, doesn't it?" Nathan met eyes with Tony who looked back up and nodded, a sober look on his face.

"Well, cheer up ... I said that's the *standard* Army definition, but it's not what I intend for *you*. I want you to *fight* with us, Tony. The men have come to think of you as one of them. But, aside from valuing you as a fighter, there's another reason I want you with us ... I wish to make a point, though perhaps a subtle one ... that

16

black men and white men can serve and fight together, and that there should be no difference."

"And what of Big George and the others?" Tony asked.

Nathan slowly shook his head. "I can only take one of you; even *that* is pushing my luck. I can't take more without the Army stepping in and putting a stop to it.

"The army wants all black men to serve only in their own special Colored Regiments with white men as officers, so the other freemen will have to serve in one of those units. The only way I can have *you* in the Twelfth is to put up a façade of you being my personal aide, though I have no intention of treating you that way. And I said 'unofficial' aide de camp, as the Army only allows generals to have such aids, and I'm only a colonel at this point."

Tony nodded, looking thoughtful.

"I'm sorry to put you in this spot, Tony, but I'm afraid you'll have to choose. Either fight with me in the Twelfth now or wait and join one of the Colored Regiments with the other freemen as they get formed up, equipped, and trained, which will likely take several more months."

Tony had gone away to think it over, and to discuss it with the other freemen. Nathan was hopeful Tony would accept; he valued the young man as one of his best fighters and as a capable leader of men, and truly wanted him in the regiment.

Still, Nathan felt badly for Tony. He knew he'd handed him a serious conundrum, and he was tempted to resolve the issue by withdrawing the option of serving in the Twelfth. But Tony was a freeman now; Nathan felt strongly that it was important for him to make his own decisions, no matter how painful and difficult.

But in the end, Tony had surprised Nathan by coming up with a compromise solution that solved the dilemma; Tony would serve in the Twelfth while the colored regiments were forming up and being trained. Then, once whichever regiment the other Mountain Meadows freemen joined was ready to go out into the field, Nathan would arrange a transfer for Tony so he could join them. That way, he could get into the fight sooner with the Captain and his men, but also could serve with the other freemen when the time came, and not feel like he was abandoning them. It was a solution that seemed to please everyone … except, of course, Rosa, who was tearful, but understanding.

Saturday June 13, 1863, 11:15 a.m. – Winchester, Virginia:

After months of mundane guard duty in and around Winchester, and only minor skirmishing against bushwhackers and small rebel cavalry units, the men of the Twelfth West Virginia suddenly found themselves in the midst of their first serious engagement. Just moments after Colonel Chambers issued the command for the regiment to stand ready, a great howling shout erupted from across the field, and a long row of rebel soldiers came boiling over their stone wall, moving at a fast trot toward the Twelfth's position, rifles with bayonets extended out front.

Looking out, Nathan quickly confirmed that this was no minor raid; the force moving toward them was of regimental strength at the least, and likely more troops were still held in reserve behind the stone wall.

"Who *are* you…?" Nathan wondered aloud, as he gazed out at the approaching enemy. There was not supposed to be a Confederate force of any significance for hundreds of miles, with General Lee's Army of Northern Virginia currently pinned down by Union Major General Hooker's Army of the Potomac over the mountains to the east near Fredericksburg, Virginia—the site of the disastrous engagement that had cost Major General Burnside his command, not to mention the lives of thousands of his men, back in December.

Nathan knew it couldn't be Lee's army, as they could never have marched a force that large such a distance undetected by the scouts, skirmishers, and cavalry patrols of the largest army in the Union.

And yet … *someone* was charging toward his regiment…

"*Present arms!*" he called out, and the order was immediately repeated by officers down the line, as blue-clad soldiers raised up from where they crouched, laid their rifles across the top of the rock wall, and pulled back the hammers. Nathan and Tom joined them, leaning out across the wall with their Henry rifles extended. Tony leaned out next to Tom with his standard-issue rifle, and Harry the Dog got up on his hind legs next to Nathan, gazing out over the wall.

"Aim!" Colonel Chambers called out, then after only a moment's hesitation, *"Fire!"*

A thunderous roar of smoke and fire poured out from nearly a thousand Union rifles. *"Reload!"* Nathan shouted, as he saw the enemy come to a halt, form up in line, aim their rifles, and return the volley. He ducked down behind the wall, ejecting the spent shell casing and loading the next cartridge into the Henry's chamber with the lever action. Bullets impacted against the wall's stones, ricocheted off the top, and sailed whistling overhead. He took a quick glance off to the left and saw that the 110th Ohio was also under attack, and had just fired off their own volley. Gunsmoke curled up in a huge plume above their position.

He then heard two large *booms* behind him and to the right: Captain Carlin, another West Virginian, had been sent out from Winchester to support them with his small artillery battery from Wheeling. This morning, expecting only a minor engagement, he'd brought only two three-inch rifled guns, which he had just fired off. Their high explosive shells detonated back behind the rebel lines to little effect. Nathan shook his head; the rebels were already too close for the big guns to target them without risking hitting their own men.

A quick glance to the sides confirmed that his men had reloaded, so he repeated the commands to fire, and another volley roared out at the enemy. The volley was answered shortly by another from the enemy, who now lay prone in the tall grass of the pasture, presenting a much smaller target to the Union rifles.

Nathan raised his spyglass and looked out through the drifting smoke at the enemy line, expecting to see it now much depleted, *"Damn!"*

"What is it?" Tom asked.

"More men are streaming out from behind their wall. They are now more than when we started..."

He lowered the spyglass and looked at Tom. "Colonel Clark, please send two companies from our left flank across to our right side ... the Ohioans guard our left, but only Captain Carlin's two small guns protect our right. I fear that with an enemy force this size..."

Tom was already moving off before Nathan could complete the sentence. A few minutes later a rifle company of just under a hundred men came trotting by, led by Captain Jamie O'Brien, his Henry rifle cradled under his left arm. He gave Nathan a quick salute and a wink as he passed by, but there was no time to exchange words. Another minute later, a second rifle company trotted past, this one lead by a promising young lieutenant named James Durham. Durham, like all of Nathan's officers, carried the Henry rifle his commander had gifted him. The lieutenant, who held a serious, determined expression, also saluted the colonel as he passed by, but didn't pause.

Tom Clark returned and resumed his position to Nathan's right. "The 110th seems to be holding its ground," Tom reported, "though they are hard pressed by a force at least the size of this one facing us."

"*Damn it, Tom!* Who *are* these guys? Our scouts this morning reported only enemy skirmishers ... not *this?*"

Tom just shrugged, and looked to their front. He knew it was a rhetorical question anyway, and he had no answer.

Several more volleys were exchanged, and though the Twelfth was well protected by their stone wall, and suffered only light casualties, the enemy, in their more exposed position out in the pasture, stubbornly refused to withdraw. Nathan found this unsettling, because it spoke to an enemy force of potentially much greater manpower than what had already been committed.

The Twelfth had just fired off another volley when Nathan felt a presence at his right sleeve. He glanced over and saw that it was Billy Creek, who immediately snapped a salute, which he returned. "Report, Mr. Creek?"

"Captain, the two rifle companies you sent to guard our right flank face a new enemy force. They are many and there is heavy fighting. There are not enough of our men to stop them; our flank will be turned," he answered calmly.

Nathan turned to Tom, "Send one of the lieutenants across to Colonel Keifer ... tell him our right flank is turned, and we must withdraw. Without our support, we recommend he do the same. We will fall back to Captain Carlin's position, and defend his artillery from a stronger point. Colonel Keifer must choose his own ground.

"Tony!" Nathan called out, and Tony stepped up and saluted, "Tony, go down the line to the right and relay my orders to withdraw. We will pivot to face the enemy force coming in on our right, so the men on the far right will fall back first, followed by the others. Do you understand?"

Tony nodded, "Yes, sir. A pivot ... just like we done when we was bustin' out o' Mountain Meadows."

Nathan smiled at the memory, and that Tony had made the connection, "Yes, just so, Mr. Anthony. Tom ... you do the same down the left flank. Tell Jim to take up the rear, and have his men come all the way down the wall to the right before withdrawing. That way we'll never have our backs to the enemy coming at us from the right flank while the wall protects our left."

"Yes, sir!" Tom saluted.

"Let's move!"

ഇ൚രുൽ൵ഇ൚രുൽ൵ഇ൚രുൽ

Though the pivot move and withdrawal took some time, and had not been carried out as smoothly as Nathan would have wished—some of his younger, greener troops broke ranks, dropped their rifles, and ran in a panic and then had to be harshly reined in by their sergeants—in the end the desired result was achieved. The Twelfth established a new, more defensible position at a place called Milltown Heights, within sight of the large Main Fort on its high hill just to the west of downtown Winchester. Here Captain Carlin had positioned his two guns in a redoubt, and once the Twelfth was out of the way, opened fire on the enemy with impunity. Nathan ordered his regiment deployed in a wide arc around the artillery for mutual defense.

Shortly after the Twelfth took up position, the 110th Ohio also arrived on the heights and positioned themselves off to the left once again.

This time, the two units were so closely deployed that Nathan was able to walk over and speak with Colonel Keifer in person. There he apologized for the abrupt withdrawal, but Keifer just shrugged, "Never worry, Chambers ... these things happen, and I do appreciate you sending a courier to tell me your intentions. If not for that we'd have been left in a rather tight spot when you were forced to pull out."

Nathan appreciated the colonel's mild reaction to the whole affair, and his calm demeanor, despite the unexpected outcome. This served to reinforce and even enhance Nathan's previous high opinion of the man.

Brigadier General Washington Elliott, currently their brigade commander, joined them after a few moments. He had been watching the action with his staff officers from a position on the hillside not far from Carlin's big guns. Elliott was also a West Pointer. He struck Nathan as a reasonably competent but none-too-inspiring leader. He seemed disinclined to aggressive action, rather preferring to do the minimum asked of him and, if possible, to simply carry out orders, whatever those might be.

"Colonels," the general greeted his two subordinate officers, "that was an unexpected surprise ... and *not* of the pleasant kind."

"Yes, sir," Nathan nodded, "not what we'd been told to expect at all, general. Any idea who they are, and where they came from?"

"None yet, colonel," Elliott answered, "but once things are back in good order out here, I intend to meet with General Milroy and ask him that very question."

Both Nathan and Keifer nodded, but there was little more to be said on that subject at the moment.

"Gentlemen, this looks like a good defensive position from which to fend off the enemy's attack." The general gazed across their defensive works then out toward the enemy's position in the distance. "Let's hold this ground until he plays himself out, then see if we can't push him back down the hill a bit, shall we?"

It wasn't a strongly worded, precise order as Nathan would have preferred, but he understood the gist: the general didn't want to return to the fort and its commander, General Milroy, without being able to report at least some small victory.

So the Twelfth endured another series of assaults, including an unnerving bombardment by some small howitzers the enemy brought forward. These fired chunks of cut-up railroad ties and spikes, which the Confederate Army often used instead of iron cannon balls to save money. These strange projectiles made odd, screaming noises whenever they passed overhead, and though they were terribly inaccurate, they caused horrific damage whenever they hit something.

But to the delight of the Union men, from this new position they were not only defended by Captain Carlin's guns; they were also now within support range of the heavy siege guns in the Main Fort.

The Twelfth and 110th had endured only a few moments of enemy artillery fire when the big Union guns uphill in the fort opened up, with their unmistakable deep, booming rumble followed by the ear-splitting concussion of their high-explosive shells detonating out toward the enemy lines. This pyrotechnic display of raw power prompted a spontaneous cheer from the hunkered down Union soldiers, and quickly silenced the enemy's big guns.

A few hours later, the enemy attacks seemed to have played themselves out, at least for the moment. Looking out with his spyglass, Nathan could see that the bulk of the enemy's troops had withdrawn down the hill, likely back behind one of several stone walls there. Out to their front he now saw only a thin line of enemy pickets laying prone in the field. They'd likely been left behind just to contest the ground, and to warn of a Union counterattack.

So, remembering General Elliott's wish to at least make a show of pushing the enemy back, he ordered Jim Wiggins to take two rifle companies and assault the picket line, the goal being to drive the enemy completely off the hillside. This Major Wiggins accomplished in short order with a quick bayonet charge, which Nathan enjoyed watching through his spy glass.

When Jim Wiggins returned to where Nathan and Tom stood, he dragged a rebel prisoner with him. Jim stopped, saluted, and then turned to the prisoner. "Go ahead, Private ... tell the Colonel what you just told me. Which Confederate units are these we're facing, how many are you, and where'd y'all come from?"

The man hesitated, looking fearful, but Jim gave him a stern look. It occurred to Nathan the man's bruised face and swollen left eye may *not* have happened during the brief battle.

But then the private looked back at Nathan, and stood up straight, a hint of pride coming into his demeanor. "Sure ... why not? Ain't nothin' you Yankees is gonna do about it anyways. Colonel ... I'm proud to say I'm of the Thirteenth Georgia, in General Gordon's brigade o' us Georgians. We's all of General Ewell's corps, all of which done marched up over the hills from away east o' these parts over the last two days."

"Lieutenant General *Richard* Ewell?" Nathan asked quietly.

"Yes, sir, that's right," the private answered, and grinned, gratified to see the reaction *this* name invoked in his enemy's colonel.

"And is General Ewell's corps the only one here or coming this way?" Nathan asked.

But the private just shrugged. "Don't know. The general ain't seen fit to share that news with me."

Nathan slowly nodded. Then, deciding he'd get nothing further of value from the man, he ordered one of the sergeants to take a couple of privates and escort the prisoner directly to General Milroy himself. Nathan penciled a quick note to Milroy concerning the news about General Ewell's arrival, and handed it to the sergeant.

Both Jim and Tom held severe looks, and Nathan had a dark frown. But Tony, who'd been listening in on the brief interrogation, couldn't help asking, "Who's General Ewell anyway, sir, and what does it mean?"

Nathan turned and met eyes with Tony. "General Ewell took command of the Second Corps of the Army of Northern Virginia when Stonewall Jackson was killed. Second Corps makes up a third part of General Lee's Army of Northern Virginia; the army that *should be* a hundred miles from here. Ewell's command likely holds ... hmm ... twenty, maybe twenty-five thousand men, and dozens of artillery pieces. And his may *not* be the only enemy force coming our way.

"Contrast that to our own meager Union garrison under General Milroy here at Winchester. We'll be lucky to field six or seven thousand officers and men."

Nathan looked down at his boots and was thoughtful a moment, pulling out a cigar, lighting it, and taking a long drag. Then he looked back up. "And what it *means*, gentlemen ... is that this Union command is in *dire* straits, and us with it."

Chapter 2. Counterespionage

"The life of spies is to know,
not be known."
- George Herbert

Monday June 1, 1863 – Richmond, Virginia:

Confederate States Secretary of War James Seddon sat in his large, well-padded leather chair and glared across his desk at Major Charles White of the C.S.A. Signal Corps, seated in the simple wood guest chair. And Seddon had to admit to himself a certain amount of annoyance, even frustration, at White's complete lack of reaction to the former's very most intimidating scowl—a look that rarely failed to strike fear into *most* lesser men. But White was an odd duck, to be sure, Seddon realized. He was also extremely intelligent and resourceful, thus ultimately worth putting up with, despite his quirks.

And as usual in meetings between the two men, the first minute or two of this one was spent in total silence, Seddon trying his best to elicit any kind of reaction from White and once again failing utterly.

"Major White," Seddon finally broke the silence. "I must confess to a certain degree of disappointment at your failure to complete the assignment I afforded you at year's end. It has been more than six months and I still do not yet have this treacherous, spying Jezebel in hand."

White was quiet for a moment, but if he was stung by his superior's harsh rebuke, he showed no sign of it.

"I too am disappointed with the slow pace of the investigation, Mr. Secretary," he replied. "I do have several interesting suspects, including one who is my focal point at the moment. But I fear our infamous lady spy has, for the most part, curtailed her activities since last we met. I will accept the blame for that, sir ... I may have been overzealous in my push to smoke out the harlot, and have instead caused her to proceed more cautiously, making it difficult to bring her to ground."

"Hmm ... I see. Well, I appreciate your willingness to accept some measure of blame in the matter, Major." Seddon then adopted a more conciliatory tone. "Let us put that behind us, and discuss how we can best proceed from here, starting with your main suspect ... Please share with me your thoughts and findings on this woman, starting with her name."

"Her name is Miss Evelyn Hanson, your honor," the major answered.

"*Oh!*" Seddon sat up straight in his chair, "*That* could be a problem..." The Secretary of War now wore a dark frown.

"Yes, your honor, I am well aware that she has connections at the very highest levels of Richmond society..."

"*Richmond society?* How about the highest levels of the *Confederate government?!* She is a regular guest at President Jefferson Davis' residence, and purported to be good friends with *Mrs.* Davis. I myself have spoken with her on several occasions at various presidential functions."

The secretary shook his head slowly, gazing up at the ceiling, "Yes ... this could be a *real* problem, all right..." He looked back down at White. "But let's set that aside for the moment ... Tell me why you suspect her, and what information you've been able to gather that might implicate her."

"Certainly, your honor. You will recall when we first met, the only solid clue we had as to this traitorous lady's identity was the rumor that she was '*the most beautiful woman in Richmond.*'

"This prompted me to conduct a very thorough survey of the upper-class Richmond ladies, in which I collected several dozen lists of ladies who might fit the bill. And Miss Hanson not only scored the highest, she was head and shoulders above anyone else."

"Well, having met her, I can't disagree with that assessment," Seddon nodded. "She is ... an *extremely* attractive and charming young lady. But it's such a subjective judgment ... it certainly doesn't prove she's our spy."

"I agree, Mr. Secretary. Which is why the survey was only the beginning of my investigation into her dealings. The first thing I did was meet with her in person to gauge her reaction to the whole matter. I confronted her with the results of the survey and told her of the nature of my investigation and the rumors we'd heard. Though her reaction seemed suspicious to me and prompted me to dig deeper, this is where I fear I may have erred, your honor; for if she is our spy, instead of smoking her out I may have encouraged her to be more reticent and less active in her espionage activities, making my investigation that much more difficult."

Seddon nodded, but waved his hand dismissively. "Never mind that, Major White; it can't be helped now. What else?"

"I discovered that she spent time with a man named Nathaniel Chambers before the Secession, at his residence in western Virginia. From what I can gather, the two of them were quite close, though it is unknown if they were ever actually betrothed."

Seddon nodded, "I'm familiar with Chambers; appointed to the state senate by Governor Letcher, then was a delegate at the Secession Convention. An avowed abolitionist and strongly opposed the Secession. Defected to the North just before the war, and now a colonel in their army. Most definitely *not* a loyal Virginian."

"Just so, your honor. At some point during Miss Hanson's visit to Mr. Chambers' residence, something happened causing her to abruptly return to Richmond. Again, I have been unable to determine what that may have been—whether it was a falling out or something planned. No one in Richmond seems to know, except perhaps Miss Hanson's mother, Harriet, but she refused to discuss the matter with me when I questioned her a few months ago."

Seddon leaned back in his chair and tented his fingers, listening intently and occasionally nodding as White continued his narrative.

"Later, Mr. Chambers and Miss Hanson were seen together on at least one occasion at a social function in Richmond during the Secession Convention. Their meeting was described to me as cordial and friendly, but not overly so. I have been trying to puzzle out what that means, your honor, but that is where I am somewhat at a disadvantage, having had little personal experience in such matters."

Seddon nodded. "It likely wouldn't matter if you had. Women are confusing even to those of us who've had plenty of experience with them." Then he chuckled. "It may be that Chambers was as baffled as anyone else."

Major White nodded and looked thoughtful, but had nothing to say to this. He then shrugged, "I fear there is little more to go on, your honor. There was an incident a little over a year ago when Miss Hanson seems to have completely disappeared from Richmond for a month or more. Of course, she has an alibi for her odd absence, but with the war raging, and the Union now holding the territory in North Carolina where she supposedly stayed during that time, I have been entirely unable to either verify or disprove her story.

"There have been other similar odd absences from the city since then, of varying durations, each one conveniently explained away, but unverifiable."

"I see. Suspicious, but not definitive, as you say. We must press harder, major ... pull out all the stops, talk to everyone she associates with, see if you can find anything more at all. Perhaps meet with her mother again, see if you can push her a bit harder and get something more out of her."

"Yes, your honor," White agreed. "And as I mentioned earlier, Miss Hanson is *not* my only suspect. Several other ladies scored high on the survey and also have varying degrees of suspicious activities and circumstances."

"Yes, understood. But perhaps your investigation will be more effective if you focus on one subject at a time. And getting back to my initial concerns ... Miss Hanson does have some *very* powerful friends. You must be discreet and tread very carefully, lest we provoke their wrath on her behalf, and are forced to curtail our probe."

"Yes, a prudent course of action. But having friends in high places is a double-edged sword; it means if she *is* our spy, she is *especially* dangerous. Not only is she connected with the president and his wife, she is also a known associate of the family that owns the shipping company Hughes Continental Freight, potentially one of the Confederacy's most vital commercial transportation resources, should we ever succeed in breaking the Union's blockade.

"And she is said to be best friends with the wife of one of General Lee's staff officers. She was also reportedly friends with General Johnston's wife and was a frequent guest in their home before the general was wounded and replaced by General Lee.

"In addition to all that, she started up a business of sorts just before the war: providing highly trained domestic slaves to the wealthiest families in Richmond, including Varina Davis. It does not take a great deal of imagination to envision these household servants as spies."

Seddon waved his hand dismissively. "Oh, I seriously doubt *that*. Slaves haven't the wit nor the education to be particularly useful in that capacity. Spreading rumors and gossip, perhaps … but actual spying? Reading and comprehending important documents? No, I'm sorry, I just can't picture it. Likely she is only using that *business* to raise funds for her other activities … assuming she is our ringleader."

White nodded his head, "I'm sure you're correct about that. It was just a passing thought."

Seddon leaned back in his chair and gazed up at the ceiling. Then he sat back up, shaking his head, "Be that as it may … you now have me worried. You are painting the picture of a veritable devil fish, with its multiple appendages nefariously reaching out for prey in all directions."

"Yes, I fear it may be so."

"If your suspicions are true," Seddon continued, "it is a *very* serious problem on several levels. Not only has she potentially had access to our most critical war intelligence, but she is a known associate of many of our most important governmental, military, and civilian men and their families. It would spawn an unimaginably devastating scandal should we have her arrested and put on trial."

"Yes, I agree, your honor. We must handle the matter delicately if and when the time comes," White nodded.

Then Seddon leaned forward, a severe frown now darkening his visage. "Let me speak more plainly, though you are *never* to repeat these words to anyone outside of this room: *if* we confirm that Miss Evelyn Hanson is our spy queen, she must *not* be arrested and put on trial."

"Not arrested? You mean to just let her go free?"

"No, you misunderstand me. If we determine she is guilty, we must bring her in quietly and secretly for interrogation, learn everything we can about her activities, and then ... she must be *eliminated!* Quietly and discreetly. Fortunately for us, she already has a reputation for disappearing without warning; this time she simply won't return. *Ever.* And no one must be the wiser."

Major White nodded, "Understood, your honor ... and agreed."

℘ℑℭℬℰℨℑℭℬℰℨℑℭℬ

Sept. 22, 1862
On the march, somewhere in Va.

My Dear Evelyn,

By now I'm sure you've read in the papers about the great battle we fought outside Sharpsburg, Maryland near Antietam Creek. I am well, and somehow survived the battle without a scratch, though for a time I lay unconscious upon the field after the concussion from an artillery shell knocked me to the ground. When I awoke, the sunken road upon which I lay was filled with the dead of both sides. The fighting had moved elsewhere, and I was all alone, save one wounded Union captain about my age. Oddly, since we were both out of ammunition, we struck up a conversation and he was a decent enough fellow.

Later I found my commander, Captain Hill, laying on the field, and thought he was dead. But he yet breathed so I carried him to the hospital, and he lived! Thank the Lord. He was sent back to Richmond to recover a few days ago.

I've seen northern papers calling the great battle a victory for the federals, but I tell you nothing could be farther from the truth.

Though we were vastly outnumbered, we inflicted such heavy casualties on the Yankees that the battle ended in a draw. And then, though we were still outnumbered and had suffered many casualties, we stood our ground and never ran away from the battlefield. After waiting an entire day for the federals to re-engage, which they clearly were afraid to do, General Lee withdrew the army in good order to the southern side of the Potomac as our provisions were running too low to stay in Maryland.

And speaking of Maryland, my dear Evelyn, you could scarcely imagine my surprise when I saw you standing in the crowd in Frederick town as our army marched down the main street on parade. I know you never saw me, as you had turned to the side and were looking in a different direction when I passed. Believe me, it took all my willpower to not break ranks and search for you in the crowd. I wandered the streets of Frederick over the next several days while we were encamped outside the town, but never found you, and nobody I asked seemed to know anything about you.

If you find time to write, it would greatly ease my mind to know you are now safely back in Richmond. I had heard there was some fighting between the opposing cavalry forces in the streets of Frederick after our departure. I have prayed that you were safely out of harm's way when that happened.

It would also appease my curiosity to hear how you happened to be in Maryland when the army passed. There must be a good story to tell in that!

I pray all is well with you, and that I will soon return south that I may visit you again.

Your faithful friend,

Jubal Collins
First Lieutenant, 27th Virginia

P.S. You may have noticed I am now a First Lieutenant, having been promoted shortly before the battle. I like to think it was because of my bravery and good conduct, but I suspect it is just that we have sadly lost so many officers in the fighting.

Evelyn read the letter one last time and sighed. She leaned out over the fireplace in her bedroom, took out a match, and set the letter aflame. Then she stood back to watch it burn.

Though she'd had several other letters from Jubal since this one, and had even answered them, she had never answered this particular one. She knew that many letters from soldiers were lost, destroyed, or simply never delivered, so likely he had thought little of it. And fortunately, Lee's army had not returned to Richmond since the battle, staying up north near Fredericksburg, Virginia after winning another great battle there at the end of the year.

She knew that she should have burned the letter the moment it arrived, as it was incriminating evidence against her, proving she was in Maryland when she was supposedly elsewhere. She could only imagine what Major White would do with such evidence. She slowly shook her head and shuddered at the thought. But she'd not had the heart to burn it, as Jubal was her friend, and it contained his heartfelt recollections of the battle, including brave and even heroic actions on his part—though he sadly fought on the wrong side, from her perspective.

But Major White, who seemed to have been elsewhere for months, was suddenly active again. Angeline had informed her that the Signal Corps Major was now interrogating everyone Evelyn was associated with, including the Hughes. So, the time had come to destroy the evidence.

33

When the fire had consumed the paper, she crushed the ashes with the fireplace poker to ensure it was completely destroyed.

Then she walked to the door, tied on her hat, and headed out to visit Angeline. It was long past time they decided what to do about the serious threat that was C.S.A. Major Charles White.

ഇൗരുവൗഇൗരുവൗഇൗരുവ

"Evelyn … I know you've resisted the notion in the past, but I think we should at least discuss it." Jonathan crossed his arms and leaned back against the window frame in the sitting room of their manor house. "When one man represents such serious danger to our organization, and we have no means of making him cease his activities, I believe it *is* a logical response that should at least be considered."

"All right, let's discuss it then, Jonathan," Evelyn scowled. "Let's say we go ahead and murder Major White, as you suggest. Then what? Do you suppose he has not shared everything he has already learned with his superiors, and likely several subordinates working for him? When they show up to finish his work, shall we murder them as well? And why stop there? Why not just go to the source? I know the Confederate White House well enough by now that I am certain I could slip in at night undetected and murder President Davis in his sleep. Sadly, Varina may be awakened by the noise and then … I'll just have to murder her as well," Evelyn shrugged mockingly, and had become red in the face in her growing agitation.

"All right, all right … Let's leave off this line of discussion," Angeline jumped into the middle of the argument. "Although you may have a valid point, Jonathan, clearly we are *not* going to go down that path, so please just let it go. And Evelyn, please calm yourself; we would never ask you to do something you are unwilling to do, which you already know well. The two of you just stop this bickering, and let's discuss what we *can* and *will* do, rather than arguing hypotheticals."

Evelyn gazed down at the floor, and felt the anger drain from her. Her face was still red, but now from a bit of embarrassment over her outburst. "Sorry, Jonathan … I guess I'm just on edge.

34

Frightened even, to be honest. I want to come up with a plan to eliminate this threat, but I don't want to even *think* about ... about doing something that would make me into someone I don't want to be ... someone I would no longer recognize. I ... I've been there before, and don't ever want to go there again."

Who am I? the long-ago voice echoed in the back of her mind. But now she could easily ignore it; now she *knew*.

"No, Evelyn, the fault is all mine. I apologize, and we'll not discuss it again." Jonathan made a short bow.

"Thank you, Jonathan." Evelyn returned the bow with a nod.

Angeline gestured Jonathan to retake his seat and smiled, "Thank you, both. Now ... let's discuss what we *are* willing to do about Signal Corps Major Charles White."

For the next few hours, they discussed various possible strategies and scenarios, but none seemed workable or had a high probability of success.

So they took a break from the discussion and moved into the dining hall for dinner.

As they were finishing up and just pushing back their chairs, Angeline put her hand on Evelyn's arm and the two met eyes, "Since we seem to be at a bit of an impasse concerning what to do about the major, there's another matter I'd like you to start thinking about. Jonathan and I have come to suspect that one of our people may be an enemy double-agent, and we'd like your help determining if it's true."

"Oh? Who is that?"

"Actually, she's a young lady about your age: Alice Spencer," Jonathan answered.

Evelyn thought for a moment, then slowly shook her head, "I'm sorry, I don't recall her..."

"A pretty young woman, thin ... long blond hair and ... hmm, I'd say about your same height...?" Angeline prompted.

"Oh, yes ... Now I recall," Evelyn nodded. "She has been at a few functions, but I haven't spoken with her much. I remember the conversation being a bit ... awkward, I suppose one might say. But tell me ... why didn't I know she was working for you?"

"Because ... to be honest, we never completely trusted her, so have kept her at arm's length," Angeline answered. "For instance, she has never even met us and doesn't even know we exist in this capacity. She certainly doesn't know anything about what *you've* been doing for us, Evelyn."

Evelyn pictured the young woman in her mind, trying to recall anything she could of their few brief encounters. Then Evelyn's eyes narrowed, and a thin smile formed on her lips; a plan began taking shape in her mind. And if it worked out as she envisioned, it just might eliminate the double-agent and the threat of Major White both at the same time.

ℰ)⊂ℰℭ℔)ℰ)⊂ℰℭ℔)ℰ)⊂ℰℭ

"Alice had been an outspoken abolitionist before the war, and an active opponent of the Secession while it was still being debated. So when she appeared at one of our Underground Railroad stations and asked if she could help, we weren't entirely surprised," Angeline explained.

"But there were also warning signs, which made us cautious," Jonathan continued, "like, how she knew about the Underground Railroad location in the first place—her explanation seemed a bit weak and was conveniently impossible to verify. And then there is the fact that her *supposedly* estranged father is Confederate Brigadier General Charles Spencer, on General Beauregard's staff. I say 'supposedly estranged' because Alice still lives at home with her mother while her father is off to the war. But she continues living there even when her father is at home on leave."

"Hmm ... yes, suspicious, but not necessarily damning," Evelyn smiled. "I recall a certain young lady who suddenly showed up unannounced at one of your railroad stations, with nothing but her word and that of a runaway slave as to how she came to be there. And that has worked out all right, I believe."

Angeline returned Evelyn's smile, and patted her on the arm. "Yes, of course, dear. And how we do thank our lucky stars you did show up when you did! But these were only our initial concerns that have caused us to move slowly with her ..."

"Yes, there have been several minor incidents since then that have increased our suspicions," Jonathan continued, "like operations that should have been relatively easy and secure being 'accidentally' discovered and disrupted by the enemy; equipment we'd stored, of which she was aware, turning up missing; and most recently one of our long-time operatives arrested on the way to a clandestine meeting with her. Could just be coincidence, or just bad luck, but ..."

"But you don't think so," Evelyn raised an eyebrow.

They both nodded. Then Jonathan added, "Most telling for me was when we had Joseph meet with her, under one of his many aliases. He spent several hours with her, and even conducted a minor operation with her. And though everything went well, he came away unconvinced, saying there was 'something' about her that didn't *feel* right. Though he couldn't describe exactly what."

"Hmm ... yes, I would tend to trust Joseph's instincts on these matters," Evelyn nodded.

"Lately she has been pressing to become more involved, and to be introduced to our inner circle," Angeline continued. "Needless to say, we have been slow-walking *that* particular request, though we don't want to flat out turn her down; she may yet prove to be a valuable asset."

"So ... obviously we need to determine once and for all whose side she is really on," Jonathan added. "And then act on that knowledge, one way or the other—though we'll definitely *not* have her murdered." He flashed Evelyn a grin.

Evelyn smirked and rolled her eyes at him. She digested this information for a few moments. "Well, I think it really should be quite simple. We just tell her details about some fake operation, something nobody else is told, and then lie in wait to see if the enemy shows up to counter it."

Jonathan gazed up at the ceiling. "Good, good."

"But it shouldn't be obvious that the operation was fake ... something whose ultimate failure is easily explained and not too suspicious," Evelyn continued.

"Why would that matter?" Angeline asked. "Wouldn't we just cut her off at that point? She really knows very little and can do us no real harm. We have already moved the one railroad station she knew about, and everyone in the organization that she has worked with has used an alias or a disguise as necessary."

"Because," Evelyn answered, "if we prove she *is* a rebel spy … then I may have *another* use for her."

ഇരുഗ്രോഇരുഗ്രോഇരുഗ്ര

Alice Spencer put the finishing touches on her French make-up, then tied on her hat with its ribbon. She stood, turning to gaze at herself in the full-length looking glass on the opposite wall of her bedroom. She turned slightly one way, then the other, examining the overall look, before deciding she approved. *Elegant, seductive, but not too formal or showy,* she decided. *Wouldn't do to look like I'm trying too hard. Not when I'm going out to meet with … him.* The thought of the dark, mysterious man who had come to so thoroughly dominate her life in the last several months always invoked a strong emotional reaction: an odd combination of fear and excitement.

She went to her closet, fetched out a matching handbag, then, after pausing for one last glimpse in the looking glass, headed out of her bedroom and toward the front door. As she crossed the broad marbled foyer she heard her mother call out from the library, "Where are you going, dear?"

"Out," she answered sharply, annoyed at always being queried about her comings and goings.

"And when will you return, may I ask?"

"You may *not.* I'm a grown woman now, and I will appreciate you minding your own affairs, Mother," she answered, and then opened the door and strode out without another word.

Meddling old biddy, she thought as she stepped down the front steps of the house and strolled out to the street. She had little respect for her mother, who'd never enforced any discipline upon her. But she was grateful that her stern, domineering father—the general—was away at war. After everything that she'd been through, he'd likely never let her out of the house again, at least not without a chaperone.

As usual, she didn't know exactly where the meeting would take place; the note just said to leave her house at precisely four o'clock and turn left on her street, walking in a southeasterly direction. She followed her instructions, walking for a block and a half before a black carriage pulled up next to her and stopped. It had dark curtains over the windows so that one could not see inside. But Alice was unconcerned, it being the usual method of transportation to these clandestine meetings. She immediately stepped up to the carriage, opened the door, and climbed up into the seat.

But she had to suppress a startled gasp, for the mysterious gentleman was seated across from her, gazing at her intently. She knew him only as Mr. Gray, though she doubted it was his real name; she had never run into him at any social events, so she had no way of confirming or denying the truth of the matter.

Always in the past she'd ridden alone in the carriage, which had taken her to a different location each time they had met.

"You startled me," she held her hand to her breast. "I didn't expect to see you in the carriage."

"Yes, I know it isn't the usual routine, Alice ... but it couldn't be helped this time. I've other business requiring my attention and haven't time for our usual ... hmm ... *more relaxed* rendezvous." He looked at her in the particular leering way of his: the cat sizing up the pet canary. This time his gaze was so intense she had to look away for a moment. She knew exactly what he meant by "more relaxed," and it sent a shiver through her. The man was really quite nefarious.

Those eyes, she thought. Those eyes had such a strange effect on her, and stirred such conflicting emotions. She knew she should despise and hate the man for what he was doing to her, but ... somehow, she simply could not summon the requisite negative feelings toward him.

It also didn't help that he was tall, lean, and darkly handsome, with neatly trimmed beard and long, flowing hair. And though he appeared to be merely in his early thirties, he walked with a cane—the effects of a devastating war injury of some kind, she presumed, though he'd never spoken of it.

"Have you anything new for me?" he asked, as the carriage continued down the lane in the direction she'd been walking.

"Oh yes, Mr. Gray. I have something I think you may find very interesting and useful," she answered, trying to sound calm and in control, but knowing she was not quite pulling it off. She reached up her sleeve, and pulled out a tightly folded slip of paper, handing it across to him.

He took it, unfolded it, and leaned out toward the window, opening the curtain a crack to give him enough light to read by. He quickly scanned the paper, then refolded it and put it in his inner jacket pocket. "It's good ... but minor." he locked eyes with her. "I need *more* ... you are clearly being kept on a short leash, only privy to their less important operations. You must push harder ... use whatever charms you may have ... work your way higher up."

Not even a thank you, she thought, feeling a bit peevish at his lukewarm response to her latest intel effort. But what she said aloud was, "Yes, of course. I will do my best, Mr. Gray. But they are very cautious ... maybe even more so than you."

He leaned back and snorted a short laugh, though there was no humor in it. "Oh, I seriously doubt *that*," he frowned. "But speaking of ... I have some new information that may help in your activities, but you must keep this strictly to yourself, lest the other side wonder how you came by the information."

"Of course; anything you say to me is always kept only between us." Just then, she realized that this time, at least, she was actually telling him the whole truth—but only because she had no one else to share their conversations with!

He nodded. "It has come to my attention that the elusive leader of the spy ring we seek may be going by the pseudonym 'The Employer.' As I said, never repeat this name to anyone, but keep your ears open for anyone letting it slip. If they do, then see if you can discreetly determine the person this name is associated with. I believe this may be the key to unraveling their entire operation."

"*Oh!* Yes, of course I will listen very carefully for it any time I am in company with the other side. And I shall be discreet, exactly as you say."

"Good. See that you are. And never forget our little ... *agreement*, Alice ... I would hate to see anything ... untoward ... happen to you or your family."

He then gripped his cane and banged the silver knob, shaped as a lion's head, against the roof of the carriage. Alice felt the vehicle slow and then turn and head back in the direction it had come.

"I'm sorry, Mr. Gray. I *will* try harder, I promise," she answered. She then leaned toward him, giving him a generous view of her cleavage, and smiled in a tentative way. "And do you think that next time we may have a ... *more relaxed* meeting once again?"

He smiled slightly, gazing intently into her eyes, and then looked down at her bosom in a meaningful way. "Perhaps. It all depends on how well you perform your ... *duties*."

A few moments later, she was let off on the street and the carriage was gone, without so much as a goodbye. *What a cruel bastard!* she thought, but then felt that same odd thrill as she recalled those dark, intense eyes. And once again, she couldn't decide if she hated him, loved him, or ... something else entirely.

She slowly shook her head, thinking back on how her life had come to this ... how carefree and exciting it had been before the Secession—those heady, exciting times when abolitionist, anti-secession young people were meeting all over town to loudly argue, debate, and carouse, until all hours of the night. She cared nothing about the actual arguments, having little knowledge or interest in politics and really not understanding what all the fuss was about. And she couldn't care less about the slaves ... Inferior dark people needed something useful to do, she figured, and God knew they were not capable of looking after themselves. But she enjoyed the attention and the edginess of the "radicals" almost as much as she enjoyed the annoyance and consternation it caused her parents.

But then ... the *incident* happened: a handsome, charismatic young man, a late night of heady debate fueled by a little too much alcohol, and a few moments of indiscretion. She shuddered to think about the shame she'd endured telling her father, and the nightmarish physical pain that she'd suffered after he'd arranged for a solution to her "problem."

Somehow, Mr. Gray had learned of it, and had threatened to expose her and ruin her reputation—and by extension, her father's—if she refused to do his bidding.

Mr. Gray wished her to use her reputation as an abolitionist—false as that may have been—to infiltrate the growing pro-Union espionage threat that was believed to be operating in Richmond.

He assumed that this ring of spies was working in close coordination with the ongoing "economic drain" known as the Underground Railroad. So that would be her starting point. And to his credit, Mr. Gray's theory had proven true. Her involvement with the Underground Railroad, which she had performed as faithfully as she could in order to gain their trust, had led directly to her being recruited by the espionage ring, just as he had hoped.

Gray had also taken advantage of his hold over her to get her into his bed. But unknown to him, she had been drawn to him from the first moment they met, despite his threats. She would have willingly come to him or spied for him had he simply asked; she had no true pro-Union or abolitionist sentiments whatsoever, so she was not feeling conflicted about what she was being asked to do.

But now, as she walked back up the street toward home, she pondered the question, *How can I work my way further into the spy network? Somehow I simply must! And I must learn who this "Employer" is. But how?*

Then in her mind's eye she envisioned how pleased Mr. Gray would be when she gave him the intel he desired. It gave her a momentary thrill and caused her to quicken her pace.

Chapter 3. A Hard Nut

"Must is a hard nut to crack,
but it has a sweet kernel."
*- **Charles Spurgeon***

Saturday June 13, 1863, 11:00 a.m. – Berryville, Virginia:

Captain Zeke Benton held his Henry rifle at the ready as he gazed down the dirt road to the south from where he crouched behind a tree trunk. A tall, lanky, red-haired former farmhand, Zeke was referred to as "the old man" by his men of the Twelfth West Virginia Regiment—though he was only in his mid-twenties.

Captain Benton had just received word via courier from Colonel McReynolds to expect an imminent attack by rebel cavalry on his position, three miles out from Berryville.

So Zeke had ordered his company of skirmishers into a line of battle; though when he thought about it, calling it a *line* was a bit of a stretch. Rather than a typical battle formation—men standing shoulder to shoulder, rifles at the ready—his men were currently spread in a broad, ragged arc on both sides of the road leading south out of town, hunkered down behind rocks, tree stumps, and in ditches—anything to provide cover. He figured concealment might give them an opportunity to ambush the rebel riders, and maybe rid themselves of the nuisance, at least for a time.

Zeke and his seventy-four riflemen of Company G had been temporarily stationed at Berryville, a small town and important crossroads ten miles east of Winchester under the command of Colonel Andrew McReynolds, a forty-something, gregarious Irishman and commander of the New York First Cavalry. When given the task of garrisoning Berryville, the colonel had had plenty of horsemen at his disposal but had been light on infantry. So he had asked several of the regimental commanders at Winchester, including Colonel Chambers, to lend him some foot soldiers.

Zeke was not overly concerned about the impending cavalry raid. He and his men had already successfully fended off several rebel mounted incursions since arriving in Berryville two weeks earlier, and he figured this time would be no different. Cavalry troopers were all flash and dash, in his opinion, but they had little stomach for slugging it out with well-positioned infantry. After a quick charge and a poorly aimed volley of pistol shots, they typically turned and scampered back from where they'd come.

But as he gazed out along the road, something strange in the distance caught his eye: a large cloud of dust drifted slowly into the sky on this hot, sparsely clouded morning. Zeke tipped back his hat and scratched his forehead. *Odd*, he thought. *Can't imagine a cavalry patrol kicking up that much dust, even in this heat.*

Zeke turned to Sergeant Dixon, kneeling behind a stump a few yards to his right. "Sergeant. Pass the word to fix bayonets, if you would."

"*Bayonets*, sir?" The sergeant looked perplexed. They'd not once needed them since they'd been deployed to the Winchester area months earlier; eighteen-inch needle-sharp spears affixed to their rifles were generally a hazardous nuisance and of little use against fast-moving cavalry. But Zeke just nodded his head out toward the rising dust cloud, causing the sergeant to turn and see it for himself. "*Oh!*" Dixon now held a look of startlement on his face.

"And Sergeant … may as well tell the men to be prepared to fall back on my command … just in case," Zeke added.

Sergeant Dixon snapped a quick salute and then scrambled off to pass the word.

Ten minutes later, the mystery was solved. From where he crouched, Zeke could see about 250 yards out along the road before it dipped out of sight. And as he watched, a large mounted double column of rebel riders rose up from the dip in the road. In a few seconds it became clear this was more than a few dozen men on a cavalry raid—hundreds of riders had appeared. But more kept coming up the road, a thousand or more, Zeke figured, and still more behind those.

Zeke reached down and gripped the binoculars he'd been gifted by Colonel Chambers and held them up to his eyes, focusing on the lead riders at the head of the column. Then he whistled softly to himself. *A dad-gummed brigadier general! Holy Jesus … what the devil's going on?* he wondered. But he immediately turned to Dixon, "Sergeant, pass the order: prepare for volley fire, then be ready to fall back." Against these numbers, Zeke knew an ambush was no longer on the table. And neither was standing and fighting it out; after all, his small rifle company was meant to be a light skirmish line, not a hardened, well-dug-in defensive line.

He glanced down the line and saw his men raising their rifles. He turned back toward the advancing enemy and raised his binoculars once more. *What the …?* He muttered. *It can't be … can it?* Next to the general rode an officer who was burly looking, with a neatly trimmed beard … and a missing left hand! Zeke fine-tuned the focus and saw a face he knew well and could never forget. *Walters … or I'm a snake!*

Captain Zeke Benton stood, cupped his hands, and yelled, *"Present arms … Aim … Fire!"* Fire and smoke belched forth from multiple concealed positions along the road.

Zeke took another quick look through the binoculars and was gratified to see that his small company had at least stirred the hornets' nest: rebel troopers were moving forward to screen their general and other officers, including Walters. Others were quickly moving off the road and taking cover. But the bulk of the column continued coming on, pulling out rifles, pistols, and sabers in preparation for battle.

Zeke looked over at the sergeant, "Well … I'd say we done gave 'em a proper West Virginia 'hello.' But now … I believe it's high time we said our fond 'farewells.'" He cupped his hands and ·shouted out, "Company G will fall back … in *good order*, boys, or you'll answer to me!" And without further ado, he reached down and scooped up his knapsack, then shouldered it and turned back toward town where they'd have artillery support, and the rest of McReynolds' brigade.

But Zeke now knew enough about fighting and battles to know that McReynolds' garrison would never be able to withstand this overwhelming rebel force, and that Company G's stopover in Berryville would be a short-lived one.

ᏚᎾᏣᎦᏣᎾᏚᎾᏣᎦᏣᎾᏚᎾᏣᎦᏣ

Saturday June 13, 1863, 2:30 p.m. – Berryville, Virginia:

C.S.A. Major Elijah Walters was feeling a growing sense of frustration as he led his four companies of cavalry at a fast trot up the heavily rutted dirt road through a thick wood, searching for the Union garrison retreating from Berryville.

C.S.A. Major General Rodes, in command of the Confederate division advancing up the eastern flank of the Winchester offensive, had rolled over the small Union town after a determined but overmatched resistance by a stubborn federal artillery battery and its equally obstinate cavalry escort. But when Rodes' foot soldiers had rushed into the town expecting to bag the entire Union force stationed there, they found the birds had flown; the town had been evacuated.

So now General Jenkins and his cavalry brigade had been sent out to cut off the federals' retreat, and that meant Walters and his mounted companies.

Damn it! How hard can it be to locate a column of over a thousand men with wagons and artillery? Walters wondered as he spurred his horse to increase the pace. *We should've found them by now...*

It was early afternoon and a hot day, though clouds were beginning to roll in, promising some relief. But Walters was in a temper, and barely noticed the weather. He knew if they could cut off the Yankees, they'd be forced to surrender, caught out on the road with no defensive works to fight behind. And Walters burned to get ahold of the Union prisoners, especially those from a company of the Twelfth West Virginia Regiment, reportedly stationed at Berryville, according to locals who'd been feeding information to the advancing rebel forces.

And Walters knew, from several Wheeling newspapers his men had taken from pro-Union civilians in the past few months, that the Twelfth West Virginia was commanded by none other than his old hated neighbor, *Nathan Chambers!* He yearned to get his hands on some of Chambers' men and squeeze them for information about his whereabouts. But the elusive Union column was *not* where it was supposed to be, retreating toward the Union forts at Winchester. *So ... where the hell are they?* he wondered.

They came to a fork in the road, and on a sudden impulse, he turned and took the right fork, moving in a more northerly direction. *If they didn't head due west toward the forts—and they must've known we would try to cut off that route, after all—then they must've swung farther north to avoid us,* he decided.

Walters currently led a portion of the Seventeenth Virginia Cavalry Regiment, of Brigadier General Albert Jenkins' cavalry brigade. Jenkins' brigade had been operating in the Shenandoah Valley in the area around Winchester for the past several months, conducting raids, seizing foodstuffs and equipment, and generally harassing Union General Milroy's command. But they'd never had enough manpower to make any real impact on the situation, and Walters had been considering abandoning Jenkins and going back to bushwhacking on his own.

But Jenkins had surprised him by offering a major's commission in the Confederate forces, so Walters had stayed. Though he cared little about military ranks per se, he did understand the power such ranks afforded. The higher the rank, the more men you commanded; more men meant more power. More power meant a greater ability to achieve one's goals. And for Walters, those goals generally included killing as many Yankees and runaway slaves as he could—but more specifically, killing Chambers and his sycophant followers. And then returning to Wheeling and slaughtering Chambers' saucy freed slaves ... then Miss Abbey, and finally, most satisfying of all ... his cheating, ungrateful whore of a wife, *Margaret!*

And now that the Confederacy had finally decided to move against Winchester in force, Walters could almost taste his revenge...

80)03 03 80 80)03 03 80 80)03 03

Saturday June 13, 1863, 6:00 p.m. – Winchester, Virginia:

Despite Colonel Chambers' report that the force now assaulting the Union fortifications at Winchester was *not* a mere cavalry raid as expected, but was in fact the entire Second Corps of General Lee's Army of Northern Virginia—inexplicably a hundred miles from their last known position—General Milroy was surprisingly upbeat.

Milroy had spent much of the day observing the actions of the 110th Ohio, Nathan's Twelfth West Virginia, and other Union regiments that had come under attack farther to the southeast from his vantage point atop a large flagpole at the crest of the Main Fort. He'd had his engineers rig up a block and tackle mechanism that could hoist him up in a wooden box some fifty feet in the air, just below the huge U.S. flag that waved from the top.

Though surprised by the Confederate numbers, Milroy had been pleased by the overall results of the day. He even declared their efforts a "victory," believing that his Union forces had so bloodied the rebels and blunted their assault that they would be inclined to give it up and bypass his well-fortified position at Winchester in favor of softer targets farther north.

But Nathan and Colonel Keifer were skeptical of this assessment, arguing that they had very nearly been destroyed by what appeared to have been only the opening probing strikes of a much larger planned assault by the enemy. Even the normally reticent General Elliott strongly urged Milroy to order a general withdrawal to the north toward Harpers Ferry, arguing that their garrison, despite its well-fortified positions, was no match for the numbers now coming against it. Several of the other senior officers present agreed.

But Milroy remained unconvinced and determined not to relinquish his position. He did, however, concede the need to consolidate his scattered forces. So he ordered a contraction of his command into close proximity of the three Union forts overlooking Winchester on the hills northwest of town. This was accomplished via a pre-arranged signal, a specific pattern fired from the Main Fort's large siege guns, which could be heard for miles around.

The Union forts at Winchester formed a defensive triangle, with each fort built on a rise, with only a few hundred yards and a steep ravine separating them. They could provide mutual defense of each other with their artillery and rifles, readily targeting enemy besiegers trying to climb the slopes or scale the walls.

The northmost point of the triangle was anchored by the so-called Star Fort with its eight heavy guns—its name derived from the distinctive star shape of its high walls. To the west and on the highest ground of the three was the aptly named West Fort with four big guns, and its adjacent artillery redoubt named simply "Battery Number Six," with two additional guns. And finally, to the south, the Main Fort, sometimes referred to as "Fort Milroy" after its commander.

The Main Fort presented a formidable obstacle to any besieging enemy, with its high walls, extensive underground storage and barracks, and its pre-positioned heavy artillery, featuring fourteen cannons, among them the massive twenty-four-pounder siege guns that could reach out and hit an enemy at upwards of two miles. The fort had been wisely constructed atop a long, sloping rise which had been kept clear of any obstructions, giving the defenders a clear field of fire, and forcing any attackers to cover a great distance uphill while utterly exposed. To complete its defenses, the Main Fort, like the other two forts, was surrounded by a series of rifle pits: trenches that could hold entire regiments of infantry, able to pour down devasting musket volleys on an enemy while relatively safe from return fire. The defenders could access the rifle pits by a series of sally ports built into the thick outer walls of the fort: small heavy iron doors that could only be opened from the inside.

But despite these impressive and intimidating defensive works, Nathan knew that an experienced and determined foe in overwhelming numbers, such as Lee's battle-hardened army, would eventually breach the fortifications. And once that happened, the game would be over for its defenders, who'd quickly be forced to choose between surrender and death.

But Nathan could also appreciate and respect General Milroy's desire to stay and put up a fight. He had to admit it was a very strong urge, even knowing it was a great risk for little reward.

And that overwhelming desire for aggressive action—taking the fight to the enemy—was, in the end, the thing that had brought Nathan and his new commanding general closer together after a rocky start to their relationship.

傩ӋՃƀ傩ӋՃƀ傩ӋՃ

Major General Robert H. Milroy, often referred to as the "Gray Eagle of the Army" on account of the tall shock of gray hair sticking straight up on the top of his head, his keen eyes, and his stern, raptor-like visage, had taken command of the Union garrison at Winchester at the beginning of the new year. He'd immediately set to work angering and alienating the town's mostly pro-Confederate civilian population by strictly enforcing President Lincoln's newly issued Emancipation Proclamation, sending wagonloads of freed slaves north across the Potomac under Army escort, and threatening that any civilian who resisted would be treated as an enemy combatant.

He was fiercely patriotic and had made it clear that he despised secessionists in general with an almost religious zealotry, labeling them all as despicable traitors. He took pride in "making the secesh tremble in fear of my cruelty," and backed his words with action: during the harsh winter months, Milroy ordered his soldiers to confiscate corn, hay, and other produce from rebel sympathizers within the region of his command, and ordered that no such goods be sold to anyone deemed disloyal to the Union. His harsh treatment of the local civilian population received widespread and vehement condemnation in Southern newspapers, causing him to be regarded as a veritable devil throughout the Confederacy. It was even rumored that Virginia residents had raised a bounty of $100,000 on his head, and several Confederate generals publicly expressed a determination to collect that reward.

By the time Nathan arrived with his Twelfth West Virginia Regiment in March, the vehemence of the local citizenry was so obvious, vitriolic, and detrimental to his own soldiers' morale, that he had spoken with General Milroy about it in person.

But Milroy scoffed at his concerns. "I must confess ... I have a strong inclination to play the tyrant among these ... *traitorous vermin*. Hell is not yet full, and I'll gladly send these secessionists to help fill it. Here in Winchester, my will is absolute law. And if that makes the secesh believe me a veritable Nero for cruelty and blood, then so be it."

Milroy also made it clear he had a healthy dislike of West Pointers like Nathan, whom he referred to as the "the royal priesthood of West Point." Milroy had finished first in his class of cadets at a private military institute called Captain Partridge's Academy in Vermont, the northern equivalent of the Virginia Military Academy, or the Citadel in South Carolina. But Milroy's attempts to gain an officer's commission in the U.S. Army before the war had been rebuffed on multiple occasions, which he blamed on the snooty graduates of the U.S. Military Academy. So Nathan's initial welcome to Winchester by its commanding general had been nothing if not icy cold.

But despite their initial mistrust, even outright animosity, Nathan began to develop a grudging respect for the general as they worked together to strengthen the fortifications and defensive works surrounding Winchester and refined the strategies for its defense. The general's intelligence, patriotism, courage, toughness, and determination served to slowly erode Nathan's negative first impressions of the man.

And when Milroy's superiors in Washington began to get nervous about what the rebels might be planning, and "strongly suggested" that he abandon the fortifications at Winchester and withdraw farther to the north, Nathan and Milroy found common ground in a strong desire to dig in and fight. Neither felt inclined to capitulate to defeatist thinking and strategy, and they balked at the idea of giving up a relatively strong, well-defended position without firing a shot.

And so it was, a month or so after the Twelfth's arrival, when one of Milroy's new anti-secessionist civilian directives rubbed Jim Wiggins the wrong way, he complained to Nathan, "He's at it again! Damn it, the man's downright incorrigible. Sorry to sound disrespectful, Colonel, but the general is one mean, crusty old bastard!"

Nathan smiled and nodded, "Yes ... maybe so, Mr. Wiggins, maybe so. But he's *our* mean, crusty old bastard!"

෨෦෬෬ඏ෨෦෬෬ඏ෨෦෬෬

Saturday June 13, 1863, 7:45 p.m. – Summit Point, West Virginia:

Walters' cavalry finally found the retreating Union garrison just as the sun was setting. They were now ten miles or more north of the normal route, out to the west of Summit Point, heading toward the Martinsburg Pike that would lead them back south to Winchester.

But rather than cutting off the Union garrison and forcing them to surrender, Walters and his men found themselves in the frustrating, helpless position of trailing the federals. And the area they now traversed was too densely wooded and hilly for them to take advantage of their greater speed to go cross country and head off the slower-moving federal column. All they could do was harass the rearguard of the garrison. And this proved more difficult and dangerous than effective, as Colonel McReynolds deployed his highly experienced First New York Cavalry against Walters' Virginians. The New Yorkers showed great resolve, tenacity, and skill, and were inflicting more casualties on the rebels than they were enduring. So Walters ordered his men to hang back, and only engage in long-range sniping, which was next to useless while riding.

And so it was that Walters finally called off the pursuit when his cavalry started taking fire from concealed Union pickets a mile or so north of Winchester. The Union garrison from Berryville had made it back to the forts at Winchester and were finally safe from rebel attack ... for the moment.

Walters sat on his horse, gazing at the Union Star Fort on its high hill, guarding the north approaches to Winchester. He raised his stubbed left arm. *This isn't over yet, Chambers … this battle has only just begun!*

Then he turned his horse and signaled for his company to withdraw.

ଈୠ୯ଌଔ୪ଈୠ୯ଌଔ୪ଈୠ୯ଌ

Sunday June 14, 1863, 3:30 a.m. – Winchester, Virginia:

A couple of hours before dawn, Colonel Chambers was awakened by the sergeant of the watch. "Sorry to disturb your slumber, sir, but I thought you would want to see who it is that has just arrived, all wore out and ragged looking—like something the dog chewed up, dragged in, and spat out."

Nathan sat up and rubbed his eyes, "Company G?"

"Yes, sir. And Captain Benton in the lead. Marched all over hell and gone from the sounds of it. But I'll let him tell it, if you care to follow me, sir. Captain Benton and the boys are havin' a bite o' chow before beddin' down for a spell."

Moments later, there were happy greetings, handshakes, and slaps on the back as Nathan, Tom, and Jim greeted Zeke and his exhausted men of Company G.

"Yep, we been marchin' and fightin' all day and night since yesterday morning. Colonel McReynolds and all of us in his command made it out by marching in a big ol' circle to fool the rebs. But it was one helluva long slog; musta hiked twenty-five miles or more, though it by rights oughta have been only ten from Berryville. Yep … *very* happy to finally be here, sir."

"Not as happy as I am to have you here, Zeke. Welcome back! Casualties?"

Zeke finished chewing and swallowing the hunk of bread he'd stuck in his mouth, then shook his head. He beamed, "None, sir; all present and accounted for. Not even a serious wound, if you can believe it. And I can't say as much for them fellas as was fightin' against us!"

53

Nathan returned the smile, "Good to hear, Zeke ... Good work. Well done, and thank you."

Jim whacked Zeke on the back and snorted a laugh, *"Damn,* Zeke ... we're gonna make a goddamned soldier out of you yet!"

Zeke laughed along with him then took another bite.

But as he was chewing, Zeke's smile turned to a frown, and his eyes widened as a thought suddenly occurred to him: "Oh ... Colonel, you ain't gonna believe this; I hardly believed it myself and I was there ... but I seen Walters."

"What? *Walters?!* Where?"

"Seen him through the binocs ... riding right behind their brigadier ... *General Jenkins,* someone said he was. And Walters was wearin' an officer's uniform this time—a major's, maybe, though I wasn't close enough to be sure."

Nathan scowled, "Are you sure it was him, Zeke?"

"Yes, sir. Burly fellow, neatly groomed, and ... missing his left hand. Plus ... I got a good look at his face 'fore the shootin' started; I'd know that varmint anywhere, having knowed him for years, well before y'all came back from Texas."

Nathan shared a dark look with Tom. But Tom shrugged. "He and his bushwhackers *were* with Jenkins in the Kanawha ... Seems like the general went ahead and commissioned him. But ... that's likely good news for the folks back home."

Nathan thought about that a moment and nodded, "True ... If he's *here*, and subject to Confederate Army marching orders, then we don't have to worry about him attacking Belle Meade again anytime soon."

"And..." Jim now wore a wicked grin, replacing the joyous one from a few minutes earlier, "if he's here ... maybe we can finally get another shot at the sumbitch!"

Nathan snorted a laugh, "One can only hope, Mr. Wiggins."

ЄƆⱭƆႸƐɄᲨЄƆႦƆჄᲨƐɄᲨЄƆⱭƆႸ

Sunday June 14, 1863, 5:30 a.m. – Winchester, Virginia:

C.S.A. Major General Jubal Early stood alone on a small rise just to the south of Bowers Hill, a mile or so southwest of

Winchester, just as the sun was peaking above the eastern horizon. The thick layer of clouds that had been building the day before had given way to a tremendous thunderstorm and an accompanying deluge just after midnight that'd made for a long, dreary night for the men of his division. But now, thankfully, the clouds were breaking up, making for a spectacular sunrise.

But Early was entirely disinterested in nature's display, focusing his attention instead on the imposing silhouette of the Union's Main Fort, looming high above the town a mile and a half to his north. As the rising sun lit its features, he let out a soft groan.

Through his binoculars he studied its thick, high walls that would have to be scaled with ladders, gun emplacements bristling with heavy siege guns, and breastworks outside the walls that could easily accommodate several regiments of rifles. All this sitting high atop a long, bare rise that would have to be traversed by his men while under devastating gunfire with no cover. And then his heart sank farther, if such a thing was possible; he realized he would not even be able to bring his artillery to bear on the fort or its defenders. Any attempt to position his smaller, more mobile guns close enough to hit the fort would immediately be met by murderous incoming projectiles from the fort's big guns, annihilating both men and equipment.

And though he burned for a victory, especially a chance to best the hated Milroy, he shuddered at the thought of wasting his precious infantry, their brave young bodies torn to bits crashing ineffectually against the fort's impregnable walls like waves on a cliff.

He steeled himself for this morning's meeting with his superior, Lieutenant General Richard Ewell. It was galling to have to admit defeat without even having made the attempt. But what could he do? The Union fortifications at Winchester just might be a nut too hard for him to crack, despite his huge advantage in numbers.

Then General Early's gaze wandered to the left, toward the smaller Union *West* Fort. *Hmm ... wait a minute ... this is interesting,* he thought. *Why didn't I notice this before? The West Fort sits on higher ground than the Main Fort, and faces heavily wooded hills out to the west...*

As he lowered the binoculars, the frown he'd held transformed into a smile, just as General Ewell stepped up to join him on the hillock. The commanding general had lost a leg, shattered by a bullet at the Battle of Second Manassas, and walked with difficulty, leaning heavily on a crutch. But despite his disability, and his otherwise unimposing appearance—rather short with a bald, dome-shaped head—Ewell projected an energy and force of will that seemed to defy his physical shortcomings. This was one of the reasons Robert E. Lee had decided to grant him Stonewall Jackson's old command.

"What are you seeing through those binoculars that suddenly makes you so cheery, Early?" Ewell asked as he came to a stop in front of his subordinate. The two senior generals' staff officers gathered together at a respectful distance near a small copse of trees in order to allow their commanders privacy in which to discuss their battle plans.

Early smiled even more broadly at this question, *"Victory,* General. I can see ... victory."

ⅺ₳Ↄⅺ₳Ↄⅺ₳Ↄ

Sunday June 14, 1863, 6:00 a.m. – Bunker Hill, West Virginia:

When Major Elijah Walters rejoined General Albert Jenkins just north of Bunker Hill, even as the sun was rising, he was expecting to meet a wrathful commander. After all, Walters had utterly failed in his mission to cut off McReynolds' retreating brigade, allowing them to escape to Winchester almost entirely intact.

But Jenkins had suffered his own embarrassing setback. The portion of the brigade the general had personally led had discovered the Berryville supply wagons at Bunker Hill, attempting to escape north on the Martinsburg Pike. But when the rebels attempted to seize the wagons, they were met by a surprisingly stiff resistance from a small Union company of about

56

two hundred infantrymen who'd been stationed at the small town to guard the roadway.

As the wagons escaped toward Martinsburg, the Union soldiers holed up in two sturdy brick churches that straddled the only road through town. And since Jenkins had brought no artillery with him, he had had no means to force the stubborn federals out of their stronghold, despite his overwhelming superiority in men.

And so a tremendous gun battle had raged all afternoon and into the evening, with the federals firing from within the churches through knocked out bricks and the rebels unable to inflict any casualties on them. So after the sun set, and a cold rain began, Jenkins had posted pickets and pulled his men back into camp in an attempt to keep them dry and warm.

But when the Confederates formed up to storm the churches in the morning, they found the Union infantry gone, having snuck out between the pickets in the dark of night and under the cover of a blinding downpour. And of course, by then, the wagons and all their precious supplies were also long gone.

But Jenkins was philosophical about it. "Major ... I must admit to a certain appreciation of the federals' determined, even heroic, stand, and their admirable escape in the middle of the night from what otherwise would've been their own tomb. And besides ... the wagons may *think* they've escaped, now safe in the Union held town of Martinsburg. But they have not!"

"Oh? And why is *that?*" Walters raised a questioning eyebrow.

"Because ... Martinsburg is our next target; in fact, I mean to take it by the end of the day!"

But if Walters thought Jenkins' mild reception was the biggest surprise of the morning, he soon learned otherwise.

"Walters," Jenkins continued, "Major James Sweeny, commander of the Thirty-Sixth Virginia Cavalry Battalion, was wounded in fighting yesterday, and was taken to the hospital."

Then Jenkins snorted a laugh and shook his head, "I heard the surgeons wanted to amputate his arm, but he pulled out his pistol and threatened to shoot them if they tried it. So they just sewed him up and splinted the arm."

Walters nodded, "Anyone that mean and stubborn deserves to live."

Jenkins laughed again. "Agreed. But anyway, the Thirty-Sixth now needs a commander, and the next ranking officer is only a captain. So, I'm of a mind to put you in command of the battalion. With a field promotion to Lieutenant Colonel ... if you are agreeable."

Walters had no need to even consider the offer; being placed in direct command of a battalion along with a promotion represented more power than he currently had. And power was the thing he needed most.

"Certainly, General. Whatever you wish," he answered mildly.

ᔕᕼᑕᔕᔕᕼᑕᔕᕼᑕᔕᔕᕼᑕᔕ

Sunday June 14, 1863, 6:30 a.m. – Winchester, Virginia:

When dawn broke over the Main Fort, all was eerily quiet. The expected daybreak assault by the rebels had not materialized, and no movement could be seen in the areas where the enemy had been observed the day before.

So General Milroy ordered the siege guns to fire a few rounds at each position previously occupied by the Confederates. To this brief bombardment the federals received no response, causing General Milroy to wonder if the enemy had indeed passed them by under cover of darkness, thinking to deal with the pesky Union garrison later upon their return from their northward campaign.

Once again, Union General Elliott was ordered to conduct a skirmish to feel out the enemy's location. Nathan's Twelfth West Virginia—less Zeke Benton's weary and footsore Company G, who were left behind to recuperate—this time accompanied by the 122nd Ohio, was chosen to march out and locate the enemy. Captain Carlin's "Wheeling Battery," Company D of the First West Virginia Light Artillery, would again provide protection for the brigade.

This time, they took a different route from the day before, crossing a lovely, sprawling estate with a stately two-story manor,

58

now deserted. They came to a halt in a pasture behind a massive stone wall, five feet high and three feet thick and nearly a thousand feet from end to end. Looking out over the wall, they immediately saw a brigade-sized force advancing toward them, so Nathan ordered them to open fire. The rebels quickly took shelter behind another stone wall a few hundred yards away and returned fire.

Captain Carlin tried in vain to find a place to position his guns, but the ground surrounding this new location would not afford him any means to target the enemy. So he retreated back toward the high ground of the fort, leaving the two Union infantry regiments to their own devices.

The back-and-forth rifle volleys continued throughout the morning and on into the early afternoon, with neither side willing to risk a charge across the deadly no-man's-land between the two walls. The 122nd had been similarly engaged with a force to their front.

Nathan began to wonder at this new behavior by the rebels. "Tom ... does it seem odd to you that the rebels are unwilling to launch an assault today and just hang back firing volleys at us, when yesterday they were aggressively advancing almost to the point of recklessness?"

Tom thought a moment, and nodded, "Yes, now that you mention it ... it does seem odd. What do you suppose it means?"

"I don't know ... but I can see the men are nearly exhausted from fighting all day yesterday, being kept up by the thunder, lightning, and pouring rain last night, and then at it again all morning. Please send to Lieutenant Colonel Granger of the 122nd and let him know I'm going to order a general fallback toward the Main Fort to allow the men some rest, if they can manage it with all the noise. That will also serve to preserve our ammunition. We'll leave two companies behind as a skirmish line to contest the ground, and I'll send them back to camp later. Give Lieutenant Durham the command of the skirmishers. He's shown a lot of promise, and I'd like to give him a little more taste of command, even if only temporarily."

"Yes, sir. I'll pass along the word."

First Lieutenant Jubal Collins, in command of Company H, Twenty-Seventh Virginia Regiment of the famous Stonewall Brigade, leaned his rifle up against the rock wall, removed his rucksack, setting it next to the rifle, then turned his back to the wall and slowly sank to the ground. It felt luxurious just to sit for a moment after marching all morning, the last several miles of which had been uphill to a place called Milltown Heights.

Jubal grabbed his canteen and took a drink, then re-stoppered it and gazed out at the view. Lush, green, rolling fields sloped off into the distance, bisected at varying distances by rock walls like the one he was sitting against. And though the Stonewall Brigade had been kept back in reserve until now, they'd heard the sounds of battle in the distance and knew that General Gordan's brigade of Georgians had fought with a regiment from West Virginia that had occupied this very spot the previous day.

Thinking of West Virginia reminded him of the young Union captain from the Seventh West Virginia that he'd met in the bloody lane at the battle by Antietam Creek the previous year. He wondered if the man was still alive. But he shook off the thought; it wouldn't do to start thinking of the Yankees as regular men like himself. They were the enemy, and it was best to keep that firmly in mind so as not to go soft on them. Besides, this regiment was the *Twelfth* West Virginia someone had said, not the *Seventh*.

As he sat enjoying his brief respite, surrounded on both sides by the men of his company, and then out beyond them by the rest of the regiment and the larger brigade, he noticed something gold-colored and shiny sticking out of the dirt by his right boot. Assuming it must be a button or insignia accidentally dropped from a Union officer's uniform, he leaned down and scooped it up, thinking he might pocket a souvenir.

But when he held it up, he was puzzled. This was no button, nor uniform insignia, nor any other piece of equipment he recognized. It was a small brass tube, about a half inch in diameter and two inches long. It was closed on one end and open on the other, but empty inside. The outside of the closed end had a minor dent on one side, but other than that it was unmarked and contained no adornments. He turned it around, gazing at it from all directions, trying to work out what it was. Then he noticed that around the rim of the open end there was a dark stain, like it had perhaps been in a fire; but when he rubbed at the smudge, it came off on his fingers. He held it up to his nose and sniffed at it.

His eyes widened and his mouth dropped open in shock as the realization hit him like a bolt of lightning: he smelled gunpowder! He held it back up, gazing at it again, then muttered, "*Sweet mother of Jesus...*"

He turned to Sergeant Evans sitting next to him, eyes half-closed and about to slip into a dream, and elbowed him wide-awake.

"What? What is it, Lieutenant?" the sergeant asked, instinctively reaching for his rifle.

"Evans, look at this. Do you know what this is?"

"No, sir, I ain't. But I seen they's a whole mess more o' the damned things right over here next to me..." The sergeant lifted his boots and Jubal saw dozens more of the strange brass cylinders scattered on the ground next to the sergeant.

"Damn and damn!" Jubal scrambled over past the sergeant, scooped up a whole handful of the odd cylinders. "This is *bad ... really bad!* I'll be right back," he headed off down the line at a run. He needed to talk with the major.

ภดพดรชชนภดพดรชชนภดพดรชช

When Jubal handed the cylinders to Major Brooks, the latter looked concerned, but not shocked.

"It's a damned repeating rifle is what it is, Major!" Jubal gasped for breath after his quick trot over to find his superior.

"Yes, I know what it is. And *damned* is right. A Henry rifle, from the looks of it. Damned thing can hold sixteen rounds in a long tube below the barrel, and one in the chamber. A man can fire off all seventeen rounds just as fast as he can crank the lever. The officers have been talking about them, just coming into use by the federals—fortunately not yet widespread." Then he snorted a humorless laugh. "They're calling it 'that damned

61

Yankee rifle they can load on a Sunday and fire all week without reloading.'"

But Jubal was not amused. He felt a shiver of dread go down his spine. "Holy Christ, sir! If the Yankees have *those* things, what chance do *we* have?"

"Not much, once they get enough of them," the major answered, shaking his head. Then he handed the cylinders back to Jubal, "Just pray to God the war is over before they make enough of these for every Union soldier. When that day comes, we are done for, Lieutenant."

ဢ)ℂℛℭ℈ℬ℧ဢ)ℂℛℭ℈ℬ℧ဢ)ℂℛℭℬ

Around noon, a delegation from the Confederate Army approached the Main Fort under a flag of truce, and all the guns fell silent. General Milroy and his staff officers came out the front gate to meet the enemy emissaries, the general not wanting to allow the rebels a look inside the fort, lest it provide them some valuable information concerning his defenses.

A Confederate Major led the delegation, accoutered in a parade dress uniform. By contrast, General Milroy wore a dirty, sweat-stained uniform tunic with pants tucked inside rough, unpolished riding boots. But the two gold stars on each shoulder and his fierce, hawklike visage left no doubt as to his rank and stature.

The major stood to attention and snapped a salute at the general, which Milroy returned smartly.

"Major ... I assume, based on the white flag you carry, that you have come here to offer your surrender?" Milroy asked with a smirk. One of Milroy's staff officers failed to suppress a quick, snorted laugh.

The major smiled, and tilted his head to one side, nodding slowly. "Well played, sir ... well played. But no, General Milroy, I am *not* authorized to offer a surrender at this time. But I am tasked, on behalf of Lieutenant General Richard Stoddert Ewell, Commander of Second Corps, of the Army of Northern Virginia, Confederate States of America, with requesting that you, sir, do lay down your arms and cease hostilities. General Ewell makes this request on purely humanitarian grounds, that unnecessary bloodshed, destruction of property, and loss of life may be averted. He wishes me to inform you that your command is currently entirely surrounded, cutoff from reinforcement, and invested in an unbreakable state of siege by his well-equipped army. An army which outnumbers your garrison by a factor of three or more to one.

"What say you, sir? Shall we have peace, and avoid paying a terrible butcher's bill over this relatively unimportant piece of ground?"

General Milroy frowned, put his hand to his mouth in a thoughtful gesture, and gazed down at the dirt in front of his boots, as if contemplating the rebel officer's offer.

But after a moment he looked back up, his face a dark scowl. "Please tell General Ewell I will consider his offer … when hell freezes over … And even then, I expect I'll just slide away on the ice!"

"But, General … be reasonable, sir. If you surrender, you, your officers, and all your men will be treated honorably and with respect, as proper prisoners of war per international convention. If you refuse … then I cannot vouch for what may happen to you and your men, sir. Very likely y'all will be annihilated."

But Milroy just nodded, continuing to glare at the major, "Then I shall see you next in hell, Major. Good day."

Milroy then pivoted on his heels and strode back into the fort. The Union soldiers who'd been listening in on the conversation from atop the wall and from nearby rifle pits began hooting, cheering, and waving their caps at their stubborn commander's bold words of defiance.

🕸🕸🕸🕸🕸🕸🕸🕸🕸

Jubal had little time to contemplate the shocking new Yankee weapon, apparently in use by some members of the Twelfth West Virginia Regiment, as the Stonewall Brigade was shortly ordered into action against several Union regiments dug in on the east side of the Main Fort. And though the brigade clearly had the federals outnumbered, their orders were to fire continuous volleys at their

63

dug-in opponents and pick them off with sharpshooters if they could, but *not* to advance, nor try to press the attack.

Jubal found these orders baffling. It made him wonder what the overall plan was; how the generals thought they'd crack this hard nut by just hanging back and firing off ineffectual rifle volleys all day long.

But he decided it was not his place to question the generals' strategy; his duty was to ensure his orders were carried out. So that's exactly what he did.

ॐ꣠ꣿ॰ꣿ॰ॐ꣠ꣿ॰ꣿ॰ॐ꣠ꣿ॰ꣿ

Nathan continued to ponder the odd rebel behavior, unable to fathom what it signified. Could General Milroy be correct? That the rebels were reluctant to commit to an all-out attack against the heavily fortified Union position, despite their huge advantage in manpower, for fear their numbers would be seriously depleted, even in victory?

He had to admit it was a possibility. He'd seen it before, when Stonewall Jackson had chosen not to engage their small dug-in force at Harpers Ferry for the same reasons.

But it didn't fit the pattern Lee's armies had shown previously, including these very same men only yesterday. A strong suspicion was beginning to grow on him that the force in front of him was only a diversion, a forceful demonstration, to deflect Milroy's attention away from a bigger threat. But from where? *Well, one thing at a time,* he decided, standing up from where he rested in a hastily dug redoubt a quarter mile from the Main Fort. He prodded Tom awake with the toe of his boot as he rose.

"Hunh? Oh, is it morning already, sir?" Tom asked facetiously, rubbing his eyes with hands so filthy, it likely did more harm than good.

Nathan snorted, "No, Colonel Clark, it is in fact three in the afternoon, and high time we got the men moving again. Let's get back down the hill and relieve Lieutenant Durham. I've an idea I'd like to run by you as we march."

And even as they were rousing the men, a courier arrived from General Elliott ordering the Twelfth to advance again, even as

Nathan was already planning to do. This time, the 122nd and 123rd Ohio Regiments would accompany them.

When the Twelfth arrived back at the now familiar stone wall, they were for the first time at full strength, with Zeke's company now rested well enough to join them. They were greeted by Lieutenant Durham, who stepped up to Nathan and Tom and snapped a salute. But Nathan and Tom were deep into a discussion concerning Nathan's theory of some kind of Confederate ruse, and Nathan paid little mind to the young lieutenant, other than to return the salute and say, "Mr. Durham ... good work holding the position..."

"Thank you, sir," Durham answered, still standing to attention, "Your orders, sir?"

But Nathan's mind was still on the conversation with Tom, and though he looked straight at Durham, he'd not really heard the question, and was still speaking with Tom, "I'd like a hard, fast assault on that rebel-held wall just below here..."

He then turned and gazed off toward the enemy's position, "See if we can't drive them off from it." He felt if the enemy put up only a token resistance, it would prove his theory that the force in front of him was only a diversion to keep their attention while their *real* danger approached from some other unknown direction. He could then go himself to General Milroy and try to convince him of his theory.

Tom's gaze followed Nathan's, so both men missed Durham's reaction to Nathan's statement. Durham's eyes widened, his face went pale, and he quivered slightly before snapping a quick salute, "Sir!" He then pivoted and strode briskly off toward where his two companies remained crouched behind the stone wall on the left end of the line.

Nathan glanced after Durham, shrugged, and turned back to Tom. "Tom, before I forget ... please order Lieutenant Durham to lead his two companies back to the redoubt for a rest, a meal, and to restock their ammunition."

♛♛♛♛♛♛♛♛♛

Lieutenant Durham returned to his small command, greeted by Sergeant Daniel Lee Allen of Company E. "What's the good word, sir?" Allen asked, but when he saw the dark look on his commander's face, he asked, "What is it, sir?"

"We're ... we're ordered to attack the enemy. Drive him from his position behind yonder wall." Durham slowly shook his head. Then he handed the sergeant his Henry rifle, "Here, you may as well use this. I will lead the charge with my saber."

"But, *sir!* They've had us pinned down here for hours. We've hardly been able to raise our heads without having them shot off. There's got to be an entire regiment down there, at the least, and we're only two undermanned rifle companies!"

"Yes ... I'm well aware of that, Sergeant. But such are our orders, and I'm not the man to question Colonel Chambers' commands ... are you?"

The sergeant gazed at him a moment, then shook his head, "Well, no ... he's ... well, he scares me a bit, sir, to be honest. I heard he was some kind of gunfighter out west before the war— killed dozens of men. He's got that steely look in his eye that says he'd not hesitate to kill a whole bunch more if he had a mind." He shuddered.

Durham nodded, "Yes, there's *that*, but ... there's more to it. The man never asks his officers or men to do something he's not willing to do himself. Back in training camp he'd march all day with the men, even when they were serving company punishment that he himself had meted out. And he never sits back where it's safe, watching the fighting like some other officers will do; he's regularly out front with the skirmishers where it's hottest. And when he orders a volley, he's right in there working his own rifle and ducking incoming rounds along with the rest of us. No ... it's not just the fear of him ... it's more like ... I don't ever want to let him down."

The sergeant nodded, "I get what you're saying, sir. But this here order ... Sir, it's suicide; we'll be slaughtered."

"Yes, Sergeant, I expect so ... That being the case, I suggest you say your goodbyes to the men. Then tell them to tighten their belts, fix bayonets, and prepare to go up over this wall."

66

Nathan and Tom were still discussing the best approach to their planned attack, with Tony listening in, when a sudden noise off to their left startled them: men screaming and shouting at the top of their lungs. They looked down the line of the wall and saw several hundred of their own men scrambling up over the top and leaping down onto the ground beyond, bayoneted rifles in their hands. When they hit the ground, they took off at a fast trot across the field, Lieutenant Durham leading the charge, a sword in his right hand and a revolver in his left.

"What the devil?! What's he doing? He'll be massacred!" Nathan shouted. They watched in horror as Durham led his company across the pasture toward the enemy's well-fortified position. They began taking incoming fire from the enemy almost immediately.

"Who gave that order?" Nathan looked over at Tom.

But Tom's eyes widened with sudden comprehension, *"You* did, sir."

"What? I never..."

"Sir, you looked right at Durham when you said you wanted to carry that enemy position. He must've taken it for an order."

Nathan slapped his hand against his forehead, "Oh my dear God! I *did* order it ... *but not on purpose."*

Nathan turned to his right, cupped his hands, and shouted, *"Twelfth West Virginia will fix bayonets, and prepare to advance on my command!"*

The order was relayed down the line, and men scrambled to obey. A moment later, Nathan leapt to the top of the wall, followed by Tom, Tony, one very large hound, and the remaining officers and men of the Twelfth. Colonel Chambers swept out his saber, held it aloft pointed out toward the enemy and shouted, *"Charge!"*

Eight hundred blue-uniformed West Virginians poured over the wall and raced toward the enemy position, where their own companies B and E could be seen already near the base of the far wall, firing off rounds from their rifles as they moved steadily forward. Enemy rifles continued to pop off their rounds, and puffs of smoke drifted in the air above the rebel position.

In moments, the men of the Twelfth swept up over the rebels' wall. But the several hundred Confederates who'd been holding it were already falling back in an organized retreat, steadily firing their rifles as they went. The West Virginians crouched or went prone, returning fire. But after a few moments, the rebels could no longer been seen, melting off down the hillside, and ducking behind additional earthworks there. So Nathan called a halt and ordered the regiment to scramble back over the wall that they might hold it as their new forward position.

Once back on the north side of the wall, he went looking for Durham, but for a time couldn't find him, and nobody seemed to know where he was. So Nathan strode back across the field, calling out, "Durham ... Lieutenant Durham! Are you out here, Lieutenant?"

He was about to turn back and order a general search when he heard a low moan off to his left, and a weak voice, "I ... I'm here, colonel."

Nathan pushed through the tall grass and found Durham lying on his back, his left arm bleeding and broken, dangling at an unnatural angle. Nathan stooped down, scooped the man up into his arms as if he were a mere child, then trotted back toward the wall, shouting, "Bring the surgeon ... Captain Jenkins ... to me, on the double!"

Once the young lieutenant was given over into William's care, Nathan, Tom, and Jim met to discuss their position. Though they'd pushed the rebels back more easily than they should have—seemingly confirming Nathan's suspicions about a ruse— even so, they were now dangerously exposed and overextended. And to make matters worse, looking through his spyglass Nathan could no longer see the two Ohio regiments that should have at least continued to hold at their previous positions, but they seemed to have instead withdrawn.

He called for Billy, but no one knew where the scout was, not even Stan, who just shrugged when asked. "He is not always telling me where he goes ... Is odd, me being his big brother."

Then he laughed and smiled his broad, toothsome grin, which rarely failed to elicit a chuckle from Nathan, regardless of the situation.

The Twelfth dug in behind the new forward wall, but soon began taking enemy fire, and not just from out past the wall; they were beginning to take incoming rounds from the left and right flanks. Soon they started taking sniper rounds coming in from up the hill behind them as well, forcing every man to lay flat on the ground, and half of them to face back toward where they'd come, trying to target the hidden enemy sharpshooters by their telltale puffs of gun smoke.

Then Billy was suddenly next to Nathan, crawling across the ground on his belly, until their faces were just inches apart in the dirt, "Good to see you, Sergeant Creek."

Billy nodded, "It is good to see you too, Captain." Billy was the only one of Nathan's men from Texas who seemed to not understand or care about Nathan's new rank, a thing Nathan chose to ignore, figuring Billy had earned the right.

"Report, Billy?"

"It is not good … The Ohio men of our side have withdrawn, and our left flank is open. The right is only guarded by distant artillery, which is to little effect."

"And the enemy?"

Billy shrugged, "They are many, though so far, they hold back. Rebels to the right of us, rebels to the left of us, rebels to the front of us, and rebels behind. And far beyond all these … *rebels*."

Nathan nodded, "Time to go, then."

"Yes, Captain," Billy agreed in his usual matter-of-fact way. If Billy felt any concern or fear from their current predicament, he didn't show it.

A difficult and dangerous hour followed, as the Twelfth West Virginia fought their way back to their previous stone wall, then continued to fall back to the artillery redoubt, where they found Captain Carlin and his big guns along with the two delinquent Ohio regiments already dug back in.

Casualties had been surprisingly light, despite the large numbers of enemy soldiers and the number of rounds expended on both sides, for which Nathan was thankful. He was also thankful to see Lieutenant Durham sitting up, leaning against the dirt wall of the redoubt, drinking from a canteen, his left arm bound up in a sling.

Nathan walked over to him, sent away the other men gathered there, and sat down next to Durham. "How's the arm, Mr. Durham?"

Durham graced him with a quick smile, though Nathan could see the young lieutenant was in a good deal of pain.

"Not too bad, Colonel, considering it's shot clean through and broken. But Captain Jenkins examined the wound and told me I was lucky, that I'd most likely not lose the arm. He felt along the bones and said the bullet passed right between 'em, and they were likely only cracked and not shattered. So, he set the bones, sewed up the bullet hole, and splinted the whole thing—pert-near good as new." He chuckled softly, but then winced at the pain. "The captain ... he's a good doctor..."

"Yes, Captain Jenkins is the most competent physician I've ever served with. We're damned lucky to have him."

"Yes, sir ... but more than that, he makes a fella feel like once he takes charge, all will be well. That's worth a lot."

Nathan nodded his agreement, then proceeded to the topic foremost on his mind. "Durham, I wished to tell you how proud I am of your conduct on the field today. That was as boldly and bravely done as any action I've ever had the honor of witnessing."

"Thank you, sir. That is gracious of you to say..."

"I mean it, Durham ... I intend to write you up for a medal when this is over. But ... I also wish to apologize to you."

"Oh? For what, sir?"

"That I never intended for you to attack with just your one company ... My intention was for the regiment to attack as a whole. But I fear I misspoke when I was addressing you, and I led you to believe you were on your own. I feel badly that it nearly got you killed."

Durham chuckled. "Thank you for that, sir. But I reckon I share some blame on it; I could've asked for clarification on your orders.

My momma always said I was a bit impetuous, and that it was like to get me killed one day. Luckily today wasn't that day."

Nathan grinned and stood. He patted Durham softly on the good shoulder, then returned to his usual position next to Tom.

ഇ)രുഗ്ലൂ)ഇ)രുഗ്ലൂ)ഇ)രുഗു

Sunday June 14, 1863, 5:00 p.m. – Winchester, Virginia:

"I hear what you're saying, Chambers," General Milroy nodded slowly as he gazed through his field glasses out toward the enemy's position, back down the hillside from the artillery redoubt currently occupied by the Twelfth and the Wheeling Artillery Battery. Milroy and his staff had ridden out for a firsthand look at the rebel action shortly after the general's rebuff of the Confederate emissary.

"And I'll admit it's a possibility." Milroy lowered the glasses and turned back toward Nathan to look him in the eye. "But I must disagree, Colonel. There's no sign of Ewell preparing a major assault against our fortifications; all his forces, save scattered cavalry patrols, are coming at us from the south and east, which we have effectively thwarted with our well-dug-in positions, and our long-range guns. I've already sent out the Twelfth Pennsylvania Cavalry to reconnoiter to the north of the Star Fort, and out past the West Fort, and they report no rebel presence in either of those directions.

"And ... one must also consider Ewell's attempt at bluffing me into surrendering," Milroy scowled. "Seems like an act of desperation to me—he knows he'll waste a great deal of his manpower and equipment trying to drive us out.

"Besides which, they've already tested our mettle, and, in part thanks to you and the Twelfth, Chambers, they've found us more than up to the challenge.

"No, I hear what you're saying, Colonel, but I can't agree with it." Milroy then softened his tone. "But ... that being said, I am inclined to have another good look ... See if we can't figure out once and for all what he's *really* up to. I've a mind to send the Ohio regiments back down this hill to have another go at them. If they can push the rebels farther back down the hill, I believe it will be proof that they aren't serious about this engagement, and are more eager to get on to the North and hit more lucrative and less heavily defended targets.

"Your Twelfth has already given good service today, so go ahead and stay put here for now. I'll hold you in reserve. But be prepared to advance on a moment's notice, in case the Ohioans get in a fix."

"Yes, sir." Nathan gave his commander a salute. But as Milroy raised his hand to return the salute, he paused and his eyes widened, and the gesture remained incomplete as his hand slowly lowered again. "*What the—?*" He stared off past Nathan into the sky.

Nathan turned to see what had caught the general's eye. And even as he did, he heard a distant *whump* of a single big gun being fired in the distance. The noise was singular and incongruous, as the guns from the Union forts had been silent for the last several hours for fear of hitting the forward Union skirmishers, and the rebels had not yet managed to move any guns within range of the Union forts. Nathan watched as a streak of light rose up from the hills beyond the West Fort, arced high over the Main Fort, and finally descended toward downtown Winchester. But before the streaking object hit ground there came a brilliant flash of light, followed by a distant concussive ... *boom!*

Milroy turned back toward Nathan, and they shared a look of shock. This lone artillery shell from the wooded hills out to the west could only mean one thing: the rebel artillery was now where none were supposed to be—and in position to pound the Union forts!

"Prepare to defend this position, Colonel," Milroy shouted, even as he sprinted toward where his staff officers held his horse. He jumped into the saddle. "Pull back to the rifle pits when you can, and bring the Ohioans. We must consolidate our forces!"

Then he yanked hard on the reins and spurred toward the Main Fort, followed by his staff officers. But his horse had not taken two strides when a great cacophony arose from out west where the first shell had originated. Twenty or more enemy guns opened fire in a tremendous volley: all were now targeting the West Fort. A great plume of gun smoke now wafted up above the wooded hills.

Nathan hadn't the time nor the inclination to enjoy any satisfaction from being proven right about the rebels' intentions. He turned and trotted back to the earthworks of the redoubt intending to order his troops into line of battle. But by the time he reached his usual position next to Tom at the center of the line, the orders had already been given by his second in command, and men were scrambling to take up firing positions in the redoubt. Captain Carlin's artillerymen were also swarming around their guns, like bees in a beehive, frantically preparing to return fire against the rebel guns, if they could target them.

Moments later, additional rebel artillery opened fire in front of the Twelfth's position. But the Twelfth and its small artillery battery weren't the intended target, and the rebel shells arced high overhead, screaming out toward both the West Fort and the Main Fort.

Leaning out over the earthworks, Nathan counted ten or more guns that the rebels had apparently moved forward during the night and carefully hidden behind obstructions throughout the day. The initial lone rebel artillery shell fired from the west hills had clearly been the signal for all pre-positioned rebel guns to open fire on the Union forts.

Nathan and his men could do nothing for the moment other than watch the spectacular thunderous display, and pray for the Union soldiers now hunkered down in the forts, enduring the tremendous barrage and scrambling to answer in kind.

Within moments, the great, thunderous guns of the Main Fort opened fire in earnest against the enemy artillery positions. They were soon joined by the smaller guns of the West Fort, the Star Fort, and various smaller forward artillery redoubts, such as the one occupied by Captain Carlin's Wheeling Battery. But what effect, if any, the Union guns were having against their well-hidden rebel counterparts, Nathan was unable to tell.

When a half-hour had passed, with no sign of an infantry assault against their position, Nathan decided it would be a good time to fall back to a less exposed position in the rifle pits just outside the Main Fort. But he knew if the Twelfth pulled out now, Captain Carlin's guns would be left undefended, so Nathan went to Carlin and ordered him to pull up stakes and withdraw into the relative safety of the Main Fort. Once the battery was packed up, the Twelfth moved out at double-time, even as the artillery duel continued to rage, projectiles screaming through the skies above them and detonating with deafening concussions all around.

Once back in the rifle pits, Nathan ordered his men to stand to their firing positions in preparation for the inevitable rebel assault that would follow the bombardment.

He said a quick prayer that his men might hold fast against the tempest that was surely coming to engulf them, which ended with one of his favorite Bible verses that seemed most appropriate under the circumstances: *When thou goest out to battle against thine enemies, and seest horses, and chariots, and a people more than thou, be not afraid of them: for the Lord thy God is with thee.*

CHAPTER 4. BESET AND BESIEGED

"They've got us surrounded again,
the poor bastards."
- U.S. Army Colonel Creighton Abrams

Sunday June 14, 1863, 5:00 p.m. – Washington, D.C.:

"What the devil is this news I'm hearing about Winchester?" President Lincoln strode into the telegraph room at the War Department and stepped up to Secretary of War Stanton.

"Good afternoon, Mr. President." Stanton rose from the stool where he'd been sitting as he read the latest dispatch.

"Is it?" Lincoln frowned, forgoing his usual polite greeting.

"No ... apparently *not*, sir." Stanton handed the president the telegram he'd been reading.

Lincoln scowled as he quickly read the paper.

"General Ewell? The entire Second Corps of Lee's army? How can that be, Mr. Secretary? According to General Hooker, he has the entire Army of Northern Virginia pinned down near Fredericksburg. That's ... I don't know ... ninety miles or so away from Winchester..."

"Yes, sir. That was our belief, but General Milroy says several rebel prisoners have now confirmed it, and the fortifications at Winchester are now under general assault by a very large, well-equipped rebel force, with plenty of artillery."

"Damn it, Edwin! How could this have happened? Telegram General Hooker at Fredericksburg straightaway, asking him if it's possible Ewell's entire command is now attacking Winchester ... and if so, how?"

"Yes, Mr. President." Stanton turned toward the telegraph at the table next to him and nodded at a young lieutenant, who immediately began tapping out the message he'd just heard, addressed to the Union general in command of the Army of the Potomac.

"And who's currently in command of Milroy's sector?"

"Major General Robert Schenck, sir, from his headquarters in Baltimore."

"Then telegraph General Schenck and tell him to order Milroy to retreat to Harpers Ferry. He'll be gobbled up if he remains; if he's not already past salvation." Lincoln slowly shook his head in consternation.

Stanton nodded and then trotted over to the next telegraph operator to relay the message.

Lincoln removed his top hat and sat heavily in a simple wooden chair behind the long table that accommodated a row of uniformed telegraph operators, mostly young officers. The president wiped the sweat from his brow, took a deep breath, and forced himself to relax.

But a few minutes later, Stanton returned to face the president. The secretary had a dark expression, and Lincoln experienced a sudden, sick knot in the pit of his stomach.

"What is it, Edwin?" he asked.

"Sir … General Schenck has informed me that he can no longer reach General Milroy. The telegraph wires to Winchester have been cut."

❧❧❧❧❧❧❧❧❧

Sunday June 14, 1863, 5:30 p.m. – Wheeling, West Virginia:

Abbey had just stepped out the front door of the farmhouse at Belle Meade, thinking to take a stroll down to the river, when she was surprised to see three riders coming up the drive. Two carried rifles slung over their shoulders and the third, riding in the lead, was dressed in a dark suit as a proper gentleman.

She was gratified to see Henry and Big George step out onto the drive, some fifty yards out from the house, rifles in hand, barring the way to the riders. Big George raised his left hand, signaling the riders to stop, and they quickly complied. Abbey could see they were conversing, and then the two freemen quickly stepped aside, allowing the riders to continue toward the house.

As they approached, she knew why they'd been allowed to pass so quickly: the two armed men were dressed in blue Union

Army uniforms. But it was the third rider, in civilian clothing, that startled Abbey: it was Governor Francis Pierpont of the Restored Government of Virginia.

When the riders came to a stop at the end of the drive in front of the walk to the house, the governor tipped his hat, "Good afternoon, Miss Abbey."

"Good afternoon, Governor," she answered with a quick curtsy. And though her instinct told her to immediately ask the obvious polite question, *"To what do we owe this honor?"*, before the words would come, a sudden frightful thought came into her mind like a bolt of lightning and threatened to drop her to her knees: *Something terrible has happened to Nathan! Why else would the governor come himself?*

But through a force of will she retained her composure, though she found she was unable to speak. The panic in her mind had her convinced that if she spoke, she'd be granting the governor permission to deliver the heart-wrenching news she never wanted to hear. If only she kept quiet, he would not be able to tell her...

"My ... I must say I approve of your security here at the farm, Miss Abbey," he waved back toward where the freemen had accosted him and his soldiers. "I'd say the rebel bushwhackers will think twice before coming onto your property again."

And just then, Cobb and Phinney stepped up to take charge of the horses. Each of the freemen carried a pistol holster at their hip, as if to validate the governor's words.

Abbey nodded, fighting to remain calm and trying to smile politely, "Yes, your honor, they are good men. They take their duty seriously ... and with good reason."

"Yes, yes, certainly ... I've heard about all the troubles you've had with *unfriendly* neighbors, both old and new ..." he glanced over at Phinney's missing arm, which he'd heard about from Nathan, but hadn't seen before.

But then the governor trailed off, noting the haunted look on Abbey's face and sensing her reticence. A serious, concerned look now knit his brow. "May I come in, Miss Abbey?"

"Of course, of course, Mr. Pierpont, certainly. Please do, sir."

Moments later, they convened in the small sitting room that served as the Belle Meade library. The governor declined Megs' offer of tea and sat across from Abbey, gazing intently into her eyes. Megs stood behind her, resting a hand on her shoulder.

"Miss Abbey ... I don't know you well, but Nathan has spoken of you such that I am well aware that you are a very perceptive, intelligent woman. So I must presume my presence here in person has caused you more than a little trepidation, for which I humbly apologize."

Abbey could think of nothing to say, and could feel her throat beginning to constrict from a fear that now threatened to overwhelm her. She could only manage a nod, allowing him to continue with what he'd come to say.

"So first let me ease your fears, somewhat ... and tell you straight off that I have no specific news that anything ill has befallen Nathan or any of his men."

At this statement Abbey felt relief roll through her like a flood, and she could no longer hold back the emotions she'd been suppressing. She put her face in her hands. "Oh, thank God ... thank God," she whispered, fighting back an urge to break down and sob.

Megs reached down, took one of her hands, and squeezed it.

"I'm sorry for frightening you so, Miss Abbey." The governor now spoke in a softer tone. "But that being said, my news is *not* good ... and I'm sorry to say it will likely cause you fear and dismay, from which I would spare you if I could."

Abbey looked back up at him, wiped away her tears, and waited for him to continue.

"Miss Abbey ... Megs ... I have received a telegram from the War Department earlier today that Winchester is presently under attack by a large rebel formation, believed to be a portion of General Lee's army."

Abbey gasped, but no longer felt overwhelmed. As dire as this news was, it at least held out some measure of hope; Nathan was not dead or seriously wounded after all, at least not yet, and he could still *fight*. And she knew with a rock-hard certainty that fighting was the thing her son knew best.

Abbey's voice was still shaky, "And ... what of the garrison at Winchester?"

"Well, the good news is, they are well supplied, and occupy a highly defensible position. I am led to understand the fortifications at Winchester are formidable, and feature high, thick walls along with very large guns that may help counter a much greater force. And so far, at least, it seems there has not yet been a major engagement, only minor skirmishing. So there is some hope the rebel army will soon give it up and go elsewhere."

Abbey nodded but could think of nothing to say to this, so the governor continued, "I'm afraid this is really all the news I have at the moment, dear ladies ... but on account of my long friendship with Nathan, I wanted you to hear it from me first, rather than reading about it in the newspapers. Though unfortunately there is very little I can do to aid them at the moment, you can be sure I will do everything in my power to do so, should the opportunity arise. And I will make you a promise to keep you informed by courier the moment I have any news, one way or the other."

"Thank you, governor," Abbey smiled, but fought to suppress another round of tears.

"Yes, thank you very kindly for coming, your honor, and not just sending a messenger," Megs added. "That was very thoughtful of you. I know Nathan will be grateful when he learns of it."

ℬ)ℭℛℭℬℬℭ)ℬ)ℭℛℭℬℭℬℬℭ)ℬ)ℭℛℭℬ

After the governor departed, Abbey steeled herself for the difficult, painful task she considered her duty: to tell everyone else on the farm the frightful news, starting with those most closely affected, the women whose men were stationed at Winchester—Margaret, Rosa, and Adilida, plus Edouard, whose son was also there. After she told each in person, one on one, she thought she'd call together everyone else on the farm for a general announcement. But Megs volunteered for *that* task. So between them, the bad news was soon disseminated.

Though the news cast a dark pall over the entire farm, Adilida seemed to be most impacted by it, and she took to her bed in tears, nearly inconsolable, convinced Thomas and Phillipe would soon be killed. The news hit her so hard she became entirely incapable of dealing with little Nathaniel, who was too young to understand what it all meant but was frightened and hurt by his mother's reaction.

Nathaniel was sitting on the floor in the hallway outside Adilida's room, head in his hands and a sad look on his face when Megs came along.

She saw him there, noting his downcast look, and it triggered a memory of another little boy long ago. She knelt down and looked him in the eye. "Nathaniel, how about old Megs reads you a story ... would you like that?" she asked.

He nodded his head, though he still held onto his pout. So Megs took him by the hand and led him downstairs to the library. She searched through the bookshelf, until she found the book she was looking for and took it down. It was an old book, and a little worn around the edges, but it immediately brought a smile to her face. She took it and sat in a chair, placing Nathaniel on her lap. She opened the book, and inside the cover was a colorful illustration of a knight in shining armor, riding a white horse, his long spear thrust forward. Nathaniel gazed at the picture, wide-eyed.

"Nathaniel, this here book was one of your Uncle Nathan's favorites when he was a little boy like you. I used to read it to him whenever he was sad ... like you are now."

Nathaniel looked up at her and nodded. "Read it?" he asked.

She chuckled, "Yes ... I will read it to you, if you wish," she answered.

"'Kay," he answered, and went back to examining the picture.

"This book is called *The Adventures of King Arthur and His Knights of the Round Table*," she began, but had to wipe a tear from the corner of her eye before she continued.

❦❧❨❩❦❧❨❩❦❧❨

Evelyn rapped on the large, elaborately carved mahogany door with its intricately detailed brass door knocker, shaped as a lion's head. She turned and gazed back down the broad stone-paved walkway that crossed the Hugheses' immaculate gardens, leading toward the cobblestone street.

A moment later, she turned and knocked again, but even as she did so, she realized it was bordering on rudeness. She knew her extreme anxiety had triggered an impatience that threatened to get the best of her. So she stepped back, took a deep breath, and waited for the door to be answered.

After another interminable moment, the door opened and the freeman butler Sam gazed out, dressed as always in formal black suit with white gloves. "Miss Evelyn," he bowed.

And then, despite her determination to calm down and behave more respectfully, Evelyn immediately stepped into the foyer past the butler. "Good afternoon, Sam. I must see Angeline or Jonathan straightaway."

But if Sam was surprised or bothered by her lack of decorum, he showed no sign of it. "Miss Angeline is in the sitting room, Miss Evelyn. I believe you will find she is expecting you." He gave her a slight smile and another bow.

"Oh!" Evelyn turned and looked Sam in the eye. "Sorry, Sam ... I am ... a bit out of sorts today. Would you please forgive my rudeness?"

"There is nothing to forgive, Miss Evelyn. Please ... come in."

She gave him a quick half-smile, then turned and stepped into the sitting room, which was just off the entryway foyer.

Angeline stood to greet her, but before she could speak, Evelyn began quizzing her, "Is it true, Angeline? Is General Lee assailing Winchester with his entire army, even as we speak? I've been hearing all sorts of rumors since early this morning but did not know what to believe. I've been going back and forth between disbelief and absolute terror since I first heard the news, so I just had to come see you, to learn if it's true."

But even before the words had rolled from her tongue in a rapid-fire stream, Evelyn knew with heart-wrenching certainty that the rumors *were* true, for Angeline held a dark, severe expression.

"I'm afraid it's true, my dear," Angeline gestured to the chair next to where she'd been sitting, sipping a cup of tea. "Please, Evelyn ... have a seat and I will tell you everything I know."

"No, Angeline, I can't possibly sit at a time like this ... It means ... it means Nathan is in *terrible* danger, along with all his dear men. The meager garrison at Winchester is no match for General Lee's *entire army!* Why, they'll be ... they'll just be ... *slaughtered...*" She was now so choked with emotion she could barely get out the last dreadful word.

And then despite her words to the contrary, Evelyn sat heavily in the chair, put her head in her hands, and began to sob such as she'd not done in many long months of never-ending fear and danger.

Angeline came and knelt next to Evelyn's chair, putting her arms around her young friend and protégé. "Yes, it's serious news, my dear, but perhaps not quite as hopeless as it seemed at first."

Evelyn looked up and met eyes with Angeline as she wiped away her tears. "What do you mean?"

"Well, from our sources, we have learned it is only a portion of Lee's army that now surrounds Winchester. Ewell's Second Corp, so ... hmm ... Perhaps only a third of Lee's Army of Northern Virginia. Still, it is a considerable force, there can be no doubt..."

"Not much consolation." Evelyn shook her head, trying to fight back the emotions that threatened to overwhelm her. "Still plenty enough to conquer Winchester. How ever did it happen? Last I heard, Lee was pinned down by Hooker at Fredericksburg ... how could a third of his army suddenly be at Winchester? It makes no sense..."

Angeline nodded and frowned, "Yes, it's a conundrum, all right, and unfortunately speaks to more incompetence at the highest levels of the Union army. As if we needed any more evidence of *that!*"

Sam entered the room at that moment with a fresh pot of tea. Without asking, he poured Evelyn a cup and set it in front of her.

"Thank you, Sam." Evelyn lifted the cup to her lips, softly blowing on it, more out of habit than conscious thought.

"You are most welcome, Miss Evelyn." He paused for a moment with a concerned look. "And ... may I say, my heart goes out to you during this difficult time. I pray all will turn out well for the good Colonel Chambers and his men."

She looked up at him and graced him with a quick smile, wiping away the tears. "Thank you, Sam. I appreciate that, very much."

Sam nodded, returned her half-smile, then bowed again before exiting the room.

Angeline returned to her own seat. "Please, Evelyn, stay here with me today. Perhaps it will be of some comfort ... and we can share any news that may come in."

But Evelyn was already shaking her head, "I can't, Angeline ... I simply can't. But thank you. I just can't sit still while Nathan is ... Nathan is..." She became choked up again and couldn't speak for a long moment. "I ... I must *do* something..."

"I understand," Angeline nodded. "But ... what will you do?"

Then the two women gazed intently into each other's eyes, and despite the tears, Evelyn now held a determined look. "If I was there, I would shoulder a rifle and fight next to him. My Daddy taught me to shoot, you know. I would rather die fighting next to Nathan than sit here in safety while he ... he..." she trailed off, unable to finish the thought aloud.

Angeline said nothing, allowing Evelyn the space to think through her answer and deal with her fears.

"But I can't fight with him ... I'm not there, and there's no way for me to get there. No ... there's nothing I can do to help Nathan. *Nothing at all...*" she slowly shook her head, gazing down at the floor once again.

Then she looked back up, "But I *can* do something to help the Union. We can no longer wait patiently; we simply *must* learn what General Lee is up to. His bold move against Winchester points to a bigger move against the North.

"I will meet with Mary, and between us we *must* come up with a way to get Lee's war plans from President Davis, straightaway."

"But my dear ... with Major White pressing his investigation ... it may be too risky," Angeline frowned, slowly shaking her head.

But Evelyn wiped back the tears and stood, "I no longer care, Angeline." She turned and headed for the door.

∞)(୫(୪∞)୫)(୫(୪∞)∞)(୫(୪

Sunday June 14, 1863, 5:45 p.m. – Winchester, Virginia:

The rebel bombardment abruptly ceased three-quarters of an hour after it had commenced. Colonel Joseph Keifer, commander of the 110th Ohio infantry, jumped up from behind the wall where he'd been sheltering in the West Fort. He'd stayed hunkered down with the rest of his regiment while a storm of fire and lead from the rebel artillery impacted all around them.

And the Union gunners had done their best to answer their adversaries, firing off high explosive shells as quickly as they could load their guns. It had been an awe-inspiring experience for the young colonel, such as he'd never before imagined. But there had been little he could do but watch as the tremendous deluge of incoming artillery rounds gradually took their toll on the Union battery, now down to just two three-inch guns and a dozen men to man them.

But Keifer knew what was surely coming next, now that the bombardment had ended. So he cupped his hands and turned to the left and shouted, "110th Ohio will stand to, fix bayonets, and prepare to meet the enemy!"

He immediately turned to his right and repeated the shouted command. He was gratified, though not surprised, when his entire regiment immediately rose as one, attached their bayonets, shouldered their rifles, and stepped up to firing positions on the wall. And he was pleased to note that the men around him held grim, determined looks, but showed little fear.

He turned and shouted at the lieutenant now in command of the artillery to load cannister in the remaining guns and prepare to fire on his command. The lieutenant acknowledged the command with a nod and a salute. Then Keifer shouted for his men to prepare for volley fire but to hold fire until he gave the command.

Keifer leaned out on top of the wall, raised his binoculars, and examined the distant tree line, 400 yards away down a long, treeless slope. Treeless, but not without obstacles, he noted with grim satisfaction; midway up the slope, a great tangle of sharpened and well dug-in tree trunks and branches, called *abatis*, presented a daunting barrier to any infantry troops attempting the perilous, exposed trek up the hillside to attack the fort. And the fort itself featured a deep trench below its thick, eight-foot-high walls—another daunting obstacle for soldiers afoot.

Keifer panned his binoculars along the tree line, moving his field of view slowly from north to south, but so far, he saw no sign of the enemy. He lowered the binoculars and gazed out at the woods expectantly—still nothing.

But then a sudden movement caught his eye due west of his position, and he raised the binoculars for a closer look: rebels by the thousands, bayonets fixed to their rifles, had just stood up from the underbrush at the woods' edge, and were now moving out into the field beyond. And then he heard a strange wailing shout rising up from the enemy position—the now infamous rebel yell. The Confederates were moving quickly down a short slope, across a narrow ravine, and then up the slope toward the fort. Keifer panned back and forth across the rebel line as the enemy continued to pour out of the woods in a great flood of humanity, uncountable thousands upon thousands. Then he focused on the banners they carried and cursed to himself, *Damn the luck ... General Harry Hays and his godforsaken Louisiana Tigers!* The regiments from Louisiana had developed a reputation for a high degree of discipline and proficiency combined with an unmatched reckless ferocity; in short, what Keifer now saw coming at him was the very last thing he would've preferred to see. But he steeled himself and thought, *But we Ohioans can fight too, Hays. Bring it on!*

He lowered his binoculars again, that he might take in the whole scene. He made a quick estimate of the numbers coming at him and gasped—five full regiments at the least, nearly five-thousand Louisianans, coming fast ... against his five hundred Ohioans ... with only two cannons remaining.

ℰℭℴℭℴℰℭℴℭℴℰℭℴℭℴℰℭℴℭℴ

The labyrinth of tree trunks and interlocked limbs, sharpened on the ends, caused only a momentary delay to the oncoming tide; the rebels climbed, clambered, and scrambled through the thick tumble of timber with astonishing speed and enthusiasm.

Keifer ordered a rifle volley that filled the *abatis* with dead rebel bodies. But this only seemed to encourage the enemy soldiers to greater efforts, and soon a great wave of Louisiana Tigers approached the fort up the slope at a run.

Keifer waved his sword at the artillery officer and the two big Union guns spoke, cutting a great, gory swath across the advancing enemy line. But the rebels closed up ranks without pause, coming on shoulder to shoulder, howling like fiends.

"One more volley men, then give them steel!" Keifer shouted. *"Present ... aim ... fire!"*

Keifer's soldiers fired their rifles—a great thunderous roar and a swirling cloud of gun smoke—then braced to meet the onslaught with only their bayonets. The rebels held their fire until they were within twenty yards of the breastworks. Then, as if on cue, they paused, formed up, and fired a massive rifle volley, forcing the Ohioans back down off the wall. The rebels then let out another tremendous shout and came on with bayonets.

The long ditch in front of the fort's wall proved only a brief obstacle; the rebels dragged their own dead up to the wall, piled them in at the base of it, then climbed over them to reach the crest and scramble over the top. Even one last-ditch round of cannister fire from the three-inch guns had little effect, the rebels simply closing ranks and continuing to come on.

86

Though a few panicked Ohioans turned and raced for the rear in the face of this incomprehensible terror, most soldiered on, fighting hand-to-hand, stabbing with bayonets, and clubbing with rifle buttstocks. Colonel Keifer, shouting and slashing with his sword like a man possessed, stubbornly refused to yield, despite the tremendous odds against him. And though they fought with courage and tenacity, the federals were pushed inexorably backward across the West Fort grounds by the great weight of numbers pressing against them.

But when the captain fighting next to him fell with a bullet hole through the center of his forehead, Keifer turned and saw that his flanks were turned, both to the right and the left. So finally, he ordered a fall back, fighting all the way out through the eastern gate and down the slope toward the Main Fort.

And though the rebels who'd breached the West Fort continued to target the retreating federals with their rifles, for the most part they did not pursue the Ohioans; the irresistible spoils of the abandoned Union supplies, including supper still hot, proved too distracting for them. This fortuitous circumstance greatly aided Keifer's escape. Within a few short minutes, the gate to the Main Fort was flung wide to allow the retreating Ohioans to enter at a trot. When the gate clanged closed again, Keifer, still out of breath from his exertions, did a quick count and realized with a shock that he had just lost a third of his men.

෯෯ඥ෪ඇ෮෯෯ඥ෪ඇ෮෯෯ඥ෪

Colonel Chambers and the Twelfth West Virginia had also endured heavy fighting from their position in the rifle pits to the south of the Main Fort, exchanging multiple rifle volleys with advancing rebel infantry units. From their regimental banners, Nathan believed these to be the very same rebels they'd been fighting the last two days, part of General Gordon's brigade of Georgians. But Nathan was reasonably sure, despite the heavy fighting, that this was once again only a distraction in the bigger rebel scheme, its main purpose only to keep the Twelfth occupied and pinned down while the main rebel assault hit the West Fort, their real target.

Nathan now realized with a sinking feeling that the rebels meant to take the West Fort and then use its higher ground to bombard the Main Fort and the Star Fort into submission. And he figured it would very likely work.

Approximately an hour after the major artillery duel had ended, and a quarter hour since the last rebel volley to their front, Nathan received a courier from General Milroy, informing him that the rebels had taken the West Fort, and ordering him to maintain his present defensive position. Nathan could only shake his head and wonder what would become of them now.

A few minutes later, another great artillery duel began; this time the rebels fired artillery positioned in the West Fort down at the Main Fort. Meanwhile, the artillery back in the west woods, and down to the south of Nathan's position, targeted the Star Fort. The rebel artillery now greatly outnumbered the federal guns in the remaining forts, whose gunners did their best to return fire. This cannonade continued unabated for another half hour.

And even as the guns fell silent once again, Tom, who happened to be looking back toward the Main Fort, caught Nathan's attention and nodded, wide-eyed, back in that direction. Nathan turned around and was shocked to see General Milroy himself striding down the hill toward him.

Nathan snapped a salute, which was abruptly returned, but Milroy was obviously in a hurry and not of a mind for the usual formalities. "Chambers ... now that they hold the high ground, I expect an all-out assault by the rebels before this day ends—they mean to annihilate us, and we shall be hard-pressed on all sides. But I mean to stop them right here and now. Have your men stand by with fixed bayonets and loaded rifles at the half-cock. Hold fire until the rebels reach the rifle pits, then give them hell ... and receive them with the bayonet!"

Major Jim Wiggins standing nearby heard the general's orders. After Milroy departed, Jim stepped up to Nathan and grinned, "Goddamn it, Colonel ... we done been outnumbered up at Rich Mountain, over to Harpers Ferry, and down in the Kanawha Valley. And now here at Winchester town. What I want to know, sir, is … when do *we* get to be the ones outnumbering them other fellas over yonder?"

And despite the dire nature of their predicament, Nathan couldn't help snorting a laugh and slapping Jim on the back. "Well, it never seemed to help McClellan much, did it?"

Jim nodded, continuing to grin, "Yeah … but *you* sure as hell ain't McClellan, sir!"

ುುುುುುುುುುುುುುುುುುುು

As the sun began to set, long columns of rebels could be seen descending from West Fort toward the Main Fort and marching up the hill from the south toward Nathan's position. And this time it would be no diversion, but rather an all-out assault, intended to overrun the Twelfth and take the fort if they could.

Nathan took advantage of the brief calm before the storm to buoy up the morale of his men, standing before them and calling out, "Gentlemen, we prepare to fight a mighty foe today, but I have faith that courage and righteousness will prevail … *Thus saith the LORD unto you, Be not afraid nor dismayed by reason of this great multitude; for the battle is not yours, but God's.*"

When the rebel columns were in position around the Main Fort, the usual rebel yell arose, and on they came. When the rebels were within thirty yards of the Twelfth's rifle pit, Colonel Chambers gave the command to open fire, and the exposed rebel advance was stalled. Nathan's officers continued to pour devastating fire into them with their repeating rifles, until the Confederates pulled back.

After a few minutes, the rebels regrouped and charged again. And once more, the Twelfth West Virginia rose up and hammered them with withering volley fire, this time staggered, company by company, stopping the charge just yards short of the rifle pits.

With darkness coming on, the rebels made one final attempt to breach the fort's defenses and came at the Twelfth with renewed determination and ferocity. This time the attack was so intense that three rebel soldiers actually pushed forward and came up over the earthworks, right in the center of the Union line where Nathan and Tom were standing.

Nathan raised his Henry rifle, aimed it at the rebel nearest him, and pulled the trigger, but the hammer fell with a *click* on an empty chamber. He dropped the rifle and swept out his sword. The man thrust forward with his bayonet. Nathan knocked the rifle aside with the saber and ran the man through in one smooth motion.

Tom Clark fired his revolver point blank at another rebel. The man crumpled to the ground.

But Nathan was still trying to pull his sword free from the soldier he'd skewered when the third rebel lunged at him with his bayonet. But the man's thrust suddenly jerked to the side and missed as the man gasped in pain. Harry the Dog had latched onto him mid-thigh with a great mouth full of sharp teeth. And at that same instant a rifle shot rang out right next to Nathan's left ear, nearly knocking him over. The rebel crumpled to the ground with the hound on top of him, still growling fiercely and shaking the body from side to side. Both Nathan and Tom turned to see Tony standing there, a fierce look on his face and smoke curling up from his rifle.

With the Confederate advance stopped and darkness setting in, all guns fell silent for the night. But the screams and groans of the rebel wounded, laying beyond help out in the fields, continued long into the night.

ᔥᏇᏇᎻᏇᏇᎻᏇᏇᎻ

An hour after sunset, C.S.A. Brigadier General John Gordon, whose brigade of Georgians had spent the last two days fighting against the West Virginia and Ohio regiments, sat in his command tent enjoying the warm afterglow of a victorious day in the field; the West Fort had been taken, and its artillery emplacements turned against the Union's Main Fort. The Union regiments had now been pushed back to the very walls of the Main Fort, leaving the Star Fort dangerously exposed, such that it would likely fall early in the morning with just a little more push.

That left only one major obstacle: the Main Fort. It was still a forbidding impediment to a Confederate victory: massive, well-defended within and without, heavy siege guns, and long,

90

exposed slopes. He shuddered at the thought of a serious attempt at breaching its walls. They'd given it a good try after the West Fort had fallen, and it'd been like breakers smashing against sea cliffs: a lot of show and noise, but little actual impact or hope of success.

But he figured General Ewell would now be content to simply lay siege to the Main Fort, seize the town of Winchester, and then move on into the North to meet up with General Lee, letting Milroy rot, penned up in impotent fury—a tempest in a teapot.

But Gordon's pleasant reverie was suddenly interrupted when Major General Jubal Early pulled back the flap of his tent and stepped within. Gordon sprang to his feet, and after a quick exchange of salutes, Early got right to business. "Gordon ... I mean to take the Main Fort at daybreak, and I want you to lead the attack. Have your men formed up and ready to strike when the sun breaks into the sky."

"But, sir ... the Main Fort ... it's ... well, sir, it's still quite strong, as we saw this evening. I fear..."

"No time for that, Gordon. General Ewell has positioned every gun at our disposal—several dozen, including those we captured from the Yankees today—to target the Union forts. I mean to start the bombardment before sunup.

"Gordon, I intend to take that fort and I'll brook no excuses. I mean to have the victory that eluded me today, and I expect *you* to get it for me. Am I understood?"

"Yes, sir!" Gordon once again saluted as Early turned and strode out of the tent.

Gordon sank back down into his chair, frowning. He sat gazing at the ground in front of him for several minutes, then reached into his kit, pulled out pen and paper, and began a letter to his wife.

My Dearest Fanny,

If you are reading this letter, it means I am no longer with you on this earth, for which I am profoundly sorry. As we must now part, I wish you to know that being your husband has been my greatest joy and honor in life...

Just before nine o'clock that evening, a courier arrived at the Twelfth's rifle pit with orders from General Milroy summoning Nathan to the Main Fort. As Nathan approached the front gate, he saw the two colonels from the 122nd and 123rd Ohio pass through just ahead of him. He knew something major was afoot if it required the attendance of the regimental commanders.

He reached the gate and passed into its large archway before he had time to puzzle it out. The walls were so thick it took several strides to reach the inner courtyard. When he was nearly through the tunnel, he passed a narrow doorway on his right that led to a small guardroom. But as he passed, he heard a voice say, "Colonel Chambers, a moment of your time, if you please…"

He immediately recognized the deep, resonant voice of General Milroy, and turned to see the general gesturing him into the room. He stepped into the small, bare, windowless guardroom that featured only a small table and several simple wooden chairs, followed closely by Harry the Dog. General Milroy stood in front of the table, gesturing for Nathan to close the door behind him. Nathan turned and pulled the thick iron door closed.

"General?" he asked, turning back toward Milroy.

"Chambers, a few minutes ago, three sergeants of the First New York Cavalry arrived at our gate, their horses all of a lather. They had ridden here at the gallop from Martinsburg; one can only imagine the courage, heroism, and derring-do it took to accomplish *that* feat, with the entire countryside simply infested with enemy soldiers and sentries."

Nathan nodded, appreciating the mettle of the young cavalrymen, but wondering why the general had felt it necessary to pull him aside to tell him this information.

"The sergeants were forced to undertake this perilous mission due to our telegraph lines being cut by the rebels," Milroy continued. "Their message was from my superior, General Schenck, who has relayed orders directly from General in Chief Halleck, Secretary of War Stanton, and the president himself. We are to abandon Winchester with all haste and make for Harpers Ferry ... if such action is still possible."

Nathan again nodded, but was not surprised; after all, it was the most reasonable course of action under the circumstances, given how badly they were now outnumbered and outgunned, with the rebels commanding the high ground of the West Fort.

"Chambers ... though my orders are clear, there is still the matter of whether or not it may still be accomplished, given the rebels' investment of the town and our fortifications. So, I have been compelled to call a council of war to decide on our course of action, which is why you and the other regimental and brigade commanders have been summoned to the fort."

Nathan could no longer contain his curiosity concerning this odd, clandestine meeting, "So ... then why are you telling me this *now*, general, when you will certainly be announcing it shortly at the council of war?"

General Milroy didn't immediately answer, but instead gazed intently into Nathan's eyes, as if taking his measure.

"Chambers ... the council may decide the best course of action is to surrender. But I will *never* surrender to any damned rebels."

Nathan shrugged. "You are the commanding general, sir. If you decide not to surrender, we must obey your orders and continue to fight. There is no need for a meeting."

Milroy nodded slowly, "In a perfect world that would be true ... but you know well that a regimental commander under extreme pressure from the enemy may choose to run up the white flag without consulting his superior, especially if he knows that the commanding general ignored the wishes of his subordinates in that regard. And once one commander capitulates, the others will quickly follow suit, and then the game is over."

Nathan nodded, acknowledging the truth of what Milroy was saying. And he could only imagine how Milroy would be publicly pilloried if it came out that he had refused his subordinates' wish to surrender and that his command suffered devastating casualties as a result.

They were quiet again for a long moment, Nathan continuing to meet eyes with Milroy. "And what is it you would have me do, General?"

"Chambers ... from working with you these past several months, I have come to believe you are the type of man who would make the attempt at breaking out of an encirclement rather than simply surrendering to the enemy. Am I correct in my assumption?"

Nathan scowled. "Yes, General ... you read me rightly. I'm a fighter, as are the men who follow me. I have no wish to spend the rest of the war in some rebel rat hole. I would cut my way out with nothing but my own sword if I had to, rather than surrender."

"Good, *good!* I am gratified to hear it, though not surprised. Chambers, at the meeting I intend to broach the subject of surrender myself, first thing ... get it out on the table. At that point, I would be grateful if you would speak up against the notion, in the strongest possible terms, even offer to lead a fighting breakout yourself if necessary. My hope is that your show of courage and fortitude will inspire the others to follow your lead."

Nathan thought for a moment, and nodded again, "I can do that ... and likely would have anyway, without you asking it of me."

"Yes, yes, I expected nothing less from you..."

"Then why bring me in here ahead of the meeting, sir, if I may ask?"

"Just this," the general answered, "if the council *does* decide to surrender, I want you to get your West Virginians together, and at their head we *will* get to Harpers Ferry, one way or the other ... or to *hell!*"

Chapter 5. Cut Off

*"The best way to escape
your problem is to solve it."*
- Robert Anthony

Sunday June 14, 1863, 8:00 p.m. – Martinsburg, West Virginia:

Though it had taken all day, and was once again a minor disappointment in that most of the Union garrison had managed to escape the siege, Martinsburg was now in Confederate hands.

After several abortive efforts to take the town with only his cavalry brigade, and even a brazen attempt to bluff the Union commander into surrendering the town or face bombardment— though he had no artillery whatsoever—General Jenkins had finally decided to wait for Major General Rodes to arrive with the infantry division.

And once Rodes arrived in the afternoon, the fate of the Union garrison was sealed; their only hope was to hold the rebels off long enough to slip away to the Potomac and cross into the North.

For Walters the good news was that with Martinsburg now secured, the noose was closing tighter on Winchester ... and on Nathan Chambers!

So when General Jenkins departed that night for Maryland, ordered by General Ewell to secure the river crossings at Williamsport, Walters delayed the Thirty-Sixth Battalion's start, hoping for his chance.

❧❦❧❦❧❦❧❦❧❦

Sunday June 14, 1863, 9:00 p.m. – Winchester, Virginia:

The council of war convened at nine o'clock in the evening, with commander Major General Robert Milroy presiding. Milroy's staff officers, brigade commanders, and regimental commanders were all in attendance. Since the Main Fort contained no meeting room large enough for such a gathering, it was held in the fort's underground mess hall.

Milroy began with a detailed description of the heroic journey by the three New York Cavalry sergeants—necessitated by the telegraph wires being cut by the rebels—bringing new orders from General Schenck. Milroy then read aloud their orders to retreat to Harpers Ferry on the instant ... *if* such a move was still possible and feasible.

There were nods, but no one interrupted the general, knowing he still held the floor.

"Gentlemen ... we are down to but a single day's rations, and our artillery ammunition is nearly spent. Given the rebel capture of the West Fort earlier this afternoon, granting them the high ground from which to bombard the Star Fort and this Main Fort, and given their overwhelming numbers in men and arms, it has become clear that our position here in Winchester is now untenable. And further, our orders are now clear: we *must* pull back to the north ... *if* such a maneuver is still possible.

"That's the issue I have brought you here to discuss: whether or not it is still an option to withdraw given our current circumstances. And if it is *not*, then we must consider the alternative of a general surrender. Thoughts?" he asked, and his eyes strayed for a moment to Nathan, who returned the look with a subtle nod.

But even as Nathan began to push back his chair to stand, Colonel Joseph Keifer, commander of the 110th Ohio regiment, sprang to his feet, "General ... if I may have the floor, sir?"

Milroy gave Nathan another quick look, then turned toward Keifer. "Certainly, Colonel ... please do." Milroy gestured for Keifer to step forward and speak.

"Thank you, sir." Keifer stepped forward and placed his hands behind his back as if in the formal at ease stance.

"Gentlemen, I for one have no inclination to surrender to this large, unruly rabble calling themselves an *army*. Though they may have breached our walls today with their subterfuge, their reckless disregard for casualties, and their overwhelming numbers, it would gall me to admit defeat before we have even *begun* to fight.

"Against crushing odds, the 110th Ohio resolutely stood its ground this afternoon, until finally our flanks were turned, and all hope of victory was lost. And even then, my men conducted an orderly withdrawal from the West Fort, displaying unequivocal honor and courage, never turning their backs on the enemy, but fighting all the way.

"I would not now tell these stout-hearted soldiers, who today lost dear comrades, that they must lay down their arms and submit themselves to the ridicule and scorn of these ... *lesser men.* I for one would fight my way out, regardless of the odds."

As Keifer spoke, he gazed about the room with a stern, hawklike visage and made eye contact with each man in turn, holding it there for a moment, as if to gauge the man's reaction and intentions, before moving on to the next. It was a gutsy and impressive performance, to Nathan's thinking, especially considering many of the men in the room either outranked Keifer or had seniority.

Colonel Keifer finally settled his gaze on General Milroy, "General ... I beg of you ... put the 110th in the van, and I swear as God is my witness, we will cut a path clear to the North, or die in the trying."

Then he turned and addressed the room again, "Who will fight with me?"

Nathan took that for his cue, and stood to his feet, "The Twelfth West Virginia will fight, Colonel!" He pounded his fist on the table for emphasis.

This started a cascading effect, and soon all officers present were on their feet, each loudly proclaiming his intention to fight. Nathan was never sure if this was on account of Colonel Keifer's masterful powers of persuasion, or if it was simply a matter of nobody wanting to look reticent or cowardly in front of his peers. Either way, General Milroy had the outcome he'd desired. He gave Nathan a quick look and a nod, before waving everyone to retake their seats.

"Very well, gentlemen ... Now that *that* matter has been put to rest, let us discuss our ways and means ... we must decide the best strategy for a general breakout—how best to force our way through the lines of the beleaguering foe."

The discussion commenced, and went on for several hours. The first order of business was determining the best route to be taken, with the rebels investing all the roads leading out of Winchester. Eventually, the council decided to head north, toward Martinsburg, rather than east toward Harpers Ferry— despite their orders to the contrary. The Martinsburg Pike had seen the least amount of rebel activity, and a Union wagon train, along with a large caravan of pro-Union civilians, had managed to get out that way earlier in the day. It seemed to present the best hope for a federal breakout.

Also, once in Martinsburg, they could join forces with Colonel Smith's Union garrison stationed there, which would strengthen their force by several thousand, allowing them a better chance of an effective fighting withdrawal across the Potomac and on into the North at Williamsport.

The debate then focused on the method of their breakout. One contingent, which included Nathan and Colonel Keifer, advocated for a powerful thrust northward, starting with the remaining heavy artillery rounds expended in one tremendous burst to open a path. Then the majority of their smaller, portable guns would be brought forth in the van to cut through any blocking enemy formations. The remaining guns would take up rear guard to prevent an attack from behind. This strategy depended upon catching the rebels by surprise in the dark of night with overwhelming firepower concentrated in a single direction, and then pushing the entire Union column through as quickly as possible to prevent the enemy from regrouping and organizing a forceful reaction.

The other side argued that such an action was a dangerous gamble with potentially disastrous consequences; the noise of such an attack would immediately alert the entire rebel force, some twenty-five thousand strong. And surely the rebels were already expecting an attempted breakout to the North, and had their troops on the alert for just such an action. A column trying to force its way out under these circumstances could be quickly cut off, and would then be exposed out on the open road with no defensive works to fight behind and artillery ammunition depleted, resulting in a horrific slaughter.

They proposed instead a silent retreat under cover of darkness. All troops to travel lightly, leaving all heavy equipment behind, spiking the artillery, cutting up harness, and sawing axles and wheels into pieces before marching out under orders of absolute silence. The idea was that this approach would allow the column to be miles away from Winchester before the rebels were aware of it, and then it would likely only face light resistance from videttes and pickets positioned along the northward road.

Nathan was skeptical that nearly seven thousand armed men, with knapsacks, rifles, and bayonets, not to mention hundreds of horses and their riders, could march out of the fort in complete silence, undetected by the enemy's pickets.

But in the end, the silent escape strategy carried the argument, and General Milroy, who'd been torn between the two strategies, went along with it. But Nathan noticed that Milroy hedged his bets by assigning Colonel Keifer the column lead as he'd requested, even granting him temporary command over the 122nd and 123rd Ohio as well, with orders to cut a path by main force if it became necessary.

And then after the meeting, Milroy pulled Nathan aside, "March your West Virginians in the middle of the column, Colonel. If there is fighting, I would keep you as a reserve … in case we still need to deploy the *particular* strategy we discussed earlier today…" The two exchanged a meaningful look, and Nathan nodded his understanding.

ಬಾಬ್ಬ ಬಾಬ್ಬ ಬಾಬ್ಬ

After the council meeting, Nathan had the unpleasant duty of ordering Wheeling Battery's Captain John Carlin to spike his guns, destroy the remaining ammunition, cut up his horses' harnesses, and saw up his gun carriages.

Carlin was furious and wasn't hesitant to say so. "Colonel, my men have done heroic service, firing more than 250 rounds per gun over the last two days. We still have thirty-five rounds each gun, more than enough to effectively cover our retreat. I beg you, sir … please, allow us to bring our guns! We can still render good service, sir … and I am certain if we leave them, we'll live to regret it … if we live at all!"

Nathan had no argument for this, but the order remained: nothing with wheels was to be brought along, and the artillerymen would ride the horses that normally pulled the artillery caissons and carriages. Carlin grudgingly complied.

፨)ᘓᑦᏻᘔᘓᑦᏻᘔ፨)ᘓᑦᏻ

Monday June 15, 1863, 12:00 a.m. – Winchester, Virginia:

At midnight, Nathan's company officers quietly roused their men from sleep in the rifle pits, instructing them to conduct themselves as silently as possible, with rebel sentries stationed only a few hundred yards away. The men were ordered to leave behind blankets, tents, and bedrolls—everything except their rifles, ammunition, and canteens. Each man was then issued several handfuls of hardtack and dry crackers to stuff into his knapsack to sustain him on the road.

When all was made ready, on a pitch-black moonless night, the eight hundred officers and men of the Twelfth West Virginia regiment filed out of their entrenchments, following Colonel Nathaniel Chambers down a long slope and into a ravine that led around the east side of the fort toward the Martinsburg Pike to the north. There they joined the long Union column already on the move, flowing down out of the fort.

As Nathan rode at the head of the regiment on his mare, Millie, next to Tom on his gelding, Jerry, he could hear the quiet treading of thousands of boots, the clinking of canteens and bayonets against buckles, the low mutterings and curses of men, the clicking of horses' hooves, and the occasional braying of mules. He shook his head in consternation; though not a word was spoken above a whisper, still there was simply no way to move a column of this size in complete silence. No matter how hard they tried, this many men moving along in almost complete darkness could not move without making a good deal of noise. And no matter how hard Nathan tried to ignore it, he couldn't help but cringe at all the sound he heard emanating from the Union column as it moved.

And somewhere out in the darkness, the enemy couldn't help but hear it too.

ℬ𝕺𝕮ℛ𝕮𝕾𝕭𝕺𝕾𝕺𝕮ℛ𝕮𝕾𝕭𝕺𝕾𝕺𝕮ℛ𝕮𝕾

Monday June 15, 1863, 12:30 a.m. – Winchester, Virginia:

Just after midnight, C.S.A. Lieutenant General Richard Ewell sat up at the small table in his command tent. He'd been unable to sleep, despite an exhaustion that he could feel right to the bone. But the excitement and trepidation about the day to come, along with the usual discomfort from his amputated leg, had kept sleep at bay. So after hours of tossing, he'd finally given it up, re-lit the oil lamp, and picked up a book to read. But he knew it was of little use; he read the words but could not absorb them.

A sudden noise and movement at the entrance to his tent startled him, and he glanced up to see cavalry Major Harry Gilmore step into the tent unannounced. The major was in a state of great excitement, his face red, and nearly out of breath, but he still remembered to snap a salute at his commanding general, and then remove his hat respectfully.

"Sorry to disturb you, sir, but I saw your light was on … and it is a matter of the utmost urgency, sir."

"Yes, Major … what is it?" Ewell asked, happy for an excuse to set aside the useless book and distract himself with some important business to attend.

"General, sir … Milroy is on the move! The federals are abandoning their forts and heading north on the Martinsburg Pike. My scouts have just reported it!"

Ewell snatched his crutch from where it leaned against the side of the table and was quickly upright, his weariness and aching leg already forgotten.

101

"Good, *good!* Now we have him, the old buzzard. Thank you, Major! Please send in Captain Foster straightaway; we have a Union army to bag."

"Sir!" Gilmore snapped a salute, but was unable to suppress a satisfied grin. He spun on his heels and hurried back out of the tent.

Moments later, Ewell's adjutant, Captain Hiram Foster, stepped in, pencil and paper already in hand. "I just heard the news, sir ... what are your orders, General?" He skipped the usual formalities and immediately took a seat at the table, preparing to write.

Ewell grabbed the map that was rolled up and laying on the side of the table opposite Foster. He quickly unrolled it on the table and began studying it intensely.

"Have General Johnson's division move north, to the right of the Martinsburg Pike with all speed, and cut Milroy off ... *here* ... which looks to be about three ... maybe four miles out from Winchester."

Foster looked over at the map, noted the route, and began scribbling on the paper.

"Next ... have General George Steuart and General Nicholls take their brigades and march to the Berryville Road, then head north to cut the Yankees off from Harpers Ferry at the least. Oh ... and have them take Colonel Andrews' artillery battalion with them—they may have need of him."

"Yes, sir ... Steuart ... Nicholls ... and Andrews ... Berryville Road. Got it, sir," Foster paused to look up at Ewell for his next set of instructions.

"And just have General Walker advance his skirmishers into town to verify the federals have left. Then have them move out from town, keeping to the east of the Martinsburg Pike to screen our movements, in case Milroy puts out scouts, and report back on the exact position of the enemy along the road. Oh ... and go ahead and have him send the Stonewall Brigade following after Steuart and Nicholls for support."

"Yes, sir ... anything more, General?" Foster asked, pushing back his chair.

"No, Hiram, that's it for the moment, thank you." Ewell then grinned. "That shameless scoundrel Milroy will finally get what he so richly deserves!"

෩෬෬෩෩෩෬෬෩෩෩෩෬෬෩

Monday June 15, 1863, 1:00 a.m. – Winchester, Virginia:

Jubal was having the sweetest dream of a beautiful blonde woman standing on a street corner in the midst of a crowd of happy, waving civilians. She seemed somehow familiar, like he should know her name. But somehow, in the dream the name wouldn't come to him. She smiled brightly, showing the most perfect white teeth, between lips of the softest pink. She laughed and reached out toward him, "Wake up, Lieutenant ... *wake up!*"

Sergeant Evans urgently shook Jubal where he lay on the bedroll in his tent. "Wake up, sir!" the sergeant repeated.

"*Hunh?* What? What is it, Evans?"

"Milroy has flown the coop. The Yankees are leaving for the North, and we're late for the party, sir!"

"Late? What? ... *Why* are we late?" Jubal sat up and rubbed at his eyes, trying to clear the fog of sleep and the vision of the lovely woman—whom he now realized had been Evelyn—from his head so he could think clearly.

"Don't know, sir ... some kind o' mix-up at the top. The major says General Walker was supposed to give us the order to march half an hour ago, but we just now got it. So we got to double-quick it to catch up with the rest of the column!"

"Oh ... all right, I'm up." Jubal pulled on his boots, stood up, and reached over to grab his gun belt and hat off the hook.

෩෬෬෩෩෩෬෬෩෩෩෩෬෬෩

Monday June 15, 1863, 2:00 a.m. – Stephenson's Depot, Virginia:

C.S.A. Lieutenant Colonel Snowden Andrews was worried. When the frantic orders had arrived at one in the morning to scramble a battery onto the Martinsburg Pike ahead of the already moving column of federals, he had only two serviceable guns

103

mobile enough for the task: a twelve-pounder Napoleon, and a six-pounder howitzer. They'd managed to get ahead of the federals and had positioned the six-pounder up on a rise overlooking a bridge over a steep-sided ravine at a place called Stephenson's Depot, a burned out and abandoned train station of the Winchester & Potomac line. A company of riflemen had arrived to cover the guns, laying prone along the railroad line a few dozen yards away.

But Andrews still had to figure out where to position the Napoleon. He just couldn't find a suitable position that would be able to rake the advancing federals while providing some measure of protection for the gun crew.

Finally, he gazed at the bridge deck itself and slowly shook his head before giving the order to position the gun right in the middle of the bridge, facing south toward the advancing Union column. He ordered both guns loaded and supplied with anti-personnel cannister projectiles.

Stepping up to the gun crew on the bridge, Colonel Andrews met eyes with Lieutenant Charles Contee, in command of the gun, and the two exchanged a salute.

"Lieutenant ... until more of our forces arrive, we'll likely be severely outnumbered and outgunned at this pinch point."

"Understood, sir," the young lieutenant answered, a concerned look forming on his brow.

"Mr. Contee ... it will be up to you and your men to hold this bridge ... and ... I expect you to hold it to the last man."

"Sir!" Contee replied, again snapping a salute.

Andrews returned the salute sharply, and had to fight down the tears attempting to form as he once again locked eyes with Contee. He nodded, then turned and strode off the bridge.

Both men knew with absolute certainty ... this was a suicide mission.

෯෩෬෯෩෬෯෩෬

Monday June 15, 1863, 2:30 a.m. – Winchester, Virginia:

To Nathan, the movement of the Union column was agonizingly slow, and he chewed anxiously on an unlit cigar as time seemed to drag to a near standstill. With every passing moment, the fear of a sudden assault out of the darkness grew ever stronger, until his skin felt like it was crawling with bugs. For the dozenth time, he reflexively reached down and loosened the pistol in its holster at his hip, and strained his eyes out into the darkness to the side of the road. But there was nothing to be seen. He could barely make out the hulking form of Harry padding along beside him.

His only consolation was the knowledge that Stan and Billy were out there somewhere in the darkness to the side of the road with their company of scouts and skirmishers, scouring the countryside for any approach, activity, or ambush by the enemy.

Then he heard the sound of horses trotting back down the line toward him, moving in the opposite direction as the column. He was surprised when the lead rider came close enough to recognize in the dim starlight: General Milroy himself. Nathan thought the commanding general looked every bit as stressed and anxious as he himself was feeling.

Nathan saluted as Milroy paused in front of him and returned the salute. "Chambers … let's pick up the pace, if we can…" The general spoke in a hush, "I wish to be well away before dawn lights the sky…"

"Yes, sir … we'll do what we can, sir," Nathan answered, knowing full well there was nothing *at all* he could do, but also understanding that the general was just venting his angst and frustration in a way that at least made him feel like he was doing something.

Milroy nodded, then spurred his horse on down the line to speak with the next commander. Nathan slowly shook his head, feeling empathy for the general; it was a thoroughly unnerving experience. He decided his demeanor was much better suited to a desperate, violent breakout such as he'd advocated … and he suspected Milroy's was as well.

And even as he was mulling over these thoughts, a sound rang out in the distance—the sound they'd all been dreading to hear: rifle fire, a great volley fired by hundreds of guns at once. And worse yet, the gun fire didn't come from behind them, fired off in frustration by consternated rebels realizing the birds had flown the cage. No, this gunfire came from somewhere up ahead. And then it got worse, as the deep, rumbling *boom* of artillery rolled through the darkness.

Nathan knew with a sickening knot in his gut that the worst-case scenario had just come to pass: the rebels had cut them off, and they were now exposed out in the open, badly outnumbered, and without their dug-in defenses or their artillery. The dangerous, dicey situation of a few moments ago had just become dire and deadly.

SÐCRCÆÐÐÐÐÐCRCÆÐÐÐÐCRCÆ

Though General Milroy had ordered him to remain in reserve if fighting broke out, Nathan immediately ordered his regiment off the road and deployed in line of battle. Though he could not tell from which side of the road up ahead the gunfire was emanating, he chose to move off to the left for the simple expedient that the right side was heavily wooded with tangled underbrush, while the left was a broad, relatively flat meadow of waist-high grass. This would allow his men to maneuver as events warranted and would prevent them from being constrained by the traffic on the roadway.

He ordered a slow advance forward, though it was not strictly speaking per his orders, figuring they would have to move in that direction eventually, and also knowing he would not be able to just sit still when there was fighting going on, regardless of General Milroy's orders.

Only moments after they'd deployed in the field, he saw General Milroy and his staff officers galloping back up the road, heading toward the front of the column and the fighting, which had now intensified. Clearly, the Union regiments were now returning fire on the rebels, and in his mind's eye, Nathan could picture Colonel Keifer aggressively pressing the enemy, attempting to punch through the blockade with his three regiments of Ohioans.

𝕭𝕺𝕽𝕮𝕾𝕯𝕺𝕭𝕺𝕽𝕮𝕾𝕯𝕺𝕭𝕺𝕽𝕮𝕾

An hour passed, and then another, and still the Twelfth had received no orders from General Milroy, though they could hear the battle raging in the near distance. Artillery continued to rumble, and rifle volleys echoed through the valley.

And as the Twelfth stayed where they were, lined up for battle, rifles loaded and at the half-cock, and bayonets fixed, there was nothing they could do. Colonel Nathaniel Chambers held a dark scowl as he paced back and forth at the front of the line, puffing on a cigar. Every few minutes he would pause in his pacing to pull up his brass spyglass and gaze out toward the battle, though there was still nothing to be seen in the dark gray pre-dawn sky, save the reflected artillery flashes in the distance.

As they stood ready for action in a broad pasture to the left of the pike, they'd seen the Eighty-Seventh Pennsylvania infantry march past at the double-quick toward the battle, followed shortly by the Eighteenth Connecticut, both regiments of Colonel William Ely's brigade. And still no orders came.

"Damn it, Tom ... what's he waiting for? We *must* get into this fight!" Nathan vented his growing frustration to his second in command.

But Tom had no answer, and just shrugged his shoulders.

Fifteen minutes more passed, and Nathan was beginning to contemplate ignoring his orders and marching forward anyway when they saw a single rider approaching from the direction of the battle. The rider peeled off from the roadway and galloped across the open field directly toward Colonel Chambers.

When the officer pulled to a stop and saluted, they saw it was Major John Lowry McGee, Milroy's chief of staff, and a capable cavalry officer in his own right. Also in McGee's favor, in Nathan's opinion, he was a fellow West Virginian. "Colonel Chambers!"

"Major. What's the word?"

"Colonel, the general's orders are for you to lead the Twelfth across the road headed due east from your present position. He believes you will meet but light resistance, likely only pickets or skirmishers. Once you have progressed a mile or so through the woods on that side of the road, you should be able to turn sharply to the north and flank the rebel line on their left. Then roll them up as circumstances allow."

"'Bout damned time," Nathan grumbled, nodding. Then remembering his manners, "Yes, we can do that. Thank you very much, Major."

"Colonel!" Major McGee snapped another salute, turned his horse, and spurred back the way he'd come.

☙✣✱✣☙✣✱✣☙✣✱✣

Sergeant Billy Creek led a company of skirmishers into the thickly wooded area on the east side of the pike, the vanguard of the overall advance by the Twelfth West Virginia. They'd advanced half a mile and had not yet met any resistance, which Billy thought odd, considering the intense battle taking place just a few miles to the north. *There should've have at least been a line of pickets*, he thought. Then his instincts, honed by years of scouting out west, kicked in, and he called the company to a halt. He crouched down, listening to the sounds in the woods. At first, he could hear nothing but the sounds of the distant battle. But then he heard the faint clink of metal on metal a few dozen yards ahead and to the left ... in a place where none of his own men would be. He stood, turned, aimed his rifle toward the source of the sound, and squeezed the trigger. Billy's men, taking his cue, stood as one and fired in the same direction.

The reaction from the enemy was sudden and overwhelming. A long row of rebels rose from behind the bushes, leveled their rifles, and returned fire. After ducking back down under cover, Billy risked a quick glance at the rebel line, which was now firing back toward the main column of the Twelfth regiment, and for the most part, no longer bothering to target him and his small party of skirmishers. In that instant, Billy confirmed what he had already suspected: this was not a mere row of rebel pickets, nor even a thin line of skirmishers; this was a rebel regiment at the least, possibly even a brigade!

And worse, as Billy's men had moved through the thick, dark forest, they had by pure bad luck passed by the rebels, who were now between them and the rest of the Twelfth regiment. Billy cursed to himself; he had failed in his most basic duty to protect the Captain, and the regiment was now being subjected to a devastating ambush. And there was nothing Billy could do about it.

✸)ᘓᘓᘕᘓᘓᘕᘓᘓᘕ

Caught by surprise in the thick tangled woods, and not yet organized for battle, the men and officers of the Twelfth scrambled to respond to the sudden massive enemy assault. But Nathan's officers were no green political appointees, nor recent military academy graduates still wet behind the ears and more used to marching than fighting; Nathan's officers were hard, experienced Indian-fighters from Texas. This was their kind of fight, and they quickly went to work.

Major Jim Wiggins and Captain Stan Volkov, who'd had the rear guard, rushed their men up to guard the regiment's left flank, while Captain Zeke Benton took charge on the right, in the absence of Billy's skirmishers now trapped behind enemy lines out to the east.

Soon, the Twelfth was targeting the enemy formation with a steady stream of independent rifle fire, immensely aided by the rapid fire from the Henry rifles of the officers.

Shortly after the ambush was sprung, Nathan, walking his horse Millie next to Tom, who'd also been leading his horse through the dense forest, had sent a private to the rear with the two animals to keep them from being shot. Now Nathan worked his repeating rifle, aiming at the distant muzzle flashes and squeezing the trigger, pumping out rounds as quickly as he could move the lever.

He'd emptied the rifle's magazine and was reaching down to pull more rounds from his ammunition pouch when a sergeant ran up and slid in next to him. The sergeant didn't bother to salute. "Colonel ... Major Wiggins says to tell you the rebels are pouring in on our left and will soon cut us off from the road and turn our flank. The major says we are up against at least two rebel regiments, and ... he saw them working to unlimber at least one big gun, sir."

"Damn it!" Nathan frowned, looking over at Colonel Clark. "Tom, we must pull back to the road and regroup. This forest is a death trap!"

"Yes, sir!" Tom scrambled off to the right to relay the orders.

Over the next hour, the Twelfth West Virginia Regiment fought a scrambling, ducking, maneuvering, fighting withdrawal, until they once again reached the roadway of the pike, and reformed a new line of defense on the other side, about 150 yards out across a pasture behind a stone wall. They prepared for an enemy advance as they caught their breath and took stock of their casualties.

Nathan knew Billy and his company of skirmishers had been cut off by the enemy, but he had faith that his old Indian scout would find his way back to them; no man on earth could do it better. But he felt a sudden sick knot in the pit of his stomach when Captain Georgie Thompson stepped up to him, and snapped a salute, "Colonel ... Zeke and Phillipe didn't make it back. Companies G and F got separated from the rest of the column off to the far right while trying to guard our flank. Somehow in the confusion of pulling back, either they didn't get the word, or the enemy cut them off."

Nathan nodded, but he could think of nothing to say to this. It was devastating news, not only losing Zeke and Phillipe, but it reduced their numbers by nearly two hundred men, leaving them severely understrength with less than six hundred rifles, and many of those remaining had been wounded in the ambush.

"There's more, sir..." Georgie frowned. "William was with them."

Nathan knew he was referring to Captain William Jenkins, Texas veteran and regimental head surgeon, *"What?!* I thought William was nearer the middle with me..."

"He *was*, sir," Georgie shrugged, "but Zeke's company took casualties at the start of the ambush, so William went to tend to the wounded and…"

"All right … let the assistant surgeons know … they'll have to take charge of the wounded now. We can … only hope Zeke and his men can fight their way out to the east toward Harpers Ferry…" Nathan trailed off, knowing the odds of escaping in that direction across a countryside crawling with enemy combatants were slim at best. The great hound Harry stepped up next to Nathan and leaned against his leg, gazing up at him as if feeling his distress.

But there was nothing Nathan could do about the lost men at the moment, so he sent a courier at the gallop to find General Milroy and tell him about their unsuccessful attempt to turn the enemy's flank and request new orders.

Perhaps if Colonel Keifer could defeat the rebel blockade, there might be an opportunity to go searching for their lost companies, Nathan thought. He said a silent prayer for his missing comrades and soldiers. And then he experienced a sudden dread of what he might say to Margaret if he had to tell her William was missing.

⏦⏧⏦⏧⏦⏧

"Damn it, William … we gotta go, *now!*" Zeke leaned down, getting right in William's face where he knelt on the ground tending a wounded man.

"Can't leave now, Zeke. Private Kelly will bleed out or go into shock if I don't keep pressure on the wound."

"William … look at him." Zeke was turning red in the face and becoming more exasperated with every passing moment in his growing anxiety. "Sorry to be the bearer o' bad tidings, William, but Kelly ain't gonna make it; that's certain. And it don't matter how hard you try. *Look at him!*"

William gazed at Zeke a moment, then looked back a Private Kelly. The front of the man's uniform tunic was covered in his own blood, which continued to ooze from a bullet hole just below the sternum where William was applying pressure with a clean white bandage, now soaked red. The man's eyes were halfway closed and unfocused, and his mouth hung open, allowing bloody saliva to slowly drip out.

William nodded, "Maybe so ... but I have to try." He looked back up and the two met eyes for a moment. "You go, Zeke. Get the company out. I'll stay with Kelly..."

Zeke stared hard at William another moment. "*Fine!* Stay, William ... stay, and see how that works out for you. *Goddamn it!*"

He stood and turned to Phillipe, "Let's move, Phillipe; we'll head east and see if we can slip outta here. Close up ranks ... Company F on the left and G on the right. Keep a sharp eye, boys ... we got plenty o' company in these here woods, and none o' the friendly type!"

And in less than two minutes, William was left alone with the bleeding private as gunfire continued to echo in the distance. He reached into his pack for a long length of cloth, thinking to wrap it around the man's chest to hold the bandage on tight. He needed to give his own aching hand a break before it cramped up.

But Kelly was heavy, and William struggled to get the cloth under him while maintaining his grip on the bandage.

"Here ... let me help you with that," a voice said. William looked up and saw Zeke stripping off his rucksack and rifle and setting them on the grass before bending down and helping lift Kelly's chest off the ground.

"Zeke! What're you doing here?" William continued to work on the bandage, securing it by tying off the ends of the cloth.

But Zeke shook his head and grinned, "Damn if I know, William. I got out there a few hundred yards with the boys and then ... I just couldn't do it, not after all we been through together. I just couldn't leave you behind. So I asked Phillipe to take the command, and I came on back."

"You shouldn't have done that, Zeke."

"Yep, I can't never argue with *you*, William ... You're right as always," Zeke rolled his eyes.

William returned a scowl, "Well, anyway ... thank you, Zeke. That was ... 'above and beyond,' as the Captain would say."

"Well, I guess you can partially thank *him* for me coming back ... when I thought of the hot scolding he was like to give me for misplacing you..." he shook his head and made a clucking sound. "That there's a mighty scary thought."

William snorted a laugh, then nodded. "Agreed."

They sat down on the ground, one on each side of Kelly, and watched over him for nearly half an hour. Then the private suddenly gasped, opened his eyes wide, coughed up a splatter of blood, then collapsed back onto the ground.

William leaned over and put his fingers to the man's neck for a moment, then looked up at Zeke, "Gone."

Zeke nodded, but he'd seen too much bloodshed recently to be overly affected by it. "Then it's time we were, too."

They stood and collected their things. But when Zeke went to sling the Henry rifle onto his back, William grabbed his arm, "Wait..."

Zeke looked at him. "What?"

"The Henrys ... we should leave them," William answered.

"Leave them? Why?"

"Because ... we're not going to fight our way out of here, not the two of us alone. Our only chance is to sneak out. But the chances are good we'll be captured, and—"

"We don't want the rebs to get their hands on them..." Zeke finished the sentence for him, nodding. "Makes sense, William. Quick, let's bury them along with the remaining ammo. And if we do need to fight, we still have our sidearms."

Fortunately, the dirt in the forest was soft and thick from years of fallen, rotting leaves, so the rifle burial was quickly accomplished, and they were soon on their way.

They'd gone a few hundred yards, scampering from tree trunk to tree trunk when they came upon a man-high ravine heading in a generally southeasterly direction. So they climbed down into it, thinking that if it continued far enough, it might provide them enough cover to slip past the roving Confederate patrols.

But they'd only been at it a few more minutes when they came to a place where a tree had fallen, blocking the ravine. And as they were clambering up over the log, a voice called out, "Hey, you damned Yankees ... where y'all think you be a goin'?"

They looked up and saw three rebel privates at the lip of the ravine, not five yards away. And all three soldiers had rifles leveled right at them.

𝕰𝕺𝕮𝕽𝕺𝕮𝕭𝕺𝕭𝕺𝕮𝕽𝕺𝕮𝕭𝕺𝕭𝕺𝕮𝕽𝕺𝕮

An hour after receiving the bad news that William, Zeke, and Phillipe had gone missing, Nathan got some good—though not entirely unexpected—news: Billy had finally returned with his company of skirmishers. They were down two men who'd been killed in the ambush, and five more who'd been wounded to varying degrees, but remained mobile. But Billy had seen nothing of the two lost companies. To avoid capture, he'd led his men miles to the east, then circled around to the south, crossed the pike, then traveled north again on the west side to reach their current position.

A few moments after Billy's return, he and Stan stood before Nathan, asking to speak with him.

Nathan removed the cigar he'd been smoking, "Gentlemen … what is it you wish to discuss?"

"Colonel," Stan stood up straight, towering over Nathan despite the latter's six-foot-three stature, "Billy and I want to take a few men and go looking for William, Zeke, and Phillipe. We are thinking perhaps they are just … hmm … lost in the deep woods, maybe. We would find our little lost sheep and bring them home."

But then Stan looked down at his feet and no longer met Nathan's eye. And for once Stan's humor fell flat, as his heart just wasn't in it. William was Stan's best friend—next to Billy, anyway—and it clearly pained him to think of something ill befalling him.

Nathan nodded his head, took another puff on the cigar, and reached down to scratch Harry between the ears. He slowly blew the smoke out again before shaking his head.

"I appreciate the offer; that is most gallant of you and does you both great credit. But I can't let you do it. It is a fool's errand at best, and more than likely a suicide mission. The chances of finding them at this point is slim, and even if you did, the woods are simply infested with the enemy, such that I am now beginning to seriously doubt the outcome of the battle. Clearly time is *not* on our side, with more rebels arriving by the minute. I have a strong feeling we will need all the men we have if we hope to cut our way out of this mess and make it home. And also..." He paused and looked each man in the eye for a long moment, "I would not trade either one of you for a whole army of *other* men ... not even for William, Zeke, and Phillipe, much as I care for them."

Moments later, another courier arrived at the gallop from General Milroy, this time a young lieutenant whom Nathan didn't recognize. The officer pulled up in a bouncing stop, kicking up a small cloud of dust before snapping a salute, "Colonel Chambers?"

"Yes, Lieutenant. I'm Nathan Chambers, Twelfth West Virginia."

"Colonel, General Milroy orders that you advance from your present position on the left, forward to where Colonel Keifer is attempting to break through on a rebel-held bridge. The general says..." and then lieutenant paused, as if uncomfortable with what he'd been ordered to say. "He says ... if you were to add the weight of the Twelfth to Colonel Keifer's regiments, it might be enough to force the bridge."

Nathan eyed the lieutenant a moment, noticing that the young officer could not meet his gaze.

"So ... that is what the general *thinks*, is it? And what do *you* think, Lieutenant?"

The young man glanced back up at Nathan, as if surprised by the question. "Oh ... well ... it's not my place to question what the general says, sir."

Nathan nodded, "Understood, and agreed, Lieutenant. But let's say—*hypothetically* of course—if you were a superior general, what would you then think of General Milroy's orders?"

"Oh ... well ... *hypothetically*..." he paused and gave Nathan a serious look. "*If* I was a major general, sir, I'd have to say it's a suicide mission and that the battle is already lost. Colonel Keifer and his regiments have done everything humanly possible to break through but have failed utterly. Colonel Ely's brigade was also thrown into the fray, but to no avail. The enemy holds the bridge with artillery and well dug-in infantry against only our rifles and raw courage. And more rebel regiments arrive every moment.

"*If* I was a general, I'd say that without artillery of our own, it is hopeless, and throwing your regiment into the breach at this late stage will avail nothing and will only get a lot of good men killed—*hypothetically* speaking."

"Hmm ... I see. Thank you, Lieutenant. Please inform the general that I have received his orders..." Nathan was certain it wasn't lost on the lieutenant that he did not add anything about his willingness or ability to *obey* those orders.

After the courier departed, Tom turned to Nathan, "So ... what will you do, sir?"

"I will obey my orders, Tom. Have the men form up and prepare to advance. But let's just send the skirmishers forward first; we must move more *cautiously* this time, to be sure we don't walk into another ambush, don't you think?"

Tom grinned, then snapped a salute, "As you say, sir."

⬥⬥⬥⬥⬥⬥⬥⬥⬥

A half hour later, with Stan's skirmishers ranging out several hundred yards ahead, the Twelfth had advanced only a quarter of a mile when another rider approached, this time at a fast trot.

Nathan was surprised to see Milroy's chief of staff, Major McGee, once again. McGee pulled up and turned his horse to fall in next to Nathan's as he walked Millie at the head of the column.

"Colonel!"

"Major, a pleasure to see you again," Nathan returned McGee's salute, expecting to receive a hot rebuke from General Milroy for the tepid pace of his advance.

But McGee surprised him, "Colonel, General Milroy has dispatched me to tell you to belay his last order and halt your advance."

"Halt the advance? And then do *what*, Major?"

"Colonel Chambers ... Colonel Ely has already surrendered his brigade, and Colonel Keifer has withdrawn from his assault on the bridge, turning to the northwest in an attempt to break the encirclement and escape. General Milroy has ... has declared the battle lost, I'm afraid ... and he has ordered the disbandment of the formation. He orders that each unit make its separate way to the North as exigencies allow."

"*Oh!* I see ... and what of the general himself? Where is he? I have sworn to see him personally to safety if I may," Nathan frowned.

"Yes ... I am aware of that, Colonel Chambers; it's why the general sent me. To tell you to escape with your men and not wait for him. He and the rest of his staff are attempting to meet up with Colonel Keifer and General Elliott with the remnants of their regiments to make their way to the North."

"Well, if he's with Colonel Keifer he'll be in good hands, anyway. And what of *you*, Major?"

"I am a West Virginian, sir ... I told the general I wished to fight my way out with you and your men, sir ... if you'll have me."

Nathan nodded, then extended his hand, "Welcome to the Twelfth, Major."

ഇ൮ൈ൮ഇ൮ൈ൮ഇ൮ൈ൮

C.S.A. Lieutenant Colonel Snowden Andrews returned to the bridge, where he'd left Lieutenant Contee and his twelve gunners four hours earlier with orders to hold the bridge at all costs. As he stepped up onto the bridge deck, gun smoke still wafting in the air, his mouth hung open in shock. The twelve-pounder Napoleon stood in the center of the bridge, still on its carriage, despite dozens of bullet holes through the wooden frame, and several of the wheel spokes completely shot away. And all about the cannon lay dead Confederate gunners, pierced by many bullets, the remains of the crew he'd left to man the gun.

Gazing out toward the far bank past the bridge entrance, he gasped in amazement; a great heap of blue-uniformed bodies, fifty or more, lay just yards from the bridge, most torn into unrecognizable pieces by cannister fire from the big gun at point-blank range.

But as he stepped up to Lieutenant Contee's body, he saw that the man's leg had been shot through and now bent at an unnatural angle. Andrews removed his hat, and knelt down to give homage to the brave, heroic young man.

But as he brushed the hair back from Contee's face, the lieutenant stirred, and opened his eyes. The colonel grabbed his own canteen from his belt, and tipped Contee's head up, giving him a swallow.

Contee coughed, then smiled, "Colonel … I have obeyed my orders … I have held this bridge to the last man."

ℰᏣᏣᏣᏣᏣᏣᏣᏣᏣᏣᏣᏣ

When C.S.A. Lieutenant Colonel Elijah Walters' Thirty-Sixth Virginia Cavalry Battalion finally arrived at Stephenson's Depot, the battle was already over, and the various Confederate units were busily rounding up and organizing prisoners. *Perfect timing*, Walters decided, and trotted up to a sergeant that looked as if he might be in charge of a large group of Union prisoners currently sitting on the ground in a large field.

"Colonel!" The sergeant stood to attention and snapped a salute.

"Sergeant." Walters pulled his horse to a stop and returned the young man's salute. "Sergeant … do you know which Union regiments these men are from?"

"Yes, Colonel … the Fifth Maryland, sir."

"Oh. All right, thank you, Sergeant." Walters turned his horse back to the road to see where other prisoners were being gathered.

"Oh! And Colonel…" the sergeant called out. "I just remembered … we also have a company or two from the Twelfth West Virginia, sir."

Walters stopped his horse and turned back around. "Which are they, Sergeant … the West Virginians?"

"Oh … that'd be them over yonder, sir," the sergeant pointed at a group of several hundred men sitting under a large oak tree over to the right of the others.

"And what of the rest of the Twelfth West Virginia Regiment, Sergeant? Were they also captured?"

118

"Not that I heard of, sir. They may have been among those as managed to break our encirclement, including that godforsaken rat, Milroy," he spat, as if disgusted by the very name of the Union commanding general. "There's various cavalry patrols out chasing them that has escaped our net, but it ain't even clear to me which direction they headed. I doubt anyone really knows, sir."

"Thank you, Sergeant." Walters turned to his second in command, Captain Roberts, "Just have the men move into that adjacent field, and dismount for a short rest. Then come with me, Roberts."

Once the Thirty-Sixth Battalion was settled into the nearby field, Walters and Captain Roberts dismounted and walked over to where the members of the Twelfth West Virginia were sitting. They stopped in the front of the downcast Union soldiers, and Walters walked along the front of the group, gazing at the faces of the men to see if he recognized any of Chambers' Texas men. But after a few moments he decided none looked familiar, so he approached the only officer of the bunch, a captain, and asked, "Name?"

"Captain Phillipe Boudreau, sir," he answered in a heavy Cajun accent, which Walters was surprised to hear from a Yankee.

"Come with me, Boudreau." Walters then looked at the sergeant sitting next to Phillipe, "You too, Sergeant, *uh*..."

"Dixon, sir. Sergeant Clark Dixon."

"Come with me, Dixon," Walters turned and strode past the large oak tree into a smaller clearing off to the side of it.

The two Union soldiers walked behind him, with Captain Roberts following behind to guard them.

When they'd reached the middle of the clearing, out of view of the rest of the Twelfth's prisoners, Walters stopped, and faced the two Union officers.

He stepped up to Sergeant Dixon, "I am looking for Colonel Nathaniel Chambers. I need to know where he was when last you saw him, how many men he has with him, what artillery they carry if any, and where they intended to go in the event the battle was lost."

Sergeant Dixon frowned and folded his arms across his chest, "Sir ... I'd not be any kind of loyal Union soldier if I was willing to answer *any* of those questions ... assuming I knew the answers, which I'll not admit to."

Walters stared at Dixon a moment, betraying no expression. Finally, Walters nodded, "Wrong answer."

He reached down, unholstered his revolver, held it up to Dixon's face, cocked the hammer, and fired—*bang!* A splatter of blood exploded from the back of the sergeant's head and he collapsed to the ground. A puff of gun smoke slowly swirled up wreathing Walters' face.

Phillipe stood where he was, staring wide-eyed at the dead sergeant, a slight quiver running through his frame.

Walters holstered the pistol, then stepped up to Phillipe, gazing into his eyes.

"Now that we *understand* each other, Captain ... I want answers to my questions..." Walters spoke in a calm, steady voice and displayed a mild expression, as if nothing unusual had just happened.

"I ... I..." Phillipe shivered.

"Just give me the information I require, Captain, and you may yet live through the day..."

"Uh ... uh, yes, sir. I..." Phillipe, closed his mouth and swallowed the hard lump that'd formed in his throat, threatening to choke off his ability to speak.

"Yes?" Walters prompted.

"Well, sir ... without the two companies that've been captured ... that leaves Colonel Chambers with about ... five hundred ... maybe five hundred-fifty rifles. Oh, and no artillery. All the big guns were spiked and left back at Winchester."

"And Chambers? Where was he when last you saw him?"

"Oh ... we were ordered to attack east into the woods from the pike ... that's about a mile south of here, I believe. We were supposed to meet only light resistance ... skirmishers was all. But we ran straight into an ambush by two or more rifle regiments. The colonel ordered a fallback toward the pike, but our two companies were too far to the east and we were cut off. So we had no choice but to continue eastward and try a break out in that direction on our own. But as you can see ... we didn't make it..."

"Hmm ... very well. And ... where do you suppose Chambers would've taken his men if he figured the battle was lost?"

"I ... I don't know, sir..." Phillipe's shaking had intensified such that he had trouble keeping his hands still.

Walters' expression never changed, but he slowly reached down toward the pistol holster.

"*But* ... but I ... I did overhear him talking with Colonel Clark about it..."

"*Clark?* Tom Clark?"

"Yes, sir ... Lieutenant Colonel Thomas Clark, regimental second in command."

Walters' bland expression darkened for a moment at mention of *that* name, but quickly resumed its previous mild appearance.

"Go on, Boudreau..."

"Well ... I recall them discussing what to do, should General Milroy's breakout go badly. I'm not certain what they decided, but they did mention some places called Bath, and Hancock."

"Hmm ... that's off to the northwest. The most difficult and longest route ... but the least likely to be heavily guarded. Yes ... that sounds like what he would do..." Walters slowly nodded, gazing down at the ground for a long moment.

Finally, he looked back up, unholstered his pistol, pointed it at Phillipe's face, and squeezed the trigger. The gun once again fired with a sharp *bang!*

ℬ﮼ℭℬℭ﮼ℬℭ﮼ℬℭ

Now that the main body of the Twelfth regiment was heading west in an attempt to escape capture, Stan's skirmishers took the lead, with Billy's unit now guarding the column's back trail off to the east. This meant Stan's eighty-three men were charged with securing a path to safety for the rest of the regiment—through force of arms, as necessary—a task that suited Stan well. And the men in his Company H had come to greatly esteem their gigantic, ferocious Russian captain who infused them with an indomitable fighting spirit, along with, ironically, an unquenchable sense of humor, even in the most extreme circumstances.

They were now moving along a dirt road that led through an area of rich pastureland, bisected by the occasional split rail fence. Only the continuing flashes of artillery fire in the distance behind them and the stars in the sky provided any illumination in the near total darkness, the moon having yet to make its appearance. They passed by several small groups of cattle as they moved through the pastures, spread out in a wide line, each man within five or so yards from the men out to his sides. This way they could keep in visual contact with each other even in the dark, could prevent any enemy skirmishers from slipping past, and could provide mutual covering fire, should a gun fight break out.

They'd moved down the road for a mile and a half without encountering any movement other than the restless, confused cattle when Stan stopped and gave the signal to halt, a loud, piercing whistle that echoed down the line, it being too dark for the usual hand signals.

He gazed forward through the murk, watching intently for the motion he'd just picked up out of the corner of his right eye. He noted they were nearly to the end of the pasture area, as the road a quarter mile or so ahead rose quickly up a hill under what appeared to be a thick forest.

Stan raised his Henry rifle and peered down its sights, scanning slowly from right to left, looking for any sign of what he might have seen; but now he saw nothing. Suddenly he shifted the barrel slightly to the left and fired. In the light of the rifle's flash, large dark forms could be seen moving across the field a few hundred yards ahead of them. Several others of Stan's men also fired their rifles at the moving forms.

But the private to Stan's right yelled, "Stop firing! Them're just the cattle. You're shootin' the damned cows!"

But then small flashes appeared where the dark shapes had been out to their front, and they heard the distinctive *popping* sound of distant rifle fire.

Stan turned toward the private and laughed, "Is stupid thing to say, Private. Whoever heard of cows shooting back?"

He laughed again, then shouted, "Give them hell, boys!" and gunfire erupted all along the Union line, targeting what was now clearly rebel cavalry out across the field, lying in wait to cut them off from escape.

After exchanging fire for only a few moments, Stan called out, "Company will be reloading and fixing the bayonets!"

Then, after a half-minute pause, he jumped up and shouted, "Come on; follow me, my fellows! These little horse boys will not stand up to us *men!*" He let out a great roaring bellow and charged forward, firing off round after round from his repeating rifle, as quickly as he could work the action, never slowing in his great stride.

And though he never looked back, he knew his men would follow. They roared across the pasture, slowing only to fire at any movement they saw, then raced on with bayonet thrust forward.

When they reached the place where the rebel cavalry had been lying in wait, they found only a handful of bodies and a few bewildered, riderless horses, which they quickly rounded up.

Stan had half the company disperse to either side of the road to guard the approach to the mountain until the main column arrived, just in case the rebel cavalry decided to return. He then led the rest of his men up the mountain trail and into the woods to secure the route that he hoped would lead to their salvation.

⁊⊃ℭℜℭ⅁⅀⊃⁊⊃ℭℜℭ⅁⅀⊃⁊⊃ℭℜℭ⅁

Phillipe flinched, then looked up cautiously, realizing he remained alive and unscathed. The shot had sailed harmlessly into the air, the pistol having been knocked skyward at the last instant.

Walters looked to his right and saw a young Confederate lieutenant holding out a saber, having just used the flat of it to deflect Walters' arm and disrupt the shot.

Walters holstered the revolver and stepped up to the officer until they were only a foot apart, nearly nose to nose. "Who do you think you are to interfere with a superior officer?" Walters spoke in an oddly calm tone, belying his obvious anger.

"First Lieutenant Jubal Collins, Twenty-Seventh Virginia ... of the *Stonewall Brigade*, sir." The young man spoke evenly, meeting Walters' eye. If the lieutenant was intimidated either by the wrath of a superior officer or by Walters' unnerving, expressionless stare, he showed no sign of it. "General Walker has tasked me with taking charge of these here prisoners, and that's what I'm fixin' to do. And I'll not have them tortured nor murdered on *my* watch ... *sir!*"

"I will do as I please with these Yankee scum, Lieutenant," Walters continued in the same expressionless tone.

"Sir, if you persist in this immoral and illegal action, then you will leave me with no other choice; I *will* order my men to shoot you down, sir." Jubal paused and gave Walters the most withering glare he could muster up. "And given all the hard fightin' we all have done together lately ... I reckon my boys'll do as I say. What do *you* think, Colonel?"

Walters glanced over and saw half a dozen dirty, raggedly dressed soldiers staring intently at the two officers as they conversed. And though these men might not look like much to a well-to-do gentleman striding down the streets of Richmond, they had grim, hard looks on their faces, and each held a rifle in his arms, loaded and at the half-cock.

Walters looked back at Jubal. The two locked eyes for another long moment, neither backing down.

Then Walters slowly nodded, "Well ... at least somebody around here has some stones..."

Jubal then took one step back and snapped a salute, "Colonel!"

But Walters gazed at him another moment before turning and slowly walking away, never acknowledging the salute.

Jubal let out a relieved breath, then looked over at Sergeant Evans standing with the other soldiers, and the two exchanged wide-eyed looks. Jubal turned and signaled his men to move forward and take charge of the federal prisoners.

⊗⊙⊰⊙⊱⊗⊙⊰⊙⊱⊗⊙⊰⊙⊱⊗⊙⊰⊙⊱

William and Zeke were marched at gunpoint by the rebel soldiers for a quarter of a mile or more through the forest until

124

they came to a large clearing. Thousands of Union soldiers stood or sat in various groups around the clearing, guarded by armed rebel soldiers.

The two men were led past the large groups toward a smaller gathering of fifty or so men in the far southeast corner of the meadow. As they came nearer, they noted that these soldiers were all officers from various regiments.

When they'd reached the edge of the group, they were met by a rebel sergeant, who took charge of them, "Good morning, sirs ... please have a seat ... we're like to be here a spell." The sergeant also took charge of their personal sidearms and officer's sabers, handed over from the soldiers who'd captured them.

They looked around for a likely dry patch of ground to sit on. At first, as they worked their way through the group, they didn't see anyone they recognized. But when they'd gone halfway through, Zeke tugged at William's arm. "Hey, there's Phillipe! Guess they musta bagged our two stray rifle companies along with all them others..."

They turned and headed toward their comrade. And when they got nearer, Zeke figured Phillipe must have been through a tough time of it since they'd last seen him. While most of the officers looked downcast and glum, as men who've lost a battle and are now prisoners will, Phillipe looked like a man devastated. His eyes were red and swollen as if he'd been crying, and his face looked pale and drained, as if he'd recently lost his lunch.

Zeke sat down next to Phillipe, and William sat on the other side. But the young captain just stared straight ahead and did not acknowledge either one.

"Phillipe ... it's us ... Zeke, and William." Zeke glanced over at William, who raised his eyebrows questioningly.

But Phillipe continued to stare straight ahead. "They murdered him, Zeke ... just plain murdered him ... and they'd have murdered me too if I hadn't ... if I hadn't..." But his voice faded off to where they could no longer hear it, if he spoke at all.

Zeke frowned, "Murdered *who*, Phillipe? Who'd they murder?"

Finally, Phillipe looked over and met eyes with Zeke, "Sergeant Dixon. They murdered him in cold blood, right in front of me ... just over there in this camp..."

Zeke scowled darkly, "*Who* murdered him, Phillipe? I'll strangle the bastard with my bare hands if I have to..."

"I don't know ... some colonel ... never seen him before. Just showed up on his horse, grabbed me and Dix, dragged us off into the woods and shot him."

Phillipe slowly shook his head, wide-eyed as if recalling the horror of the event in his mind's eye. "Would've killed me too, except ... I..."

"You did *what*, Phillipe?" William jumped into the conversation for the first time.

"I ... I..." Phillipe stuttered, then stopped. He took a deep breath, "I was saved by that young lieutenant."

"Which lieutenant?" Zeke asked.

Phillipe looked up and pointed toward a rebel officer standing out past where the sergeant had met them when they'd arrived at their present location. The rebel lieutenant was speaking with some other Confederate soldiers gathered around him.

"Well, by damn, I'm going to get to the bottom of this!" Zeke rose to his feet. "Murder *my* men, will they? We'll see about that!"

"What're you doing?" William grabbed Zeke's tunic sleeve.

"Going to speak with that lieutenant ... This ain't right, war or no war. They can't just murder a man who's already a prisoner. And by God, I ain't gonna just sit here and take it. You stay here, William. Look after Phillipe ... See if you can ... *help* him a bit," Zeke gave William a hard look, which the latter acknowledged with a nod.

Zeke turned and pushed straight through the other Union officers, not bothering to acknowledge nor apologize to any he incidentally bumped in his urgency. And when he reached the edge of the group, he continued to stride right out across the meadow.

To his surprise, no one moved to stop him, until he was nearly up to the group of rebel soldiers surrounding the lieutenant. He was only few yards away when one of the soldiers spotted him and stepped up to block Zeke's way with his rifle held out sideways. But Zeke was fighting mad, and continued to push his chest against the man's rifle, until two more soldiers joined the first, seizing him by the arms and holding him fast as he continued to struggle.

The young lieutenant looked up at him, a bemused expression on his face. Zeke met eyes with him, "Lieutenant, I want to know why y'all think you can *murder* my men in cold blood—them as was already prisoners!"

The officer gazed at him a moment, then to Zeke's surprise, he addressed the men holding him, "Let him go."

The rebels stepped back and released Zeke, who stood still a moment, looking about in amazement and shaking his suddenly freed arms. Then he stepped up to the lieutenant, who astonished him by saluting, which Zeke returned, more out of habit than anything else.

"Captain … walk with me, if you please." The lieutenant turned away from the group of soldiers and began walking out away from where the prisoners were gathered. When they'd gotten out of earshot, he turned to face Zeke, "I'm sorry about what happened, Captain. It wasn't my doing, and I would've stopped it if I could."

Zeke could see the sincerity, even regret in the man's eyes, and felt his anger melting away. "But … what *happened*, Lieutenant? I'm Captain Zeke Benton, Twelfth West Virginia, by the way."

The rebel officer extended his hand, "Jubal Collins, Twenty-Seventh Virginia. Good to meet you, Captain, though I wish it were under better circumstances."

Zeke took the lieutenant's hand and shook it.

"To answer your question, Captain Benton, I don't really know how it happened. A Confederate cavalry battalion arrived, led by a lieutenant colonel, and took a short rest near where we were gathering the prisoners. I thought little of it at the time, but next thing you know I hear a single pistol shot. When I went to investigate, I found this colonel had already shot one of your men, a sergeant, and was getting ready to shoot another one who was a captain. Happily, I was able to prevent *that* travesty ... but was too late to help your sergeant.

"I *am* sorry; and believe me, I was sore angry about it at the time. I was a policeman before the war, so I take a bit o' pride in treating my prisoners proper-like; don't much care for an officer marching in here and murdering a man I'm tasked with guarding. No, sir; that didn't sit well!"

"All right, but who was this colonel, Lieutenant? The scoundrel ought to be brought up on charges. Such behavior ain't allowed in any army I ever heard of ... not even a rebel one like y'all's."

Jubal chose to ignore the slight against his army, given the circumstances, so again he shrugged, "Never seen him before, Captain; that's God's truth. And he left directly after, which I was happy about at the time, him being one of the scariest sumbitches I ever saw; figured I was gonna have to shoot him. I never thought to try and get his name until after he was gone."

But something the lieutenant said stirred a thought in Zeke's mind ... "You say he was *scary*? What'd he look like?"

"Hmm ... 'bout six feet, couple hundred pounds, but not fat ... sort of burly—strong looking. Forty-something, dark hair, neatly trimmed beard. But ... what an *odd* look he had ... like the man don't never feel a thing. Not happy, not sad, not angry, just ... *nothin'*."

Zeke began nodding, though his face was now a dark scowl, "Anything else you notice about this fella?"

"Yes, now that you mention it ... he was missing his left hand."

"*Damn it!* I shoulda knowed," Zeke removed his hat and slapped it against his knee. "Goddamned *Walters!*"

"Who?"

"Elijah Walters ... was our neighbor down Greenbrier way. Had a blood feud with my colonel, Nathaniel Chambers, back before the war. Only he's carried it on into the war. Doubt he cares about anything beyond killing the colonel ... and all of us that're his men—the bastard."

Jubal nodded, "Well, that now makes a bit more sense, anyhow. From the little I overheard, I expect he was trying to gather information about the whereabouts of your Colonel Chambers and his regiment.

"Tell you what, Captain, I will file an official report on the matter, with a complaint against this Colonel Walters. Likely nothing'll come of it with the war raging, but you never know.

"Now, Captain … if you would kindly return to where the other Union officers are seated, I'd be much obliged…"

ℬꙅ)ℭꙅℭꙅℬꙅ)ℬꙅ)ℭꙅℭꙅℬꙅ)ℬꙅ)ℭꙅℭꙅ

C.S.A. Lieutenant Colonel Elijah Walters felt almost giddy at his prospects, the momentary annoyance at the interfering young Stonewall Brigade officer already forgotten. After all, he'd gotten the information he required, and killing the captain from the Twelfth West Virginia would've only been a bonus, of sorts—not necessary to his plans.

He led the Thirty-Sixth Battalion northward past Martinsburg at a trot. With any luck, the fully mounted cavalry should move fast enough to cut off Chambers' slower moving foot soldiers, allowing them to set an ambush somewhere between the western Virginia hill country and the town of Bath.

And he not only had Chambers outmanned this time, with nearly eight hundred against five hundred and fifty, he also brought with him three six-pounder horse-drawn howitzers that he'd captured during the attack on Martinsburg and secreted away for future use, along with a caisson filled with anti-personnel grapeshot and plenty of powder.

As he rode and contemplated these secret weapons, Walters couldn't suppress a quick, evil grin when he thought, *And now is the perfect time for their use! Finally, I will have you, Chambers!*

Chapter 6. The Road Less Traveled

"I took the road less traveled ...
that has made all the difference."
- Robert Frost

Monday June 15, 1863, 5:00 a.m. – North Mountain, West Virginia:

Nathan and Tom rode at the head of the long column of soldiers trudging up the mountain on a narrow, twisting dirt road, hemmed in tightly on both sides by huge trees and thick underbrush. They'd started the uphill trek in the dark of the night, but now dawn was finally emerging, the inky blackness giving way to an eerie, eye-straining whiteness. A strange, thick fog had settled over the mountain during the early morning hours. So now, despite the growing daylight, they could still see but little ahead of them, even on the rare occasions when the trees parted for a short distance.

Tom figured the unusual summer fog must be due to the heavy storms of several days ago, with the heat of the rising sun trying mightily to dry up the saturated forest, drawing all the moisture up into the air. He decided he'd have to discuss the specific details of it with William later; being the scholar of the company, he'd likely understand the science behind the phenomenon.

The continuing lack of visibility contributed to the uncomfortable feeling that they were being watched by unseen enemy eyes—that they might at any moment stumble into a deadly ambush. The soldiers marched with rifles in hand— loaded and at the half-cock with bayonets fixed. They gazed about with wide eyes, straining to see anything moving in the woods as they pushed along. It reminded Tom of the anxious feeling they had had when traveling through the deep, dank western Virginia woods during their long breakout from Mountain Meadows. An intense, frightful night of fighting had given way to a long, fearful morning of marching, with as yet no end in sight.

And though Billy and Stan's scouts were spread out ahead and to the rear of the column, screening the march, Tom knew that was never any guarantee against sudden, unexpected attack, especially since the narrow winding trail prevented any protection out to the sides. Tom knew the thick trees and heavy undergrowth could potentially hide thousands of enemy soldiers only a few yards away.

They'd been riding steadily uphill for several hours, and Tom was about to suggest a short rest for the weary men afoot, when he felt the slope suddenly level off, and even begin to slope slightly downhill; they'd at last made it to the top of the pass. And as if to emphasize that change, the trees suddenly thinned, and the soldiers now rode through a mostly open area, though they still could see but little in the murk.

Tom was gazing off to the left when he noticed what appeared to be the roofline of a small house up a slight rise in that direction. He could only faintly make it out, but he thought he saw a thin wisp of smoke coming from its chimney, though he saw no lights in the windows.

He leaned over and tugged at Nathan's sleeve to get his attention, then pointed at the house. Nathan nodded but said nothing.

Tom stared at the house, trying to make out the details through the swirling mist, and nearly missed Nathan suddenly raise his right fist, signaling the column to a halt. Tony, who was walking and leading his horse as he typically did when on the march, had also been looking off to the side and nearly bumped into the back of Tom's horse. The column came to a halt, and a sullen silence settled over the mountain, broken only by the heavy breathing of men and the nickering of horses.

Nathan rode Millie a few steps forward, followed closely by his huge, ever-present hound. He stopped again, leaning forward into the darkness. Tom moved up near him, keeping back a pace, and reached down to unbutton the flap on the pistol holster at his right hip.

Straining his eyes into the fog, Tom finally saw what had caused Nathan to stop: someone approached them on the road. A moment later, Tom could see that the figure was a woman. She stepped up to within a few paces of Nathan and stopped, gazing up at him. She was willowy thin, and dressed in a simple woolen dress with a shawl around her shoulders, but no shoes nor any covering on her head. She was a young woman, with light brown hair and a pretty face, though not overly so, to Tom's thinking. Her face was smooth and unblemished, such that Tom couldn't decide if she was only a youth of fourteen or so, or fully a woman of twenty or more years.

She raised her right hand, "Greetings, sir."

"Lady ... I am Colonel Chambers," Nathan tipped his hat. "What is your name, and what, may I ask, brings a young woman out in the fog all alone? It has been an evil night with much death and violence. Some men who may be about are not to be trusted, and would likely do ill upon a defenseless young lady."

She tilted her head at this statement, as if pondering it. "I am called Anna. And to answer your second question, I saw you coming ... a long way off, and knew you needed my aid. And of your warning, I can tell by your kindly face, and the uniform you wear, that you are *not* one of the evil men of which you speak, but rather a gentlemanly and righteous man."

Tom found her speech odd, almost archaic, likely the result her folks' long years of isolation up on the mountain. Nathan looked at her for a moment, "Yes, all that may be so ... but I would *not* be kindly or gentle with an agent of the enemy. You can be sure such a one would quickly feel the sting of my wrath."

"As it should be, Colonel; I believe you are not a man to be trifled with. But you already know from my face and by my words that I am *not* of the enemy. And if I'm not mistaken, your heart also confirms it. To the contrary, as I said, I am here to *aid* you, and to warn you of great danger that lies ahead."

Nathan nodded, and Tom thought he had an odd, thoughtful look. But he said nothing, waiting for the lady to continue.

"The enemy you speak of watches this road some ... hmm ... thirty-five miles hence," she turned and gestured down the road in front of them. "If you continue on this path, many of you—or perhaps even all of you—will perish, including you, Colonel."

"I see ... and what would you have me do, then, Anna? Clearly we cannot turn back, for that way leads to death or imprisonment, which, given the way our enemy treats captives, are nearly indistinguishable."

"No ... I would not send you back that way either, Colonel, though I can promise you that an even worse fate lies ahead.

"But fear not, good sir. For behold, I bring you good tidings; there is yet another way. And though there may still be danger, it is a path rarely used and known to few, so it may remain unguarded by the enemy—safer for you and the men you lead."

Tom realized he'd been listening to this odd conversation as if mesmerized, and suddenly shook his head to break the spell. He looked back at the other men and saw many wide-eyed looks and intent stares, men listening attentively to every word as if their very fate hung in the balance.

"Very well," Nathan broke the long, thoughtful silence. "I will choose to trust you. My heart tells me there is no evil in you, but again I must warn you: if you betray me, it will go ill for you and for your people; I am not opposed to returning to this vale and burning everything in it, including your family's home."

But if the young woman was startled or frightened by this blatant threat of violence, she showed no sign of it, smiling in answer, "I will not betray you, sir ... never in life."

Then Tom noticed for the first time that the dog Harry seemed relaxed and unconcerned with the lady's presence. Harry sat next to Nathan's horse panting heavily, his huge tongue hanging out; but he was clearly at peace with the stranger. Tom took this for a good sign; the hound had always been a keen judge of character. Harry had instantly taken to trustworthy, honorable men like General Rosecrans, Governor Pierpont, and even the president, but had immediately disliked George McClellan and his boot-licking staff officers; such men immediately raised his hackles and made him bristle.

The young woman turned and began walking away, then paused and looked back, "Tighten your belt, sir, and pull your boots on tight, for the path is rough. And the morning is yet cool ... Wrap your cloak around your shoulders and follow me."

133

Nathan looked startled for a moment, "What of *you*, lady … does the morning air not chill you as well? You haven't even any shoes…"

She gave another slight smile. "Oh, I am used to the high places, Colonel … the cold does not bite me. But I thank you for your concern. Please … come…" She gestured, then turned and walked away down the road. Nathan turned in his saddle, gave the signal to march, and the entire column moved into motion once more.

Here the road undulated slightly up and down, and bent to the left, then the right, and back again, but was overall relatively flat and straight. She led them on this road for another quarter mile, then stopped, turned to face Nathan, and gestured to the right side of the road toward what looked like the start of a game trail.

"This is the path of which I spoke, Colonel. It is narrow, rocky, and steep, but both men and horses may pass, though you will have to dismount and come on in single file." She turned and without pause started up the trail. Nathan exchanged a look with Tom, then shrugged, and dismounted from Millie.

For the next four hours, she led them along the narrow, twisting path, which scrambled over rocks and fallen tree trunks amidst towering trees that let in little daylight from the rising sun. The trail led generally in a north-by-northwest direction and always downhill but had so many turns and switchbacks that Tom would have been completely turned around if it weren't for the occasional glimpse of the sun through the trees, telling him which way was east.

There had also been many side branches and forks in the road, but Anna led them steadily without pause, as if she knew these trails like the back of her hand. Tom was also impressed with her stamina; though the foot soldiers marching along behind looked weary and footsore, Anna seemed to move down the trail with a tireless ease. Surprisingly, Harry had chosen to follow closely behind her, out in front of Nathan, as if entirely comfortable in her presence and eager for her company.

Finally, they came to a wide clearing, and here the fog suddenly lifted, giving way to a sparkling blue sky with only a few scattered, fluffy clouds. To Tom, this sudden change to bright daylight seemed like waking from a long, nightmarish dream to discover you were safe after all. They moved across the clearing to its edge, and from there they could see a broad valley below, stretching for miles off into the distance. A sparkling blue stream meandered through a broad, green meadow, with no sign of human habitation. But at the foot of the hill, below where they now stood, a dirt road could clearly be seen, following the northward flowing stream on its east side.

Anna turned and once again stepped up to Nathan, "From here you can clearly see the road that lies ahead. It will take you to the North, and with good fortune you may encounter but few of the enemy along the way."

Nathan tipped his hat to her. "Thank you, dear lady; you have proven true and steadfast, and I shall not forget, though I can't imagine how I might ever repay your kindness. You should return to your home now. Can I send some of my men with you to keep you safe?"

She smiled again but shook her head. "There is no need, Colonel, I have no fear of the enemy. All will be perfectly well. And if I encounter your scouts along the way I will tell them where you have gone and how to find you." And to Tom's amazement, Harry the Dog sat down next to Anna, allowing her to pat him on the head, his prodigious tongue hanging out of his mouth to one side.

Nathan nodded thoughtfully, "Thank you again, Anna. This appears to be a good road, devoid of our enemies. But if we do encounter them, I am confident we can fight our way through to the North from here."

But she looked up toward the sky, as if thinking about this statement, then slowly shook her head. "Not by might of arms, nor by the power of your will alone shall you make it through Colonel, but rather by the Spirit of the Lord. Never forget, good sir: *God has given*."

Once again, Tom noticed an odd, startled look on Nathan's face, but didn't know what to make of it.

Nathan slowly nodded his head, then reached into his pocket for a cigar, and stuck it in his mouth. He tipped his hat to Anna, who nodded and smiled slightly in return, then he spurred Millie forward and didn't look back. Tom followed, but after only a short distance, he looked back to see what the girl was doing and was taken aback by what he saw.

Many of the officers and men were greeting her as they passed, tipping their hats politely and saying a quiet word of greeting or thanks. That was not especially surprising; after all, the girl had likely helped to save them from grave danger. The thing that startled Tom was that nearly all of the soldiers were laying coins, paper money, or other valuables at her feet as they passed, though she had never asked for any reward. She smiled at each man in turn, and thanked him, but seemed entirely unsurprised by this singular event.

A short scramble down the remaining hillside ended with the trees parting and the path leading across a beautiful green meadow of thick, waist-high grass to the dirt road they'd seen from above. Nathan immediately turned to the right, heading north, with the slowly moving stream off to their left. This wider dirt track allowed them to once again walk two abreast, and the soldiers quickly formed into columns without being told.

Nathan was deep in thought, smoking a cigar as they rode, and Tom did not feel inclined to intrude on those thoughts. They'd traveled only a few miles along the roadway when Tom heard the sound of riders approaching from behind at a trot. He looked back and saw Billy on horseback, leading a half-dozen mounted scouts.

When they pulled up to the front of the column, Billy slowed his horse to a walk next to Nathan.

Nathan returned Billy's salute, "Good to see you, Billy. I assume the girl told you where you could find us?"

But Billy seemed confused, "*Girl*, Captain?"

"The young girl who showed us this path ... she lives in that small house at the top of the pass. She said she would keep a watch for you and let you know that we had moved off the main road and were taking a new route."

But Billy just shook his head, "I saw no girl, Captain. But I would not need someone to tell me where you had gone." He grinned and rolled his eyes. "Five hundred men marching and a dozen more riding are not hard to follow. Even a blind child could do it."

Nathan snorted a laugh and nodded, acknowledging the absurdity of what he'd just suggested.

But then Billy said something that left Tom bewildered: "Also, Captain ... there is no house at the top of the mountain."

"Yes ... it's just as you crest the rise," Nathan gestured back toward the mountain. "There's a clearing there where they've cut back the trees. The house sits on a small rise twenty or thirty yards off to the left of the road. Both Tom and I saw it through the fog— it had a slate roof, and we could see a thin wisp of smoke rising from the chimney."

But Billy just stared at him, "Captain ... you know I am not one to boast, but there is one thing I am good at, and that's scouting. When I tell you there is no house at the top of the mountain pass..." he shrugged, then gave Nathan a hard look, leaving the sentence unfinished. Then he saluted and spurred his horse forward, the other scouts following closely behind.

Tom looked at Nathan, "What do you make of that, Colonel?"

Nathan didn't answer for a long moment, looking thoughtful as he continued to smoke his cigar, "Tom ... did you find there was anything odd or unusual about the girl, Anna?"

Tom thought about the question a moment before answering, "Well, yes ... several things, actually. First, she seemed amazingly calm and unconcerned despite the circumstances—all alone and suddenly confronted in the thick fog by half a thousand desperate, armed strangers. Most grown men would be reticent, much less an innocent young lady.

"I also noticed her unusual manner of speech—antiquated, it seemed to me.

"And I also found it amazing how all the men seemed to be naturally drawn to her, though she was no great beauty, to my thinking. When we were parting from her, they showered her with gifts she had never asked for. Oddly, she seemed entirely unimpressed by it."

Nathan nodded, "Anything else?"

Tom thought for a moment, "Hmm ... I remember her saying she had seen us from a long way off, but at the time I thought she was surely making that up; our entire trek up the mountain had been either in the black of night or in that thick morning fog. So I don't see how she could've seen us from more than a few dozen yards away.

"But I had noticed Harry seemed to approve of her, so I figured at least she was harmless."

"Harmless?" Nathan shook his head. "I wonder..."

"Why? What are you thinking, sir?"

"*Be not forgetful to entertain strangers: for thereby some have entertained angels unawares*," Nathan answered cryptically.

Tom nodded, "So ... you think maybe this Anna was an angel, sent by God to help guide us to a safer path? What gives you that impression?"

"Firstly, the odd things you've just mentioned. But also ... many of the things she said seemed eerily similar to quotations from angels in the Bible," Nathan answered.

Tom contemplated this for a moment before answering, "I can see the similarities. But I've been thinking about that, and it has occurred to me—what with her almost total isolation up on that mountain—she probably learned her letters and gained much of her education through reading the Bible, likely the only book her folks owned. So, it stands to reason she'd tend to repeat words and phrases she has read and studied, likely over and over again for years."

Nathan was quiet a moment, continuing to puff on the cigar and nodding his head slowly. "Yes ... *could be*, could be..."

Then Nathan tossed down the stub of the cigar and turned to meet eyes with Tom. "Tom ... you were with me the entire time, and no one but you and I spoke with the girl until we parted, agreed?"

"Yes ... that's true."

"And ... did I at any time ever speak my *given* name to her, or did you use it in her presence?"

"No, certainly not," Tom shook his head. Nathan had simply introduced himself as "Colonel Chambers," and nobody else in the regiment would ever dare address him using his first name. Tom himself had only done so on rare occasions, and then only to get his full attention in the most dire emergency.

"Do you recall the very last words she said to me ... *precisely?*" Nathan continued.

Tom thought for a minute, picturing in his mind the last moments of their conversation. "She said ... uh ... 'God is great'? ... no ... that's not quite right ... hmm..." He thought for another minute, then answered, "She said, 'Never forget, good sir; *God has given.'* I remember at the time thinking it was an odd turn of phrase for one to use in parting. But I wrote it off as just another example of her quirky, antiquated manner of speaking."

Nathan was again quiet for a moment, but now had an odd, inscrutable look on his face, "Tom ... in Hebrew my given name, *Nathaniel*, means 'God has given.'"

Tom's eyes widened, and he felt a chill run down his spine, "*Oh!*"

⚜⚜⚜⚜⚜⚜⚜⚜

Tuesday June 16, 1863 – Wheeling, West Virginia:

Miss Abbey and Megs greeted the young Union private out on the driveway in front of the Belle Meade farmhouse. He tipped his hat to them from where he sat on his horse. "Good afternoon, ladies."

"Private. Welcome back to Belle Meade," Abbey said, recognizing the soldier as one of those who had escorted the governor on his recent visit.

The private seemed pleased that she recognized him. "Thank you very kindly, ma'am." But then, seeming to remember the seriousness of his mission, he reached into his tunic pocket and pulled out a folded piece of paper.

"His honor the governor has tasked me with delivering this message into your hands, ma'am," he handed the paper down to Abbey.

She took it and thanked the soldier, who tipped his hat and then departed.

Megs and Abbey sat down right on the stairs to the farmhouse. Abbey unfolded the letter and began reading it aloud:

June 16, 1863
Wheeling, West Virginia

Dear Abbey,

I am sorry to be the bearer of bad news, but we have received word today of the fall of Winchester. During the early morning hours yesterday, Union forces under Major General Robert Milroy attempted an ultimately unsuccessful breakout from the besieged town.

And though I say unsuccessful, there are reports of individual units making their way separately to safety across the Potomac into Maryland, though it is still unclear which these might be. Other regiments have been, either fully or in part, captured by the enemy, and there are unfortunately reports of many casualties on both sides. The only thing that is clear and certain is that the Union garrison at Winchester has ceased to exist as a fighting force, and the enemy now controls the town and its forts.

Of course, I will inform you immediately of any news concerning our men of the Twelfth. In the meantime, we must pray for their safe return, and keep our heads up and never lose faith or hope.

Very sincerely,
Hon. Francis Pierpont, Governor
Commonwealth of Virginia

When Abbey finished reading, she heard a soft gasp behind her. She looked back and saw Margaret kneeling in the grass at the edge of the driveway; she'd come up behind them unnoticed and had overheard Abbey reading the letter. Margaret now held her hand over her mouth as tears flooded her eyes. Without a word, she stood and walked back into the house.

Ⓢ❁Ⓢ❁Ⓢ❁Ⓢ❁Ⓢ❁Ⓢ❁Ⓢ

Tuesday June 16, 1863 – Stephenson's Depot, Virginia:

William and Zeke queued up with the other Union officers waiting to begin the long, sad, uncomfortable journey to the Confederate capital of Richmond, where the prisoner of war camp awaited them.

A rebel sergeant had them write their name, rank, regiment, and hometown on a list which was intended to eventually make its way to the Union War Department for notification of kin and for a potential future prisoner exchange. He then checked through the officers' rucksacks, dumping each out onto a small folding camp table and examining the contents before putting everything back.

When Zeke handed over his pack, he was surprised when the sergeant withheld nothing, not even the paper dollar bills from his last trip to the paymaster. "Not that I'm complainin', mind … but you ain't even gonna take my money?" Zeke couldn't help but ask as the sergeant stuffed the bills back into the pack.

Zeke knew that United States dollars were highly valued by *both* sides, as Confederate dollars were notoriously subject to ruinous devaluation; their desperate government simply printed more paper bills as needed, and each Confederate state was allowed to print their own. The last Zeke had heard, a single U.S. dollar could be exchanged in the South for twenty Confederate dollars or more.

"Nope. Not that I have any love for you Yanks. But I have my orders from the lieutenant; only weapons are to be seized, but no personal items, *especially* not money. They say Lieutenant Collins used to be a policeman back in Richmond. So I reckon he's a bit of a stickler for the law," he concluded with shrug.

141

Zeke smiled and nodded his head, remembering his earlier positive interaction with the same Confederate officer. "Mighty decent of him," he concluded, then he slung his pack back over his shoulder and stepped forward into the group of officers waiting to begin their march back to Winchester.

But when William dumped his pack out, the sergeant frowned upon unrolling a small, tightly wound canvas cloth and seeing the shiny contents within. He picked up a small, slim, razor-sharp knife, and looking up at William asked, "What we got here?".

"I'm a surgeon, Sergeant. That is an operating knife, clearly."

"Well, it looks like a weapon to me," the sergeant set it to the side.

"And what about this?" The sergeant held up a small, shiny, inwardly curved tool with an eight-inch-long serrated blade, also razor sharp.

"It's a saw ... for cutting bones," William frowned.

"Another weapon..." the sergeant set it too aside.

"Sergeant! Did you not hear me? Those are *medical* instruments, and I am a surgeon. If you deprive me of those tools, you will very likely be sentencing men to die who might otherwise receive my life-saving services."

But the sergeant shrugged, "Thank the Lord I ain't never been inside the surgeons' tent, so I don't know nothin' 'bout that, Captain. But I *do* know what a weapon looks like, and these're them."

"But—"

"No use in arguin'." The sergeant stuffed the remainder of William's items back into his pack, after picking out another wicked looking, pointy-nosed set of pliers.

"Belay that, Sergeant," a voice said, and they both turned to see Lieutenant Jubal Collins step up to the table.

"Did you not hear the man, Sergeant? He's a surgeon, not an assassin. These are the life-saving tools of his trade. You will kindly return them to his pack."

"Yes, sir," the sergeant shrugged and proceeded to do as ordered, seemingly not at all put off by the mild rebuke from his commander.

"Thank you, Lieutenant," William met eyes with Jubal. "That was handsomely done, and speaks highly of you."

Jubal nodded. "It's the least I can do after what happened to that poor sergeant of yours. God speed to you, sir."

William could think of nothing more to say, so he nodded and stepped over to where Zeke waited with the other officers.

ဢဢၶ႙ၷဢဢၶ႙ၷဢဢၶ႙ၷ

Tuesday June 16, 1863 – Richmond, Virginia:

"But, Miss Evelyn … I don't understand what you want of me." Mary's tone was beginning to reflect a growing sense of frustration. "I've been following the plan we *both* made … *together* … right here in this room not even a month ago." Mary frowned across at Evelyn. The young black woman had been serving as a domestic slave in the house of Confederate President Jefferson Davis since the previous fall. At least that's what Davis's wife Varina believed she was; in reality she was Evelyn's spy, a freeman surreptitiously obtaining valuable information on the president's comings, goings, and meetings, and occasionally reading his private communications and government documents.

Evelyn closed her eyes and took a deep breath, attempting to quash a growing feeling of dread.

"Sorry, Mary … You're right … You're right. I'm being unfair. It's not your fault, it's just…" She removed her hand from her face and met eyes with Mary. "I just heard this morning that Winchester has fallen to the Confederate army … and Nathan was there with all his men…"

"*Oh!* Oh, Miss Evelyn … I'm so sorry; I didn't know!" She came across the room and grasped Evelyn's hands in her own and gave them a squeeze.

"Is Nathan…?"

"I don't know … there is no news yet with any specifics. All I know is the Union has tried to break out of Winchester but failed, suffering many casualties and surrendering most of their troops. There is some small hope; it seems several Union units and

143

numerous individual soldiers have escaped, apparently including commanding General Milroy himself."

"What can I do to help, Miss Evelyn?"

"I ... I just need to *do* something ... something to help our side, even if there's nothing I can do to help Nathan."

Mary sat back down and nodded. "I think I understand, Miss Evelyn. Though you can't help Nathan directly, if you do *something* ... something *significant*, it will feel like you are doing everything you can to help.

"Tell me what it is you want me to do, and I will try to do it," Mary gave a determined-looking nod.

"Thank you, Mary. Thank you for being so understanding. What I want to do is ... I want to learn what General Lee plans for the coming campaign ... and this time I mean to get the information straight from President Davis himself!"

"*Oh my!*" Mary's eyes widened.

📖❦📖❦📖❦

"With an honest old friend, and a merry old song ... And a flask of old port, let me sit the night long ... And laugh at the malice o' those who repine ... That they just swig porter, whilst I can drink wine!" The old man belted out the verse from his favorite drinking song, then paused to punctuate the song's theme by taking another swallow from the jug he held in his right hand.

As he lowered the jug, he reached up to wipe his mouth with his left, which he momentarily forgot was holding the reins to the horse pulling the wagon, causing it to jerk a bit to the right before righting itself again with a toss of its head.

"Hey, Wilbur ... watch yer steerin'." The younger fellow sitting next to him grabbed his arm. "Yer like to send us right off the bridge into the water."

"Ha! Ain't done it yet in all m'long years," the old man snorted a laugh. "I kin drive this wagon better drunk than any other fella kin cold sober!"

"Yeah, and you're just drunk enough to believe yer own lies," the younger man chuckled, shaking his head.

But the old man just grinned and took a deep breath in preparation for belting out the next verse. But the younger man clapped his hand over the old man's mouth, "Shhh ... you hear that?"

"Hear what?"

"Old Sally ... I can hear she's startin' in to limpin'. Reckon she's done throwed a shoe again..."

The old man listened for a moment, but he couldn't hear anything over the sounds of clanging pots, pans, tools, and other odd implements coming from the back of their own wagon.

"Nah ... like as not just the usual hitch in her get-along, the old nag," he shook his head, then took another swig.

"I'm telling ya', Will ... she done throwed a shoe. Pull up now and I'll go have a looksee."

"All right ... all right ... I'm stoppin'. Whoa! Whoa, Sally! There's a good ol' gal now." The wagon rumbled to a stop on the boards of the wide bridge.

It was sometime around midnight, and the long length of Mayo's Bridge spanning the James River from Richmond south to Manchester was dark, save the gas lamps at the entrances on both sides of the river, and devoid of traffic save their own tinker's wagon.

"Damn ... too dark to see." The young man lifted the horse's left front hoof and squinted at it. "Just light the torch and bring it 'round," he called out.

"All right ... all right, hold yer horses ... Ha! Hold yer horses ... that's a good one!" The old man started laughing as only a man more than half drunk will.

But then, suddenly they were no longer alone on the bridge; a Confederate soldier stepped up to them out of the darkness from the Richmond side of the bridge.

"You fellas get this wagon off the bridge, now!" He sounded cross and more than a little impatient.

"Oh ... hello there, Sergeant," the old man called out from where he continued to sit on the wagon, the requested torch now forgotten. "Where'd *you* come from, sir?"

"Never mind that, old man ... and I'm not a sergeant, I'm a private ... You daft or something?"

"No, sir ... never been accused o' that afore." He struck a mock offended pose.

"He's just drunk as a skunk," the younger man shrugged while still examining the horse's hooves.

The old man laughed. "Well, now ... *that* I have been accused of, on occasion ... Guilty as charged, officer!" He held the bottle up toward the private in mock salute before taking another swig.

Suddenly, three other soldiers appeared out of the darkness, with rifles in their arms.

"The colonel says to get this wagon off the bridge, if we have to toss it over the side," one of the new privates addressed the first.

"You heard him, you damned old coot. Move this wagon or we'll do it for you," the first private ordered.

"We're goin', we're goin', yer honors," the younger man nodded his head at the soldiers, grinning broadly, "No need fer no violence, good sirs." He clambered up into the wagon and sat next to the old man.

"C'mon, Will, you heard these soldier boys, let's get old Sally off this-here bridge and then we kin finish that bottle in peace down the road a spell ... and take a good look at that throwed shoe."

"All right ... we're gettin'." The old man snapped the reins to get the horse started.

Ten minutes later, out of earshot of the bridge, the young tinker turned to the older one, "Well, I'd say that was fairly definitive, wouldn't you?"

"Agreed." The older man no longer slurred his speech. "And did you notice? The Richmond side of the bridge was fairly crawling with soldiers, though they were trying their hardest to stay quiet and hidden."

"Well, I have to admit I haven't your keen eye for observation, Joseph, but even I couldn't help but notice when four armed soldiers walked up to us and drove us off the bridge by force," the younger man grinned.

146

Joseph nodded, "Looks like you were right about Alice Spencer, Jonathan."

"Yes," Jonathan nodded, "with Alice serving as the courier making all the arrangements, she ended up being the only person, other than us, who knew everything about this business."

"Nobody else involved knew anything more than a single piece of the puzzle," Joseph agreed, "so they couldn't have betrayed it—"

"Proving without question that Alice is indeed our double-agent," Jonathan finished the thought for him. "And Evelyn's scheme worked to perfection ... not surprisingly."

Joseph nodded his agreement, "She has become quite good at this, to be sure. It seems to come naturally to her. Like how she decided to use our *real* operation to blow the bridge—that we'd planned and then abandoned some months ago—as the bait to catch the rebel double-agent.

"Oh, and I'd be remiss if I didn't thank you for helping out this time, Jonathan. It was good having you here. And for not being a regular field operative, you pulled off your part flawlessly."

"Thank you, Joseph; I appreciate that. It means a lot coming from you. It felt good to be out in the field and to be finally doing something in person. Just do me a favor, will you please?"

"Yes?"

"Don't tell Angeline ... She worries so over me, and will no doubt chastise the very hide off me if she learns of *this*." Jonathan's eyes widened in mock terror.

Joseph snorted a laugh, "Never fear ... I always do as my *employer* orders!"

Two hours later, at the north end of Mayo's Bridge, a Confederate sergeant stepped up to the officer in charge of the operation, Confederate Signal Corps Colonel Grayson, a tall, dark-haired man of stern demeanor who leaned heavily on a walking stick tipped with a silver knob shaped as a lion's head. Unknown to the sergeant, Grayson was also a man who typically performed his clandestine duties dressed as a civilian, using the pseudonym, "Mr. Gray."

The sergeant snapped a salute, which was returned with less enthusiasm by the colonel.

"Report, Sergeant?" the colonel held tightly to a frown that lurked above dark, intense eyes.

"We found a wagon, sir ... less than a hundred yards from the bridge on the Manchester side, parked behind an old warehouse. A dozen barrels of gunpowder, several hundred feet of coiled rope, and enough good long fuses to safely set the whole thing off."

The colonel nodded, but said nothing.

"We could not find the horse that pulled the wagon, nor any sign of the saboteurs. Nobody else out and about anywhere along the waterfront. Looks like them damned old drunken tinkers scared the saboteurs off, like we'd feared."

The colonel looked thoughtful for a moment. "So it would seem."

✂︎✂︎✂︎✂︎✂︎✂︎✂︎✂︎✂︎

Tuesday June 16, 1863 – In the hills of West Virginia:

The Twelfth now marched through an area of low, wooded hills, interspersed with pretty little valleys through which sparkling streams flowed. Here and there, a lonely farmhouse and its outbuildings dotted the landscape, which was otherwise devoid of men.

As Nathan led them down yet another winding, sloping hillside trail, Stan appeared out front, trotting toward them on his great stallion, Groz. He pulled up and snapped a salute as Nathan raised his hand to halt the column.

"Colonel, my scouts have spied a large group of soldiers in the next valley. They appear to be resting beside a stream there. There are ... hmm ... a thousand, maybe more—of various regiments, from their flags. And also several hundreds of cavalry. No artillery that I saw, but..." he shrugged.

Nathan thought a moment. "Are they aware of us yet, do you think, Stan?"

"Oh, no ... is not likely. They seem very ... how you say? Lackadaisical? Is this correct word? Yes, I think is right ... lackadaisical ... no scouts, no sentries, though some scattered cavalry patrols roaming around ... mostly soldiers just lazing about, eating, pissing, and whatnot." Again he shrugged.

"All right, then we should be able to get a jump on them, despite our lesser numbers. Either destroy them outright, or at least disperse and scatter them so we can continue on our way north," Nathan rubbed his chin, already working out in his mind a scheme of attack.

But then Stan started laughing. Tom and Nathan looked at him questioningly.

When Stan caught his breath he explained, "Sorry, Colonel ... sorry ... I laugh because you are misunderstanding me ... Is my fault. Sometimes speaking the English, I am forgetting ... these little details of things. Like, this time I am forgetting to tell you that these slovenly soldiers are wearing *blue* uniforms!" Then he laughed again, slowly shaking his head.

"Oh!" Nathan and Tom joined Stan's laughter. "Well, in *that* case, I suppose we'll not attack them after all. Though when I've finished with them, they may *feel* like they've been attacked." Nathan now scowled darkly.

Tom nodded, knowing his commander's long-standing intolerance of sloppiness and poor discipline, especially in a potential combat zone. *Yep, they're going to catch hell, all right!* he decided, and grinned at the thought, remembering the first time he'd met Nathan Chambers and had caught that very hell himself for being more than a little disorganized and untidy. *Yep, this ought to make for a good show.*

A half hour later, as they approached the broad field containing the large contingent of Union soldiers Stan had reported, they were greeted by a platoon of cavalry troopers led by a major.

"Colonel Chambers! I can't tell you how good it is to see you again, sir," the major snapped a salute, which Nathan returned.

"Major Adams," Nathan recognized Alonzo Adams, the second in command of the New York First Cavalry. "Which units have you here in this valley?"

"Well, sir ... we seem to have gathered together a little bit of everything. Now that you're here, looks like yours may be the largest contingent, followed by something like five hundred men of the 116th Ohio. Then, let's see ... we've got a few hundred troopers of the Twelfth and Thirteenth Pennsylvania Cavalries ... something like a hundred men from the 123rd Ohio Infantry—oh, and they brought along thirty-five rebel captives, God knows why—and your own Captain Carlin and about fifty of his artillerymen from the Wheeling Battery, though what they'll do with no big guns to wrangle I can't imagine. A few other drips and drabs from other units that've tagged along. And several hundred teamsters and civilian evacuees from Winchester. That's pretty much it, sir."

Nathan nodded, "And supplies?"

"Well, sir ... in addition to no artillery, we have no food, no fodder, no tents, and very nearly no ammunition. 'Bout the only thing we have plenty of is water ... oh, and empty bellies," he grinned, despite the seriousness of their present circumstances.

"I see. Who's the senior officer?"

"That'd be Colonel James Washburn, 116th Ohio, sir."

"Take me to Colonel Washburn, Major. Tom, give the men a brief rest, and have them refill their canteens. But don't let them get too comfortable ... I want to be moving again within the hour."

"Sir!" Tom saluted and turned to carry out his orders.

ЄꝈԀꞬꞠꙄꙄꝈԀꞬꞠꙄꙄꝈԀꞬꞠ

As Nathan rode across the meadow with Major Adams, they approached a group of a hundred or so soldiers lounging by a sparkling stream. Several of the men had stripped off their tunics and taken off their shoes, and laid about on the grass by the stream.

Nathan pulled his horse to a stop next to a captain, who was lying next to several privates and a sergeant.

"On your feet, soldiers!" Nathan ordered.

The soldiers jumped up, stood to attention, and saluted.

Nathan looked down at them with a dark scowl. "Captain ... get these men dressed, armed, and in good order before I return. And spread the word to any other nearby units ... We're still in a battle zone, and must be prepared to fight at any moment."

"Yes, sir," The captain continued to hold the salute. "But ... sir, we ain't got no ammo, nor any food..." The captain trailed off lamely as he seemed to realize he was eliciting no sympathy from the stern-looking officer.

"You've got bayonets, Captain. And you've got guts. I suggest you start using them." Colonel Chambers returned the salute before spurring Millie forward.

The captain gazed after him, immediately started buttoning up his tunic, and turned to his men, "You heard that colonel: snap to, you lazy rascals ... or there'll be hell to pay!"

A nearly identical scene played out as they passed various other groups of disorganized soldiers, such that by the time they finally reached Colonel Washburn, Major Adams was beaming broadly and slowly shaking his head, working hard to suppress a growing chuckle. But Nathan was smoking on a cigar that was tightly clenched in his teeth, accompanied by a stern frown.

Nathan dismounted, stomped out the stub of his cigar, then stepped up to Colonel Washburn, where the latter sat on a stump. The colonel stood and the two men exchanged a salute, and then a handshake.

But Nathan was in no mood for pleasantries or small talk, "Colonel ... what was the date of your commission, sir?"

Washburn seemed startled at first, and then nodded his understanding, "August thirteenth, 1862. And yours, Chambers?"

"Backdated to April twelfth, 1861."

"Ah ... beginning of the conflict. Good to have friends in high places," Washburn shrugged. "Very well, Colonel; that puts you in command by seniority. What are your orders, sir?"

"The battle's not over yet, Washburn," Nathan frowned. "The enemy is still in the field, and would like nothing better than to bag another Union formation. We march within the hour. But first, we must organize ourselves into a fighting force. This rag-tag, straggling group of derelicts won't do, Colonel. If we meet the enemy, I mean to make a good accounting of ourselves."

"Yes, sir ... but you should know we're very short of ammunition and food ... and morale is ... Well with the devastating defeat they've just endured, it's pretty much non-existent—"

"Yes, yes ... I've heard it already, from pretty much every officer here. But frankly, Colonel, I don't give a damn. We'll use our bayonets and the butts of our rifles if we have nothing else, and we'll cinch up our belts if we're hungry. And as for morale; I find if you treat men like men, they'll respond in kind."

"As you say, sir," Washburn nodded.

"Now ... who's the senior cavalry officer present?"

"Oh, that'd be me, sir," Major Adams jumped into the conversation for the first time.

"Very well, then. Major, I'm placing you in command of all brigade cavalry forces. Get them organized into companies, and prepare to screen our advance to all sides as we march. I've had ... *specific intelligence* ... of a rebel force somewhere out ahead that is preparing an ambush. Obviously, it's your job to make sure that doesn't happen."

"Yes, sir!" Adams saluted.

Then Nathan turned back to Colonel Washburn, "And you, Colonel, I'm placing in command of all infantry regiments."

"Including the Twelfth West Virginia?" Colonel Washburn raised an eyebrow.

"Of course, including the Twelfth. Lieutenant Colonel Thomas Clark will take regimental command under your brigade-level command." Nathan then stuck another cigar in his mouth, strode back to where Millie stood cropping grass, and remounted.

Major Adams also remounted his horse.

Nathan then turned to them. "Gentlemen, you have your orders ... Let's get this brigade moving ... *now*."

ಬಂಣಲಲಜಾಬಂಣಲಲಜಾಬಂಣಲಲ

152

Four hours later, Nathan met up with Tom Clark again, pulling his horse up next to Tom's, where the latter rode at the head of the Twelfth West Virginia regiment. Nathan was riding back down the line, checking on the discipline and morale of the various marching companies as he went, and had finally reached the Twelfth.

"How's the new brigade coming together, sir?" Tom asked.

"Looking better ... much better than when we first found them all downcast and listless out in that field. I'm starting to see a little pride back in their step, and a return to the belief that they can still whip the enemy if given a chance."

"Good to hear it, sir." Tom then snorted an incongruous short laugh.

"What?" Nathan asked, wondering what Tom found humorous under the current circumstances.

"I was just wondering if you'd heard what the men have taken to calling your new command, sir..."

"No, I've not heard a thing ... What are they calling it?" Nathan returned Tom's grin with a questioning eyebrow.

"They've dubbed us the *Hodgepodge Brigade*, sir."

Nathan chuckled, "That sounds about right." He gave Tom a quick salute and continued on down the line to check on the next regiment.

When Nathan had nearly reached the back of the column, he heard multiple gunshots in the distance back to the southwest, so he stopped to look and listen, pulling out his spyglass and standing in the stirrups. He could see nothing at first, but then on a low ridgeline several miles away he saw a sudden large puff of smoke roll up into the sky. This was followed a few seconds later by a low, rumbling, *boom!*

Since his brigade had no artillery, that could only mean one thing: Major Adams's cavalry was under attack by the rebels. He immediately spurred Millie forward, and she leapt into motion. He ran at the gallop for several miles, but he surprisingly had heard no more artillery fire and only a smattering of small arms.

Then as he rounded a corner in the road, he slowed to a walk as he saw Union cavalry troopers riding toward him at a trot, led by Major Adams. And next to Adams rode Sergeant Billy Creek.

As the cavalry troop neared Nathan, he turned Millie around and fell in with Major Adams as the column continued to move.

"What happened, Major?" he asked.

Adams grinned, "We gave them rebels hell; that's what happened, Colonel." Then he snorted a laugh, "Your man Creek here spotted their ambush, just as you'd warned us of, and came to find me. The rebs were guarding the wrong roadway, thinking we'd be farther out to the west."

"Anyway, we were able to ambush their ambush," Adams continued. "Were riding right down on them before they knew we were even there. They only managed to fire off a single shot from one o' their howitzers, but that was poorly aimed and did no damage. Then we were on them, driving them off their hill in a panic with saber and pistol shot. Unfortunately, they were too many for us to press the assault, so we had to pull back, but not before spiking one of their two big guns.

"Couldn't destroy 'em, but gave 'em a good bloody nose. From their banners, they looked to be some o' Jenkins' cavalry," Adams concluded. "Thirty-Sixth Virginia Battalion, I believe."

"Hmm ... I'm not familiar with that one," Nathan admitted with a shrug.

Then Nathan looked over at Billy, "You have anything to add?"

"Yes, Captain. I recognized their leader; he is one I know well—a snake I have hunted in the winter hills with Stan. A snake who now has only one hand, thanks to us." He snorted a laugh.

"*Walters?!* He's here?" Nathan raised his fist, signaling the cavalry column to a halt. He turned Millie and faced Billy.

"Yes, Captain. He now wears a lieutenant colonel's uniform, like Sergeant Clark. And when he shouts orders, these rebel cavalrymen obey."

"*Damn...*" Nathan muttered, slowly shaking his head, gazing at the ground ahead of him.

"Who's Walters?" Adams asked.

Nathan growled, "Someone who needs killing, Major. What's his troop strength?"

"Looked to be about eight hundred, more or less," Adams shrugged, then looked over at Billy who nodded.

"All mounted. No infantry, and now only the one big gun on a horse carriage," Adams concluded.

Nathan turned and looked back toward where he now knew Walters lurked. He took out a cigar, stuck it in his mouth and chewed it for a moment, a dark frown knitting his brow.

Then he pulled it out, turned to Adams, and said, "Major, send a rider at the gallop to Colonel Washburn. Tell him to about-face the brigade and prepare for battle. Have your rider inform the colonel of the enemy's troop strength and last known disposition. Then have your cavalry guard our flanks as we advance, and just move enough troopers forward to see if you can cut off his retreat."

"Sir!" Adams snapped a salute and began giving orders to his officers, who immediately moved into motion.

Billy saluted, then turned his horse and trotted off to continue scouting the enemy.

Nathan sat on Millie, waiting for the arrival of Colonel Washburn and the infantry. He lit the cigar and smoked it as he ruminated on the battle to come. *Finally, we come to grips, you murderous son of a bitch. Finally, I have you where I want you ... and this time there will be no escape.*

😖☻∞😖☻∞😖☻∞

The Hodgepodge Brigade moved into motion against Walters' cavalry battalion with the unmatched enthusiasm of men who've recently been bested in battle and burn for a chance at redemption, and a measure of revenge.

Nathan was gratified to see grim smiles on the faces of the men who marched past him, several groups even cheering him as they passed, especially the men of the Twelfth.

Stan laughed as he passed, "So Billy has found our snake, eh, Colonel?"

"Yes, so it seems, Mr. Volkov."

"Is good, Colonel … is good. Maybe I can take off his other hand this time!"

Nathan grinned and nodded as Stan snorted another laugh.

Adams sent back a lieutenant to report the brigade's cavalry had successfully maneuvered into a position to Walters' rear, effectively cutting off the enemy's retreat.

When Colonel Washburn and his officers reached his position, Nathan turned Millie and joined them as they trotted forward.

"A rebel cavalry battalion?" Washburn asked.

"Yes, and Adams has them cut off from escape, so we should be able to have our way with them."

"*Good!* Excellent, Chambers," Washburn beamed, also seeming excited by the prospect of an action that might go their way for once.

As the brigade advanced, scouts reported that the enemy had pulled back onto a small rise, and seemed to be digging in behind several intersecting stone walls near the top of the hill.

Nathan dispersed the infantry into three main groups, with a reserve force to cover any gaps or exploit any breakthroughs. The cavalry continued to guard the flanks and prevent the enemy from running.

The Union skirmishers moved forward and engaged the enemy pickets, quickly driving them inward.

The Union brigade moved into position at the bottom of the hill, on top of which several hundred yards away sat the Confederate cavalry battalion, now dismounted and dug in behind the rock walls.

Nathan sat up in the saddle, pulled out his brass spyglass and held it to his eye. The first thing he saw was a burly looking Confederate officer sitting on a horse, looking right back at him through binoculars. The man slowly raised his left arm and appeared to shake his fist at Nathan. Only the arm had no hand to clench.

Nathan growled and cursed under his breath. He prepared to shout out the order to advance.

But then, just beyond Walters, something caught his eye: the enemy's cannon, what appeared to be a six-inch rifled field gun. *They'll have it loaded with cannister, no doubt.*

It was an advantage for Walters that Nathan had no good way of countering. He knew the only way to defeat it was a quick charge to capture the gun and thus minimize the time the enemy had to reload and fire. In the meantime, men would die, cut down in horrific swaths by the deadly projectiles.

He gazed up the open slope to the enemy's position. *No cover. Three, maybe four hundred yards …*

He did a quick calculation in his head … how long it would take to traverse the ground, uphill, under heavy rifle volleys and subjected to deadly cannister fire from the field piece until they could put a stop to it.

Then he turned to Washburn, "Colonel … how many rounds do the men have … on average?"

Washburn shrugged, "Not many, Chambers … two or three rounds a piece, I should think. Of course, many have none at all. But they all have bayonets … and rifle butts, as you recently pointed out."

"Hmm … not especially effective against that field gun." Nathan turned back to gaze at the enemy.

"Never worry, Chambers … with our numbers, there can be no doubt we'll carry their position, even with our lack of ammunition and despite having to take out that gun."

Nathan turned back toward Washburn and they locked eyes. "Yes, certainly, Washburn. But at what cost? And for what *gain?*"

Washburn shrugged. "For victory. To gain a measure of revenge against our hated enemy."

Revenge? Nathan thought and smiled ruefully. *Yes … it's all about revenge…*

"One would hope to gain some strategic advantage," Nathan slowly shook his head. "But here there is none. Our current mission is to make our way back to the North and live to fight another day. There is nothing this meager cavalry battalion can do to stop us. There is nothing to be gained here. Call off the attack, Colonel."

"*What?!* But Colonel Chambers, I must protest! We have them dead to rights. Pinned down and helpless. Desperately outnumbered. A good strong push and they'll collapse and surrender, mark my words."

Nathan shook his head. "Not this guy … He'll never surrender to me. He'd rather die. I'll not sacrifice hundreds of our men just to kill him, much as he deserves it.

"Call off the attack, Colonel. We continue our march to the North."

⊱ ⋆ ⊰ ⊱ ⋆ ⊰ ⊱ ⋆ ⊰

Elijah Walters watched the departure of the Union brigade through his binoculars, fighting to maintain his typical expressionless visage in the face of a thoroughly bewildering turn of events.

One minute cutoff, surrounded, and under imminent threat of assault by a vastly superior enemy force—led by his most hated enemy—and the next minute … *this!*

He lowered the binoculars and slowly shook his head, trying to digest what had just happened; the whole thing was nearly unbelievable. Walters prided himself on knowing people, knowing how to manipulate them by applying just the right amount of pressure. And Chambers had always been one of the easiest reads of all; if you prodded him hard enough, he would fight, period. He never failed in that regard. Never showed any hesitation, never seemed concerned about possible casualties or consequences. Never backed down. He was a thoroughly dependable enemy.

But this time … he had me outnumbered. He could've taken out my entire command, while only suffering a few hundred casualties on his side—a number he could've easily absorbed. I … just don't understand it. Is Chambers, losing his nerve? Afraid of a hard fight? A goddamned coward?

⊱ ⋆ ⊰ ⊱ ⋆ ⊰ ⊱ ⋆ ⊰

As the column once again resumed the northward march, Major Adams approached Nathan, brought his horse to a halt, and saluted. Nathan noted that the major still appeared in good humor, unlike the foot soldiers who now gave him sullen, downcast looks.

"Major, let's keep a close watch on that enemy cavalry formation as we move northward. I wouldn't put it past Walters to take another crack at us before we're done. Especially when we're most vulnerable, like when crossing the river."

"Already ordered, sir. They'll not take a piss in the creek or a shit in the woods without us knowing of it," the major answered with a chuckle.

"Good! See that it's so, Major."

Then Nathan thought of the odd mountain girl Anna, their meeting with her on the road, and her warning not to continue into the west. If they had, they'd have missed joining up with the rest of the Hodgepodge Brigade and would've likely marched right into Walters' ambush. He said a quick silent prayer of thanks to whomever had arranged *that* fortuitous meeting.

∞CЯ∞∞∞CЯCЯ∞∞∞CЯCЯ

Tuesday June 16, 1863 – Hancock, Maryland:

The motley Hodgepodge Brigade stopped in the small town of Bath for a few hours in the late afternoon to rest and refill their canteens, though there was no food to be found. Either the residents were hiding what they had, or it had already been taken by some other passing army formation. And many of the soldiers took advantage of the opportunity to bathe in the town's famous sulfurous waters.

Then, as the sun was setting, the brigade waded across the Potomac at a place called Millstone Point near the confluence with St. John's run. The First New York Cavalry continued to guard their rear against Jenkins' cavalry, which had shadowed their march the whole way but had not attempted another serious engagement.

But as Major Adams reached the north shore of the Potomac, the last man of the brigade to do so, and was greeted by Colonel Chambers, they looked back and saw a rebel officer sitting on his horse on the far bank along with a small group of riders. The officer held up his left arm, which was missing its hand. Then he turned his horse and was gone. Nathan gazed after him, nodding.

From that point, the brigade marched five miles downstream to Hancock, Maryland and were welcomed joyfully by the townspeople and the small Union garrison stationed there.

After posting sentries and ordering a continuation of Major Adams' cavalry patrols, Nathan ordered the brigade to bivouac in and around the town for the night wherever they could find shelter. And now that they'd be stationary for a few hours, he assigned the other necessary brigade command duties to specific officers: an adjutant general, a provost marshal, quartermasters, and commissary officers. He was careful to choose these important posts from each of the disparate army units in order to help with overall unit cohesion and to prevent any potential divisiveness.

With these critical posts assigned, the town was quickly organized, and the soldiers were finally fed and rested, and whatever ammunition was available in the town's stores was quickly distributed.

And then Nathan fired off a series of telegrams, first to the War Department, giving his action report, present force disposition, and requesting further marching orders.

Next, he telegraphed Governor Pierpont reporting the happy news of the Twelfth West Virginia's escape, along with that of the Wheeling Battery—minus its big guns—and the other bits and pieces of regiments from various other states.

Finally, he sent a telegram to Miss Abbey to let her know they were safe. This one was the most difficult, as he struggled with what to say when it came to the fortunes of the Twelfth, not yet knowing the fate of William, Phillipe, and Zeke. In the end, he decided to say nothing about that, as it was still possible that they escaped in a different direction with the other two missing Twelfth companies. If that were the case, then he would've worried the folks back home for no purpose. And if in the end it turned out to be bad news … well, there would be plenty of time for that later.

ℰᎧᏣᏝᏟᏐᏇᎧℰᎧᏣᏝᏟᏐᏇᎧℰᎧᏣᏝᏟᏐ

Tuesday June 16, 1863 – Wheeling, West Virginia:

In the late evening of the same frightful day on which the residents of Belle Meade Farm learned of the downfall of Winchester from Governor Pierpont's letter, Abbey received a telegram. And to her delight and relief, this one was from Nathan himself.

After a quick read through, she called together the members of the family who were most affected: Megs, Rosa, Margaret, Adilida with little Nathaniel, and Edouard, so she could read it again aloud. Later she planned to read it to a gathering of the entire farm, but once again thought it proper to give the news first to those with loved ones in the fighting.

> *Hancock, Maryland*
> *June 16, 1863*
>
> *Abigail Chambers*
> *Belle Meade Farm, Wheeling, W. Va.:*
>
> *Dear Momma, the 12th has escaped the battle at Winchester. Now safely north of Potomac. Joined with other Union forces into a capable fighting force. Relatively few casualties. Leaving this place shortly, will send more news from next station.*
>
> *Nathaniel Chambers,*
> *Colonel, 12th W. Va. Infantry*

When she finished reading, a spontaneous cheer went up from the gathering, and there were tearful, happy embraces, handshakes, and pats on the back all around.

But Abbey noticed that Margaret did not seem as excited as the others, so she approached and quietly asked why.

"Momma … I don't know … I just have a *bad* feeling about this, though it's seemingly wonderful news. Like Nathan has told only *part* of the truth," she answered. "I would feel better if I could hear something from William himself."

But Abbey could think of nothing to say to this, so she just gave Margaret a long, warm embrace, while her adopted daughter softly cried.

Chapter 7. Many Paths and Errands

"Far ahead the road has gone ...
where many paths and errands meet.
And whither then? I cannot say."
- J.R.R. Tolkien
The Road Goes Ever On

Wednesday June 17, 1863 – Hancock, Maryland:

Despite Nathan's intentionally optimistic telegram to Miss Abbey, the situation the Hodgepodge Brigade found itself in was a precarious one at best. At first light, the alarm sounded, warning of a Confederate attack on the C&O Canal that ran parallel to the river just south of downtown Hancock. Union cavalrymen of the Thirteenth Pennsylvania were the first to respond, and quickly drove off the rebels, but not before the enemy had burned all the canal boats moored there.

An hour later, 700 Confederate horse soldiers attacked upstream of Hancock, crossing over near St. John's Run in an attempt to flank Union forces at Hancock. But this time, the First New York Cavalry counterattacked, forcing the rebels back and preventing them from destroying a large culvert over the canal, which would've effectively blocked all canal traffic westward.

Major Adams reported that he believed these rebel cavalry troopers were of Brigadier General John Imboden's Northwestern Brigade. Nathan wasn't convinced, remembering the distant sight of the one-handed Confederate officer on the far bank of the Potomac. *Walters again; I'd bet money on it.*

But the rebel cavalry raids were not much more than an annoyance with the forces Nathan currently had at his disposal. The real fear was the impending advance of Major General Ewell's Second Corps of the Army of Northern Virginia, the same twenty-five-thousand-man-strong force that had just captured Winchester. If the Hodgepodge Brigade was still at Hancock

163

when even a portion of that army crossed the river, it could go very badly for them, very quickly.

At noon, Nathan received marching orders from Major General Schenck, in command of the Middle Military District, which included West Virginia and the Shenandoah Valley. The general reported that the War Department, and the North in general, was in a panic over the expected rebel attack into Maryland, Pennsylvania and beyond. Schenck ordered all Union troops at Hancock to march north into Pennsylvania immediately, to rendezvous with other retreating formations at a town called Bloody Run, some thirty-three miles to the north, and once there to await further orders. Schenck reported that Ewell's main force had not yet crossed the river, but that was expected at any time. It was feared that General Lee might advance as well, linking up with Ewell north of the Potomac as part of a general offensive.

Nathan scowled when he pulled out a map and saw where they were heading; it seemed clear to him that General Schenck — likely wanting to avoid another debacle under his command — was now erring on the side of caution. Bloody Run was not only north, but also west of their current position, well out of any northward path Ewell or Lee might be expected to take. Nathan shook his head in annoyance; though he appreciated keeping his men out of harm's way after the near disaster they had just endured, he now had a reasonably capable fighting force at his command. If they could be re-equipped, they could join with other Union forces off to the east and help defeat the advancing rebels. But all he could do was shake his head and shrug his shoulders; he had his orders.

General Schenck warned in his message that the Hodgepodge Brigade should be on the lookout during its march for rebel cavalry raids, as it was reported that C.S.A. Generals Jenkins and Imboden were already in force on the northern side of the river.

When Nathan read that last line, he snorted a laugh and rolled his eyes, *Thanks for the warning, General; we could've never figured that one out on our own!*

Fortunately, Nathan had anticipated the general's order, given the perilous situation they were currently in, so he had already directed his commanders to prepare for another march at a moment's notice.

Clearly, that moment had arrived.

Friday June 19, 1863 – Woodstock, Virginia:

William, Zeke, and Phillipe were tired, hot, thirsty, and hungry, having marched almost nonstop since sunup on the fourth day of their captivity. It had been a scorching hot day, triggering an almost unbearable humidity as the sun burned off the remains of the previous day's rain showers.

After they'd first been captured and marched back to Winchester, they'd spent the rest of that day and the following one in a makeshift outdoor prisoner camp while the Confederates rounded up and brought in more captives.

Then, on the third day of their captivity, they had lined up for the long march to Staunton, some ninety-five miles to the southwest, where they could then board a train for Richmond. And despite their unhappy circumstances, their journey started out on a hopeful note when a Confederate colonel stepped up in front of the men and made a short speech to the guards: "I am Colonel Francis Board, commander, Fifty-Eighth Virginia. Men, these Yankees have fallen into our hands by the fortune of war. I want them treated like gentlemen. If I hear of any insults or abuse, it *will* be punished."

But once out of sight of the town, most of the guards seemed unconcerned with the colonel's stern warning and proceeded to liberally apply both insults and abuse. And the local population, being mostly pro-secessionist, did not hold back their vitriol in the least, pelting the unfortunate prisoners with sticks, rocks, and plenty of insults. "Damned Yankees … Milroy's thieves … Y'all ought to be hung … I hope y'all rot and die in prison," were typical invectives.

At first, it had been almost shocking, and brought home to them just how hated Yankees were—and General Milroy in particular—among the pro-Confederate civilians. But the young officers were fighters, and despite their recent defeat, most were still feeling vigorous and defiant. So they soon began firing back their own insults, or would burst into pro-Union songs as they marched, just to annoy the rebels—"Yankee Doodle," "Battle Hymn of the Republic," and "The Star-Spangled Banner" were among the favorites.

It was now the end of the fourth day, which had been terribly hot and humid. But if they had entertained any prospects for a more comfortable evening, those hopes were soon dashed; a dark thunderstorm rolled in just as the sun was setting, bringing with it a drenching rain and a frigid, gusty wind.

The Confederate guards hustled the 109 Union officers into an old log barn a few yards back from the road in order to escape the deluge. But it was too late to prevent an uncomfortable dousing, which would make for a sodden, unpleasant night's sleep.

After a quick inadequate bite of the small crust of cornbread provided by their captors, William figured he was exhausted enough to sleep through almost anything, including his soggy clothes. But even as he was drifting off to sleep on a lumpy, musty layer of hay, he heard a slap and a curse next to him.

He rolled over and opened one eye to see Zeke sitting up, scratching furiously at the back of his neck and then his arms.

"What is it? What's the matter with you?" William asked, feeling more than a little annoyed at being kept awake by the commotion.

"Ain't you felt them?" Zeke continued to scratch. "Damn it, William, I'm being eaten alive!" Zeke held out his left arm so William could see it.

But William had to reach over and put on his spectacles to see anything more than a blur. He sat up and examined the proffered arm, then gasped. Zeke's arm was crawling with tiny insects: fleas! Hundreds of them.

And then William felt them too, itchy and crawling inside his shirt and on his scalp. But he resisted the urge to scratch, knowing it would do no good and would only irritate the skin worse than was already being done by the tiny host of hungry invaders.

166

He looked around and saw that the other prisoners, including Phillipe, had also begun to notice their diminutive attackers, and were now busily stripping off shirts, swatting, scratching, and cursing.

But William laid back down and closed his eyes.

"What're you doing?" Zeke asked.

"Sleeping." William's exhaustion overcame his discomfort, and he found himself in a restless dream of endless marching, thirst, hunger, and untold thousands of biting insects.

ℰℬℭℛℭℬℭ℧ℬℰℬℭℛℭℬℭ℧ℬℰℬℭℛℭℬ

Saturday June 20, 1863 – Wheeling, West Virginia:

Arthur Ingram Boreman had served previously in the House of Delegates for the Commonwealth of Virginia as a circuit judge for Wood County and as the president of the Second Wheeling Convention, which voted to form the Restored Government of Virginia in defiance of the Secessionist government in Richmond. He'd now been sworn in as the first governor of the state of West Virginia on the day it officially became the thirty-fifth state of the United States of America. He walked deliberately up the steps of the Linsly School building—a beautiful newly constructed brick structure the fledgling state had leased for use as its first state capitol building—to address the large crowd gathered there.

Miss Abbey leaned over to Margaret and whispered, "I still don't understand why Francis Pierpont couldn't be the governor for West Virginia, after all he's done to create the new state…"

Margaret nodded. "The president simply couldn't allow it. The new state government must be separate from the Restored Government of Virginia in order to keep everything legal according to the U.S. Constitution. For the same reason the new state government couldn't use the Customs building for its capitol. But don't worry, Momma, Mr. Boreman is a good man too. I believe you'll like him … Let's listen to what he has to say, shall we?"

"Yes, of course … Thank you, dear," Abbey patted Margaret on the arm as the two shared a smile.

At first glance, Arthur Boreman seemed the very antithesis of the loud, gregarious, larger-than-life Francis Pierpont. Boreman was slight of build and short in stature, stern, and serious-seeming—looking more like a clerk than a governor. But after expressing his gratitude for the honor the people of the state had bestowed upon him, he launched into a rousing speech that not only expressed the grievances the western half of Virginia held against their former government in the east, but also vilified those who would take up arms against the federal government and their fellow Virginians in the west:

"...Our State has been invaded by traitors in arms against the best government that a kind and beneficent God ever inspired man to make; they have applied the torch to public and private property; they have murdered our friends; they have robbed and plundered our people; our country is laid waste, and, to-day, gaunt hunger stares many families of helpless women and children in the face. This picture is not overdrawn. It is a simple statement of facts.

"Yet, notwithstanding all this, the Union men of West Virginia have not looked to the right or the left, but through all these difficulties and dangers they have stood by the Government...

"We want no compromise: we want no peace, except upon the terms that those in rebellion will lay down their arms and submit to the regularly constituted authorities of the Government of the United States. Then, and not till then, will the people of West Virginia agree to peace.

"We have done much and suffered much already, but we will do more, and suffer on for years, if need be, rather than consent to a dissolution of the Union, which would be nothing less than a surrender of the last hope of human liberty on the face of the earth..."

When Governor Boreman concluded his speech, he was met with thunderous applause and enthusiastic cheers from the throng assembled there. When the noise finally died back down, Abbey looked at Margaret and smiled, "Yes ... you were right, dear ... I *do* like him!"

"Me too," Megs agreed. "The man has backbone; that's certain. It's exactly what the new state's needin' right now, same as Mr. Pierpont: a man who will *fight!*"

As they headed back toward the carriage where Cobb awaited them, a young clerk named Jacob from Governor Pierpont's office, stepped up to them and tipped his hat, "Miss Abbey ... Miss Megs, Miss Margaret."

"Hello, Jacob," Miss Abbey greeted him with a smile, "A momentous day, wouldn't you say?"

"Oh, yes, ma'am. A wonderful day ... truly wonderful," he agreed, smiling brightly and nodding vigorously. He then seemingly remembered his mission, "Governor Pierpont thought I might find you here ... he has asked me to give this into Miss Margaret's hands." He held out a telegram.

"And, Miss Abbey, if you would be so kind as to deliver this other one to Mr. Edouard Boudreau at Belle Meade Farm, I would be most grateful, as it would save me the long ride." The clerk handed Miss Abbey another folded sheet of paper. He then wished them a good day and withdrew that they might read in private.

Margaret shared a frightened look with the other ladies before slowly unfolding the paper and reading the contents:

Bloody Run, Pennsylvania
June 20, 1863

Margaret Chambers
Belle Meade Farm, Wheeling, W. Va.:

> *Dear Sister, 12th is now safely in Pennsylvania. Only minor skirmishing along the way. But I write with unhappy news that I did not share before for not wanting to worry you.*

> *After the Winchester battle two companies of the 12th became separated, including William, Zeke, and Phillipe. We have just learned they were captured and sent to Richmond.*

> *I am truly sorry and will do all in my power to see that they are exchanged soon. Sincerely,*

Nathaniel Chambers,

Colonel, 12th W. Va. Infantry

When Margaret finished reading, she handed the sheet across to Miss Abbey, who held it out so she and Megs could read it together. When they'd finished, the three of them shared a tearful hug. But when she stepped back, Margaret nodded and smiled through her tears, "At least they aren't dead ... I have lived in dread that William was dead since Nathan's last telegram. But now I know he yet lives and is no longer in the fighting, so all will be well."

ၷၩ၅ၷဎ၅ၷဎၷၩ၅ၷဎ၅ၷဎၷၩ၅ၷ

Wednesday June 24, 1863 – Staunton, Virginia:

By the time they reached Staunton, the captive Union officers were nearly done in. The march had been particularly hard on the cavalry officers, who were more used to riding than marching, and whose heavy riding boots were meant for stirrups, not hiking. Footsore young men limped and hobbled along like broken-down old men. Some now walked barefooted, deciding it was a better alternative to cast off the cumbersome footwear even in exchange for cracked and bleeding soles. William was, for the first time, grateful that Colonel Chambers had always insisted that his officers march alongside the enlisted men and lead their horses when not in combat.

Many of the Union officers had now fallen sick, or were beginning to succumb to infections from minor wounds or injuries from the fighting. William did what he could whenever they stopped for the night, but his resources were extremely limited.

The lack of food was the biggest issue, in his view; he could do nothing whatsoever about that. His only consolation was that their Confederate guards seemed not much better off. Clearly, from their bony limbs, sallow faces, and baggy clothes, they'd been on short rations for quite some time now, though from time to time they did benefit from the largesse of pro-rebel civilians handing out food along the march—milk, butter, cheese,

170

vegetables, chickens, and bread. But if the guards shared with the prisoners at all, it was only the scraps.

The good news was, now that they were in Staunton, they would no longer have to march. The bad news was, they would be packed into windowless, stifling-hot freight cars for the 135-mile train ride to Richmond. The officers were divided between two freight cars, but they were the lucky ones; the roughly 2,000 Union-enlisted prisoners were divided into groups of eighty soldiers for each car.

William could hardly imagine what eighty in a car was like; fifty was quite bad enough. They were packed so tightly together they could not lie down, but had to sit with their knees tucked up under their chins. To occasionally stretch their legs, they had to extend them up over the shoulders of the man in front of them.

Adding insult to injury, the freight cars had not been swept out after their last usage, and from the smell and the evidence on the floor, their car had previously been used to haul cattle. After several hours of this noisome, hot, crowded misery, one of the officers called out, "Cheer up boys, the worst is yet to come!"

He was right; a journey that might've taken a day on a modern, well-run Northern rail line like the B&O, took them three days on the Virginia Central Railroad. The route wound through the Allegheny Mountains, and cars tilted sickeningly as they rounded the corners. And because the rail line was in heavy use by the rebel army for the transportation of food, equipment, and troops, the prisoner train had to pull off on every siding and wait for numerous trains to pass going north before continuing on their southbound journey.

Worst of all, they received no food, and the only water was whatever they'd brought with them in their canteens, which they had to carefully ration. Their stomachs ached and cramped for lack of sustenance and their throats were parched and swollen.

The relief at finally arriving in Richmond and debarking the horrid train was immediately offset by the reception they received from the local population lining the streets as they marched. If anything, the citizens of Richmond were even more hateful and angry than those they'd encountered outside of Winchester.

William was convinced these civilians would've murdered the prisoners with their bare hands if the guards would've allowed it.

They finally arrived at their destination, a large three-story brick warehouse with the inauspicious sign on the side reading "Libby & Son, Ship Chandlers & Grocers."

ဢ)റ୫୯ঙ୫ঢ଼ঢ଼ড়ঢ়റ୫ঢ଼ঢ়

Sunday June 28, 1863 – Richmond, Virginia:

They had arrived at Libby Prison, a name that was already infamous in the North for its mistreatment of Union prisoners. William and Zeke exchanged a dark look. It was little consolation that Libby contained mostly officers and that the enlisted men were sent to a different place—an outdoor prison on the ironically named Belle Isle in the middle of the James River—that was said to be even worse than Libby, if possible.

A group of young boys hovered around the column of captives, laughing and taunting them with chants of, "Fresh fish! Fresh fish for the kettle, boys!" The Union soldiers, now thoroughly numbed to the continuous insults of the enemy civilians and soldiers alike, simply ignored them. The Union officers were now being marched into the open door of the building, but the line had come to a halt. Zeke assumed this meant that each prisoner was being processed inside.

Then something fluttering caught the corner of Zeke's eye, and he instinctively reached out and snatched it, thinking it was another biting insect attempting to further torment him. But when he crushed the thing in his hand, he felt it was a tiny piece of cardboard. He opened his hand and gazed at the thing, surprised to see writing on it. He read, "Hide your greenbacks!"

He looked up and saw faces in the windows above, staring down through the iron bars of the opening.

Zeke glanced over at the nearest guard to make sure he wasn't looking their way, then tapped William's arm and slipped the tiny note into his palm. He saw William glance down at the thing, then subtly nod, and pass it on to Phillipe, who did likewise, passing it on to the next man in line.

Zeke knew that both Union and Confederate soldiers referred to the highly prized United States dollars as "greenbacks." From the note, he assumed that the guards at Libby were not as ethical as Lieutenant Collins had been back at Winchester.

Zeke immediately slipped his hand up inside his shirt where he'd pinned his paper dollars, grabbed them, and stuffed them into his mouth. After the bills had become wet and pliable, he tucked them up between his upper lip and gums with his tongue.

And once inside, the truth of that concern became immediately clear; the prison inspector methodically searched each man and stripped him of everything of value: canteens, haversacks, gum blankets, pencils, combs, pocketknives, watches, and money. Private papers, pocket diaries, lists of dead and wounded, and even last written messages from the dying were taken. Only bare essential clothing was left to prevent nakedness.

When Zeke saw the inspector prying men's mouths open and carefully examining inside, he shrugged his shoulders and swallowed the precious bills he'd hidden up under his gums. He was not particularly concerned about it; he'd been raised on a farm, where dealing with piles of manure was part of everyday life. Recovering the bills later would be just more of the same, and of little bother to him. But he wondered how the others might deal with it, especially the more fastidious Frenchman, Phillipe.

When it was William's turn, there was no honoring the previous convention of respecting the tools of a surgeon's trade; he was stripped of everything, including the badge of his profession, his surgical instruments, and all his medicines. When he tried to protest, the captain of the guard unholstered his pistol, and raised it above his head threateningly, and then spoke up for all present to hear, "If anyone attempts to withhold any valuables, he'll be shot down like a dog!"

Once past the inspector, they were led down a dark hallway, then up a set of stairs to the second floor, where they entered a large, open room, reeking of sweat, vomit, and sewage. They gazed about at the gaunt, hopeless faces of the hundreds of men already in the room, all in ragged uniforms infested with lice. Most of these sat crowded together on the hard wooden floor with no bedding, cushions, nor furniture. They showed little interest in the newcomers; simply more grist for the voracious mill.

Zeke turned to William, "I heard they've stopped exchanging prisoners on account o' President Lincoln's emancipation ... so you'd best start using that big ol' brain of yours to figure us a way outta here. Else wise ... we're gonna die in this place, William."

William gazed at him wide-eyed, then looking around once again at the room full of downcast, emaciated prisoners, he turned back and nodded.

ΣΟΘΣΘΟΣΟΘΣΘΟΣΟΘΣΘ

Wednesday June 17, 1863 – Richmond, Virginia:

"I'm surprised, Evelyn, that you aren't more elated by this news." Jonathan sat across from her in the elegant sitting room at the Hugheses' manor house. "Our sources have just confirmed that Nathan Chambers and his regiment have miraculously managed to escape intact from the disaster at Winchester and are now safely north of the Potomac in Maryland, and on their way to Pennsylvania. And yet you seem ... well, *unenthused* would not be too strong a term," he frowned.

She returned his look with a thoughtful one of her own before answering. "You misunderstand me, Jonathan ... Of course I'm relieved that Nathan is safe—*for the moment*. The problem is the 'for the moment' part ... He is clearly still in harm's way, and— along with the rest of the Union Army—will be tasked with confronting Lee's army as it moves north."

She looked down and slowly shook her head. "No, Jonathan ... there is no safety for Nathan and his men as long as Lee is on the offensive, and all indications point to this being even bigger and more devastating than his Maryland Campaign last year. And despite getting rid of McClellan, the Union Army command seems as ineffectual as ever."

She set down her teacup, only half empty, and stood to her feet. "All the more reason I must push forward with my scheme, despite the risks. We simply *must* learn the details of the planned

174

offensive. And for Nathan's sake, that is now more vital than ever."

"All right, all right. Just … *please*, be careful." He rose to escort her to the front door.

ॐ

Friday June 19, 1863 – Millwood, Virginia:

C.S.A. Major Oliver Boyd had been interrupted in his duties by one of the clerks, a young lieutenant, who informed him a major from the Signal Corps wished to speak with him. As Ollie was Lee's unofficial intelligence officer, it was routine for him to meet with members of the Signal Corps to exchange vital information concerning the enemy's movements. But he was a little surprised at the newcomer's rank; typically, majors didn't make an appearance this far afield, preferring to operate nearer the capital. But he shrugged, and told the clerk to bring the major in.

After months in the field, having become accustomed to the grit and grime of an army in an active combat zone, Ollie was startled at the man's appearance: gray parade uniform, spotless and impeccably ironed and pleated. The major's elegant officer's hat showed none of the usual stains, spots, and creases. Ollie thought it unlikely that General Lee could come up with such a fine uniform out here in the field. Even the flashy cavalry general Jeb Stuart, as fashion-conscious as he was, would have a hard time pulling it off.

Ollie stood, exchanged the obligatory salute, then shook hands with the man, who introduced himself as Major Charles White. The man was older, in his mid-forties, with thick glasses which helped add to an odd, unreadable expression; his smile seemed more reflexive than sincere. Ollie gestured to the camp chair opposite his desk, "Major … please, be seated. How can I assist you, sir?"

"I am making certain inquiries, Major Boyd, on behalf of the government. To be more specific, I am tasked with certain counterespionage activities—intended to root out and

175

exterminate Union spies operating within the Confederacy." Major White spoke in a quiet even tone. When he'd completed the statement, he gazed at Ollie intently, as if gauging his reaction.

But Ollie just shrugged. "Seems a reasonable assignment for a Signal Corps officer, Major. And don't get me wrong, I certainly appreciate the importance of the service y'all are performing; but with a major campaign underway … well, to be blunt, counterespionage is fairly low in my priorities. I am more focused on ascertaining the numbers and movements of the Union Army. So again, I must ask, how it is I may assist you, sir?"

Major White did not seem put off by Ollie's attempted dismissal, smiling thinly before continuing. "I am investigating rumors of a particular spy ring operating within Richmond itself. Would you have any information about this matter, Major?" White once again stared at Ollie in the same odd manner as before.

Ollie was surprised by this question, and suddenly had a tingling feeling that this meeting was not of the usual routine nature. Major White's unexpected inquiry, and his odd, intense gaze gave Ollie the same feeling of impending danger he always got just before the start of a battle. *Odd*, he thought, *considering we're supposed to be on the same side here.*

Ollie just shrugged, "As I said before, Major, I have little time to delve into counterespionage activities. So, *no*, I know nothing of any spy activities in Richmond. In fact, I have only been in Richmond a few short weeks these past two years, being out in the field with the army the remainder of that time."

The major nodded slowly, but his expression did not betray his thoughts. And if the previous question had surprised Ollie, the next one fairly shocked him.

"Do you know a woman named Evelyn Hanson, Major Boyd?"

Given the topic of conversation, Ollie was certain his jaw must have dropped open before he caught himself, straightened up, and answered, "Of course I know her. She's my wife's best friend. I've known her for years. She was maid of honor at our wedding. But I'm guessing you already knew all that. What's this all about, Major? Why are you asking me about Miss Evelyn?"

But rather than answer, Major White immediately asked another question, "When was the last time you saw Miss Evelyn Hanson, Major Boyd?"

"Well, I..." Ollie started to answer, then a shocking, startling thought flashed through his mind: he'd seen Evelyn, inexplicably, in Frederick, Maryland during the Antietam Campaign. *What was she doing there? And why did she suddenly turn away from me?* he wondered for the dozenth time, though he'd not thought about the incident in many months.

He'd meant to ask her about it, but hadn't been back to Richmond since, and had nearly forgotten about the whole thing. But Major White was now asking about Evelyn in connection with a Union spy ring ... *Is it possible?* Ollie wondered.

Then he shook his head, and pulled himself from his reverie, realizing Major White was gazing at him expectantly, waiting for an answer.

"I was just trying to remember ... whether or not I'd seen her the last time I was in Richmond. I ... I was visiting various people with my wife, Belinda. I think it likely we saw Miss Evelyn then. That would've been ... hmm ... June of last year, I believe. Why do you ask, Major? What does Miss Evelyn have to do with any of this?"

On the spur of the moment, not knowing the truth of the matter, Ollie had decided to give Evelyn the benefit of the doubt, for the sake of their long friendship. He feared that mentioning seeing her in Frederick might get her into some kind of trouble, for reasons he couldn't quite fathom.

But rather than answer his questions, Major White simply stood and saluted, "Good day to you, Major." Then he turned and strode from the tent.

An hour later, with no explanation, Ollie received written orders from General Lee via a courier that he was to accompany Major White to Richmond and, once there, was to report directly to the War Department. Further, Ollie was not to speak with any other officers or other persons of any kind prior to his departure, and he was to leave all his paperwork behind, including any and all personal correspondence.

Friday June 19, 1863 – Richmond, Virginia:

Mary scowled bitterly, folding her arms across her chest. But despite the rising heat and frustration she was feeling, she noticed that for first time since they'd met and started working together as domestic "slaves" at the Confederate White House, the stern, commanding head butler, Hank, did not snap back at her and seemed less certain of himself. It gave her the spark of confidence she needed to continue her argument.

"Look, Hank … I understand you had an … *arrangement* … with Miss Eve. But time has marched on since then … and unfortunately, so has General Lee. Now it's time to choose which side you're on: Will you stand with the slavers, or will you stand with the men who're fighting—and dying—to free our people … and to free you?" Though Mary was still feeling heated, based on Hank's reaction, she knew she'd hit the nerve she'd been aiming for.

He slowly shook his head, but said nothing, finally breaking eye contact, and gazing at the floor. He'd agreed to meet with her in the basement where they could talk with no fear of being overheard. Now Mary was wondering if Hank was regretting that decision. But then she saw a look of distress forming on his usually strong, unflappable visage, and her heart softened.

"Look, Hank … I understand that you take pride in your work, and rightly so; I doubt there's a better butler in all of Richmond. But … *please, look at me, Hank…*"

He looked up, and again met eyes with her, the anguish in his expression now plain to see.

"Hank … think how much better you'll feel, when you can take pride in your labors as a *free* man, working where you choose, for whom you choose, and making your own money—with no regrets, no conflicted feelings … especially knowing you did your part to help free us all."

He gazed up at the dark, cobweb-covered beams of the basement with eyes faraway and unseeing that were slowly welling with tears. Finally, he looked back down at her. They met eyes for a long moment, unspeaking, his expression now unreadable. Mary feared he would just turn and walk away without giving her an answer. But then he nodded, "Yes … you're right, Mary … You're right; it's time. What is it you need me to do?"

Mary's preparation for the current operation was almost identical to that which Evelyn had gone through, now more than a year and a half ago. On one of Mary's regularly scheduled "re-training" sessions, Evelyn had snuck her into the Hugheses' manor house, where they'd previously recreated Jefferson Davis's office in a spare room, complete with an identical copy of his desk.

This time, Evelyn conducted the training, lacing the mockup office with official-looking but phony government documents, interspersed with innocuous personal letters and writings. Evelyn had the advantage of once having been in the president's office, so she could arrange things more in keeping with reality.

And as Evelyn had done before with Jonathan, Mary went into the fake office to search through the desk and around the room to find the information they sought, and memorize as many of the details as possible within a specific time limit—seven minutes, the same as on Evelyn's first visit. Now she was looking for anything that might hint at what General Lee had planned for his next offensive.

Mary felt exhausted but pleased when they'd completed the exercise, especially when Evelyn praised her efforts. "I'm impressed, Mary. I thought I'd done well before, but you are much better at this than I am. Your searches were thorough, logical, and quick. And your ability to separate the 'wheat from the chaff,' as they say, is really quite remarkable, not to mention your ability to memorize important details. I'm feeling very confident that this will go well!"

That had been a week ago, and now that the time had come to actually carry out the plan, Mary was feeling much less confident and much more anxious. She'd never felt fear before during her long placement in the Davis home, despite technically being a spy. She realized now that she'd never been asked to do anything dangerous or risky before. Evelyn had only asked her to keep her eyes and ears open to anything of importance that might be said in her presence, between the president and his wife or anyone else in the house. And if the occasion presented itself, to read a letter or document that might be left out in plain sight.

Never before had she been asked to rifle a desk, or to look for some specific information; and now that it came down to it, she realized she was more frightened than she'd ever been before in life. It had been something of a game before, pretending to be an illiterate but highly skilled house slave—when she was in fact a college educated freeman.

But now, it was no longer a game. She had no legitimate reason to be in the president's office when he was gone; this time she would be spying for real, and if they caught her, they would kill her. No prison, no trial, just a swift, painful death and a secret burial, she realized. They'd never risk the devastating scandal of handling it otherwise. She shuddered at the thought but was determined not to back down from her task, no matter how frightful it had become.

They'd waited until President Davis was out of town on some sort of army business, and Varina Davis was out at a social function to run the operation.

Mary calmed herself by focusing on the details of the task at hand, and by reminding herself that she had a huge advantage over what Evelyn had had when she'd attempted the same thing: rather than being *caught* by Hank, she would be *guarded* by him. And that was crucial; as head butler, Hank was in charge of all the household staff, and could order them about as he pleased. He'd already arranged to have everyone busy at other tasks while they conducted their particular clandestine business.

She stood with Hank in the hallway leading to the president's office, and the two met eyes. To her surprise, the normally stoic butler smiled at her reassuringly and nodded, indicating it was time. She returned the nod, and the smile, then turned and walked to the door of the president's office and entered.

As she'd practiced, she first went directly to the president's desk and started by searching the two hidden compartments. The first was entirely empty. She remembered Evelyn reporting the same thing, so she closed it and moved on.

But the second compartment contained a stack of a dozen or more letters. She quickly scanned through them and noticed a pattern: these were letters from various Confederate generals to the president, appealing to him on several matters—asking for additional troops or equipment, complaining about the performance of a subordinate officer or even a superior one. Mary thought about this a moment and realized these letters had been hidden because they had circumvented the normal chain of command, a thing the president apparently encouraged. Likely, given his previous experience as United States Secretary of War, he saw himself as more knowledgeable and expert at military matters than his generals or the Confederate Secretary of War, Seddon. She shook her head at the man's apparent arrogance, and was about to put the letters back when she noticed the signature at the bottom of the last one. Her breath caught when she realized its significance. So she laid it out on the desk and read through it carefully:

> *Fredericksburg, Va.*
> *May 15, 1863*
>
> *His excellency, President Davis:*
>
> *Dear sir,*
> *I wish to address Secretary Seddon's recent request to transfer units of my army, specifically two brigades of Gen. Pickett's division, to the west in support of Gen. Bragg, by arguing that the best method of relieving pressure on our troops out west, and in other theaters, is a large-scale campaign into Maryland and Pennsylvania.*
>
> *Such a campaign will serve not only to relieve the northern Virginia area of the devastating presence of two major armies, but will serve to draw Union forces away*

from other regions in order to support the Army of the Potomac, which will be forced to pursue us into the North.

I am in the process of drawing up detailed plans to circumvent Hooker's army by passing through the Shenandoah Valley, relieving said area from the noisome thrall of Union occupation in the process, by re-taking Winchester on the march northward.

My hope is to draw the Union Army into battle at a place of our choosing somewhere in Pennsylvania, likely either Chambersburg, York, or Gettysburg.

The alternative is unacceptable; the North has the superiority in numbers, resources, and means of carrying on the war. Staying still, we grow weaker by the day, as livestock and other foodstuffs are sorely depleted, and recruitments are no longer keeping up with desertions.

To stay in Virginia is to be inexorably forced back toward Richmond by the slow but certain buildup of enemy forces, until our situation devolves into a state of siege, confined to our own capital city. A siege from which there can be no relief, and in which I fear the inevitable outcome will not be in our favor.

For these reasons, I beseech you to keep my current forces intact, and if anything, further strengthen them as much as resources and circumstances allow.

Your obedient servant,

R.E. Lee
Commanding General
Army of Northern Virginia

Her heart beat faster when she realized this was likely exactly what Evelyn had been looking for: specific evidence that General Lee planned an attack against the North, the probable route, and the most likely targets.

She read it through again, this time committing each paragraph to memory—not word for word, that was too difficult, time-consuming, and ultimately unnecessary. She concentrated on memorizing the important gist of each statement, rather than the exact wording. In this case, it would be enough.

She had finished going through it for the third time and now closed her eyes and repeated the whole thing to herself, confident she'd gotten it down, when she heard a noise out in the hall. Voices. Hank's voice and another man's.

Then a chill of fear ran down her spine when she heard Hank say, "Welcome home, Mr. President. We were not expecting you today, sir…"

ಬಿಂಕಾಟಿಯ ಬಿಂಕಾಟಿಯ ಬಿಂಕಾಟ

Mary thought she was dead. But she hadn't considered the full impact of having Hank's active involvement in their scheme. He was not just the man in charge of all the household servants, he also knew the master and mistress probably better than anyone else.

So, when the president had returned home unexpectedly, Hank hadn't panicked. Knowing the president's usual habit of skipping meals, and generally taking poor care for his health while traveling, it was a simple matter for him to deflect the president away from his office, straight toward the kitchen for a much-needed meal. Mary returned the letters to the secret compartment, then rushed to the door and listened as the two men's voices faded back down the hallway. She slipped out of the door, and taking the back servants' passage, hurried along to the kitchen, arriving just before Hank and the president.

She curtsied to President Davis and shared a quick look with Hank—who seemed amused, to her annoyance—"Mr. President, welcome home, sir. I heard you'd arrived and thought it likely you'd be half-starved, sir, so have come to see to your supper."

"Yes, yes … Thank you, Mary. Hank was saying that very thing only a moment ago. And I'd not be foolish enough to argue with either one of you in that regard," he chuckled, removing his hat and coat, then handing them over to Hank. He took a seat at

183

the informal kitchen table, as the kitchen staff scrambled to prepare him a meal at Mary's direction.

Evelyn's own role in Mary's operation was a simple but important one: she was to attend the same function as Varina, and make sure the first lady didn't leave early for any reason.

Or if she did, to provide warning via a pre-arranged courier, Tad, a twelve-year-old freeman boy, whom Evelyn had employed to run errands for her. He was quick and industrious, knowing all the shortcuts and back alleys in Richmond. He'd be able to get to Varina's house and warn Hank well before Varina could arrive in a carriage. And nobody would pay any attention to his comings and goings. And even if they did, he always had a pre-arranged alibi.

But Tad's services had proved unnecessary; Varina seemed to be enjoying herself at the event, and did not seem inclined to leave early. So Evelyn decided to indulge her other goal for the evening, this one more out of curiosity than any specific purpose: she wished to formally meet the double-agent Alice Spencer and gauge for herself the woman's character, demeanor, and potential capabilities, without exposing any of her own.

Evelyn approached Alice when the latter was standing alone, sipping a glass of brandy. Evelyn held a glass of her own, the same she'd held all evening but had never taken a sip of.

"Good evening … *Alice*, isn't it?" Evelyn asked, smiling brightly.

"Yes, that's right … I don't believe we've met before, Miss…"

"Evelyn. Evelyn Hanson. And no, I don't believe we've ever formally made acquaintance, though I believe we may have spoken a few words on a few other occasions.

"But seeing you from across the room just now, I thought simple good manners required that we rectify that unfortunate circumstance; wouldn't you agree? Besides which, seeing that you look absolutely lovely, and that we are of a similar age, I trust that we shall become the very closest of friends once we've become better acquainted." Evelyn graced Alice with her warmest smile.

184

Alice returned a smile. "How sweet of you to say, Evelyn. But surely you are the most beautiful woman here?" she asked.

Evelyn resisted the urge to wince at that particular question, it being the very verbiage used by Major White in his ongoing investigation of her. Instead, she smiled and answered, "Oh, certainly *not!* But very kind of you to say, my dear. Shall we take a seat and become best friends, even as I have predicted?" Then Evelyn again flashed her most winning smile and gestured toward an elegant padded bench off to the side of the room, far enough from the quartet of musicians to afford enough quiet to talk.

After they'd indulged in the usual small talk, Evelyn launched into the conversation she'd pre-selected for this specific meeting with Alice; given the young lady's reputation as something of a troubled youth before the war, she thought it might pique her interest.

Evelyn gazed about the room, then looked back at Alice, "Seems odd that we are surrounded by such splendor, luxury, and excess while the rest of the city, the entire country even, goes without? Many now walk the streets in ragged clothes, or without shoes. I've heard that many are forced to make do with the simplest of fares, or even none at all. It's like we live in a whole other world from the common people…"

Alice nodded, "Yes … it is odd … ironic, even. I'm just happy to be on this side of it, aren't you? Imagine, living in some hovel … cold and hungry." She shuddered, as if repulsed by the thought.

"Oh, yes, certainly," Evelyn agreed, "but we mustn't feel guilty about it; after all, even if we gave away all that we see in this room, and went hungry for the evening, it would scarcely make a dent in the general lack that surrounds us."

"True," Alice concurred, "and I read in the *Examiner* that we must continue living the traditional, genteel, Southern life, even in the face of general want, lest the morale of the republic suffer."

"That makes complete sense to me." Evelyn had adopted a thoughtful expression. However, in contrast to the role she was playing for Alice's sake, Evelyn *did* feel badly about all the suffering in the city. But she also knew the war was ultimately the cause of all the suffering, not these ridiculous, opulent events, as wasteful and excessive as they might be.

But she raised her glass and smiled, "Here's to doing our part for morale." Then she finally took a sip of the brandy, deciding it was quite good after all.

Alice giggled. "To keeping up morale." She took a sip of her own.

By the end of the evening, Evelyn and Alice were chatting like lifelong friends, and parted promising to stay in touch. Evelyn felt certain that Alice had accepted her proffered friendship at face value, likely welcoming it, as she seemed to have a general dearth in that regard. But Evelyn came away from the meeting feeling certain that Alice would *never* be her best friend, and that she was everything Joseph, Jonathan, and Angeline had said she was … including a Confederate double-agent.

When Evelyn finally bade her carriage driver goodnight and entered her darkened house, she was feeling fairly done in. All the freemen had gone to bed, per her orders. She would not have them waiting up for her for no good reason.

And as anxious as she was to learn the results of Mary's mission, she knew she would have to wait until morning. She had already arranged for Tad to help deliver groceries from Varina's grocer to the Confederate White House, which would allow Mary to send a message. By noon, she would know one way or the other. Until then, a good night's sleep suddenly appealed greatly.

She picked up a small oil lamp and moved down the hallway toward her bedroom, moving quietly so as not to disturb the other sleepers in the house. As she moved along in the dark, she heard a noise, and a movement to her side in the large, common room. She looked and saw the outline of a bulky man standing there in the shadows—definitely *not* one of her people. He took a step toward her. She gasped, and instinctively pulled the small pistol from its hiding place up her sleeve, pointing it at his face.

He stopped and held up his hands, saying, "Don't shoot, Evelyn!"

The voice sounded familiar, but she couldn't immediately place it. She held up the lamp to illuminate the man's face.

"*Ollie!* What in the world are *you* doing here?" Evelyn immediately lowered the pistol. And not only was his presence unexpected, but so was his appearance. The last time she'd seen him he was sitting on a horse, riding in a parade next to General Lee, looking handsome and proud in a neat, gray major's uniform.

The man who stood before her now had an entirely different appearance: dressed in rumpled and dirty civilian clothes, his hair was disheveled, and he looked like he might be unwell. She thought he had a frightened look about him.

And then, oddest of all, rather than offering some explanation for his sudden, unexpected appearance and raiment, he scowled darkly, "Evelyn ... what in *hell* is going on?"

໖ͻ໖ͻ͵໖ͻ໖ͻ͵໖ͻ໖ͻ

A half hour later, once the entire household had calmed back down from the unexpected late-night commotion—which had triggered a fully-armed response from Evelyn's major-domo, Jacob—Evelyn and Ollie sat together in the common room, sipping hot tea in the light of a larger, brighter oil lamp.

"How did you get in here, Ollie?" She was baffled as to how he'd managed it without alerting the normally reliable Jacob.

"I ... I've been hesitant to come see you, for fear of ... being followed. So I decided to come at night, and see if I could sneak in an open window. Which I did—the one in this room." He pointed to the window, which was now closed with the curtains drawn.

"Ollie ... *who* are you concerned is following you, and more importantly, *why*? And why are you in Richmond, and in civilian clothes, rather than out in the field with the Army?"

But he answered her question with a question, "Do you know a man named Major Charles White, with the Signal Corps?"

"Major White? Yes ... yes, I have met him ... Why do you ask?"

Ollie was quiet for a long moment, gazing intently into her eyes. Then he slowly nodded, "I can hardly believe it, Evelyn ... but it's true, isn't it? The things Major White implies about you ... they're true, aren't they?"

187

The entire event had been so unexpected, Evelyn was entirely at a loss as to what to say. Ollie was her friend, and obviously in pain, and in trouble. And he was clearly appealing to her for help. Could she just lie to him and deny everything? Treat him like just another of her rebel "targets"?

But before she could think of an answer, he surprised her again, "I saw you, you know … at Frederick, up in Maryland. At first, I disbelieved my eyes. But when I thought on it later, I *knew* it was you. You … aren't exactly *common*, you know. A man does not simply forget your face, nor mistake it for another—and I've seen that face a lot, over the course of many years. So, then I wondered why you were there. And if you were there for some *legitimate* reason, why didn't you call out to me, or greet me when we met eyes? Instead, you ran away."

She slowly nodded. "And … *if* it's true … what will you do, Ollie? Will you turn me in to Major White?"

He gazed at her for a long moment, and then tears filled his eyes, "I could never … I could never do that to you, Evelyn … never … *never!*" He slowly shook his head. "I have refused to tell him anything—not that I know much. But they now think I'm in league with you, that I'm a traitor. I … I don't know what to do…" Then he buried his head in his hands with a groan.

Evelyn felt a tight knot of guilt that she could no longer ignore, "I'm so sorry, Ollie … I never meant for you to get caught up in any of this … I never meant for you to see me in Frederick. This is all my fault. You must just turn me in and save yourself."

"It's too late for that now, Evelyn. Major White grilled me with questions the entire ride home, making it clear he believed I was a traitor and a spy, in league with you. He also said I should confess during the ride, because otherwise … his methods would be 'less gentle' once we reached Richmond. Those were his words … and judging by the man's demeanor, I can imagine I wouldn't have liked to learn the true meaning of them.

"So, when we arrived in Richmond, and were close pressed by a crowd on the streets, I leapt from my horse and ducked into a narrow alley. We were down in the warehouse district near the waterfront, and after a desperate scramble, I managed to find an open door and slipped inside. Fortunately, it was nearly dark and the place was deserted for the day. So I hid in the old warehouse for several hours. Then I searched around and found a pile of dirty laundry in a back room, and donned the clothing you see me now wearing. I stuffed my uniform behind a loose wall board, then headed back outside, keeping a sharp lookout for searchers. I was nearly caught by a group of soldiers, but managed to lose them in the dark.

"I thought about going home—I dearly wished to see Belinda and tell her what had happened—but I dared not, fearing the house would be watched.

"Then I thought of you ... and that I needed to find out the truth. And though your house might also be watched, I thought I might slip in unseen after dark. So ... here I am."

Evelyn returned to her seat, slowly shaking her head. "You must hate me ... a traitor and a spy..."

But he looked up and met eyes with her, a more determined look now on his face. "No, Evelyn. No! What I *hate* is this damned war ... the secession ... the slavery ... the horrible suffering ... the blood. All of it! I've done my best to be a good soldier ... but I have hated it all from the beginning and wish it had never happened.

"So you chose to help the *other* side ... the *correct* side, I'm now thinking ... It shows you had the moral courage I've lacked, just going along with something I didn't agree with. Going along so people would like me ... so my father would finally be proud of me ... None of it for the right reasons. None of it because I believed in what we were doing, in why we were fighting."

"What will you do now, Ollie?"

He gazed at her a long time without answering. Then answered in a pleading tone, "I don't know, Evelyn. I was hoping *you* could tell me."

ಶಿ)ಲ್ಡಿಲ್ಡಿ೫೨)ಶಿ)ಲ್ಡಿಲ್ಡಿ೫೨)ಶಿ)ಲ್ಡಿಲ್ಡಿ

Evelyn had decided the best thing she could do for Ollie that night was to give him a hot meal and a safe, hidden place to sleep.

189

She figured he'd be in better condition to discuss next steps come the morning.

Fortunately, her house was ideal for both purposes, being, among other things, a former way station on the Underground Railroad. The cook, who'd been awakened by the commotion, prepared Ollie a hot meal from what had been left over from dinner. Then he was escorted to one of the secret back rooms that had been used to hide escaping slaves, where he could get a much-needed night's sleep.

In the morning, just after first light, Evelyn brought Ollie his breakfast with a steaming cup of coffee and the two broke the fast together on a little table in the hidden room.

"Feeling better?" she asked after he'd pushed back his plate.

"Yes, much. Thank you ever so kindly, Evelyn," he answered, giving her a wan smile.

"Yes, I know ... much better *considering*..." she held a thoughtful frown. "Let's talk about what comes now, Ollie, shall we?"

"Yes, please, Evelyn."

"Ollie ... I am sorry to have to do this, as you are already in such obvious distress, but I am compelled to ask ... after what you've just been through, and from the things you told me last night about your *true* feelings, are you prepared to now aid our side? And before you answer, let me assure you I will help you out of this predicament as best as I can either way. After all, I have gotten you into this mess, and I mean to get you out again."

He gazed into her eyes for a long moment, slowly nodding. "You know ... I had thought about deserting and joining the other side on several occasions, believing we were fighting for the wrong cause, and destroying untold lives in the process. But three things always stopped me. The fear of how it would affect Belinda was foremost, of course ... and then there was my father. He'd have been devastated.

"But the third thing, and maybe more impactful on a day-to-day basis, was General Lee. I greatly admired him, and he treated me with respect ... like he believed in me, and what I was capable of doing. He treated me better than my own father ever had ... or any other man, for that matter. The thought of betraying him was … *unthinkable*. But now…"

He shook his head and gazed down at the floor. Once again, she could see his eyes watering up. "He … he just sent me away on Major White's word, without even a goodbye. Didn't stand up for me, didn't defend me … nothing. Just a written order to leave his command and—presumably—never come back."

He looked up at Evelyn again, "Seems to me *that* decision has now been made for me, Evelyn. They're convinced I am in league with you, and have joined the other side. So, I may as well do what I am already accused of, and what my conscience tells me to do. It's too late to worry about what Belinda or my parents will think; seems like there's nothing I can do about that now."

Evelyn shook her head slowly and didn't immediately answer. "Ollie … I'm mulling over the beginnings an idea … that maybe we can clear your name and put you back in good standing with the Confederate Army, if you wish, while aiding our side in the process."

"What? How could you do that, Evelyn?"

"I'm not sure yet … let me work on that awhile. In the meantime, we will have to hide you—but not here; that'd be too obvious—and somehow let Belinda know what's going on. Unfortunately, I can't just go visit her as I'd like; it'd look too suspicious given what's just happened to you. I'll have to come up with some other way. Somehow, we need to get her away to her parents' house. They're important enough citizens that the major will have to leave her alone once she's there."

"I would be much obliged if you can help her, Evelyn," Ollie answered.

"Oh, never mind that, Ollie. I just shudder to think how Belinda will hate me when she finds out about all this."

"Belinda won't hate you either, Evelyn. Likely, she'll be confused and hurt that you didn't confide in her, but she won't be completely surprised. She has mentioned on several occasions your ambivalence toward the secession and the war. And you've not been especially good at hiding from her your continuing strong feelings for Captain Chambers, who fights for the Union. Oh ... *Colonel* Chambers now, I understand."

Evelyn slowly nodded, then smiled slightly, thinking first of Nathan, and then of her lifelong friend, Belinda. Evelyn was a little surprised at how much it meant to her that in the midst of all this madness, that her best friend might finally know the truth—and might not hate her for it, after all.

"Now, Ollie ... if you're sure you're ready to help me ... help to save the Union ... I wish to know everything you can tell me about General Lee's offensive."

But even as Ollie opened his mouth to respond, there came a soft knock at the secret door, which had a latch on this side, but appeared as only a section of wall from the opposite side. Evelyn stood and stepped to the door, opening it a crack. The freeman maid Bess on the other side whispered, "Miss Evelyn ... sorry to disturb you, ma'am ... but there's an officer at the door, and he insists on speaking with you. He gives his name as Major White..."

₧₧₧₧₧₧

Saturday June 20, 1863 – Bloody Run, Pennsylvania:

The day after the Hodgepodge Brigade arrived in Bloody Run and set up camp, Nathan sat in his tent reviewing and signing requisitions for ammunition and equipment, when he heard a commotion outside.

Tony stuck his head in through the tent flap, "Uh, sir ... I think you're gonna want to come see this..."

"Oh, all right, I'm coming," Nathan stood up and grabbed his hat. He was so happy for an excuse to set aside the paperwork that it never crossed his mind to ask Tony what it was all about. Harry raised his head from where he'd been napping under the table, saw Nathan heading for the door, and jumped up to follow.

When he stepped out of the tent, followed closely by the dog, he was surprised to see several hundred of his soldiers lined up on both sides of the road, standing to attention as if for inspection, and more pouring in to join them by the moment. And there arose

192

a spontaneous cheer, mixed with raucous laughter and loud chatter.

As Nathan strode closer, the mystery solved itself: a tall, fierce-looking general, with a great shock of gray hair, was riding his horse down the middle of the road, bowing and doffing his hat to the soldiers, acknowledging their shouts and cheers with smiles and shouted responses.

Nathan pushed through the line and stepped out into the middle of the road in the path of the rider. There he stood to attention and snapped a salute. Harry sat down in the road next to him. The rider stopped his horse, replaced his hat, sat up straight, and returned the salute smartly. And though the general had a smile on his face, Nathan thought he looked haggard and … sad, somehow.

Nathan stepped up smiling, and shook hands with the rider, "General Milroy! What a pleasure to see you again, sir!"

"Colonel Chambers! Good to see you as well, my good sir," Milroy beamed.

"I'd heard you'd made good your escape to Harpers Ferry, General, but that you'd been sent on to Baltimore to meet with General Schenck. We'd not been told when to expect your return."

"I wasn't sure myself, Chambers, but as you can see, I'm back. And I must give credit where it's due: Ohio's Colonel Keifer once again proved his intrepidity. When it looked as if the rebels would cut us off and capture me, my staff, and all the companies with us, Colonel Keifer bluffed the enemy with an aggressive charge, though he was entirely out of ammunition. Happily, his ruse worked, and they gave way before us. Likely they believed his force was made up of fresh Union reinforcements arriving from the North."

"Good to hear it, sir. Colonel Keifer is one of the finest officers I've ever had the honor of working with, so it doesn't surprise me in the least.

"And I am pleased and honored to say, that the brigade—such as it is—is yours to command, sir," Nathan held the general's horse while he dismounted.

"Thank you, Chambers. And I would be remiss if I didn't congratulate you on your own escape from Winchester, bringing a good portion of my division with you. Clearly Colonel Keifer was not the only excellent officer within my command." Milroy patted Nathan on the shoulder. They retired to Nathan's tent, where the two men spent the next several hours discussing the state of the Hodgepodge Brigade, Milroy's precarious situation with his superiors, and the war in general.

෨ඟ෬ඟෳ෨ඟ෬ඟෳ෨ඟ෬ඟ

But Milroy's resumption of his command was short-lived, as he was recalled to Washington several days later, and reports were that he'd been placed under arrest by General in Chief Halleck and Secretary of War Stanton for alleged dereliction of duty resulting in the downfall of Winchester.

Nathan and Tom discussed this disconcerting news in the command tent of the brigade, which had reverted once again to Nathan's command, pending a permanent replacement for General Milroy.

Tom shook his head in disgust, saying, "I can't believe they're blaming him for the whole affair; what about the Army of the Potomac, who allowed Ewell to march his entire corps nearly a hundred miles to attack us, right from under their very noses, giving us no warning?"

"Agreed," Nathan scowled. "And further, one might argue that Winchester was the linchpin to the entire Shenandoah Valley for the Union; why not reinforce it better? Place two or three more divisions there, which would've not only defended it, but given the Union another point from which to attack northeastern Virginia, even as General Rosecrans had proposed doing two years ago?"

Tom nodded, "And … didn't you tell me the last orders General Milroy received from General Schenck before the rebels cut the telegraph lines was to hold the fort? I don't see how they can now blame him for the loss when he was just following his orders, and had been given no warning and insufficient forces. Seems like they're just bowing to pressure from a disappointed public and looking for a scapegoat. Maybe Milroy could've done this or that better, or more timely … but being arrested for negligence? It's unconscionable."

Nathan chewed on a cigar, a frown knit across his face. "Easy for men to second guess the general in hindsight after the battle is lost. But they weren't there, forced to make the hard, life-or-death choices in the heat of the moment, without the advantage of knowing the final outcome."

Chapter 8. The Hunt for Lee

"So far as I was enabled to judge ...
Lee meant to cross the upper Potomac,
or to throw his army between
mine and Washington."
- **Union Major General Joseph Hooker**

Friday June 26, 1863 – Richmond, Virginia:

Evelyn didn't know whether to laugh or cry. Her efforts to obtain specific information about the present location of Lee's army and his battle plans, then pass that critical intel along to the Union Army, which seemed to be bearing such abundant fruit at first, had in the end amounted to nothing. She snorted a quiet, mirthless chuckle as she sipped a cup of tea in her sitting room. *Almost Shakespearian*, she decided. *Either* Much Ado About Nothing, *or else maybe* A Comedy of Errors!

First, just as she'd received the unexpected "gift" of Ollie Boyd's arrival and agreement to tell everything he knew of Lee's plans, and even as she awaited word from Mary about her efforts to search Jefferson Davis's desk—due any moment from her covert courier Tad—Major White showed up at her door and insisted on speaking with her.

He proceeded to grill her for hours, asking for details on all her comings and goings, making her account for her several odd, long absences from Richmond, her relationship with Ollie and Belinda, when they'd last seen each other, whether she knew his present whereabouts, and various questions about other individuals in Richmond high society, some of whom she barely knew. It was frustrating, maddening, and exhausting, but there was nothing she could do about it. He simply refused to leave until all his questions were answered.

When the major finally departed in the late afternoon, one of the freemen maids, Pegg, reported that Tad had arrived mid-morning, wanting to speak with Evelyn, but had left after waiting more than an hour, promising to return the next morning.

And with much of the day now wasted, it had become critical to make arrangements to move Ollie to a safer place; Major White could return at any moment with a troop of soldiers to tear the place apart. Evelyn was under no misconception that her secret rooms would remain secret for very long under such scrutiny; especially with Major White supervising. And, of course, she now had to fear that her house was being watched.

She'd managed to get Ollie out of the house by pure subterfuge and distraction; she'd had Jacob arrange for a series of workers to come and go all day long, delivering goods, making various repairs, doing gardening, etc. and at one point Ollie simply walked out in the midst of a group of workers with directions to make his way to Elizabeth Van Lew's house, where he would be kept until Evelyn could figure out a solution to his problem.

When Tad had arrived the following morning, he'd delivered a neatly folded slip of paper from Mary, summarizing Lee's letter to Davis. It had seemed like another "Holy Grail" moment, but she now needed to meet with Ollie to verify its contents. This required another intricate deception on her part, this time involving inviting ladies to tea at her house, then walking out in their company, with her hair pinned up and a hat pulled down low to disguise herself.

She met with Ollie at Elizabeth's house, which also had a secret room in the attic, and he confirmed the information in the letter was valid and still applicable. He also added more detail, and updated information on Lee's plans.

She arrived back home feeling buoyed up, already pondering how to get her latest intel to the Hughes, when she had a sudden, sinking thought; the enemy now suspected Ollie, and knew that he had escaped their clutches. The Confederates were now aware that anything Ollie knew of Lee's plans could potentially be in Union hands shortly. So … now Lee would likely change them. Ironically, what seemed like a godsend, Ollie's defection, had turned out to be the opposite, as it negated the information they had just gained by reading Lee's letter to Davis.

But she'd gone ahead and arranged to meet up with Angeline to pass along what she had learned, in case it might in some way still benefit the Union commanders. But Angeline put the final nail in the coffin of the failed operation, informing Evelyn that the Union Army had, ironically, so effectively closed the river crossings against rebel scouts and spies that Jonathan's men were being prevented from reaching Washington in the usual manner. So there was, at present, no way to get the information to the Union War Department, or even to the Union commanding General Hooker, without great risk of being shot trying to cross the Rappahannock or the Rapidan.

The only small consolation she had was that Ollie's absence from his role as intelligence officer would leave a gap, and that could ultimately hurt Lee, at least to some degree. Ollie confirmed that Lee was distrusting of other officers in that regard, and it had taken a long time to win him over and gain his trust. Likely with the suspicion now surrounding Ollie, Lee would be even more reticent than before to trust one of his officers with vital intelligence.

It was *something* ... but little enough solace when she thought of the terrible danger now inexorably approaching Nathan and his men. And now there was *truly* nothing she could do about it.

ഇറ്റൈ

Friday June 26, 1863 – Bloody Run, Pennsylvania:

"Hullo, Colonel," Georgie saluted Nathan, who sat at a folding table in his command tent. "You wanted to see me, sir?"

Nathan returned the salute and stood, handing Georgie a folded sheet of paper containing a telegram. "Georgie. Just received this from Miss Abbey ... it's addressed to you, but I must confess to having read it already."

"Oh, that's okay, sir. God knows I got no secrets from *you*, sir, after all the things we been through," he grinned. "What's it about, anyways?" But then he noticed the serious look on his commander's face, and his grin faded.

"Best you just read it, Georgie," Nathan frowned.

198

Georgie unfolded it and quickly read it through. "Oh! Sounds bad all right. My momma ain't one to get all worked up in a panic just 'cause a fella's got a cough or a snuffle. Reckon my dad must be in pretty bad shape. Dyin' more'n likely," he frowned, refolding the paper and putting it in his pocket.

"Sorry, Georgie. I've already written up your furlough papers so you can go visit him before ... well, before things get any worse, I suppose..."

"Thank you, sir; much obliged," Georgie held out his hand, which Nathan accepted and shook firmly.

"Please ... before you go ... have a seat, Georgie. I'd like to discuss your route," Nathan returned to his chair and pulled out a rolled map, which he spread out on the table.

"So ... we're *here*, at Bloody Run ... and where your folks live is off to the east of us ... *here* at Gettysburg." Nathan pointed to the two points on the map.

"Yes, sir. It's country I know well," Georgie nodded. "'Bout seventy miles, give or take..."

"Yep, that looks about right. The problem is..." Nathan shrugged. "*Where in the devil is Lee?* Amazingly, despite Ewell driving us out of Winchester, and the entire Union Army out looking, General Hooker has been unable to locate the bulk of Lee's army."

Georgie shook his head in disbelief, "That's a heck of a big ol' thing to lose track of, sir. Occasionally I'll misplace one o' my boots, or a sock, maybe ... but the whole danged Army of Northern Virginia? That don't just accidentally get kicked under the table when one ain't lookin'."

Nathan chuckled, "True enough. Once again, our high command is not exactly shining. I pray this isn't a sign of things to come."

"Yes, sir."

"Anyway, the point is, Lee's column could show up just about anywhere between here and Washington. You could ride right into them with little or no warning. I suggest you leave your uniforms behind and travel as civilians—just in case. The only people who will recognize you are the Gettysburg locals, and presumably they're all on our side. Maybe use your old ruse of riding a mule dressed as a farmer, or something of the kind."

"That seems prudent, sir."

"Still, it's a risk … if they do capture you and discover your true identity, they could hang you for spies, being out of uniform. Up to you…"

"I think the civilian clothes make sense, sir. And there's no reason they'd figure out who I really am. As you say, all the folks that know me are loyal to the Union. But … just now you made it sound like I'd be having some company with me on this trek…?"

Nathan smiled, "Well, I don't expect I'd be able to keep Mr. O'Brien here once he found out you were going, unless I was willing to tie him to his bunk and place an armed guard over him. Or several…"

Georgie returned the smile, "No … I reckon *not*, sir. Thank you also for *that*. It'll be a great comfort to have him there … and he is also quite close to my dad, having practically growed up in our house."

"Never mention it, Georgie. Just be careful out there, and return to us as quickly as circumstances allow."

"Yes, sir; will do."

₧

Saturday June 27, 1863 – McConnellsburg, Pennsylvania:

The first day of Georgie and Jamie's journey had been uneventful, and they spent the night camping out just east of the small town of McConnellsburg on the pike that led eastward to Gettysburg.

They laid out under the stars with just their saddle blankets thrown over them. They'd brought nothing with them that might give them away as soldiers, so they'd neither tents nor bedrolls. Not to mention guns, sabers, binoculars, cooking utensils, or many other things they'd become used to carrying practically night and day, since years ago out in Texas. To complete the disguise, they'd even bought well-worn work boots from some local farmers outside Bloody Run, paying more for them than a new pair would've cost.

Fortunately, it was a pleasant evening, so they didn't suffer the cold, nor did any sight or sound of war disturb their rest.

The next morning, as they rode east along the pike toward the next town called Chambersburg, about twenty-four miles distant, the countryside held an odd, expectant feeling amongst the hot, still air. Like something momentous was about to happen. The few civilians they met seemed nervous and in a hurry, though no one they spoke with reported seeing any soldiers from either side. Even the birds and beasts seemed wary and furtive, like their instincts were telling them the earth was about to experience a cataclysmic upheaval. Georgie thought it felt like it did when a thunderstorm was brewing. Yet there were no clouds in the sky.

The odd feeling eventually affected the usually lighthearted young army captains. They soon abandoned their usual banter, adopting instead a quiet, sullen demeanor. And through unspoken agreement, they found themselves continuously halting to reconnoiter the next valley, or to scout out beyond the next bend before proceeding along the road.

And then as they passed several farmhouses approaching the outskirts of Chambersburg, they saw a large cloud of dust rising a few miles away in the direction of the road leading south from the town.

So they left the roadway and traveled cross country in the direction of the dust cloud until they reached the foot of a rise, where they tied their horses to a tree. They crept to the top of the hill, crawling the last several yards on their bellies.

Gazing out through the tall grass, they saw a vast column of gray uniformed soldiers, rifles on their shoulders, marching northward on the pike. To their left they could see the column marching into the small town, then taking the righthand turn onto the eastbound pike. To their right, the column stretched southward as far as they could see, uncountable thousands of rebel soldiers.

They met eyes and shared a dire look; General Lee's missing army had been found at last. And it was marching directly toward Gettysburg!

Georgie shook his head, "We gotta ride straight back and tell the colonel!"

"Agreed. But what about your dear old dad, Georgie?"

"Dad's gonna have to wait. This here's the whole damned war—or could be, anyway. Dad'll understand."

Jamie nodded, and they crawled backward down the hill, being careful not to stir the grass as they went, until they were far enough not to be seen from the other side. Then they stood and moved back down the hill.

But as they trotted toward where their horses were tied, five riders came out from where they'd been hiding behind a copse of trees. The riders quickly surrounded the two men afoot and pointed revolvers at them. Georgie and Jamie raised their hands in surrender.

The rebel's leader wore a gray lieutenant's uniform, while the rest of the men wore only bits and pieces of uniforms, mixed with various items of ragged-looking civilian clothing. All had hard, dark looks on their faces.

"Well, now," the Confederate officer leaned down in his saddle and looked in their eyes. "What're y'all boys doin' out here a spyin' on the troops, anyhow?"

ॐॐॐॐॐॐॐॐॐ

Sunday June 28, 1863 – Chambersburg, Pennsylvania:

Jamie was impressed with the story Georgie spun for the Confederate cavalrymen. He told the rebels that the two of them were just locals from Gettysburg—that part was true enough, them having grown up there—and that they'd been out visiting Georgie's old uncle Willard in McConnellsburg one last time before the two of them enlisted in the Union army—pre-answering the obvious, unstated question as to why two healthy young men in their twenties were not already in uniform. Jamie realized that Georgie had been wise to say they were joining the

Union Army as it served to make his tale more believable; Pennsylvanians claiming they were getting ready to join the *Confederate* Army would've stretched credulity. After all, Pennsylvania was an unequivocally pro-Union, Northern state, and the rebels knew it.

"But we ain't been spyin'," Georgie claimed, "we was just curious, is all. Never seen a *real* army before, with big *cannons* and all," Georgie lied, with a big grin and wide, excited-seeming eyes.

Georgie was *so* convincing, Jamie found himself nearly believing it! And when the Confederates searched them and their horses, they found nothing at all incriminating, as intended—just a couple of local farm boys out for a visit to a relative. The Confederate lieutenant seemed convinced, so much so that they figured he was about to just let them go on their way, saying, "I'm inclined to believe you boys, and since you ain't yet enlisted, I can't rightly take you in for captured soldiers.

"But … I have my orders … any male civilians, aged thirteen to sixty, caught observing our troop movements are to be brought in for interrogation—no exceptions. Sorry, boys," he shrugged.

So though they were treated respectfully, and not bound or restrained in any way, they were forced to saddle up and accompany the rebels on the march toward Gettysburg. Luckily, it was where they wanted to go anyway, though they'd have preferred not to have the Confederate Army for an escort.

During the course of the march, they overheard enough to determine that this was General Longstreet's Corps, and that it would be meeting up with General Ewell's Corps somewhere along the march. Of the other corps, under General A.P. Hill, they heard nothing.

So when the rebel army made camp several miles outside Gettysburg that night, Georgie and Jamie were placed in a tent with a single armed private guarding the door. Georgie asked the guard, "What're we doin' here? How long do we have to wait? Who's gonna question us, anyway?"

The guard just frowned at him. "Y'all ask too many questions. All's I was told was y'all was to wait 'til General Lee calls you in for interrogation."

"General Lee? You mean *the* General Lee? *Robert E.* Lee?"

"Yep, the very same. Must be your lucky day…" the private grinned. "Now y'all keep quiet in there 'til it's time." He stepped out of the tent and pulled the flap closed.

"Well, how about *that?*" Georgie softly whistled. "Old Man Lee himself! I'll be damned! Dad won't hardly believe it…"

"Aye … odd that is. You'd think he'd have some lower-level officer for such doin's—him bein' so high and mighty and all. Makes me almost sad we won't be here to see him," Jamie shook his head in mock sadness, rolling his eyes as he did so.

"What do you mean?"

"Well, boyo," Jamie grinned. "They now got us pegged for just a couple o' local yokels—sure and certain…"

"Well, they ain't taking us for a pair of old Indian fighters from Texas, nor full-fledged Union officers, that's for sure," Georgie agreed, "So…"

"Exactly," Jamie winked. "And speakin' o' your dear old dad, I am thinkin' it's well after time to be goin' to call on him. Shall we?" he gestured toward the tent flap.

Georgie stood and grinned, "After *you*, my good sir…"

Jamie stood and took a step toward the tent flap, then called out to the guard, "Hey … hey, there *Sergeant* … when you ever gonna let us outta here?"

The private flipped back the tent flap with the bayonet of his rifle, and took one step into the tent, "I told y'all knot heads to keep it quiet in here. And I done already told y'all, I'm a *private*, not some gul-durned serg—"

Georgie's right fist smashed into the side of the man's head. He crumpled toward the ground, Jamie catching him and grabbing his rifle before either could hit hard enough to make a racket.

They laid him down, then decided they ought to gag and bind him, lest he regain consciousness before they could get well away. But they had no rope, so Georgie pulled off the man's belt and strapped the fellow's hands behind his back with it. Jamie then reached down and pulled off the man's pants.

"What're you doing *that* for?" Georgie asked.

"It'll buy us more time, laddie … he'll be too embarrassed to run out o' the tent, or start shoutin' for help when he realizes he's got no pants."

But for good measure, Jamie also pulled one of the man's socks off and stuffed it into his mouth for a gag. Georgie then pulled the strap off the guard's rifle and used it to tie his feet to his hands by looping it around the belt and pulling it tight before twisting it into a knot.

Then they searched him for anything useful. Georgie found a small pen knife and used it to cut a three-foot vertical slit in the back of the tent. Jamie picked up the rifle, and Georgie grabbed the man's ammo pouch and his pants, then they headed out the tent hole and into the night.

Their first stop would be Georgie's folks' house in Gettysburg to visit his dad, and there get new horses. Then … they'd try to somehow get around the rebel army and make their way back to Colonel Chambers to tell him they had found General Lee.

ജ〇ക൙ᏟᏰᏞᎥᏔ〇ക〇ക൙ᏟᏰᏞᎥᏔ〇ക〇ക൙ᏟᏰᏞᎥᏔ

Monday June 29, 1863 – Gettysburg, Pennsylvania:

"Get your sorry hides outta here, you rebel scoundrels, 'less you're wanting a taste of buckshot! You already stole everything worth stealing," the woman shouted from where she stood on her back porch. Though the light from the windows was dim, and the sun had not yet risen above the hills to the east, they could make her out well enough to see she wasn't bluffing; she held a long, double-barreled fowling piece, and both hammers were cocked. Though she was an older woman wearing a simple dress and an apron, with gray hair tied up in a bun, she was yet stout and sturdy on her feet. And the scowl on her face confirmed she meant business.

"Don't shoot, Momma … it's your boy Georgie!"

"And Jamie too."

Both men raised their hands, palm outwards.

"*Georgie-boy? Jamie-lad!* Oh, will wonders never cease! My goodness, come in, come in now, 'fore them damned rebs see you," she lowered the barrel of the shotgun and de-cocked the hammers.

"Dang, Momma … you could've kilt us."

"And would've, too, if you'd been more of them damned thieving secesh. That villain General Early rode through town three days back, sitting up all high and mighty on his horse. Ordered his men to strip the town of every horse, hammer, and horseshoe nail! Cleaned out our stables, and the smithing shed, 'til there weren't nothing left but the anvils … *the scoundrels!* So, yes … I'd o' shot you."

"Darn it, Momma … who'd o' thought it'd come to this, right here in Gettysburg? Nothing important ever happened here before." Georgie shook his head in disbelief as they stepped in the back door and made their way toward the kitchen. "I can't even remember the last time anything was took from anyone … likely never."

When they'd got inside, Mrs. Thompson leaned the gun up against the wall, then turned and squeezed Georgie so firmly that his feet nearly left the ground, despite his great advantage in height. Then she stepped back, patted him firmly on his arms, then turned and gave Jamie the exact same treatment. "Oh, my dear boys … it does an old woman's heart good to see you two again, it truly does…"

"Us too, Mrs. Thompson," Jamie beamed.

"Good to see you, too, Momma," Georgie echoed Jamie's broad smile.

"And just look at you two! Skinny little teenagers no more … You're grown-up men, with muscles and all. My, my…" she gazed at them admiringly, for several moments, with a wistful smile on her face, causing the two men to blush.

"How's Dad? I want to see him … He back in the bedroom?" Georgie gestured back down the hallway.

But Mrs. Thompson didn't immediately answer, looking down at her feet.

"*Oh…*" Georgie went quiet for a moment, also gazing down at the ground, his eyes growing watery.

Jamie reached over and patted him on the back. "When did he go?"

"He passed day before yesterday ... I've not had the heart to bury him, and what with all the upheaval in town, haven't been able to get any help; most of the neighbors have left town on account of the troubles. Dad's laid out in the smithing shed on the table. Since you two are here now, do you think you could...?"

"Of course, Momma. We'll dig him a grave and then we'll get him laid to rest proper, don't you worry," Georgie sniffed and wiped back a tear with his shirt sleeve.

But then he looked around as another thought hit him, "Hey ... where are the *girls*, Momma?"

She knew Georgie referred to his two youngest sisters who still lived at home. The rest of his siblings were already out living on their own, including his two older brothers, Christopher and Joseph, who were enlisted in the Forty-Fifth Pennsylvania Infantry, currently out west fighting for General Grant at the siege of Vicksburg along the Mississippi River.

"After Dad passed, with all these rebs roaming about, I sent 'em away to Aunt Susie's over to Lancaster when some of the neighbors were heading that way. Don't trust those secesh to not try ... well, *you know* ... with a couple of pretty young girls around..."

"Mmm ... good thinking, Momma. Best to get 'em out of harm's way. But *you* should've gone with 'em."

"And who's gonna feed the chickens and slop the hogs if I leave? Or keep 'em from being taken, more's the point. I'm not afraid of southern hooligans ... and as you can see, I know how take care of myself perfectly well!"

They both nodded their agreement to that statement, having personally experienced her robust defense out on the porch.

Mrs. Thompson ushered them to the kitchen table, set plates in front of them, and immediately started heaping bread, cheese, and slices of cold ham on them, which the two men dove into with great enthusiasm, having not eaten a thing since their capture.

Several minutes later, with a mouth still half-full of food, Georgie sat up and asked, "Hey, Momma, you seen any *Union*

Army boys around here? Since you got no horses for us to borrow, we may need to see if we can hook up with some other fellas from *our* side before the damned rebs sniff us out and catch us again."

"Mind your manners and don't talk with your mouth full, Georgie-boy," she scolded mildly, with a playful slap on the arm.

Georgie rolled his eyes, but then swallowed, "Yes, ma'am."

"To answer your question: no, I've not seen any. But if I was inclined to be the wagering type—which I certainly am *not*, bein' a good Christian woman—I'd say with all these rebs sniffing around it's only a matter of time before our boys in blue come a calling to see what all the fuss is about."

Georgie nodded his head, "You got a good point there, Momma." He turned and met eyes with Jamie, "Which way you figure the main column of the Army will be coming in from when they do?"

"Well, it's got to be from the south, doesn't it?" Jamie rubbed at the stubble on his chin, realizing he hadn't had a shave since they'd left Bloody Run, and he was now badly in need. "They would've crossed the Potomac well to the east o' wherever Lee crossed, don't you think? Old General Hooker would've wanted to keep his army between Lee and the capital, I reckon. So, it's got to be coming on up the south road, I'm thinkin'."

"Makes sense. So, soon as we get Dad laid to rest, let's see if we can't head out that a way and find some of our boys. Then we can lead 'em back here and give these ornery rebs a fight!"

ℬᴑ☾ℛᴕℬᴑ☾ℛᴕℬᴑ☾ℛᴕ

"You're saying those two farm boys escaped before I could interrogate them?" General Lee turned away from the stack of papers on his camp table to gaze up at his aide de camp, Major Charles Marshall, who stood above him. Lee rubbed at eyes that felt the strain of a long day, threatening to bring on a blinding headache if he kept at it much longer. "How did *that* happen?"

"Sorry, sir. Apparently our cavalry troopers were taken in by a ruse, and these fellows were *not* what they seemed at all. Based on the ease of their escape, and the skill of the methods they employed, we are now assuming these men were highly

208

experienced enemy agents. Likely scouts sent out by the new Union BMI—the Bureau of Military Intelligence—which we've been hearing rumblings about. The poor private posted to guard them really didn't stand a chance, I'm afraid."

Lee slowly shook his head, "Well, that's a most bitter pill ... Now we must assume these enemy spies have gotten clean away, and will report everything they've heard and seen of this command to General Hooker. Damn the bad luck ... if only Oliver Boyd was still here ... likely he would've been able to speak with them sooner and would've seen through their subterfuge. I feel so blind without an intelligence officer, trying to do it all myself. And speaking of being blind, where in hell is Jeb Stuart?" He looked down at his boots and absently kicked at the dirt in the floor of the tent.

But Marshall knew the general's question was only rhetorical, speaking out loud the thought that had been troubling his entire command for the past several days, ever since General Stuart and the bulk of the Confederate cavalry had failed to meet up with the army at the expected rendezvous point. Without them, the Army of Northern Virginia was almost completely deaf and blind to the Union Army's movements, and had no way to screen their own movements from its spies.

Lee looked back up, slowly shaking his head, and repeated the question, "Where the hell is General Stuart?"

ℬↄℭℜℭჰℬↄℬↄℭℜℭჰℬↄℬↄℭℜℭჰ

Tuesday, June 30, 1863 – Bedford, Pennsylvania:

When Nathan finally received marching orders for the Hodgepodge Brigade from General Schenck, he snorted derisively; once again, he felt he was being sent in the entirely wrong direction. While everyone expected Lee's army to strike somewhere out east, anywhere from Harrisburg, Pennsylvania to Washington City, he was once again being ordered to march west, with no explanation.

"Damn it, Tom … if I didn't know better, I'd say Momma has friends in the War Department and is intentionally keeping us out of harm's way!"

Tom chuckled, "Or maybe Adilida … or Evelyn."

Nathan snorted, "Yes … Evelyn is the most likely to have the connections … but the least likely to send us marching off in the wrong direction; she wants to finish this thing as badly as we do, maybe more so."

"True. From the little I know her, I'd agree; she's a fighter."

There was nothing for Nathan to do but follow his orders and lead the ten-mile march west up the Juniata River to Bedford, Pennsylvania.

But Nathan's initial reticence and resentment concerning his new orders quickly gave way to pleased satisfaction when the brigade arrived in Bedford and he met with the provost marshal there, followed by the quartermaster. He immediately called a pause to the pitching of tents and setting up of camp and marched the troops to the train station where his nearly three-thousand men queued up for new uniforms and blankets for the first time since before the battle of Winchester, after which they lined up to receive their back pay from the paymaster.

It led to a very happy, festive mood that evening in camp, and Nathan was grateful there was no great quantity of alcohol available, or they might've had a very long night of it.

Nathan retired to his tent late in the evening, and as usual tried to think happy thoughts of Evelyn, along with saying his usual prayer for her safety and good health.

He found he could not, however, sustain a good humor, despite the positive events of the day; a nagging, disturbing doubt would grant him no peace. It had even begun to haunt his dreams at night: *Where is Lee?*

☩☨☯☮☩☨☯☮☩☨☯

Tuesday June 30, 1863 – Gettysburg, Pennsylvania:

The previous day, after burying Georgie's father, Georgie and Jamie had headed out, going due south on the Taneytown Road, figuring it was the most likely approach to Gettysburg for the Union Army. Their efforts were frustrated and hindered by the lack of any horses in town after General Early's earlier plundering, so they were limited to the distance they could walk out and back in a day, not wanting to leave Gettysburg and risk losing contact with Lee's army altogether.

But finally, after a long day of trudging in a blazing hot sun, they had had to turn back, having seen no soldiers at all, neither blue nor gray. Oddly, they'd not seen any civilians either; there had been no traffic on the road at all, which was unusual in the extreme. It was almost as if *something* major was about to happen, and people were instinctively avoiding it.

Today, their second day in Gettysburg, they had decided to try the Baltimore Pike, which headed more southeasterly. But once again, their efforts bore no fruit and they were forced to turn back to Gettysburg empty handed. It was puzzling and confounding. How could the entire rebel army be camped out in rural Pennsylvania without eliciting a quick and violent response from the Union army? Or any response at all?

They reached town, just as the sun was setting, and were surprised to see Old Man Taylor, who ran the general store on Main Street just down the block from the Thompsons' blacksmith shop and home. He was standing out in front of his store waving to them.

"You boys missed all the excitement," Taylor motioned them over to the bench on the walkway outside his store.

"What excitement, Mr. Taylor?" Georgie removed his hat and wiped his sweaty brow before gratefully taking a seat next to Taylor. Jamie plopped down on the other side of Taylor with a grunt.

"Union Cavalry, that's what!"

"What? Where? When? How many?" Georgie sat up straight, gazing intently down at Taylor, who beamed, obviously pleased with the reaction his news had elicited.

"They came riding up the Emmitsburg Road around … hmm … eleven or thereabouts this morning. Thousands of 'em, all dressed in blue. Prettiest sight I ever saw, I must say."

Georgie and Jamie shared a look, and Jamie rolled his eyes, "From the *southwest* … the last damned place we'd o' thought to look for 'em."

"What happened when they got here?" Georgie met eyes with Taylor once again.

"They were led by a stern-looking general … *Buford*, I think he said he was."

"Brigadier General John Buford, that'd be," Georgie, nodded. "First U.S. Cavalry Division."

"Yep, that's him. Anyhow, the general gets down off his horse and asks if anyone has seen the enemy. So, I tell him that you two fellas had told me you'd seen a whole flock of rebels back along the Chambersburg Pike up to Cashtown. He then asks me where you two were, as he wishes to speak with you on it. But I says you'd gone out looking for *him* and his troops early in the morn, and had headed south. Since nobody else knew anything more than I did, he thanks me, saddles back up, and rides out of town, heading northwest."

Jamie and Georgie were quiet for a moment, absorbing this news and processing the frustration of having missed the thing they were working so hard to find, knowing if they'd have just stayed put, they would've found it.

"Well, one thing's certain, boyo," Jamie sat up, grinned and slapped Georgie on the back and stood up from the bench.

"What's that?"

"We know for sure where *we'll* be come first light on the morrow!"

Georgie answered Jamie's grin with a chuckle and a nod as he too stood.

ॐᏣᎦᏋᏬॐᏣᎦᏋᏬॐᏣᎦᏋᏬ

Wednesday July 1, 1863 – Fayetteville, Pennsylvania:

C.S.A. Lieutenant Jubal Collins felt an aching weariness that he'd rarely felt before. He feared the years of almost nonstop marching, camping outdoors, and fighting was finally taking its toll, despite his relative youth, having just turned twenty-three years old last month. He shook his head and smiled ruefully when he considered that the men of Company H that he commanded commonly referred to him as "the old man."

As usual on this campaign, the Stonewall Brigade, now led by Brigadier General James A. Walker, seemed to be late to the party, and scrambling to catch up, along with the rest of Major General Edward "Allegheny" Johnson's division. Jubal understood it was part of the strategy, that General Lee needed a unit he could trust serving as rearguard to his army, but it had become a wearisome task.

And General Walker's usual sour disposition didn't seem to benefit from the duty either; the officers and men down the line knew he was best avoided, lest one invoke his wrath. Fortunately, the Twenty-Seventh's regimental commander, Lieutenant Colonel Daniel Shriver, was of a more agreeable temperament, which worked out well for Jubal.

This day, they'd been up before dawn, breaking camp outside the village of Fayetteville, Pennsylvania, eating a cold, tasteless breakfast of hardtack before shouldering their packs and hitting the road one more time. This time they were headed to another small town in Pennsylvania that Jubal had never heard of named Gettysburg, which was said to be about twenty-four miles away.

Though the day had started out pleasant enough, as the hot summer sun slowly rose in the sky, it began to beat down on their heads and shoulders like a hammer on an anvil. Jubal's clothing was quickly soaked through with sweat and covered with a thick coating of dust, adding to what had already been accumulated during the previous days' marches. He chuckled to himself, a mirthless laughter, as he wondered how many extra pounds all that dirt added to his tiresome burden. His only thought about their destination was hoping there'd be plenty of shade and a cool stream to wet their parched throats.

It was now late in the afternoon, and the Stonewall Brigade had been toiling up a long, gently sloping hill for several hours. Jubal could feel the slope beginning to ease, and looking ahead over the heads of the Fifth Virginia Regiment in front of them he could see that they were finally cresting the rise. He felt a welcome relief, as that meant the next several miles would be, thankfully, mostly downhill.

But even as he reached the crest, he heard a rumbling in the distance immediately followed by another, and another, and another in rapid succession. Artillery fire, there could be no doubt. Then he heard the unmistakable rattle of musket fire, a rapid popping sound as if an entire field of ripe corn were going up in flame and popping off thousands of kernels all at once.

Jubal turned and met eyes with Sergeant Charles Rollins, who was walking next to him. Rollins grinned and said, "Well, Lieutenant ... evidently someone has found the Yanks!"

঺৩৵৵঺৩৵৵঺৩৵৵

Wednesday July 1, 1863 – Uniontown, Maryland:

In the pre-dawn darkness, Captain James Hawkins dragged himself from his bedroll, and began the thankless task of rousing his men. Several hard kicks, and much grumbling and cursing later, his men were up and moving, grabbing a quick breakfast of dry biscuits and canteen water before shouldering their rifles and haversacks to continue the seemingly endless march northward. They'd marched 250 miles nonstop at the double-quick in the past two weeks, and James Hawkins could feel every mile of it right down to his bones.

The good news, if there was any, was that this day they would finally be crossing into Pennsylvania, what the Union soldiers had started thinking of as the beginning of the "true North" where the civilians were entirely and enthusiastically pro-Union, unlike their almost evenly divided counterparts in Maryland. That not only meant they'd receive a warmer welcome, but there was now the possibility of a warm meal, or other highly appreciated assistance from the local population.

The nightmarish march for the Seventh West Virginia, along with the rest of what had become known as the Gibraltar Brigade under General Samuel S. Carroll, had begun on June fourteenth in Falmouth, Virginia, where General Hooker's headquarters had been before the Army of the Potomac had moved out to hunt for

214

General Lee's army. The Gibraltar Brigade, which had received its nickname for its courage and steadfastness during the Battle of Antietam, was one of the last units to move out of camp, being assigned as rearguard for the rest of the army.

The men had marched for a solid week at a quick pace, sunup to sundown, from Falmouth through Gainesville, then past Leesburg before crossing the Potomac at Edwards Ferry. Then it was due north to just south of Frederick, Maryland, camping at the Monocacy River Bridge where the soldiers enjoyed a bath in the cold river—the first they'd had since leaving Falmouth, if one didn't count the dousing they'd received wading the Potomac.

The march north had been so grueling, with minimal rations, that many of the less stalwart soldiers simply dropped out of the march, laying down beside the road and refusing to move any further. Even some of the healthier men began to straggle, such that at times there were so many stragglers at the back of the brigade that they seemed to have formed their own regiment. Captain Hawkins began to fear that he'd have no men fit to fight by the time they reached their final destination, wherever that might be.

So far, they'd had no news of Lee's location, though they'd heard dozens of conflicting rumors. The only concrete news they'd heard was that General Hooker had resigned as commander of the Army of the Potomac, replaced by Major General George Meade. James Hawkins had no idea what this meant, or why it had happened, but he was hopeful it would be an improvement given Hooker's lackluster record to date; at least he chose to believe that, having little alternative.

By the time the Seventh had neared the Mason-Dixon Line and camped at Uniontown, Maryland, the officers and men of the regiment were completely worn out. But there would be no rest for them this day.

So now, with Pennsylvania's mountains looming ahead of them, the Seventh West Virginia once again forged on. They reached the small town of Hanover, Pennsylvania in the early afternoon. There they were informed that a major portion of Lee's army had been encountered out west near the small town of

Gettysburg, another fifteen miles' march. So after a brief rest, and another cold, tasteless lunch, the brigade shouldered its gear once more and headed west.

And as the sun began to set, and they grew closer to Gettysburg, they began to hear the rumbling of artillery in the distance, and the whistling, buzzing noise of musket fire—the unmistakable song of battle.

Captain Hawkins soon realized he had quickened his pace without conscious thought, and as he looked around, he realized the rest of the men had as well. There was no more complaining or straggling, and all the aches and pains were driven away by the surge of adrenaline at the thought of finally encountering the elusive enemy in battle.

Apparently, the long, exhausting hunt for General Lee was over at last.

Chapter 9. Gettysburg

"...we here highly resolve that these dead shall not have died in vain ... that government of the people, by the people, for the people, shall not perish from the earth."

- Abraham Lincoln

The Gettysburg Address

Wednesday July 1, 1863, 7:00 a.m. – along the Chambersburg Pike:

Jamie and Georgie had started out from Gettysburg well before the break of day, after a hearty meal and a tearful goodbye from Mrs. Thompson, whose final words to them were, "You boys go ahead and run those rebs off now, y'hear? They got no business bein' here 'bouts, and I for one am *done* with 'em. And ... just do keep your heads down, my darlings..."

Being very familiar with the surrounding environs, they were confident they could find their way even in the dark, and were anxious to locate General Buford before he rode headlong into Lee's entire army, a move that would likely spell disaster for his cavalry division, being outnumbered more than ten to one with only light artillery.

But their concerns proved unfounded, and General Buford proved himself a more than competent and capable commander.

They'd traveled more than three miles along the road toward Cashtown, where Lee's camp had been when they'd made their escape, but so far had seen no one. But just as they were beginning to wonder if Buford had somehow headed off in some other direction, and Old Man Taylor had got it wrong, they heard the sounds of galloping horses, coming fast in their direction from just around the next bend—hundreds of horses, and likely supply wagons or artillery caissons.

Not knowing whether these riders be friend or foe, they dived into a ditch, then crawled up to the lip in time to see a cavalry troop coming along the road at a fast trot, leading several teams of horses that pulled six light artillery pieces behind them, and an artillery caisson. Of course, it was not lost on Jamie and Georgie that these cavalrymen wore blue uniforms, nor that they were moving with a great sense of urgency.

After these artillerymen had passed, another group of a thousand or so cavalry rode past, led by a dark-haired, stern-looking brigadier general whom they assumed was General Buford. The general pushed his men hard past where Jamie and Georgie lay in the ditch. Then a few hundred yards farther, Buford ordered his troopers off the road where it rose up a rocky ridgeline. Here the artillerymen quickly unlimbered and deployed the big guns facing back toward Cashtown, from whence the enemy would likely come. The cavalry troopers dismounted and immediately began digging in, cutting timbers, and digging trenches with short-handled shovels.

Another larger group of cavalry, several thousand strong, followed these, giving ground more slowly. These troopers turned back by companies to point their pistols and short rifles, called carbines, toward the direction from which they'd come. Clearly, these units were serving as rearguard, ready to hold back the enemy as the rest of the regiment dug in on the hillside. But so far, there'd been no gunfire and no sign of the enemy.

When this last regiment of riders was nearly even with them, Georgie started to rise up out of the ditch, intending to flag down one of the troopers that they might join up with them. But Jamie grabbed Georgie by the belt and dragged him back down into the ditch.

"You daft, Georgie?"

"What'd you do that for? We want to join 'em, don't we?" Georgie rolled over and scowled up at his comrade.

"Well sure we do … but look at us! We look just like damned rebs. They'll just shoot us down and ask their questions after, don't you know."

Georgie gazed at Jamie's clothes, then down at this own, and it hit him for the first time: they didn't just look like local farm boys, they looked exactly like most of the rebel soldiers, many of whom wore no proper uniforms, and often went without any shoes.

"Damn me. You're right … They'll shoot us for sure. We'll have to somehow sneak up on 'em and surrender before they can think to put a bullet in us."

So they stayed hunkered down as the Union cavalry passed by, then waited to see if the enemy might be closely following. The majority of these new Union riders also dismounted and began digging in when they reached the hillside. Only a small portion of the original cavalry brigade remained mounted, and these divided into two groups, each deployed on opposite wings of the dismounted troopers to intercept any flanking attacks.

Georgie's hard military experience and training from serving with the Captain had given him a keen understanding of what was unfolding before his eyes, a scene that a civilian or even a less experienced soldier might not comprehend. He appreciated the cleverness and bravery of the Union cavalry general, Buford. By deploying his artillery and dismounting most of his cavalry troopers, he gave the appearance of a large, well dug-in infantry division supported by artillery—a much harder nut to crack than an outnumbered, hastily retreating cavalry brigade. Georgie turned to Jamie and grinned, "That fellow Buford's smart, and's got some kinda backbone. That's as neat a ruse as I ever hope to see!"

Jamie nodded, "Sure hope it works. But, Georgie-boy … why is he doing it? What's he hoping to gain? Seems like he found Lee all right, and now knows what he's up against; why not run, beat it out o' here? Why stand and fight? Why here?"

Georgie thought about that a moment. "Only one reason I can think of: he knows more Union troops are on their way, probably enough to give Lee a good fight, and he wants to buy them time to arrive."

Jamie nodded, "Makes sense. Still … the man's got to have icy water in his veins to try a stunt like that."

"Yep. Speaking of … I *ain't* got that kind of veins, so I reckon we ought to beat it outta here before those Southern boys pay us a visit."

"Agreed, boyo. Let's go."

But making their way back to the Union lines without getting themselves shot for enemy scouts proved harder at first than they'd imagined. It soon became apparent that General Buford had previously scouted this very spot and had already chosen it as a hard point that would be easy to defend in the event he needed to fall back. Not only did it have a rocky slope on which to dig in, but the slope had been logged at one point, and it now featured a broad meadow at the foot of it, several hundred yards across and wide enough to reach beyond their present view in both directions. Their only option was to work their way through the trees to wherever the clearing ended, then try to sneak past the scouts that would undoubtedly be watching the flanks.

But they'd not gone more than a few hundred yards through the trees heading north when they heard a single rifle shot that echoed eerily through the woods. They both immediately stopped to listen. For a moment, there was nothing further ... then a rifle volley burst forth from the Union side, which was immediately answered by one from the enemy. Georgie and Jamie took cover once again, this time in a dry streambed.

The Battle of Gettysburg had begun...

ॐ∂Ҩ℘ℬℭ∂Ҩℭℬℭ∂ҩℬℭ℘Ҩℭℬ

General Buford's ruse appeared to work; looking back toward the road over the lip of the stream bank, Georgie could see that a huge enemy cavalry formation, several divisions strong, had arrived along the road. But rather than immediately thrusting forward to push their great advantage in numbers, they paused and dismounted, taking cover in the trees and sending forward a skirmish line to feel out the enemy position. These skirmishers took up positions at the edge of the trees and began targeting the Union position, firing at will.

Georgie watched the action intently, trying to decide if they should risk another go at getting to the Union lines. But before he could make up his mind on it, he was startled by a sudden movement next to him, making him jump. A half dozen men with rifles had just jumped down into the streambed next to them.

220

These rebels quickly scrambled up to the lip of the streambed and began firing at the hillside.

Their sergeant, the only one of the group wearing an actual gray uniform, glanced over at Georgie and Jamie and said, "Hey … what's the situation out here, anyhow? And … where the hell are y'all's rifles?"

Once again, Georgie proved his ability to spin a tall tale, this time using a heavy Texas twang he'd picked up during his years out west, since it wouldn't do to sound like a Pennsylvanian. He convinced the sergeant that he and Jamie—whose Irish accent didn't require disguising since there were Irishmen on both sides of the conflict—were scouts sent out earlier by General Lee to reconnoiter the road. And they'd gone unarmed intentionally so that if they were confronted by Union soldiers, they could claim to be local farm boys, just watching the action out of curiosity.

It was such a creative twist on the real story, and with enough elements of truth thrown in to make it plausible, that the sergeant seemed satisfied and left them alone after the two reported they'd spent the morning "spying out a very large Union infantry division that had been busily digging in on the hillside, supported by several dozen heavy artillery pieces," to the Confederate sergeant's chagrin.

ॐ૭ଓ૭ଓ૭ॐ૭ଓ૭ଓ૭ॐ૭ଓ૭ଓ

Wednesday July 1, 1863, 2:30 p.m. – along the Chambersburg Pike:

Once the rebel skirmishers moved on to another position, Georgie and Jamie slipped out of the streambed and moved off into the woods, continuing to the north. And though a bright sun shone above, it was dark under the shade of the trees and the woods were now crawling with rebel skirmishers, making for a slow, harrowing task.

They'd managed to make it what they reckoned was about a quarter of a mile from their original position to a place that seemed quieter. From here, they thought they might risk moving out of the woods across the grassy field at the base of the slope, then up toward the Union lines.

As they approached the open field where they would lose the forest's cover, they paused every few yards to watch and listen. But they saw and heard no movement. They figured they'd need to climb several hundred yards up the mostly barren hillside before they might encounter the Union pickets. Then they'd just have to pray they'd not be shot before they could explain themselves.

But when they reached the treeline, figures suddenly stood up from the cover of bushes and out from behind trees. Five men blocked their way, but in the deep shade of the forest with the sunlight behind, they appeared only as silhouettes, though the steely glint of their bayonets was unmistakable.

Georgie and Jamie raised their hands in surrender. Georgie figured they'd had it this time for sure, and likely no amount of tale spinning would convince these rebel sentries of their innocence.

But then Georgie noticed something other than bayonets was sparkling in the shadows: *Brass buttons! These guys are wearing uniforms with … shiny … brass … buttons! In a neat little row, right down the front of their tunics!*

He laughed out loud and saw the man in front of him tilt his head in confusion at the sound, "What's so funny?"

But Georgie continued to chuckle, "What's funny is … *man*, are we ever happy to see you fellas!"

"And why might that be, Johnny reb? You boys deserters?"

Jamie slowly lowered his hands, "We aren't goddamned secesh, Private. We're Union officers, so show some respect!"

❦❧☙❦❧☙❦❧☙

Wednesday July 1, 1863, 3:45 p.m. – Gettysburg – Seminary Ridge:

Jamie and Georgie were brought to a Union command tent up on Seminary Ridge, which was a beehive of activity, with officers and scouts coming and going in a steady stream. Brightly colored U.S. and regimental flags on long poles planted in the ground around the tent gave the scene a surreal, almost festive air. But the newcomers knew the business being conducted here was of the most deadly-serious nature.

They were brought into the tent, where a stern-looking major general sat behind a folding table. It occurred to Georgie that this man reminded him of Colonel Chambers: exceptionally handsome with dark, intense eyes and dark hair. He also sported a mustache along with a goatee beard, and the two were of roughly the same age and build.

Though Georgie and Jamie wore no uniforms, they immediately stood to attention in front of the general and saluted.

"Captain George E. Thompson, Twelfth West Virginia, reporting for duty, sir!"

"Captain Jamie O'Brien, Twelfth West Virginia—also reporting for duty, sir!"

The two of them continued to hold their salutes, awaiting the general's response.

The general gazed at them with curiosity, remaining seated, "Major General Winfield Scott Hancock, Army of the Potomac." He returned the salute smartly, "At ease, gentlemen. Now, you will please explain to me how you have come to be here, and why you are out of uniform." He pointed to Georgie. "You first."

"Yes, sir … we're on furlough, though we never brought our signed papers nor our uniforms in case we were captured by the rebs—which we were—but made good our escape last night, and then snuck our way through to your lines just now."

"Hmm … I see. That being the case, I must verify that you are who you claim to be before we speak further. But I must warn you, I am *very* familiar with the commanding officer of the Twelfth West Virginia, having served with him in Mexico; my regiment fought next to his during the Battle of Molino Del Rey. So it will do you no good to prevaricate."

"*Prevari … what?*" Jamie turned to Georgie with raised eyebrows.

"He means it won't do us no good to make up some big ol' lie," Georgie told him, then looked back at the general. "But there ain't need for us to lie, sir. Jamie and I have known Colonel Chambers for years, ever since we served with him out in Texas at Fort Davis, part of the U.S. Eighth Infantry, where he was our captain and commander. When his papa died and he decided to come back east, we were among those of his men that volunteered to come with him. And then when the war broke out, we stayed with him to help get the new state started up."

"*West* Virginia..." General Hancock prompted.

"Yes, sir. We were serving sort of like ... hmm ... a special police force, I guess you could say, up to Wheeling, fightin' rebel bushwhackers, helpin' Governor Pierpont put the new state in order—though we was itchin' to get into the fight proper. Finally, this spring we all o' Captain Chambers' men from Texas joined up together into the Twelfth West Virginia. We two were made captains, along with most of the others, and Captain Chambers was made our commanding colonel, though we all think he by rights ought to be a major general—no offense to *you*, sir."

"None taken," the general smiled. "And I happen to agree with you on that point."

"Aye," Jamie nodded. "And after, we had ourselves a nice little gunfight down Winchester way when General Ewell came callin' with some o' his Southern boys."

"True enough," Georgie nodded his agreement.

"And what did Colonel Chambers do during the Winchester battle?" the general asked.

"Fought like a tiger, is all," Jamie answered. "But we were too badly outnumbered for it to do us no good. Then when it came time to bust outta there, he led us over the mountains to where we picked up the rest o' the Hodgepodge Brigade. Then we marched through Bath, crossed the river to Hancock, and from there were ordered on to Pennsylvania."

"Then while we were up at Bloody Run, I got a telegram sayin' my old dad had taken ill, here in Gettysburg where us two growed up," Georgie added. "So Colonel Chambers kindly gave us furlough to go visit him."

"Oh, and how *is* your father?" the general asked.

Georgie glanced down at the floor. "Sorry to say, he passed 'fore we arrived, sir."

224

"Oh ... Sorry for your loss, Mr. Thompson," the general frowned.

"Thank you, sir. But my momma is well, though fightin' mad on account o' all these rebs in her town, and that they stole all her horses and blacksmithing equipment, along with every shoe and nail, whenever General Early passed through here a few days back."

Then Georgie looked back up and chuckled, "She told us to go shoo them rascals away from her town, so ... here we are, under *orders* you might say, to do whatever we can to help lick them rebs, sir."

General Hancock had an amused look in his eyes as he gazed at each of them in turn for a long moment. Then he turned toward the officer standing to the left side of his table, "Lieutenant, please obtain sidearms and proper uniforms for these two men, if any are to be had." Then he looked back at Georgie and Jamie, "And do be sure their tunics have captain's bars on the shoulders."

After the lieutenant departed, General Hancock gestured toward folding camp chairs leaning against the side of the tent, "Now, gentlemen ... pull up a couple of chairs, and get comfortable, if you please. I wish you to tell me all you've seen and heard of the enemy, and *everything* there is to know about the terrain in and around Gettysburg, Pennsylvania."

ഇരുകൂട്ടരുംഇരുകൂട്ടരുംഇരുകൂട്ടര

Georgie and Jamie spent the next several hours with General Hancock and his staff, poring over, annotating, and often correcting, maps the general had of Gettysburg and environs. They also provided detailed descriptions of various roads and geographical features of the surrounding area. But most important, they verified that the high ground Hancock now commanded was where he and the Union Army must stay, at all costs. It commanded the terrain for many miles around, and could ensure a path of communication and re-supply for the army by controlling the main roadway southward.

They learned during the course of the evening that Hancock had specifically been sent to Gettysburg by General Meade — who had taken over from General Hooker—to determine if the Union Army should attempt to engage Lee here, or retreat to another defensive line in Maryland. And when Hancock had completed his interrogation of them, he gazed again at the map in front of him. "Thanks to your timely arrival, I shall send word to General Meade to bring up the entire army; we shall have our fight right here at Gettysburg."

Georgie thought of his mother and cringed, wondering what she'd say if she knew her son had just helped to convince a Union general to wage a major battle right in her own backyard.

But even as Georgie and Jamie stood to depart, a lieutenant strode into the tent, snapped a salute, and said, "Sorry to disturb you sir, but ... there's been a terrible tragedy. Major General Reynolds has been killed, sir!"

ᏚᎧᏨᏨᏫᎳᏚᎧᏨᏨᏫᎳᏚᎧᏨᏨᏫᎳ

Wednesday July 1, 1863, 6:15 p.m. – Gettysburg – base of Cemetery Hill:

By the time C.S.A. Lieutenant Colonel Elijah Walters, commander of the Thirty-Sixth Virginia Cavalry Battalion, received his orders—orders that had started out from General Lee to General Ewell as a vague and indecisive order to attack the Union position on Cemetery Hill "if practicable," and had then been forwarded to General Jenkins, then finally to Jenkins' subordinates—the order came across to attack the Union position "as exigencies allow."

Walters listened to the verbal orders from Jenkins' courier, a young lieutenant, and simply nodded. General Jenkins had already been wounded in the earlier action, and was, according to what Walters had heard, unable to mount a horse. He was now relaying orders from a hastily erected command tent.

Walters gazed long and hard through binoculars up at the hill, which someone had said was, appropriately enough, called Cemetery Hill. There, unknown units of the Union Army were dug in, supported by unknown numbers of artillery pieces—the very place his orders implied he should attack *if the opportunity presented itself.* After a moment, he turned to his second in command, Captain Roberts and said, "I believe we will move off to the left, through the woods there, and see if that presents us with an opportunity to flank the enemy position."

The captain gazed in the direction his commander indicated, then looked back and nodded, "That seems prudent, sir."

So, the Thirty-Sixth Virginia Cavalry Battalion moved slowly off into the woods to the left of the Confederate line until they reached a place where a small meadow provided a relatively large open space.

Walters raised his right fist to call for a halt, then turned to Captain Roberts and said, "Roberts, the men have been fighting hard today … I believe they require a brief … *respite* … before we attempt to engage the enemy. Have the men dismount and rest themselves for a spell."

"Very good, sir. And when shall I have them re-mount and advance?"

"Hmm … I'm thinking it shall be … when I say so, Captain."

The captain grinned, and saluted his commander, "Yes, sir!"

It occurred to Walters that the captain likely assumed his reticence to engage the formidable enemy position was out of an altruistic concern for his men. He inwardly laughed at the thought. He was concerned for his men, true, but only because a hopeless, pointless assault against a strongly held enemy position would most likely result in a serious depletion of his force, and so diminish his power. He cared nothing for his men as individuals, but as the sum of their parts they were invaluable—invaluable if he wished to kill more Yankees, slaughter more escaped slaves, and ultimately … to kill Nathan Chambers and all of his men.

ॐ

Wednesday July 1, 1863, 6:30 p.m. – Gettysburg – Cemetery Hill:

When the men of the Seventh West Virginia were a few miles out from the town of Gettysburg and the cacophony of battle was growing ever closer, a halt was suddenly called, and an order inexplicably came down the line to remove hats and stand to respectful attention. Captain Hawkins exchanged a puzzled look with Lieutenant James Titsworth, who marched next to him, but neither man had any idea what this was about; nothing like it had ever occurred before, especially not when fast approaching an active battlefield.

But the mystery was soon solved as an open wagon rolled by, escorted by a half-dozen cavalry troopers. In the wagon, the lifeless body of a soldier lay, with a blood-soaked flag draped over the lower half of his body. But this was no ordinary soldier; the slain wore an officer's tunic with two stars on each shoulder — a Major General! Hawkins later learned to his dismay that this was Major General John F. Reynolds, commonly considered one of the best generals in the Army. It was a sobering sight for the men of the Seventh; if a Major General had been killed in the fighting ahead, what kind of hell were they marching into? If this killing field was already claiming the highest of their command, what chance did a common soldier have?

But by the time the Gibraltar Brigade — consisting of the Fourteenth Indiana, Fourth and Eighth Ohio, and the Seventh West Virginia — reached Cemetery Hill just south of town, the day's fighting was dying down. They could see that Union forces held the high ground south of the small town, and that artillery batteries were already dug in. The brigade was met by Major General Oliver Otis Howard, currently in command of all Union forces in General Meade's absence. Howard, who'd lost his right arm in the Battle of Fair Oaks during the Peninsula Campaign, ordered them to make camp and get some food and rest, telling them, "Your business will likely be hot and heavy, come first light tomorrow."

Nobody doubted the general's word on *that* point, but now that the earlier surge of adrenaline had subsided, they once again felt the exhaustion of weeks of hard marching, such that Hawkins had a hard time even caring what the morrow might bring.

But as he stood next to their regimental commander, Lieutenant Colonel Jonathan Lockwood, he was surprised to see Major General Winfield Scott Hancock approaching them on his horse.

Hancock stopped in front of the colonel, and the two exchanged a salute. General Hancock then surprised Lockwood with a grin, "Colonel … I have a little gift for you. These gentlemen are looking for a regiment to fight with and have already given good service here at Gettysburg, providing me with invaluable intelligence concerning our battleground and the surrounding environs. I trust you will find a use for them…"

He then gestured behind his horse, waving two officers forward. When they stepped around the general's horse, Georgie and Jamie stood to attention, and saluted the officers of the Seventh West Virginia, whom they had helped to train at the beginning of the conflict. The two young captains could not suppress broad grins at the sight of so many joyfully surprised, familiar faces.

ಐ಼ೞ಼ಐ಼ೞ಼ಐ಼ೞ಼ಐ಼ೞ಼ಐ಼ೞ಼

Wednesday July 1, 1863, 6:30 p.m. – Gettysburg:

As the Stonewall Brigade approached the outskirts of Gettysburg with the sun setting behind them, Jubal could tell that the heavy fighting they'd heard earlier on the march was beginning to die down for the evening. Only intermittent rifle fire could now be heard over toward the far side of town, away to the south.

So far, all they'd seen of the Yankees were downcast groups of Union soldiers being marched to the rear under guard. He'd have taken this for a very favorable sign if it weren't for the fact that they were also seeing a growing stream of their own wounded flowing past—some walking, others carried on stretchers or transported in overfilled ambulance wagons.

The division was ordered to halt near the Carlisle Street rail station while General Johnson went to meet with General Ewell to receive his new orders.

Jubal thought it prudent to take advantage of the respite and restock their depleted stores before heading into battle. So he sent a platoon of his company out to locate a source of water to refill

229

their canteens and to forage for supplies among the abandoned stores and warehouses in the district.

He initially thought these efforts were proceeding nicely, as several members of the platoon came back shortly with full canteens, prompting the other members of the company to follow them back in order to refill theirs. But as these men returned, something tickled at his old policeman instincts: his men were behaving oddly, smiling and laughing as if sharing a private joke, and glancing furtively at the sergeants.

Jubal marched over to the closest group of men, held out his hand, and said, "Hand me that canteen, private."

Jubal uncorked the canteen, took a sniff, then turned it upside down, emptying its contents onto the road. The private looked disappointed, and somewhat embarrassed, but said nothing, only shrugging.

"Sergeant Evans!"

"Sir!"

"Line the men up for inspection … *now*, if you please." And then to Evans questioning look he added, "Someone has apparently discovered a barrel of whiskey…"

"*Ah!* Yes, sir!"

Moments later, the entire company stood to attention, with Jubal and his two sergeants standing out front of them.

"Company will unstopper and empty all canteens on my command." Jubal scowled at his men, though he felt no particular anger toward them, knowing they'd more than earned the pleasure. But he also knew that allowing them to indulge in such a diversion might very well lead to disaster. "*Empty … canteens!*"

A sullen company of men dumped the contents of their supposed water containers onto the ground under the watchful eyes of their sergeants.

"Now … refill your canteens on the double … with *water* this time, please. Company dismissed!"

The fact he'd not ordered any company punishment had not gone unnoticed, and he received several furtive grins and nods in recognition of that fact.

Wednesday July 1, 1863, 7:30 p.m. – Gettysburg – Culp's Hill:

General Johnson's division had received its new marching orders from General Ewell, and Jubal thought them oddly indecisive: that they were to "take possession of Culp's Hill only if you find it unoccupied."

When they arrived at the base of the hill, just southeast of the town, it was already getting dark. But it was still light enough for Jubal to see the hill and to understand its significance; it was the easternmost piece of high ground overlooking the place where the Union Army was now encamped and digging in on Cemetery Hill just to the west. To Jubal's thinking, having control of Culp's Hill could spell the difference between victory and defeat for the Confederate Army, as it would allow them to bombard and attack the Union position from equally high ground. Otherwise, they'd be forced to fight an uphill battle—quite literally.

And yet ... General Ewell's strangely unaggressive orders ... When Jubal had spoken with Colonel Shriver about it, Shriver said he overheard Generals Johnson and Walker talking about it, and Johnson was complaining that Ewell hadn't just gone ahead and ordered the assault. Johnson said that General Jubal Early had argued in favor of the action, saying that they could either take the hill tonight, or pay for it in thousands of more lives later. But General Ewell was apparently unmoved by the argument.

And now Jubal had just been informed that the scouts had confirmed the Union was in fact occupying Culp's Hill and was digging in. So, per their orders, they were *not* to attempt to take possession tonight, but would instead withdraw and set up camp for the evening.

Jubal shook his head in consternation and prayed the Stonewall Brigade would not be the ones to have to pay those thousands of extra lives later. And then it occurred to him to wonder what Stonewall Jackson would've ordered under these same circumstances, were he still alive and in command. He was pretty sure he knew the answer.

That evening, as Jubal sat on his cot in his tent, he contemplated the great battle that had started that morning and was likely to continue growing ever larger and more destructive in the coming days as more units from both sides joined the fray. For the first time since his enlistment, he seriously considered the possibility that he might be killed in the coming action. And that thought made him consider the things he cared about in life, which inevitably led to thoughts of Evelyn. His desire and longing for her had never diminished, and, if anything, had grown ever stronger during their long, forced separation.

Now he feared he might never see her again, might never have the chance to see if a deeper, more meaningful relationship between them might be possible. So he picked up his pen, set his inkwell on the ground between his feet, took out a crumpled sheet of paper which he spread in his lap for lack of a table, and wrote:

July 1, 1863
Gettysburg, Pennsylvania

Dearest Evelyn,

We are in all probability on the eve of a terrible battle. The two contending armies lie close together and at any moment may commence the work of death.

Great results hang upon the issue of the battle. If we are victorious peace may follow. If not, we may look for the continuation of a long and fierce war.

Although we may be victorious many must fall, and I may be among that number. If it is the Lord's will, I trust I am prepared to go.

I wish for you to know, however, if the worst happens, that my only regret in life will be to never see you again, nor to ever again hear your voice. And that we may never have the opportunity to see where our friendship might possibly lead in the future.

I wish you continued good health and every happiness in life.

Your sincere friend,

Jubal Collins
1st Lt. 27th Virginia

∞）෭ധ∞）෭ധ∞）෭

Wednesday July 1, 1863, 9:00 p.m. – Gettysburg – Cemetery Hill:

Captain James Hawkins had two extra cots added to his tent in order to accommodate his unexpected but highly welcomed guests. It made for tight but happy accommodations, as the three men spent the evening lying on their bunks, swapping stories of their various adventures since they'd last been together more than two years earlier in Wheeling.

During a pause in the story telling, Hawkins suddenly chuckled, "You guys may be amused to hear what the men of the Seventh are saying about your arrival…"

"Oh, what's that?" Georgie rolled over on his cot and looked over at Hawkins, who now sported a grin.

"The word has gone 'round that 'two of Captain Chambers' legendary Indian fighters' have come to help the Seventh fight against Lee."

"*Legendary,* is it?" Jamie snorted a laugh.

"Legendary Indian fighters, hunh?" Georgie chuckled, "Well, at least *part* of it's true. What else they sayin', Hawkins?"

Hawkins shook his head, "Well, to hear them talk, now that you two have joined us, the battle's practically already won. They're saying there's no possible way the Seventh can lose now!"

The three shared a laugh.

But then Jamie's face became more serious, "If only it were that easy, lads … if only…"

∞）෭ധ∞）෭ധ∞）෭

Jubal was roused from a dark, frightful dream by the popping of musket fire. He sat up on his cot, but for a moment could not focus nor remember where he was. But outside, the call *"to arms, to arms!"* echoed across the camp, and the full, cold reality of his current circumstances came flooding back into his mind.

He stood and stretched, ignoring his sore, complaining limbs, then grabbed his hat, tunic, and gun belt. He stepped over to the tent flap, reached down to pull on his boots, then stepped out, briefly wondering if this might be his last day on earth.

After the occupation of Culp's Hill had been called off the previous evening, the Stonewall Brigade, along with the rest of General Johnson's division, had been relocated into the hilly rural region to the east of town. There, they'd bivouacked on one of the many farms that were interspersed between thickly wooded areas—this particular one owned by the Wolf family.

Once again, the Stonewall Brigade's experience and reliability backfired, ensuring they were assigned some of the most difficult and dangerous duty in the battle—this time defending the Army of Northern Virginia's left flank.

Guarding the flank was a job that by rights should've been handled by the Confederate cavalry, but General Jeb Stuart remained AWOL, to everyone's consternation. And it occurred to Jubal that General Lee had little faith in General Jenkins' cavalry, which had the reputation of being poorly trained and highly undisciplined; Jubal had heard several officers refer to them derisively as "mounted infantry" rather than actual cavalry.

So this morning, with the sun barely peeking above the horizon, the Stonewall Brigade formed up in line of battle and advanced into the trees to the order, *"As skirmishers … forward!"* to face whatever the Union Army saw fit to send at them.

As Jubal moved forward through the farm with his loaded rifle held across his chest, crossing the field with a thin line of men from the Twenty-Seventh Virginia, he continued to hear sporadic gunfire nearby—from the number of gun shots, he assumed it was only long-range sniping at their pickets, up to this point. But that was about to change with the arrival of the brigade's skirmishers.

Jubal's men moved from the pastureland into a wooded area only about a quarter mile wide. When they neared the edge of these woods, after which a wide field spread out for several hundred more yards, Jubal ordered his men to take cover near the edge of the trees and wait. Then he noticed well off to their left, about fifty yards into the field, an old stone farmhouse, and next to it a large barn. So he ordered a dozen of his men to sprint over and occupy these structures, preparing to target the enemy at long range from that direction.

Only a few minutes went by before a thin line of Union soldiers stepped out from the far tree line and came slowly across the field.

Jubal waited until the enemy soldiers were completely clear of the trees before giving the signal to fire, by aiming and firing his own rifle. His single shot was followed by a rapid crackling of musket fire right down the Confederate line.

Across the way, the Union soldiers immediately went to ground, then began returning fire by raising up in the grass, firing their muskets, then diving back down to reload while lying on their backs.

Jubal glanced over toward the farmhouse and was gratified to see multiple puffs of smoke rising from its windows, and also from the hayloft of the barn. These sharpshooters were now catching the Union skirmishers in the flank with enfilading fire.

The blue-clad soldiers were soon driven from the field. *First round to our side*, Jubal thought...

But he knew the day's fighting had only just begun.

めのぐ᪴のみのぐ᪴のみのぐの

Thursday July 2, 1863, 7:00 a.m. – Gettysburg – Cemetery Hill:

"What's this place called, anyway, Georgie?" James Hawkins took stock of the terrain where the Seventh had been positioned as a reserve unit at the back of the Gibraltar Brigade.

"We call it Zeigler's Grove." Georgie waved back toward the ridgeline to their left. "On account o' them big trees over yonder.

235

I reckon the place belonged to the Zeigler family once, but that was before my time. Guess the name just stuck.

"This hill down here we call Raffensperger's Hill, though I guess all the Union troops have taken to calling it Cemetery Hill, it bein' the town graveyard, with that big ol' brick arch at the gatehouse."

"And what about this ridgeline up above us?" Hawkins gestured to their left to where the hillside became steeper and rockier.

Jamie chuckled, "We don't have a name for that part, but … if this here's gonna be called Cemetery Hill, then I guess we can just call that *Cemetery Ridge.*"

"That works." Hawkins nodded and turned back to their front. "No sign of activity from our friends yet." Although they could hear the sounds of battle in the far distance—a smattering of rifle fire and the occasional thumping of artillery—there was still no action to their front, or anywhere they could see from their position. "Wonder how long we'll have to sit here in this hot sun. I expect it'll be another scorching hot day before the end."

Jamie snorted a laugh. "*Hot?* This here ain't *hot*, boyo … You shoulda been with us out in Texas … now *that* was hot!"

"He's right about that," Georgie grinned, "I remember a time we'd been out on patrol for three or four days, had emptied our canteens and could find no water. My face felt like it was on fire, and my throat felt like I'd swallowed a mouthful o' cotton. We had to squeeze the juice outta cactus to survive. Nasty stuff … No, sir … this don't feel hot at all after what we been through."

"Glad to hear you're enjoying it." Hawkins rolled his eyes and returned their grins with a rueful one of his own. "But seein's how I'm *not* a 'legendary Indian fighter,' I reckon this is plenty hot enough for me. I just hope the damned rebs get on with it soon, so we aren't just sitting here frying all day with nothing to do."

Jamie's grin turned to a frown, "Careful what you wish for, boyo … Careful what you wish for."

ᏸᏓᏒᏣᏸᏛᏸᏓᏒᏣᏸᏛᏸᏓᏒᏣᏸ

Walters stood on a tall rock, gazing through his binoculars out toward Culp's Hill. He'd been watching the progress of the Confederate assault on the hill for more than an hour.

And what he saw convinced him that the Yankees were going to eventually win the battle at Gettysburg. General Lee, for whatever reasons of his own, had decided to enter a winner-take-all battle against a well-dug-in, well-equipped, and more amply manned army which currently held the high ground. *What is the man thinking?* he wondered. *Who knows ... But I want no part of it. And from what I can determine, Chambers isn't even here. I'll not waste my men on a doomed battle and end up with no command, or worse, rotting in some federal prison. No, never that! It's time to head back to Virginia while we still can.*

Fortunately, with General Jenkins wounded and confined to his tent, Walters had been able to avoid him and his couriers, and thus ensure that he never received orders requiring him to take some action he'd prefer not to take—such as actually engaging the enemy.

And the men under his command were none the wiser. Only Captain Roberts knew they'd not received any orders from the general since shortly after their arrival at Gettysburg. But he seemed to agree with Walters that discretion was the better part of valor, in this case.

Walters lowered the binoculars, stepped down from the rock and approached his second in command, "Roberts ... new orders. We're to move out to the west ... screen the army from that direction, in case the Yankees attempt some sort of ... roundabout flanking maneuver with their cavalry."

Roberts nodded, and a slight grin betrayed his reaction to these new "orders," that had clearly *not* come from General Jenkins. "Seems prudent, sir. I'll get the men mounted up."

Two hours later, the battalion had worked its way around the north side of town and was now ranging out to the west. And though the sounds of battle echoed in the distance away to the south, the woods in this area were mostly devoid of any activity.

Walters figured they'd move a few more miles to the west before looking for a suitable route that would take them south into Maryland and eventually home to Virginia. He had briefly considered trying to somehow obtain Union uniforms so they could pass through the northern states unhindered. But he'd decided it was unnecessary; likely any Yankee units in the area were now drawn into the fighting at Gettysburg. Except, ironically, Chambers, whose location he'd been unable to determine despite having interrogated a number of Union prisoners. Nobody seemed to know anything about the Twelfth West Virginia, even men from various other West Virginia regiments. It was frustrating and confounding, but there was seemingly nothing he could do about it.

They were passing through a thickly wooded area on a narrow, winding path when they suddenly came face-to-face with a group of Union soldiers walking along the trail. The soldiers were unarmed, and immediately raised their hands in surrender.

"What're y'all doing out here?" Walters glared down at the first man in line.

"We, uh … we got ourselves separated from our regiment, sir. And was … uh … thinkin' to just head on home…"

Walters nodded, "*Deserters…*"

The man he'd been interrogating looked down at his shoes and appeared embarrassed, but didn't bother denying the accusation.

Walters briefly considered what to do with these men. He had no desire to take them prisoner; prisoners were of no use to him.

"Captain, we have no time for prisoners, and since these men are cowards and deserters—no longer legitimate enemy combatants—we are under no obligation to take them into custody."

Captain Roberts nodded, but said nothing.

The young Union soldier Walters had been speaking to seemed pleased by this statement, likely thinking they'd be allowed to continue on their way.

Walters gazed at him, expressionlessly, for a long moment, "Captain … give the order … Shoot down these men."

"*Sir?*"

Walters turned and locked eyes with the captain, "Do you have a *problem* with my orders, Captain?"

Roberts was wide-eyed for a moment. "Uh ... no, sir.

"You heard the colonel, men. Shoot down these Yankee cowards!"

The Union soldiers screamed and tried to run off into the woods, scrambling in different directions. But multiple gunshots rang out, and soon all the blue-clad soldiers lay dead on the ground.

Walters gazed at the bodies a moment, then nodded, "Let's move out, Captain."

ॐॐॐॐॐॐॐॐॐॐ

Thursday July 2, 1863, 12:00 noon – Gettysburg – Brinkerhoff's Ridge:

As the morning wore on, the Stonewall Brigade's skirmish line became hard-pressed to hold back the mounting pressure from the Union forces being sent against it. Shortly after nine o'clock, one of Jubal's forward scouts returned and sank down on the ground next to him, exhausted and covered in sweat and dirt.

"Lieutenant, it's bad, sir ... Made it to a high spot and climbed a tree ... I seen three different Union formations gathered to our front, not more'n two miles out. Division-sized they was, and sendin' out row after row of skirmishers."

Jubal nodded but could think of nothing to say. Donaldson was one of his most reliable scouts, and not prone to exaggeration as some others were, so it was unlikely he was mistaken. It meant that the Stonewall Brigade was now facing off against Union skirmishers with a differential of ten to one.

And though Jubal's men fought like tigers, giving ground only grudgingly and then sometimes regaining it again with a sharp counterattack as circumstances allowed, still he knew they were being pushed inexorably inward, and if something didn't change soon, the Confederate left flank would be turned, and the entire battle might be lost.

But then, at just a few minutes after ten, Union trumpets sounded in the distance. At first, Jubal feared it was the signal for an all-out assault by the Union infantry divisions, and that his command would soon be annihilated. He was about to order a fallback, but then he listened more closely. He realized with a shock that the trumpets were not signaling an advance, but rather a recall. Within minutes, the Union skirmishers they'd been dueling all morning simply vanished.

Jubal's hopes for at least a brief respite from the fighting were quickly dashed, however, when another of his men reported that a Union cavalry division had just arrived to their front, had dismounted, and was digging in on Brinkerhoff's Ridge out to the far left of the Stonewall Brigade's skirmish line, once again threatening to turn their flank.

Minutes later, General Walker relayed orders that they were to drive the federal cavalry off the ridge as quickly as possible, that the brigade was needed elsewhere—apparently General Ewell had finally ordered the assault on Culp's Hill, and he needed more men for the task. Jubal shook his head; they were being asked to fight one dangerous, difficult battle—and win it quickly—just so they'd be available to fight another. *Some reward for accomplishing a hard, hazardous task!*

The brigade turned and moved off to carry out its new orders, trudging through the trees to the base of the hill. Jubal could see a low stone wall at the crest of the ridge and assumed this was where the Union troopers were now ensconced.

He scowled; this would be a tough nut to crack, as the slope was mostly devoid of cover, having been logged at some point. The good news was that the Confederate infantry had longer, more powerful rifles than the Union cavalry, who typically carried the smaller, short-range carbines and pistols. He prayed it would be enough advantage to make the difference.

The order to attack came down the line, and he moved his men forward to obey. The lack of cover soon had them crawling up the hill on their bellies, rising up only long enough to fire their guns, drop back down, and roll onto their backs to reload. Jubal couldn't ever remember a time he so much wished to be thinner, just to lay flatter to the ground.

Then, as a bullet impacted just in front of him, showering him with dirt and rocks that stuck to his sweat-soaked face and uniform, Jubal decided this was going to be a *very* long day.

Thursday July 2, 1863, 4:00 p.m. – Gettysburg – Cemetery Hill:

Georgie, Jamie, Hawkins, and the rest of the Seventh West Virginia had endured a long, hot, monotonous day dug in near Ziegler's Grove when without warning a tremendous, concussive blast knocked them to the ground and covered them with dirt and rocks.

Hawkins sat up, brushed himself off, and looked to his comrades.

Jamie was on his hands and knees, spitting dirt from his mouth, but appeared to be unharmed.

Georgie sat with his back to their earthworks, rubbing his head, but he met eyes with Hawkins and nodded to indicate he too was not seriously injured.

When Hawkins placed his hand on the ground, preparing to rise, he felt something sharp stab him in the hand and he flinched. Gazing at his wounded hand, he saw a laceration, as from a knife, with a thin line of blood streaming out. He looked down and saw a jagged, twisted chunk of metal with a shiny piece of broken wood attached. Examining it more closely, he was shocked to realize the thing was a foot-long piece of what had once been a rifle.

He heard shouts for the surgeon coming down the line a few yards away, and he stood to see that one of the privates was down. Hawkins grimaced when he realized the man had been impaled by a flying bayonet with half of a broken off rifle still attached.

A short distance away from the earthworks, he saw a smoldering crater where an artillery shell had impacted, with bits and pieces of broken rifles laying all around the pit. He guessed that the shell had landed right on top of a stack of rifles, sending deadly shards in all directions. Miraculously, there had been few injuries, and nobody had been killed outright.

241

Several more high-explosive rounds burst in their vicinity, but the Seventh did not appear to be the intended target, likely just collateral damage from poorly aimed enemy artillery fire directed at other Union formations farther up the hill. The men of the Seventh hunkered down and stayed under cover while the sporadic bombardment lasted.

A few hours later, as the sun was moving toward the horizon in the west, they heard what sounded like a major enemy assault off to the northeast of their position, but they could see nothing from where they were.

But then, even as twilight darkened the battlefield and the clamor of battle was so intense they could scarcely converse, there came a moment that James Hawkins would never forget. On a rise above their position, a rider suddenly appeared, lit by the last rays of the setting sun. Hawkins realized with a start that this was Major General Hancock himself, now in command of their entire sector, including the Gibraltar Brigade, of which the Seventh was a part.

General Hancock cupped his hands and shouted, "Men of the Gibraltar Brigade, your fellow countrymen are sorely beset and in grave peril for their lives. This is the hour of our nation's greatest need; the time to rise up and stand tall, to show your mettle, and to prove your true devotion! *Fix bayonets, men ... and follow me!*"

His horse reared even as he swept out his saber. Then he turned and led them down the hill, toward the growing conflagration. With a great shout, the three regiments of the Gibraltar Brigade leapt up and rushed after him.

After the initial surge of excitement, the brigade's officers quickly formed them up into an organized column that moved at the double-quick down the hill following after General Hancock. At the Cemetery Hill gatehouse, the column split in two, with the Seventh West Virginia moving to the left and the other regiments to the right. They crossed a gravel roadway, then made a left-face into line of battle.

The three young captains exchanged meaningful looks and nods before facing to the front once more. Hawkins held his saber in his right hand and his revolver in his left, while Georgie and

Jamie each carried a rifle with fixed bayonet, having left their sabers back at the Twelfth's camp with Colonel Chambers for safe keeping—along with their highly prized, and now much missed, Henry repeating rifles.

General Hancock rode his horse out in front of the brigade once again, though now the twilit battlefield had become so dark they could barely make him out only a few yards in front of them. Hancock raised his sword, then chopped it downward, shouting, "*Charge!*"

The Gibraltar Brigade rushed forward as one in a desperate bayonet charge to drive back the enemy and save their severely beset fellows. Hawkins shouted wordlessly as he ran, with no idea what he was about to face, but he assumed it would likely involve overwhelming odds against them. He suffered a sudden premonition that he was running straight to his own death, and yet he never slackened his pace.

છૐલ૭ૐ૭ૐ૭ૐ૭ૐ૭ૐ૭ૐ

Thursday July 2, 1863, 8:30 p.m. – Gettysburg – Cemetery Hill:

As he closed upon the scene, Hawkins could scarcely make sense of the swirling maelstrom he was witnessing: in the near darkness, blue-clad Union artillerymen fought a hand-to-hand, free-for-all battle against gray-accoutered rebel infantrymen wielding bayonets and occasionally firing rifles. The artillerymen fought courageously with whatever they had at hand—handspikes, rammers, and even one soldier who Hawkins watched brain a Confederate with a large rock—but clearly their plight was becoming more desperate by the moment.

The Gibraltar Brigade crashed into the melee like a great wave upon the shore. James Hawkins found himself in the midst of a chaotic, nightmarish fight so obscured by darkness that it was difficult to tell friend from foe.

Hawkins slashed and hacked with his saber, and occasionally used the pistol. But even as he pushed forward toward the beleaguered Union artillerymen, Georgie and Jamie were ever in advance of him, cutting down their adversaries with bayonet, rifle butt, or pistol shot, in a display of ferocity and efficiency that was a grim pleasure to witness.

Guess that's what legendary Indian fighters look like in action, flashed through Hawkins' mind and he grinned, even as he knocked aside a bayonet thrust with his saber and fired his revolver into another man's face at point-blank.

As he pushed and hacked, it came to Hawkins' mind that this was no modern battle at all, rather an ancient Greek hoplite contest, Spartans versus Athenians, pushing with shields and prodding with spears, muscle versus muscle, and steel against steel.

The battle hung in the balance for several agonizing moments, and Hawkins' right arm began to ache from the strain of wielding the heavy saber. He was beginning to wonder how much longer he could keep it up before being forced to succumb to the inevitable.

But the weight of the Gibraltar Brigade's all-out assault had tipped the scales in the Union's favor; suddenly, the rebels were disengaging and falling back, moving swiftly down the hill.

A hundred yards down the slope, the Confederates attempted to regroup and take a stand behind a rock wall. But Colonel Shriver, commander of the Seventh, shouted for the regiment to rally and form up in line of battle. He ordered a full rifle volley targeting the rebels behind the rock wall. With a tremendous blast that momentarily lit up the night and covered the hillside in gun smoke, the Confederates were driven from the wall, and scrambled back down the hill in disarray.

The Union line had held—thanks to General Hancock's timely intervention and the Gibraltar Brigade's gritty heroics—but only for the moment … Though Hawkins breathed a sigh of relief, he knew that the battle was far from over, and the rebels were far from defeated.

ℬↃ☾ℛℭℬↄℬↃ☾ℛℭℬↄℬↃ☾ℛℭℬ

The Union cavalrymen who'd dug in at the top of the ridge had proven stubbornly resistant to the Stonewall Brigade's attempts to drive them off. What was supposed to be a quick charge to overrun the Union position had devolved into an hours-long, back-and-forth slugfest, with counterattack following attack, and push being equally answered by shove, and neither side able to gain any ground.

And as the sun had nearly set, Jubal realized with a growing sense of frustration and futility that he was right back in the same spot at the base of the hill that he'd been at the beginning. He scrambled back behind the remains of a broken tree so he could sit up and dig his binoculars out from where he'd stuffed them inside his shirt for safekeeping. After a quick rub down of the lenses—an act rendered nearly useless by the fact that everything Jubal wore was thickly coated in dirt—he slipped around the tree trunk and took another look at the enemy's position.

As he gazed intently, he heard heavy footsteps and a deep, resonant voice behind him, "What's the situation, Lieutenant?"

Assuming it was one of the privates come up to quiz him, he didn't bother looking up. "Damned discouraging, is what. These Yank cavalry are a stubborn, determined lot. Gotta hand it to 'em, though; they've taken everything we've thrown at 'em and keep right on givin' it straight back!"

"Hmm … have you tried an oblique attack up that left flank?"

"Well *yes*, of course I…" Then it suddenly occurred to Jubal: *that* was not the type of question a private would *ever* ask.

He lowered the glasses and looked up, then suffered a shock. An elegantly uniformed major general stood over him, gazing up at the hillside.

Jubal sat up and saluted, "*General!* General Stuart, sir. Sorry, sir, didn't know it was you." Though he'd never been this close to the man before, there was no mistaking the style and bearing of Major General Jeb Stuart, commander of the army's cavalry.

"Never mind that, Lieutenant, you've got a battle to fight and no time for entertaining generals. Do carry on, mister."

"Yes, sir!"

Jubal turned back toward the hill, once again examining it through his binoculars.

After a few moments, it occurred to him to see if the general had any other thoughts about dislodging the stubborn enemy, "Sir … I was thinking … what if we … *sir?*"

He turned back to look at the general, but Stuart was gone. And then, despite the lack of immediate help, he felt a sudden sense of relief as the full impact of what he'd just witnessed hit home: General Stuart, with the entire Confederate cavalry, had returned from their long and unexpected absence. This was good news beyond measure, and it also meant the Stonewall Brigade would no longer carry the dangerous, difficult, and tedious task of guarding the army's left flank.

Then he suffered a sobering thought: with the arrival of the cavalry, the Stonewall Brigade would soon be freed up to assault Culp's Hill, a thing General Early had said would likely cost thousands of lives.

ﭤﭤﭤﭤﭤﭤﭤﭤﭤﭤﭤﭤﭤ

Friday, July 3, 1863, 4:00 a.m. – Gettysburg – Culp's Hill:

Jubal and the other men of the Stonewall Brigade had little opportunity to sleep at their new camp at the base of Culp's Hill; with only the slightest hint of dawn in the eastern sky at four o'clock in the morning, Union artillery opened fire with some two dozen guns in a furious bombardment of solid shot, high explosive shells, and cannister that screamed, exploded, and tore through the woods that contained the massed forces of the Confederate army gathered there.

Jubal and his men hunkered down behind trees, stumps, or in any available depression in the earth, covering their heads against deadly flying splinters. Glancing up at the hill, Jubal's eyes were dazzled by the flames leaping up from the big Union guns, as if the very earth itself were on fire.

In the light of the blasts, he noted the general terrain of the hill for the first time. He estimated the crest of the hill at some two-

246

hundred feet above the creek that ran along its eastern base where he had been camped. Its slopes were heavily timbered with oak and chestnut, though there was no undergrowth. The steep slope was broken by various worn and rounded rock outcroppings and boulders, which Jubal imagined as hundreds of elephants sleeping under the trees. The Union earthworks dominated the hillside about halfway to the top. This was an obstacle the Confederates would have to overcome.

When the Union guns fell silent, Confederate forces attacked with such fury—while screaming out the rebel yell—that any idea the Union corps had of launching an assault of their own was likely abandoned, as it was all they could handle to prevent being overrun by the oncoming rebels.

But a sheet of flame leapt up from the Union lines, and a thunderous noise and smoke followed, as the federals let loose a tremendous rifle volley that checked the rebel advance and sent the southerners scrambling for cover behind any available rock or tree, from which they quickly returned fire.

A half hour later, the Stonewall Brigade was ordered to advance again, this time advancing up the hill to other Confederate forces behind a section of Union earthworks that had been captured the previous day.

From this relatively protected position, the Stonewall Brigade traded rifle volleys with the federals up the hill for several hours until ordered to renew the assault on the Union breastworks. Jubal risked a quick glance up over their own protective log wall and noted the Union line was some thirty or forty feet higher up than their present position, and a hundred yards or so away.

He met eyes with a grim-looking Sergeant Evans, who nodded and reloaded his rifle. Up and down the line, men braced themselves for the coming assault. When the order came to advance, three brigades moved out as one. They were met with a tremendous barrage of Minni balls and explosive artillery shells, such as Jubal had never before seen in the war, despite the many battles they'd already endured. The very air seemed alive with deadly missiles screaming past, and as Jubal ran forward, keeping his head as low as he could, he could not imagine how any of them would survive this terrible firestorm.

But somehow, he found himself slamming against the logs of the Union breastworks, along with hundreds of other Confederate soldiers. He paused a moment to catch his breath, then turned and attempted to scramble over the top.

But the Union infantry rose up on top of the wall and began pouring down rifle fire onto the rebel troops massed below. Bodies began to pile up, until bugles sounded the recall. Jubal scrambled to obey, falling back several dozen yards to a point where a rock outcropping provided cover. He was shocked to find Sergeant Evans next to him, already rising up to fire his rifle. Jubal had feared that none of his men had lived through the deadly assault. He looked around and saw that most of the brigade had somehow survived, and had taken cover to return fire on the federals.

Another hour of continuous fighting went by, and Jubal was now running out of ammunition. They'd long since used all they'd carried with them, and he and Sergeant Evans had already risked their lives several times crawling out on their bellies to search the dead for spare ammunition. But now, that too had been exhausted. So Jubal cupped his hands and called out for volunteers to go back for more ammunition.

A half dozen fearless young men answered the call, leaping up and sprinting back down hillside, zigzagging and ducking behind anything that might provide cover in an attempt to avoid the enemy's sharpshooters as bullets impacted all around them.

ഇരുജ്ഞരുജ്ഞരുഇരുജ്ഞരുജ്ഞരുഇരുജ്ഞരു

Friday, July 3, 1863, 1:00 p.m. – Gettysburg – Cemetery Hill:

After enduring another long, hot, tedious morning in the earthworks on Cemetery Hill with only the sounds of distant fighting off to the east, Georgie, Jamie, and James Hawkins witnessed one of the most awe-inspiring, spectacular, and frightful scenes of the entire war. At just after one o'clock in the afternoon, the massed rebel artillery—more than 150 guns

248

positioned in a wide arc over two miles long—opened fire on the Union Army.

Fortunately for the three young captains, the Seventh was not specifically targeted by the barrage, so they were able to witness the magnificent battle scene with little fear for their own safety.

Hawkins had never seen anything like it, and figured this bombardment must be the biggest ever seen in North America. And then … it suddenly doubled in scope as the Union artillery answered with an equal number of guns. The deafening thunder, dazzling fire, and swirling clouds of smoke from more than three hundred big guns dueling over the battlefield was exhilarating and mind numbing.

And Hawkins now had enough battle experience to know what was coming next: once the rebel bombardment had run its course, an all-out infantry assault was sure to follow…

ℬↄℭ℧ℬↄℭ℧ℬↄℭ℧ℬↄℭ℧

Friday, July 3, 1863, 2:00 p.m. – Gettysburg – Culp's Hill:

Restocked with ammunition, the Stonewall Brigade was pulled back and shifted four hundred yards to the right of their earlier position, replacing another brigade, which had been on the front line since the first shots were fired in the morning. Jubal looked up toward the federal line and winced; from this new position, the Yankee's breastworks were even higher than those they'd faced in the morning, and the ground in front was much steeper. They were also now closer to the middle of the Union line, so presumably the Yankee defense would be even stiffer.

When the order came down to advance, Jubal already held a deep sense of dread, which would soon manifest with the imminent assault. As the Twenty-Seventh moved forward, a long row of Union muskets leaned over the wall above, aimed at the approaching Confederates, and opened fire.

Jubal, who had on many occasions been exposed to devastating artillery and infantry fire, including some of the most intense he'd ever experienced earlier that morning, quickly realized he had never before encountered anything so frightful and so destructive to human life as what he was now encountering. Every battle he'd previously fought was mere child's play in compare. The roar of cannon and rifle fire was deafening, and the dense, swirling smoke gave the impression that the Stonewall Brigade was assaulting hell itself.

Men were cut down in swaths, and those not hit by rifle and artillery fire in front of them were felled by devastating enfilading fire from the side.

The attack soon stalled, only halfway to its objective. Men took to the ground, using whatever cover they could find. Jubal watched a private next to him duck down behind a rock, followed immediately by a sound like a hammer hitting a chunk of meat; Jubal looked over and witnessed the back of the man's head explode as a bullet made its exit upon impacting his face.

The wounded and the dead lay all around Jubal's position, and he looked over to his right to see Sergeant Evans lying just six feet away. He'd been hit in the chest, and he gazed up at Jubal as if imploring him for help. But there's was nothing Jubal could do for him, and after a few moments, Evans shuddered, closed his eyes, and never opened them again.

But Jubal looked down the slope and saw another surge of Confederate soldiers coming up the hill. Thinking they might have a chance to make it, he joined the charge when they reached his position. But this line too was subject to ferocious and deadly fire from above, and eventually faltered just fifteen yards short of the Union defensive works.

Now unable to advance or retreat, Jubal and those around him took shelter behind rocks and tree stumps and hunkered down, trying to keep from exposing themselves to the deadly fire raining down upon them.

Someone raised a piece of white cloth for a flag of surrender, but others of the Confederate men threw rocks at him to make him lower it. But Jubal could see the writing on the wall; with a large group of men pinned down and helpless, it was only a matter of time before surrender would be the only option. And Jubal had no intentions of sitting out the war as a prisoner.

So he discarded his rifle and his rucksack, lay down on his belly, and slowly crawled back down the hill. He had decided that whatever else might happen, whether he lived or died, his battle this day was over.

✲✦✲✦✲✦✲✦✲✦✲✦✲

Friday, July 3, 1863, 2:30 p.m. – Gettysburg – Cemetery Hill:

Georgie, Jamie, and Hawkins gazed over to the northeast of their position, where for the better part of an hour they'd watched transfixed as the rebel army slowly, inexorably advanced despite being subjected to extreme duress by the Union gunners.

Jamie let out a long, low whistle, "Damn me if that ain't one helluva gunfight … The biggest I ever seen."

"Yep," Georgie continued to pan the scene through his binoculars, "seems like old Bobby Lee was fixin' to win or lose it all on one big ol' roll of the dice. Looks like the whole damned rebel army is marching right into the teeth of ours."

Hawkins lowered his binoculars and turned to gaze out to the north and west of the Seventh's current position. He again raised the binoculars to his eyes and panned slowly across the enemy-held ground. "Still nothing stirring to our front."

"Seems like we ain't been invited to the party this time." Jamie continued watching the rebel attack that was now only a few hundred yards from the Union front lines, at a place where two stone fences met at a ninety-degree angle, creating a sharp outward bulge in the federal line.

Then, as they watched, thousands of rebel soldiers jumped up from the roadbed with fixed bayonets, let loose the rebel yell, and came charging at the angle where the Union fences met.

And though the rebels were taking a horrific beating, it looked like they just might have enough momentum to breach the Union lines. If they did, they'd split Meade's forces, and then the battle would quickly devolve into every unit for itself, much as it had during the disastrous attempted Union breakout from Winchester.

Then, to James Hawkins' dismay, the Union regiment guarding the fence-angle salient abandoned their position in a sudden, panicked stream, leaving a large gap in the federal line. It was then he glimpsed General Hancock through the thick, swirling smoke, up at the front lines, sitting tall in the saddle despite the raging battle. He seemed to be attempting to rally the troops to fill the sudden gap.

Jamie looked over at his companions and scowled, "I never much cared for just sittin' back and watchin' when a fight was goin' on..."

Georgie nodded, "That's what I always liked about you, Jamie; ever since we was ornery little boys, you never once shied from a fight, even when they was much older and bigger."

Jamie nodded and gazed back down at the action, a grim frown creasing his brow.

James Hawkins looked back to his left to see if he could see Colonel Shriver, that he might convince him to take action to help General Hancock. But the intervening trees and terrain prevented him from seeing the rest of the regiment. Company C was in a sector of their own at the moment, on the far-right flank of the Seventh. He turned and met eyes with Georgie and Jamie for a moment, as the three shared a serious look.

Hawkins nodded, then turned, cupped his hands to his mouth, and yelled out, *"Company will fix bayonets, and follow me at the double-quick!"*

ഇഇരുൽഇഇരുൽഇഇരുൽ

Friday, July 3, 1863, 2:45 p.m. – Gettysburg – Cemetery Hill:

General Hancock rode his horse toward the sudden breach in the Union lines that was about to be penetrated by the rebels. But as he crested a low rise overlooking the disputed angle of rock walls, something hit him like a hammer just below his belt on the right side. For a moment, he fought to stay in the saddle, and to steady his startled mount. He glanced down and saw that his saddle horn had been shot clean away. *A close call*, he thought.

Then he turned to see where he might gather troops to fill the gap in his line.

But as he turned, a searing pain racked his body, emanating from the place where he'd felt the blow near his belt buckle. He searched with his hand, and it came away wet and red. *Not now! Not now ... please, dear God ... they cannot spare me. I must not leave them now...*

And then his staff officers appeared next to him. He'd left them behind when he saw the gap suddenly form in his lines, and now they'd caught up after running down the hill after him.

Captain Snyder was the first to arrive, stopping with his hands on his knees, panting hard, straining to catch his breath, "What ... what's the status, General? *General!* You're hit, sir!"

"Yes ... I know I'm hit ... *damn it!*"

"Here, sir ... let me help you down from your horse," Snyder reached out to take Hancock's arm.

But Hancock shook him off, "Not now, Snyder. Not until the battle is decided. I must not be seen leaving the field."

"But, sir..." Snyder looked up at his commander with a pale, frighted expression.

But Hancock ignored him, gazing back toward the fighting. He was gratified to see the men on either side of the gap resisting furiously in a clash of rifle fire, bayonets, and even bare fists, fighting to prevent a complete collapse of the line. But rebels were now pouring through the gap and had already seized several big guns. They were busily turning the guns around that they might be used against the Union forces.

And then, to his shock, Hancock saw his old friend, General Armistead, saber in hand, leading the Confederate charge, ordering the guns being turned.

Hancock's head began to swim, and he felt he could no longer stay in the saddle. Strong hands reached up and grabbed him as Captain Snyder and the other staff officers helped him from the saddle and laid him on the ground.

"No ... no ... sit me up, at least ... I must see the battle," Hancock coughed.

So his men dutifully sat him up, and held him in the upright position, even as they attempted to bind up his wound. And as he viewed the center of the action, a group of several hundred Union soldiers came rushing forward past him, and with a yell they plunged into the breach, bayonets thrust forward, fighting hand-to-hand with the rebel forces there. To his surprise, Hancock recognized among them the two young captains from the Twelfth West Virginia, Thompson and O'Brien, who had helped him draw up maps of the battlefield two days earlier.

And then, even as everything around him began to swirl and fade, he witnessed, to his everlasting horror and sorrow, Captain Jamie O'Brien point his revolver at General Lewis Armistead's chest and pull the trigger. Armistead collapsed to the ground.

With their leader down, the Confederate breakthrough quickly collapsed, and those left alive withdrew from the breach and joined the desperate retreat of rebel soldiers back down the hillside. Lee's assault was over.

♔ ♕ ♖ ♗ ♔ ♕ ♖ ♗ ♔ ♕ ♖

Jamie O'Brien had seen General Hancock being lifted from his saddle even as they charged past to attack the rebels in the gap. So as soon as the rebel general went down and the gap was secured, he grabbed Georgie and Hawkins and rushed back to check on General Hancock.

When they arrived, the general was lying on the ground, a folded tunic under his head and one of his staff officers pressing a bandage into an oozing wound at his pelvis.

Jamie stepped over and looked down at the general. To his surprise, Hancock's eyes were open, and he seemed to be aware. He gazed up at Jamie with sudden recognition.

"O'Brien!" Hancock rasped.

"Yes, General. Captain O'Brien again, sir. Please rest easy, General, the surgeons are on their way, I'm sure…" He looked up at Captain Snyder, who nodded.

But Hancock raised his head and frowned up at Jamie, "O'Brien … you killed my friend…"

254

"I *what?*" Jamie looked over at Georgie and Hawkins, who both just shrugged. Jamie figured the general must be hallucinating due to the pain from his severe injury.

"The Confederate General ... Lewis Armistead ... my dear friend ... *you killed him.*"

Jamie's eyes went wide with a sudden understanding, but he looked down at the general and shook his head, "No, sir. I never killed no *friend* of yours. I did, however, kill a rebel general who was about to overrun your command, sir ... and to slaughter a whole lot o' your good and brave soldiers."

The general nodded, then laid back and closed his eyes. A surgeon arrived with two privates carrying a stretcher. They loaded the general on the stretcher and carried him away to the hospital.

Jamie gazed back down the hill and saw the enemy formations streaming back toward Seminary Ridge in disarray. Lee's gamble on an all-out assault had failed. The Union Army had held, victorious.

He had a sudden strong feeling that this was likely the farthest Lee's army would ever get in the North—their high-water mark, so to speak. *After this, it's the Union's turn to take the battle to the South, I'm thinkin'. And this time, God willing, we'll put an end to it, for good and all!*

CHAPTER 10. RACE TO THE RIVER

"The men now know that
Lee's Army is not invincible
and that the Army of the Potomac can
win a victory if it is allowed to."
- Augustus Van Dyke
Fourteenth Indiana Infantry

Friday, July 3, 1863 – Bedford, Pennsylvania:

Colonel Chambers received orders to march his brigade at first light on July third, headed to Gettysburg to join up with the Army of the Potomac, where he'd temporarily be under the command of Major General Meade. Nathan wasn't clear about what had happened to General Hooker, but he took it for a positive change, given Hooker's less than stellar record as commander. Meade had a reasonably good reputation, but his ability to command an army of this size was still a big unknown.

And though it wasn't mentioned in the orders, Nathan had to assume Meade had located Lee's army and was even now conducting operations against him. But information was maddeningly scarce concerning what was happening. Once again, he found himself in the uncomfortable position of blindly obeying marching orders with little idea of the goal or what he might encounter on the march. As was his habit, he ordered a widely spread screen of scouts, videttes, and cavalry surrounding his brigade as it marched.

From Bedford, they first passed back through Bloody Run, then continued on a few miles past the small town of Breezewood, where they camped for the night in a drizzling rain. At dawn, they were on the march again, with Nathan anxious to push forward as quickly as they could. So he drove the men harder than he normally would have, despite the worsening weather making the roads ever muddier.

As they passed through McConnellsburg in the late afternoon, one of the foot soldiers came trotting up to him where he walked at the front of the column, leading Millie. The soldier snapped a salute, then fell in beside him. "Private Johnson, sir, Sammy Johnson, 116th Ohio, Company D."

"Johnson…" Nathan returned the salute.

"Sir, I found this in the street as we marched. Showed it to the sergeant, and he sent me to the colonel, who said I should bring it to you, sir, straightaway." He handed Nathan a wet, dirty, torn scrap of paper that clearly had been torn from a newspaper.

Nathan glanced at it and turned it over to see both sides, then looked up at the private questioningly.

"Sorry, sir … that's all there was of it," the private shrugged. Then he reached over and pointed at something on the page, "Read it, sir … uh, I mean … if you'd care to read it, sir, I believe you might find it … *interesting.*"

Nathan looked to where the private was pointing. The headline was torn off and mud was splattered on the paper, but he could still read portions of it:

> *…great battle, at small town of Gettysb … with Union forces under Maj. Gen. Meade … ickett-led charge … driven back at great loss. Casualties extremely high … sides. Gen. Lee's … killed or wounded … left the field with … cavalry in pursuit. Details unknown at presstime but … pray for the Union soldi…*

Nathan handed the scrap of paper to Tom who walked next to him, and they shared a dark look. Then Nathan turned to the private, "Thank you, Johnson; you've done well. And tell your sergeant I thank him for sending you straightaway."

"So … what now?" Tom handed the paper back to Nathan who stuck it in his pocket.

"I figure we'll camp at Loudon tonight and see if they have a working telegraph. Hopefully we can gain some more news about this battle there."

"But, sir … Georgie and Jamie were at Gettysburg…" Tom's brow held a concerned frown.

Nathan nodded, "Of that I am *painfully* aware, Tom. I have already said a prayer for their safety, and I'd recommend you do the same."

"That I will, sir," Tom answered.

They reached Loudon by nightfall, where they made camp once again. Nathan went looking for a telegraph operator and was able to get through to General Schenck, who confirmed there had been a great battle at Gettysburg, that Meade had been victorious and Lee had been driven off but not destroyed. The Army of the Potomac was regrouping, preparing to pursue the enemy.

Nathan's new orders were to discontinue his march to Gettysburg and turn south to Mercersburg, there to await further orders.

When they arrived at Mercersburg midday in a driving rain, they saw the first physical indications that indeed a great battle had been waged; as the brigade slogged into town on the muddy road, they could see a freight train being unloaded. It was filled with hundreds of wounded rebel prisoners, most of whom were being carried off to makeshift hospitals.

Nathan once again fired off a telegram to General Schenck, but the orders he received back were, to his mind, vague and subject to broad interpretation. He handed the telegram across the camp table to Tom, who read:

> *Baltimore, Md.*
> *June 5, 1863*
>
> *Col. Nathaniel Chambers*
> *Mercersburg, Pa.:*
>
> *Lee's column moves south in strength. Gen. Meade pursues. Expect rebel cavalry activity your sector, screening Lee's march. Prepare brigade for action and proceed as exigencies allow and dictate.*
>
> *Maj. Gen. R.C. Schenck,*
> *Commander, Middle Military Dist.*

Tom snorted a laugh, then looked back up at Nathan, "Not very helpful, is he?"

"No, he's not." Nathan chewed on a cigar and stroked the whiskers on his chin, a thoughtful look on his brow. "On the other hand..."

"What're you thinking, sir?"

"I'm thinking ... the general has just given me a free hand to do whatever I damned well please."

Nathan now sported a broad grin, which Tom immediately reflected, "I believe you're right, sir. That being the case, what are your orders, sir?"

"We march at first light, that's what. Now ... pull out those maps and let's figure out where in the hell we're going."

ಶಃಯಃಞಃಶಃಯಃಞಃಶಃಯಃಞ

Monday, July 6, 1863 – Hagerstown, Maryland:

"What did you find, Billy?"

"An enemy convoy, Captain. Hundreds of wagons, stretching for a dozen or more miles. The tail end is just a few miles to the west of us. Mostly wounded men in the wagons, I think, though some may hold food and other supplies."

"And the escort?"

"Cavalry only. A brigade, more or less, guarding the rear. They are ragged and undisciplined. Likely more of the same kind farther down the line."

"Hmm..." Nathan shared a look with Colonel Washburn and Tom. "Not exactly the fight I was looking for. Driving off cavalry then capturing wagonloads of wounded men and supplies is hardly going to end the war..."

"True," Washburn nodded. "But we can't always choose our fight, Chambers."

Nathan nodded and gazed out toward where Billy had reported the enemy wagons, but with the rain and low clouds there was nothing to be seen. He took out a cigar, lit it, and took several puffs. "Gentlemen, prepare the brigade to—"

Nathan's orders were interrupted by the arrival of a horseman, who pulled up short of him in a splatter of mud. There was no mistaking the new arrival; both horse and man were gigantic.

"Colonel," Stan snapped a salute, water streaming down his sleeve from the pouring rain. Nathan smartly returned the salute. "Lee comes from the north—his main column, maybe. Couple of cavalry brigades out front, screening. Four, maybe five miles out." He shrugged. "A large Union cavalry force is shadowing them, and may get here first. Wherever *here* is ... what *is* little town called, Colonel?"

"Hagerstown," Nathan now gazed back in the direction Stan had come from. "It may not look like much, but by my thinking, holding it could make all the difference; it controls the roads to the river crossings at Williamsport and Falling Waters."

Nathan turned to the two colonels and grinned with the cigar clenched between his teeth. "Well, gentlemen, now *this* is a battle a man can sink his teeth into! Let's get ready to greet General Lee, shall we?"

❦❧❦❧❦❧❦❧❦❧

When Union Brigadier General Judson Kilpatrick arrived in Hagerstown at the trot with his entire cavalry division, he was pleased to see Nathan's Hodgepodge Brigade already there, and formed up for battle.

"Colonel, happy to see you here," the young general beamed. "Didn't expect to have any infantry on our side in this one. We're expecting Jeb Stuart shortly, and it'll be good to give him a proper reception."

"You'll get no arguments from me on that, General." Nathan returned Kilpatrick's grin. The two quickly exchanged thoughts on the best disposition of troops for the coming battle, and then Kilpatrick deployed his cavalry in a wide arc across the northern end of the town, awaiting the arrival of Jeb Stuart's cavalry.

They did not have long to wait; within the hour, Stuart's horsemen drove in Nathan's skirmish line, and then began exchanging gunfire with Kilpatrick's cavalry troopers. The battle for Hagerstown was on.

For the next four hours and more, the streets of the tiny town were rocked by warfare. The city's residents took whatever shelter they could as men and horses jammed the streets, with saber-wielding cavalrymen hacking at the prodding bayonets of foot soldiers. The battle quickly devolved into a hand-to-hand street brawl, where the battle lines were jumbled together and cavalry troopers often dismounted and fought afoot, slipping through alleyways and climbing up on rooftops to fire down on their enemies using pistols and carbines.

But for Nathan and his men from the West, this was their type of fight, and they stubbornly held their ground against greater numbers, inflicting heavy casualties on the cavalrymen of Jeb Stuart.

Eventually, the battle had settled into a near stalemate when a rider appeared in front of Nathan and snapped a salute, "Colonel Chambers, General Kirkpatrick sends me to say we must withdraw, sir."

"*Withdraw?* Why?"

"Sir, the general says our scouts report Lee's main column of infantry approaches the town and will be here within minutes. Two divisions at the least. With artillery."

"*Oh.*"

಄ಶಃ಄ಶಃ಄ಶಃ಄ಶಃ಄ಶಃ಄ಶಃ಄ಶಃ

Tuesday, July 7, 1863 – Clear Spring, Maryland:

"Too bad about losing Hagerstown," Tom sat across from Nathan in his tent, the day after the battle. When forced to withdraw at the approach of Lee's main army, the Hodgepodge Brigade had moved away in the only direction open to them, off to the west. They'd forded Conococheague Creek and set up a well-dug-in, heavily guarded camp just outside the village of Clear Spring. Nathan had figured the rebels would use the creek as their defensive line in the west, so getting on the western side of it would put a little distance between them and Jeb Stuart's cavalry.

Nathan nodded, "Yes ... it's a bitter pill for our side. Whoever controls that town controls the river crossings, and now that's Lee. Damn it, Tom! Where the hell was Meade? If he would've sent one or two infantry divisions to our aid, the battle would've been ours, and by now Lee would be entirely cutoff from the river."

"Yes, it's a damned shame. Seems like Meade has contracted a case of *McClellan's* disease."

Nathan snorted a laugh, "Yes, that sounds about right. But fortunately, all this wretched rain has swollen the rivers. There's no way they can ford the Potomac the way it is now. They'd all be swept away and drown. That should buy Meade a bit more time ... if he'll just show up!"

"It would, but I understand the rebs have built themselves a pontoon bridge at Williamsport. Likely they can still cross on that, regardless of the flood."

The two were quiet and thoughtful for a moment.

Then Nathan looked up and said, "Tom ... what do you reckon would happen if somebody put a match to that pontoon bridge and burned it up?"

Tom nodded, "Well, I figure a thing like that would set Lee back the better part of a week at least. But Lee will know that too, I'm afraid. I'd have to believe the bridge is heavily defended."

"Hmm ... yes, very likely so. But..." Nathan chewed on a cigar and wore a thoughtful expression. "They'll be guarding it against the most likely Union attempt to take it out: a large-scale cavalry raid. I reckon it'd take a full division at the least to even make the attempt."

"True ... So, what're you thinking, sir?"

"I'm thinking ... that these rebels have no idea who they're dealing with. They're not prepared to counter men like ours — men of the wild West who're trained to fight Indian-style. Where a major assault might fail, a half-dozen or so highly skilled and determined men may well succeed."

Tom slowly nodded, a grin spreading across his cheeks.

⁂

Wednesday, July 8, 1863 – Williamsport, Maryland:

Confederate Private Silas Higgins stopped at the end of his midnight picket march, took a quick glance out across the dark waters of the Potomac, barely visible in the flickering torchlight, sighed heavily, then pivoted and began pacing back in the direction from which he'd come. Fifty yards off, he could see that his partner on picket duty, Jethro Tubbs, had just likewise turned, and was now coming in his direction.

Moments later, the two men neared the meeting point of their respective routes, and Higgins decided it was time for a brief rest, so he came to a stop as Tubbs was only a few yards away.

Tubbs stepped up in front him and also came to stop.

"Damned if this ain't the most tedious business we done yet, Tubbs."

"Yep. Ain't nothin' to keep a man's mind from wandrin'. Just march one way, and then t'other. 'Twas more to my liking when we was raidin' Yankee farmhouses and stealin' their chickens."

"Amen to that, Tubbs. Can't figger why good old Gen'ral Lee had to go'n spoil all the fun by havin' a big ol' battle with the Yanks. Don't seem like no good come o' *that*."

"Nope. Sounds like our boys took a beatin' too. At least we mostly missed out on *that* sorry business. Makes one almost happy havin' this here safe duty, boring though it may—"

Higgins gazed at Tubbs, wondering why he'd stopped talking so abruptly, and was now looking down at something on his shirt. In the dark, Higgins couldn't quite make out what the thing was at first. Then, in a shock, he realized the thing sticking out of Tubbs' chest was covered with feathers. *A goddamned arrow! What the hell?*

Tubbs gasped and looked up at Higgins, then his eyes rolled back into his head and he collapsed to the ground.

"Hey—" Higgins shout was cut off by a hand over his mouth and nose. He tried to struggle, but he was held by an iron-hard grip. A sudden sharp pain in the center of his chest was the last thing he felt before his world went black.

Stan carefully laid the guard's body on the ground and wiped his knife blade clean on the man's shirt before re-sheathing it. He picked up the man's rifle, slung it over his own shoulder, and began marching, taking the same line the guard had been tracing.

Billy and a half-dozen men from his scout company sprinted past Stan out onto the pontoon bridge deck, slowed only slightly by the heavy cans of kerosene they carried with them.

Stan could just make out the others of their party—Colonel Chambers, Jim Wiggins, and Tom Clark—spread in a wide, defensive arc a few dozen yards farther toward shore. They'd each taken out their pickets with knives, and now marched in the rebel guards' places so that anyone glancing out toward the bridge from the Confederate camp would see that all was well … at least until the moment it would become readily apparent that it was not.

Stan marched in a steady, relaxed manner that belied the boiling cauldron of emotions he felt inside—the nearly uncontrollable urge for immediate, violent action. But he had a job to do, and thanks to his many years serving in the army under Nathan Chambers, he had learned just enough discipline to carry it off.

In what seemed like hours, but was in reality only a few minutes, the would-be arsonists returned from their quick foray across the bridge. Stan noted with satisfaction that only Billy still carried his kerosene can, and it was clearly now almost empty. When they reached shore, Billy turned and emptied the remainder of his can over dozens of wrist-thick ropes securing the bridge to the shore.

When he was satisfied, Billy dropped the kerosene can and pulled out a long, thick stick from the pack on his back. Then he turned toward the rebel camp and made a loud bird call.

The call was immediately answered in kind.

Billy struck a match, lit the oil-soaked rags on the end of his torch, lit the ropes, then tossed the torch out onto the bridge deck. In seconds, flames leapt up.

Stan, Billy, and the scouts strolled casually away as the flames flickered. In moments, Colonel Chambers, Lieutenant Colonel Clark, and Major Wiggins joined them, and together they walked back to the banks of Conococheague Creek. They waded back across at the same point they'd crossed a short while earlier.

Stan glanced down and saw the bodies of the rebels that'd been guarding the crossing, still lying at the water's edge. In the dim light, he could barely see the arrows sticking out from their bodies. For a moment, he toyed with the idea of retrieving the precious projectiles, but then thought better of it. Colonel Chambers was anxious to keep moving and would likely frown at the attempt.

They had re-mounted and were nearly a mile away, moving at a swift trot, before they heard the sounds of the rebel camp coming to life—shouts, screams, and bells ringing.

Stan glanced back over his shoulder and grinned at the lovely sight of firelight flickering off the low, heavy clouds over the Potomac.

ം⳿⳿⳿⳿⳿⳿⳿⳿⳿⳿⳿

Sunday, July 12, 1863 – Clear Spring, Maryland:

After three long, anxious days with no news since the destruction of Lee's bridge, Nathan sent Stan and Billy out to reconnoiter Lee's army. Nathan needed to know exactly where Lee was, and what he intended. And he could think of no better men to find out for him than those two.

Two hours later, the duo stood on top of a ridge, their quarry plainly in sight below.

"Seems like Lee's whole army is being here," Stan scanned the valley with his binoculars. He could see a vast encampment, with artillery redoubts well placed, defending the approaches from the east, surrounded by regiments of riflemen dug into long trenches built up with log breastworks out front.

Billy said nothing, but grunted his agreement from where he crouched behind a bush to Stan's right.

265

"River is still up … too high to ford, maybe," Stan continued, "Seems to me rebs are stuck here, for now. Wait … look … they are already working on new bridge … farther downstream from burned bridge."

Billy nodded, but gazed up at the blue sky sporting only a few scattered cloud with a warm sun beating down, sending steam off the grass in the fields. "Hmm … river drops quickly this time of year once the rains stop … could be they can also cross by the ford, tomorrow … maybe the next day."

"Yes … and new bridge may also be finished by then," Stan scanned along the far-off riverbank.

Then Stan lowered his binoculars and looked over at Billy with a frown, "And where the hell *is* Union Army? Lee is dug in, yes, but he's pretty beat up from what we heard … not near enough men left to stand against whole Union Army; could be lambs to the slaughter."

"Lee thinks the Union Army is somewhere out east, from the way his guns are pointed," Billy shrugged. "Or maybe the Union Army command has lost track of Lee once again; it seems to be their habit," he snorted derisively. "Come, Stan, let's get back and tell the Captain where we found Lee. He'll know what to do."

"Is true … the Captain will know. I mean, the *colonel!* There, now you have *me* doing it too!" He shook his head in mock annoyance, but grinned.

Billy just shrugged, *"What?"*

But as they crept back down the hill toward where they'd left their horses, Billy stopped, "We have company…"

Stan looked in the direction Billy was gazing and saw a group of five riders, coming fast up the hill in their direction. Clearly they'd been seen, and the rebel cavalrymen were now coming to investigate. Stan and Billy wore their blue Union army uniforms, so if captured they'd not be hanged for spies. But they had no intention of being captured. Not now … not ever.

Stan turned and continued striding down the slope toward his horse. "Is my turn."

Billy tilted his head in thought, "I am not remembering that…"

"Yes, yes ... you killed those two fellows with bow ... this morning, when we are crossing little stream. You remember now?"

"Oh ... yes; I had forgotten. All right, your turn," Billy agreed.

Stan nodded, stepped up to Groz, and yanked the Henry rifle from its sheath strapped to the saddle.

Billy also retrieved his repeating rifle and stood beside his horse, holding the reins, ready to assist Stan if needed.

Stan chambered a round with the lever action, then grabbed the horse's cheek piece and turned him until the horse stood between Stan and the approaching riders, who were now less than a hundred yards away and quickly closing the gap.

"*Easy* now, Groz ... there is good boy..." Stan growled as he laid the rifle across the horse's shoulder, just in front of the saddle horn. He took aim down the hill, and squeezed the trigger, *boom!* The well-trained and experienced warhorse didn't flinch at the gunshot, but stood like a great statue, the only indication he'd noticed the gun being fired off his back was the twitching of his ears.

Without awaiting the result, Stan ratcheted another round into the chamber, adjusted his aim, and fired again, *boom!* Three more shots followed in rapid succession: *boom ... boom ... boom!*

Gun smoke drifted slowly away as Stan stepped out around Groz and gazed down the hillside. There he saw five horses, now riderless, trotting away, headed off in different directions.

He looked over at Billy, who just nodded. Stan reached into the ammunition pouch and quickly reloaded the five spent rounds to keep the rifle's magazine topped off, then shoved the weapon back into its sheath. The two men remounted and left at a quick trot heading northwest, back toward where the Hodgepodge Brigade was bivouacked.

ഇ൝ഡ൝ഇ൝ഡ൝ഇ൝ഡ

Monday, July 13, 1863 – Hagerstown, Maryland:

"The scouts have returned, sir," C.S.A. Major Charles Marshall stepped up in front of General Lee, who immediately gestured for his aide de camp to take the seat opposite him in the command tent.

"Excellent … so, where is Meade preparing to attack?"

"Well, sir … the short answer is … he's not."

"Not *what?*"

"Not preparing to attack. At least not at the moment. The scouts report the federals are digging their own entrenchments out beyond ours."

"*What?!* They mean to besiege us? Here? Where we can slip across the river whenever we're ready?"

"That appears to be the case, sir."

Lee scowled and shook his head, "I was prepared for another battle; this is a very strong defensive position, now that we've had time to dig in, and I thought our chances good. But a *siege?* That will take too long; I cannot wait for that."

He stood and strode out of the tent, then stopped and shaded his eyes against the bright morning sun as he gazed out east toward where the federals were now digging in.

After a few moments, he turned back around and met eyes with Marshall, a frown still knitting his brow, "*Pah!* These Union generals … they have but little courage."

Lee looked down at the ground in front of him for several moments, as if deep in thought. Finally, he looked back up. "What is the situation with the new bridge?"

"Nearly complete, sir. The engineers say it will be ready by nightfall."

"And the river?"

"It has dropped a good deal since the rains have stopped and the sun has come out. Fording it will still be dicey, but we'll make it across if we need to."

"Good. Issue the necessary orders; we begin our crossing one hour after nightfall."

⅏⅏⅌⅍⅏⅌⅍⅏⅌⅍

Monday, July 13, 1863 – Clear Spring, Maryland:

Nathan, Colonel Washburn, Major Adams, Tom, Tony, and Jim sat in the brigade's command tent, with Harry curled up under the table, as Stan and Billy gave their report. They'd arrived just as the sun was setting, and Nathan had immediately called together his subordinate commanders and his most trusted men. When they finished, Nathan stood and paced the floor, his face a storm cloud as he chewed on an unlit cigar.

"Damn it! Lee is trapped on this side of the river, and yet once again the Army of the Potomac hesitates to attack and finish him," he grumbled. "And not even McClellan this time! I had high hopes for Meade after his victory at Gettysburg. And yet here we are, another day wasted while the enemy prepares to escape to the South!"

He sat back down and rubbed the bridge of his nose as if suffering a headache. Then he sat up, reached for a map and unrolled it on the table and began gazing at it. "Stan, Billy ... show me where you stood when you were overlooking Lee's camp."

The two men stepped around the table and stood behind the colonel, gazing at the map over his shoulders.

"We crossed this small stream about ... here," Stan pointed, "and then moved southeasterly for four, maybe five miles to ... around here, don't you think Billy?"

Billy gazed at where Stan was pointing and nodded, "It's close ... maybe a little farther south. There is a slight rise there. It would be a good place to launch an attack if we could get there without being seen. All the enemy's big guns are pointed the other direction, toward the east, and his rifle pits are also facing that way. Rebel line runs from little town to edge of river."

"Makes sense," Nathan continued to gaze at the map, "East of there is where the Army of the Potomac is most likely positioned, preparing for an attack." Then he scowled, "...and preparing, and preparing, and preparing, apparently."

Then he folded his arms and stared at the map, continuing to chew on the cigar. Finally, he sat up, and turned to his second in command.

"Washburn ... send a courier to General Meade ... I expect he will be found out east of Hagerstown by now. Tell the general I mean to attack at daylight tomorrow. Our brigade will engage the enemy from behind in an attempt to delay his crossing if we can, though we are too few to entirely prevent it without the general's support ... which we *humbly* request..."

Jim whistled, and shook his head, "You sure about this, Colonel? We been outnumbered before, I'll grant you ... but *this*? That'll be something like three thousand of us in the Hodgepodge Brigade against ... oh, I don't know ... *fifty thousand* or more in Lee's army, give or take ... with hundreds o' big guns against our half-dozen or so small howitzers."

"No, Mr. Wiggins, I'm *not* sure about this ... but it infuriates me to think of Lee slipping away once again without anyone doing anything to stop him. Perhaps we can shame the commander of the Army of the Potomac into taking action. If not..." he shrugged.

He left the rest unsaid, but nobody questioned his orders, so they all left the tent and went out to spread the orders for a march to battle, to commence in the pre-dawn darkness.

ഗ‌‌‌‌‌‌‌‌‌‌‌‌‌‌‌‌‌‌‌

Tuesday, July 14, 1863 – Hagerstown, Maryland:

When the Hodgepodge Brigade arrived at the hilltop where Billy and Stan had observed Lee's army the day before, they were greeted by a completely different sight: the rebel gun emplacements were now empty, and the rifle pits deserted. Only discarded equipment and broken wagons remained where the Army of Northern Virginia had been dug in just the day before.

Nathan raised his spyglass and gazed off to the south toward the river crossing at Falling Waters and its new pontoon bridge. He could see a column of soldiers marching across, but a much larger mass of troops gathered on the far bank of the river, moving off to the south in a steady stream.

"Damn it ... a day late!" He panned the spyglass back upstream and then stopped. "Hmm ... but not all are gone, yet. Look over there, Washburn..."

Colonel Washburn raised his binoculars and looked where Nathan indicated. "Another large rebel formation ... mostly infantry ... I'd say a division, at the least. Must be the rearguard."

Then Tom tugged at Nathan's sleeve, "Look, sir! Out to the east..."

Nathan turned and looked where Tom had indicated, "Horsemen ... Union cavalry. A fairly large formation..."

Washburn shook his head as he too now scanned the approaching Union riders, "But where's the damned infantry? The cavalry will be too little ... and too late."

"Maybe ... or maybe not," Nathan lowered the spyglass and met eyes with his officers. "Gentlemen, I mean to engage that rearguard. With the help of the Union cavalry, we can hit them hard ... maybe hurt them badly enough that Lee will be forced to about-face and come to their aid. Perhaps that will be enough to get Meade's attention."

Tom just shrugged, and Washburn raised a questioning eyebrow, but neither man had a better notion.

"Let's move," Nathan said, already following his own directive, striding back down the hill to the awaiting troops.

80)CR03EU80)CR03EU80)CR03

Tuesday, July 14, 1863 – Falling Waters, West Virginia:

"General Lee, sir!" a cavalry captain pulled his horse to a stop in front of the commanding general and his staff officers, who were also mounted, sitting beside the road watching the long column of Confederate infantry pass by heading south. The captain snapped a salute, which Lee smartly returned.

"Sir, I have just forded the river on General Heth's behest. He wishes me to inform you that he is assailed by both infantry and cavalry, and his division is sorely beset and his mission to guard our rear is now seriously threatened."

"*Infantry?* What infantry? Did Meade finally launch his assault?"

"No, sir. Still no movement from Meade's position out to the east, other than cavalry. No, this infantry caught us with our guard down as they attacked from the *west*, where we were but lightly defended."

"From the *west?* Who are they, anyway? And how'd they get out there?"

Major Marshall stepped his horse up next to Lee, "I believe I may have the answer, sir. You will recall when General Stuart pushed the federals out of Hagerstown, he reported a brigade of Yankee infantry was also in the battle."

"Oh, yes ... I'd nearly forgotten about that. So, you think this may be them?"

"Well, after the battle we lost track of them, I'm afraid. So, we just assumed they'd fallen back to the east with the rest of Meade's column. But I was doubtful of that explanation, because they would've had to fight through our cavalry division to do so, and no such battle took place."

"Hmm ... so they've been lurking out west all this time, unnoticed, and now have decided to attack? A brigade with cavalry against Heth's entire infantry division? That's bold. Do we know who they are?"

"Well, sir, if it's the same outfit, we know from prisoners captured at the Hagerstown battle that the brigade is made up of the remnants of various Union formations that escaped the Battle of Winchester: some of Milroy's men."

Marshall chuckled. "The prisoners said the ragtag outfit has dubbed itself the *Hodgepodge Brigade*, and from what I hear, it sounds fitting."

"Hmm ... that doesn't sound like much of a threat. Who's their commander, did they say?"

"A colonel named Chambers."

"Chambers? *Nathaniel* Chambers?"

"Hmm ... I believe that was the name, sir. They said he was the commander of the Twelfth West Virginia ... Why? Do you know him, sir?"

Lee turned and redirected his gaze back to the north, where Heth was now engaged in a fight at the rear of the army. "Yes … I know him. He was one of my very best officers out in Texas before the war."

"Oh! Trouble, then?"

Lee turned to Marshall and gave him a hard look, "Yes, likely big trouble for General Heth. Let's just say if Nathaniel Chambers had been put in command of the Army of the Potomac instead of McClellan, the war might've ended two years ago—and not in our favor."

"Oh! Then shall we send reinforcements to General Heth? Have one of the infantry divisions recross the river and render aid?"

Lee was thoughtful for a moment, then slowly shook his head, "No … I don't think so. If I know Colonel Chambers, he's trying to bait me into turning around and engaging in battle so I'll be caught on the wrong side of the river. No … I'll not take the bait.

"Captain, return to General Heth and tell him he must fight his way out and make his way across the river as exigencies allow. We'll not be able to send him any reinforcements."

The captain saluted, turned his horse, and headed back toward the river.

ഇറ൪ദ൪൪ഇറ൪ദ൪൪ഇറ൪ദ൪

By pure good fortune, the march of the Hodgepodge Brigade and the ride of the approaching Union cavalry were both hidden from the rebel rearguard division by the natural rolling terrain between them, such that the disparate federal forces were able to meet and conduct a coordinated attack.

The resulting combined assault by the same Union forces that had fought together days earlier at Hagerstown caught the rebel rearguard division almost completely by surprise. The Confederates, who'd been up all night with little sleep, responded sluggishly, and were soon driven back toward the river in disarray. Between the heavy firepower of the Hodgepodge infantry and the speed of the Union cavalry, the rebels were in serious jeopardy of being completely routed. Heavily beset rebel soldiers began throwing down their rifles and surrendering in droves.

But Nathan didn't want to just capture or destroy them; he wanted to place them in dire straits and then keep them there as long as possible in order to force Lee to respond. He hoped to entice his adversary into sending back the bulk of his army to rescue the rearguard division. Maybe then, Meade would join the fight in earnest.

The Confederate officers finally managed to rally their troops, and then fought a slow withdrawal toward the river. When they reached the water's edge, the Union cavalry attacked in earnest, and Nathan saw a Confederate general fall from the saddle into the water, mortally wounded. The battle continued out across the water until the Union cavalry finally gave up the pursuit.

Nathan sat atop Millie at the north bank of the Potomac, a few yards from the pontoon bridge, as the Union cavalry waded back to shore. His face held a dark frown; despite his best efforts, Lee was gone.

Nathan turned and met eyes with Tom, who'd just ridden up beside him. "Tom … I had hoped we could force a final battle with Lee's army today—maybe end the war right here. But it was not meant to be…"

Tom nodded, "What now, Colonel?"

Nathan took out a cigar, lit it, and took a puff before answering. "Now … the war goes on…"

𝕾𝕺𝕮𝕽𝕮𝕾𝕺𝕾𝕺𝕮𝕽𝕮𝕾𝕺𝕾𝕺𝕮𝕽𝕮𝕾

Wednesday, July 15, 1863 – Hagerstown, Maryland:

The following morning, a courier arrived informing Nathan that the Army of the Potomac would be passing through their camp that afternoon on its way to Harpers Ferry. Nathan had received no orders to march with them, so he ordered the officers and men of the Hodgepodge Brigade to fall out in parade formation to salute the victors of Gettysburg as they passed by on the road.

274

About an hour after the Union cavalry had trotted through to take up their position as forward vanguard, Major General Meade led the infantry procession himself, along with his staff officers. Nathan stood in front of his brigade, and when he saluted the general, his entire brigade did likewise. This seemed to please the general, who smiled as he rode past, and returned the salute without pausing.

Nathan had half expected General Meade to stop and chastise him for his presumptuous courier message entreating the general to attack Lee's retiring army at the crossings of the Potomac. Nathan couldn't decide if he was disappointed Meade hadn't confronted him over it—that he might've had the opportunity to vent his dissatisfaction with the general's inaction—or whether he was relieved to just let the matter drop.

But if the general remembered the incident, or even knew who Nathan was, he made no acknowledgment of it and continued on his way.

Some of the common soldiers who marched behind Meade found the show put on by the Hodgepodge Brigade amusing, teasing the brigade soldiers about their relatively new uniforms, calling them "Sunday soldiers." By contrast, the Army of the Potomac had been in the field for more than a month chasing and then fighting Lee, with no opportunity to do laundry, much less acquire new uniforms. By this point, they were a motley looking bunch, with well-worn and tattered uniforms covered in mud, blood, and dust.

But despite the recent devastating fighting, the Army of the Potomac was still a tremendous fighting force of well over 100,000 men; it took hours for them to march entirely past Nathan's position. So once General Meade and the first several regiments had passed, Nathan dismissed most of his soldiers, requiring only his staff officers and regimental commanders to remain. These saluted the commander of each division, brigade, and regiment as he passed.

They'd been at it for more than an hour when an officer passed that Nathan knew well: Lieutenant Colonel Jonathan Lockwood, now commanding the Seventh West Virginia infantry in the absence of Colonel Snider, who'd been wounded at Chancellorsville back in May.

It was a happy reunion with the officers of the Seventh, whom Nathan and his men had trained for battle, now two years ago. Lockwood stepped his horse out of formation to talk with Nathan, Tom, and Jim, as the rest of the Seventh continued their march.

But after initial greetings were exchanged, Lockwood grinned brightly at Nathan, "Colonel ... I have a joyful surprise for you ... a little gift ... I trust you shall be well pleased, sir." He turned and gestured back toward the marching troops. Nathan was indeed pleased as he met eyes with Captain James Hawkins, with whom he'd had a special relationship, having recruited the young man away from another regiment back at the beginning of the conflict. The two men had exchanged many letters since, but this was the first time they'd met face-to-face since the Seventh had officially mustered into service and departed Wheeling.

But before Nathan could even greet or shake hands with Hawkins, the young captain swept off his hat and bowed from the saddle, gesturing toward the two men riding just behind him. Nathan's look of shock made Colonel Lockwood laugh with pleasure, as the three captains, James Hawkins, Georgie Thompson, and Jamie O'Brien broke ranks and trotted their horses over to the group of Hodgepodge Brigade officers and dismounted.

It was, of course, a joyful reunion; until that moment, Nathan, Tom, Tony, and Jim hadn't known what had become of Georgie and Jamie, whether they yet lived or had been killed in the fighting.

"Well, I'll be a three-eyed horny toad!" Jim Wiggins beamed from ear to ear as he vigorously shook hands with the two captains. "You two ornery juvenile delinquents have given us one heckuva scare, ridin' off into the middle o' just the biggest goddamned battle ever! *Damn*, but it's good to see y'all!"

Colonel Lockwood bid farewell before trotting his horse back to the head of his column, "Thank you for lending us your two excellent captains, Colonel Chambers ... they were a great inspiration to the men, and we shall miss their company."

That night, a celebratory mood permeated the Twelfth West Virginia Regiment due to the unexpected return of their two beloved officers, who'd not only survived the great battle, but had apparently acquitted themselves heroically in it.

Nathan sat back and watched the festivities with his feet propped up and a smile on his face, slowly smoking a cigar. He longed for a sip of whiskey, but he wouldn't break his own rules in that regard; he never allowed his officers or men to imbibe liquor while on campaign. So he settled for rubbing Harry on his prodigious, furry head, surprised at what a calming effect that simple, affectionate act had.

He decided that the return of Georgie and Jamie was a fitting, and happy ending to the whole Winchester-Gettysburg chapter of the war. But he worried what would come next.

And as was his habit in the still of the evening every day of the year, regardless of the weather or circumstances, he thought of Evelyn, and prayed for her continued good health and happiness. And he wished the war could be over that he might hold her in his arms once again. And this time, he'd never let her go.

CHAPTER 11. CAUGHT IN THE ACT

"Spying is like a game of chess;
sometimes you have to withdraw,
sometimes you have to sacrifice one of your pieces to win —
preferably a knight rather than a queen."
- John Rhys-Davies

Wednesday, July 15, 1863 – Richmond, Virginia:

It had been nearly two weeks since the great battle had been fought up north in Pennsylvania near the previously unknown town of Gettysburg. And although the Richmond papers tried to portray the outcome in the best possible light, Evelyn knew from reading between the lines, and from the reports she'd seen from Jonathan, that the battle had been a disaster for General Lee and the Confederate Army. But also, that it had taken enough out of the Union Army to allow Lee to escape with his army mostly intact, and so the war would go on.

Evelyn's enthusiasm for what should have been excellent news of a Union victory had been almost completely dampened by her inability to find out anything about Nathan and the Twelfth West Virginia: whether they'd been in the fight, and if so, how they had fared. Though she could find dispatches listing other units, including several from West Virginia, it was as if the Twelfth no longer existed. This thought left a gnawing doubt in her gut that burned and twisted like a living thing, even when she tried to concentrate on other matters to distract herself.

And adding to her trepidation was the lack of news from Jubal, whose Twenty-Seventh Virginia, along with the rest of the Stonewall Brigade, had reportedly been in the thick of the fighting, taking a terrible beating at a place called Culp's Hill. The reports said the Stonewall Brigade had suffered casualties as high as fifty percent. Evelyn shuddered at the thought of all those courageous soldiers suffering horrible pain and death. Though he could never take Nathan's place in her heart, she truly cared for Jubal and feared for his safety.

Evelyn set aside the latest copy of the *Richmond Examiner* and sighed. *Nothing new...*

She gazed out the window, thinking of Nathan and his men, and of Jubal ... she fought hard to push down a paralyzing dread and a growing hopelessness.

Then she shook her head, attempting to physically force down the evil thoughts that were flooding in. *Think of something else, Evelyn ... Think of what you can do, now ... what you need to do now...*

She turned her thoughts to the ongoing espionage campaign against the Confederate double-agent, Alice Spencer. Ever since she'd met with Alice, Evelyn had been searching to find out anything she could about the enigmatic young lady.

The Employer's clandestine contacts had provided scant information, though what they had provided was interesting—hints and suggestions of a possible connection with an unnamed officer in the Confederate Signal Corps. Of course, whenever that particular unit was named, Evelyn's mind immediately went to the ever-lurking, ever-dangerous Major White. But no matter how hard she pushed or dug, she could not discover anything specific, nor verify the truth of the matter.

And then there was the much more voluminous, forthcoming, and free-flowing—though totally unreliable—Richmond upper-class rumor mill. From these rumors, one could learn almost anything one wanted to know, the problem being that almost none of it was true. Evelyn smiled ruefully, knowing she herself had taken advantage of that specific shortcoming to spread any number of false tales intended to mislead her enemies.

The trick was to glean the few shining nuggets of truth from the vast, muddy sludge of falsehoods and exaggerations. From this dubious source, Evelyn had been searching for anything that might hint at why Alice would risk her personal well-being in a dangerous game of double espionage. The one solid clue that she'd been able to confirm as at least partially true was that Alice had dallied with a young gentleman who'd been a radical, highly vocal opponent of the secession, and proponent of abolition. It seemed that Alice had been very close to this man at one point, and then … she had mysteriously disappeared for a time after which the young man had been arrested by the new Confederate government, charged with sedition.

Apparently, the reason for Alice's absence had been an illness of some sort. And the rumors ruthlessly suggested Alice had been with child and hinted that unethical, illegal methods had been obtained to quietly resolve that inconvenient situation.

Evelyn tried to picture the scenario in her mind … a wild dalliance … the horror and shame of an unexpected pregnancy … a stern father with a reputation to protect, arranging the unthinkable … and finally … *what?* A ruthless, amoral Signal Corps officer learning of the incident and blackmailing the young woman into cooperation? Or did she have some other, completely different motivation?

If the rumors were true, Evelyn almost felt sorry for Alice … *almost.* She reminded herself that Alice was working for the enemy, whether voluntarily or against her will was of little matter in the end. And … Alice had proven herself a self-centered, arrogant socialite, with little or no sympathy either for the slaves, or for her less fortunate fellow Confederate citizens.

No … I just can't brew up much empathy for the little brat … Evelyn decided. *And I'll stop beating myself up over trying to put her out of business, as she so richly deserves.*

She gazed at the oil lamp burning on the side table for a long moment, lost in thought.

"Oh!" she said aloud, rising to her feet. *Now I'm late, and that won't do! Not tonight … Damn it, Evelyn … pull yourself together!*

She rose from her seat and hurried to the front door.

 இல்ல்லாஇல்ல்லாஇல்ல

Major Charles White pulled his collar up a little tighter to fend off the chill of an unseasonably cool evening as he gazed out from behind a streetlamp post toward the door he'd been watching for the past hour, even as the sun began to set. He'd dressed in civilian garb tonight, and suddenly missed his warm wool uniform tunic.

According to the information he'd gathered, the Union spy queen he'd been seeking, known only as "the most beautiful woman in Richmond" was finally going to re-engage in her nefarious espionage activities after some frustrating months of relative inactivity.

The trail had suddenly turned warm a week earlier when one of the Signal Corps' spies, a Confederate double-agent, had reported that a Union spy ring had been in contact with him through various intermediaries, working on a plot to steal documents from the War Department. All was supposed to be handled through couriers and ignorant third parties, such that arresting any of them would have resulted in nothing of value, beyond a few meaningless executions.

But then, only this morning, an unexpected break came in the case; a dirty young street urchin appeared at the War Department, saying that he'd been running errands for an upper-class lady, and that he'd figured out these errands were for the purpose of spying against the government. He claimed he was hungry, and offered to tell all he knew in exchange for a few dollars, to which the Signal Corps duty officer had quickly agreed.

The boy had told them he'd been the go-between in helping to arrange a meeting between a courier and a man—a man that the boy didn't realize was a Confederate double-agent—for the exchange of some kind of important documents. But the spy ring courier had taken ill at the last moment and was bed-ridden. When the boy had reported this to the upper-class lady, she'd been extremely agitated, saying she'd then just have to go herself.

And though the boy didn't know the lady's name, he did know where she would be, and the way he described her—young, blonde, beautiful, and stately—there was little doubt in White's mind of whom the street boy was speaking.

And so Major White now waited, watching the door of an upper-class house. Though he rarely allowed his emotions to get the better of him for fear that they might cloud his better judgement, White had to admit to a certain feeling of ... impending *satisfaction? Excitement,* even, at the thought of finally capturing his elusive quarry — of finally laying hands, figuratively speaking, on the elusive spy queen, *Miss Evelyn Hanson.*

In her haste, Evelyn nearly forgot to put on her hat. But as she stepped into the foyer, Jacob stepped out and handed it to her with a bow.

She nodded, and rolled her eyes, "Thank you, Jacob. Whatever would I do without you?"

"I don't know, Miss Evelyn … and hopefully you'll not need to find out," he gave her a quick grin, which she returned in kind.

Evelyn tied on the hat, pulled tight her shawl, and stepped out the door. She had an important meeting, and was running late. She looked up at the sky — already twilight, and becoming chilly, though it was high summer. She pulled the hat brim down in front to block the wind as she hurried down the stairs, and she turned to stride up the street, heading north.

She glanced back down the street to see if anyone followed, but saw no one. Jacob had offered to accompany her, but she had declined, not wanting to risk anyone else being caught up in the activity lest something go wrong. But now, as the night began to close in, and a stray dog stepped out of an alleyway and snarled as she hurried past, she wondered if she'd made a bad choice.

Out of habit, she felt the hard lump up her sleeve under her left forearm: the reassuring presence of the tiny but deadly .22 caliber Smith & Wesson revolver. She quickened her pace.

And then, as she reached the street corner and turned, she thought she caught a glimpse — out of the very corner of her eye — of someone following. So when she reached the edge of the red building, she stopped and turned, peeking around the corner back the way she'd come.

Again, she thought she saw a furtive movement in the dark street behind her, but she couldn't be sure. So she turned, shrugged, and continued down the street.

Half a block away, a man stepped out from behind a hedgerow and walked down the street in her direction…

Major White made his way down the street, watching his quarry carefully, ready to move out of sight at the slightest hint of a backward glance. Any doubts he'd had about the subject of his attentions had been dispelled the moment the woman had stepped out of the front door. Though it was becoming dark, and he was several dozen yards away, he'd had a momentary, clear glimpse of a pretty young face, a swirl of long blond hair, quickly tucked up under a fashionable hat. She was also well dressed, and tall with a lean, curvaceous figure of the type gentlemen typically admired.

Though he was not one to count his chickens before they were hatched, he was feeling confident of success. And that success would be just the thing to ingratiate him with his superiors; it would give him a leg up on his chief rival in the Signal Corps, the annoyingly arrogant and condescending Colonel Grayson.

Grayson had pooh-poohed the idea of a "spy queen," insisting instead that the real leader of the Richmond spy ring was a man known only as "The Employer." And Grayson had made it clear he though little of White's skills or ability to carry out his mission.

White was fairly certain Secretary Seddon had intentionally set up the two men as rivals, hedging his bets, uncertain himself as to which theory was the correct one.

Seddon had even hinted that White might expect a promotion, properly backdated to give him seniority over Grayson, if he were successful. White wondered what incentive Seddon had offered Grayson, but he decided it didn't matter, since he, White, was about to win this particular contest.

They were now moving through a more densely built-up area of downtown Richmond, and as White reached the fourth street corner, he paused and peered around it.

He saw the woman step up to the door of a red brick industrial-looking building and knock on the door. The door opened, and she stepped inside.

White sprinted across the street and stepped up to the door. He paused a moment to unholster his pistol, put his left hand on the door handle, and turned. The door was unlocked, and opened easily…

ᏚᎧᏣᎷᏣᏅᎯᏚᎧᏣᎷᏣᏅᎯᏚᎧᏣᎷᎯ

Evelyn had just removed her hat and was beginning to remove her coat, and had not even had time to properly greet the man who stood before her when the door behind her opened unexpectedly, and a man stepped inside from the street.

Evelyn turned and gasped.

ᏚᎧᏣᎷᏣᏅᎯᏚᎧᏣᎷᏣᏅᎯᏚᎧᏣᎷᎯ

Major White stepped into the room, which was well lit by several oil lamps in notches on the brick walls. It was a small sitting room in the entrance area of what appeared to be a warehouse.

He took everything in almost immediately: a man holding a stack of papers, gazing up at him in surprise—presumably the Signal Corps agent, though White didn't personally know him—and a woman with her back turned to him, just removing her coat.

"I have you at last," White held the pistol out, aimed at her back. "Do nothing stupid … I am armed and will not hesitate to end your treasonous life, if forced to…"

The woman turned to face him, a look of shock on her face.

But then it was Major White's turn to be shocked, "*Oh!* Who are you?"

The woman before him was young, blonde, and beautiful … perhaps even "the most beautiful woman in Richmond" … but she was *not* Evelyn Hanson.

ᏚᎧᏣᎷᏣᏅᎯᏚᎧᏣᎷᏣᏅᎯᏚᎧᏣᎷᎯ

Evelyn gasped, then smiled. "Joseph! I should've known you'd be following me. Old habits die hard?"

"Yes, something like that," he chuckled and removed his hat, stepping into the room and closing the door behind him. "Brrr … getting chilly out there." He shivered and rubbed at his sleeves.

"You should've worn a coat, my dear," she scolded mildly.

"Yes, yes, *mother!* So … what are you doing out tonight anyway?" Joseph moved over and sat down heavily on a bench to the side of the room, still rubbing at his shirtsleeves.

"Finishing up a little business." She tossed her coat over the back of the bench next to Joseph, then looked over at the black man standing in front of them. "Willy, would you please go fetch our guest?"

"Yes, ma'am."

The man, a freeman, who was one of Evelyn's helpers, went out another door, returning a moment later with Ollie Boyd in tow.

"Ollie, thanks for coming … please meet Joseph; he's a good friend of mine and in the same … *business*."

The two men shook hands, then Evelyn gestured for Ollie to take a seat, and she did likewise.

"Now … it's time to begin the final phase of our operation…" Evelyn grinned, but not in her typical, warm, friendly manner.

ಬೃ಄ೞಬ಄ಬೃ಄ೞಬೃ಄

"My name is Alice Spencer," the woman frowned, looking up at the perplexed major.

"*Alice Spencer* … yes … yes, you were on my list, though not especially high on it. You might've gone beneath my notice for a *very* long time if you'd not made this one fatal misstep tonight."

"Misstep? Whatever do you mean, sir? And who are you … and why, in the name of heaven, are you pointing a gun at me?"

Major White smiled thinly, "Oh come now, Miss Alice … We both know why you're here. I am Major White of the Confederate Signal Corps, and this man is a Confederate agent. So, you see, your reason for being here is already known to us. It will do you no good to deny it."

"But I … I … I am also on *your* side. I … I also work for the Signal Corps."

"Oh? And is there anyone at the Corps who can vouch for that?"

"Yes … I … well, I don't know his *real* name, of course … but he goes by the name Mr. Gray."

285

"Gray? Hmm … I know of no one in the corps by that name. But come, we shall see…" White reached into his pocket and brought out something shiny and metallic.

Alice shuddered when she recognized the object: a set of hand shackles.

ℰℭℛℭℬℰℭℛℭℬℰℭℛℭ

When Major White arrived back at the Signal Corps headquarters with Alice Spencer in tow, he locked her in an interrogation room, then walked back down the hall toward his office, intending to change back into his uniform.

He was surprised to be met halfway down the hallway by Colonel Grayson himself, who, for once, greeted him amiably.

"White … there's someone here I think you'll want to speak with," Grayson gestured toward his own office.

White nodded, gazing into Grayson's eyes, "Interesting coincidence, Colonel, since I also have someone whom I wish you to meet. But … let's do yours first."

When he stepped into Grayson's office, it was the second time that evening White had suffered an unexpected shock. There at Grayson's desk sat Major Oliver Boyd, dressed in civilian clothes.

"Major Boyd…" White stepped into the office and was surprised when Boyd stood and extended his hand.

"Major White … please, come in … I owe you an apology, sir."

White looked at the proffered hand, but rather than take it, he stepped up and took a chair opposite Boyd and sat.

"Go on…"

"I … I apologize for running away from you when we reached Richmond." Boyd slowly sank back down into his seat. "I was … confused, and felt betrayed, knowing I'd done nothing wrong, having faithfully served my country. And … well, frankly fearing you intended to put me to some … *distress*, shall we say?"

Colonel Grayson scowled, but White just shrugged, "Sometimes sterner methods are required in our business, it's true."

"Yes … certainly…" Ollie shrugged. "Anyway, after giving it some thought, it occurred to me you were suspicious of me because I hadn't been entirely truthful with you back at General Lee's camp."

White nodded, and tilted his head to one side, but said nothing.

"I … I actually thought I had seen Miss Evelyn Hanson once, up in the North … at Frederick town in Maryland." Boyd looked from one man to the other, as if gauging their reactions. "I was bewildered, and feared getting my wife's dear friend into some kind of trouble that I didn't understand. But I'd had only the briefest glimpse of a pretty, blonde woman on a crowded street. Having had time to reflect on it, I have realized it was not Miss Evelyn I saw after all, but rather another woman from Richmond whom I know."

"Oh? And who would that be?" White folded his arms and leaned back in his chair.

"Another high-class socialite, and the daughter of one of our own generals: Miss Alice Spencer."

ℬ)☾☙ℬ)☾☙ℬ)☾☙

Having released Major Boyd, White and Grayson returned to the interrogation room where Alice Spencer waited.

Alice immediately sprang to her feet, "Mr. Gray! Oh, thank God you've come! Please tell this major I work for you … Tell him I'm on *your* side…"

But Grayson frowned, then turned to Major White, shrugged, and said, "I'm sorry, I've never seen this woman before in my life."

ℬ)☾☙ℬ)☾☙ℬ)☾☙

Wednesday, July 22, 1863 – Richmond, Virginia:

"My goodness, Ollie, it's so wonderful to see you once again looking so dashing in your dress uniform." Evelyn graced her guests with the special smile she reserved for those dearest to her before having another sip of tea.

Belinda gripped Ollie's arm and leaned into his shoulder, "Yes, he certainly does look handsome, don't you think?"

287

Ollie blushed, as he always did when Belinda paid him a compliment. "Well, I don't know about all that … but it is good to be out from under the dark cloud that seemed to be hanging over my very existence of late. And that happy change in circumstance is all thanks to you, Evelyn."

But she frowned, "Well, I hardly think you should thank me, considering it was me who got you into this mess to begin with."

It was Belinda's turn to scowl, "No, Eve, it wasn't your fault. It's this stupid war … oh, how I wish it was just over for good and all!"

"Amen to that, dear," Evelyn nodded, taking another sip. "And thank you for saying so, Bel. And especially thank you for … for not being *angry* with me…"

"Oh, Eve … you're my best friend in the world … I'd rather be angry at myself than at you. Besides, Ollie and I have talked it over, and we agree that you've been on the *right* side all along. The slavery, and the secession, and all … it just never seemed right.

"But I must confess to being a little surprised at your invitation to come here today for tea, after all that's happened. Aren't you concerned that meeting with Ollie will raise suspicions again?"

"No, I don't think so," Evelyn gazed up at the ceiling a moment. "I think maybe it would be more suspicious if we *didn't* meet, since Ollie already told Major White that we're close friends. If we never met again, it might look as if we had something to hide.

"Besides, I understand you've been cleared of all charges, Ollie, including going AWOL. Is that not so?"

"Well, yes and no," Ollie shrugged.

"What do you mean?"

"*Officially* I've been cleared for duty, yes, but … there's been no answer to my request to rejoin General Lee, and they've assigned me to a desk in the darkest corner at the war department. It's about as tedious and mundane a duty as one could imagine. I can only assume it means they still don't entirely trust me, and don't want to put me anywhere that I might be able to do some harm or acquire any damaging information."

"Ah, I see…" Evelyn looked down at the floor. "Yes, that does seem telling. I'm sorry, Ollie, I truly am."

"Don't be, Evelyn. It has helped me decide what I need to do."

"Oh?"

"Yes," Belinda interrupted, "Ollie and I have decided we need to defect to the North. And we thought … well, we thought *you* might know how to do it."

"*Oh!* Are you sure about that? It's a dangerous, risky business at best, at least for Ollie. If you travel separately, you shouldn't have any trouble, Belinda. But an officer? It would be considered treason, and if he was caught…" Evelyn shook her head.

There was a long, awkward silence, finally broken by Ollie, "Evelyn … I've considered the risks, but I believe it's the right thing to do. I can no longer pretend to support the Confederacy, and no longer wish to contribute to its war effort, regardless of how trivial that contribution may now appear to be."

"Very well, if you're determined—"

"I am."

"All right. It may take a while to plan and then to arrange, but I will start working on it straightaway. And Belinda … we'll have to pretend to have a falling out—something very loud and public—and then not see each other again until the war is over. Otherwise, they will arrest me for sure once Ollie defects and you leave the South."

Belinda frowned, and began to tear up, but nodded her understanding.

"In the meantime, shall we not lighten the mood and celebrate a little? Not only Ollie's wonderful change of fortune, but I have just received news that Nathan and his men of the Twelfth West Virginia are safe and well, and were never in the great battle after all!"

"Oh! That *is* wonderful news, Eve!" Belinda beamed and leaned in to give Evelyn a hug. "Yes, let's *do* celebrate … And I'm thinking we've had just about enough tea … Where's your brandy, dear?"

Chapter 12. The Fight for Freedom

*"People will never fight for your freedom
if you have not given evidence
that you are prepared to fight for it yourself."*
- Bayard Rustin

Wednesday July 1, 1863 – Cabin Creek, Indian Territory:

Union Colonel James Williams, commanding officer of Fort Scott, Kansas, frowned as he gazed out at the rain-swollen, swirling stream in front of him, marked as *Cabin Creek* on the map he held tucked under his left arm. And though the restless, brown, surging waters represented a serious obstacle to the two hundred supply wagons he was responsible for safely transporting from Kansas to Union-held Fort Gibson in the Indian Territory, he was much more concerned about what now lay just beyond the ford. Stretching out for nearly a mile to either side of the point where the road crossed the stream, ran a series of hastily dug earthworks, behind which a sizable enemy force lay armed and ready for battle.

"They's pretty well dug in, sir," Sergeant Ned Turner stood next to the colonel, delivering the report he'd just received from the Union scouts. "Scouts reckon at least five hundred rebs, likely more. But so far, no sign of artillery."

"Well, that's some good news, anyway," Williams said. "That'll give us a bit of an advantage, given we *do* have a half-dozen Napoleons at our disposal. And we also have them outnumbered, seemingly."

Colonel Williams turned and directed his gaze to the terrain on his side of the creek, carefully taking in every detail. He lowered the glasses and looked over to meet eyes with Captain Mathews. "It's too late to start an assault today, especially as I'm not liking the way that creek's looking; we'll hit them first light in the morning. That'll give us good light for crossing the stream, and all day to carry the position, if necessary.

"Captain ... let's go ahead and position our artillery on that ridge over yonder this evening. Should give us a good vantage point from which to hit the enemy on the far bank tomorrow when we launch our assault."

"Yes, sir!" Mathews, very likely the highest-ranking black man in the entire Union Army, snapped a salute, then pivoted and trotted off to relay the colonel's orders to the artillery officer.

"Sergeant Turner, please relay my orders to the regimental commanders—that I wish to have the brigade set up a fortified camp straightaway, in case the enemy gets any wild notions to pre-empt us during the night."

"Sir!" Ned also saluted, then turned and trotted off to pass the word to begin setting up a defensive camp, which implied several hours of chopping trees and digging trenches before anyone could even start *thinking* about setting up a tent, preparing a meal, or getting any sleep. But Ned, being a field slave his entire life until being freed just before the war started, was used to long, hard labor, so he thought little of it.

Though the First Kansas Colored Regiment had now seen plenty of action, mostly against bushwhackers over on the Missouri side of the border, this current assignment was a novelty for them; it was the first time a colored regiment would serve side by side with white soldiers, as the First Kansas had been joined by detachments from the Second Colorado Infantry, the Third Wisconsin Cavalry, the Sixth and Ninth Kansas Cavalry, and, most interestingly from Ned's perspective, the Third Indian Home Guard.

Captain Mathews had explained to Ned that the Indian Home Guard infantry regiments had been recruited by the Union Army from the so-called "Five Civilized Tribes of Indian Territory." And though the leaders of the five tribes, Cherokee, Choctaw, Chickasaw, Creek, and Seminole Indians—who'd set up semi-autonomous governments in the Indian Territory—had signed treaties to support the Confederacy at the start of the war, many of the tribal members had supported the Union side instead. This pro-Union element had been forced to flee to Kansas or Missouri, where they volunteered with the Union Army, intending to eventually retake their home territory, by force if necessary.

Ned, remembering the fighting skill and tenaciousness of Billy Creek, already had a healthy respect for Indians, and these volunteers had so far done nothing to disappoint him. Applying their own unique style of headwear, warpaint, and various leather and bead Indian accouterments to the standard issue blue Union uniforms and kepi hats, they were impressive, intimidating-looking fighting men.

They also exuded a boundless enthusiasm for combat, speaking of little else. Ned just hoped when it came down to the actual fighting, they'd live up to his expectations. Now, standing on the edge of Cabin Creek in Indian Territory, gazing across at a dug in, determined enemy, Ned had a strong feeling he was about to find out.

࿇ᏫᏧᏫᏧᏫᏫᏧᏫᏫᏫᏧᏫ࿇

"Hey, Ned ... wake up..." Ned felt a strong hand grip his upper arm and give him a shake. He groaned in response.

"C'mon ... time to rise and shine, Sergeant Turner!" the same voice said in a tone that seemed much too cheerful given that it was not yet even close to daylight in the camp. Ned recognized the jovial voice of their youthful company commander, First Lieutenant August Gordon, whom everyone called "Auggie."

"Well ... I reckon I'll rise, all right," Ned pushed himself up into a sitting position, tossing the blanket back from his bedroll, and rubbed at his eyes, "but I ain't about to do no shinin'..."

Auggie snorted a laugh and slapped Ned on the back, "That's the spirit ... Come on ... I'm gonna need your help rousting out the others..."

"All right, all right ... I'm comin', Lieutenant," and then Ned grinned in spite of himself, shaking his head at the wonder of his present circumstances; against all his experience and stubborn determination, Auggie's unabashed enthusiasm and relentless good humor, combined with an unequaled measure of personal courage and fighting skill and knowledge, had completely won Ned over. So much so that at one point, Ned had come to realize

292

for the first time in his life that he liked a white man so much that he no longer thought of him as a white man at all, only as a very *good* man. *Well, I reckon now pert-near anything's possible,* was all he could think about that when he considered it.

And he knew that the other freemen in the company felt much the same about Auggie. Ned understood for the first time why it was that Captain Chambers' men from Texas seemed willing to lay down their lives for their leader without hesitation or question. Chambers was "The Captain" to his men. And likewise, Auggie Gordon, a slender, blond haired, blue eyed, baby-faced young man had become "The Lieutenant" to Ned and the rest of the freemen of Company G, First Kansas Colored Infantry. Ned now knew, if it came right down to it, they'd do anything Auggie asked them to do, knowing he'd be right there in the thick of it with them.

৪৩৫৫৪৩৫৫৪৩৫৫

When the first cannon shot was fired, Ned flinched at the thunderous sound; he'd heard plenty of rifle fire, starting back in their breakout from Mountain Meadows—what now seemed like a lifetime ago—but this was the first time he'd been in a battle with artillery.

He felt slightly shamed by his reaction, and glanced over at Lieutenant Gordon to see if he'd noticed. He had. Auggie was looking right at Ned, beaming. "Great fun, ain't it, Ned?" he said, and slapped Ned on the arm.

"Oh, yes, sir. *Great* fun." Ned rolled his eyes, and Auggie laughed.

The bombardment from the Union guns continued for a half-hour, with Auggie occasionally glancing at his pocket watch. Finally, there came a pause in the firing, and the lieutenant took one last look at his watch, stuck it back in his pocket, cupped his hands and shouted, *"Company G will fix bayonets, and prepare to charge on my command!"*

Above the sound of bayonets sliding onto rifle barrels and clicking into the locked position, the lieutenant's command could be heard repeating down the line. Ned imagined the same was taking place in the other companies and infantry regiments.

Moments later, Auggie leapt up on top of the earthwork logs in front of them, his saber pointed at the enemy, *"Come on, men. Follow me!"* And without a backward glance, he was down on the other side, sprinting toward the creek. The eighty-three men of Company G boiled up over the earthworks and followed without hesitation, bayonets thrust forward.

ഇ)രുകൗ™ുഇ)രുകൗ™ുഇ)രുകൗ

Though Cabin Creek was not especially wide, the recent rains had given it a depth and volume that slowed the charge to an agonizing slog, as Ned forced his way across, water up to his armpits, rifle and ammunition pouch held above his head. He felt terribly exposed in the middle of the stream, there being no cover except for the other soldiers around him. He could not keep himself from imagining a bullet speeding straight for his forehead.

But Colonel Williams once again proved his competence and leadership in battle; rather than trying to send the entire force across the creek at once and risking them bogging down and being slaughtered, he'd ordered the Third Wisconsin Cavalry on the left, and the Ninth Kansas Cavalry on the right, to dismount, move up to the bank, and pour volleys of carbine fire into the enemy earthworks on the opposite shore, forcing the rebels to keep their heads down for the most part. Williams had also placed dozens of sharpshooters at strategic locations in the trees or hillocks near the creek to target any rebel soldier or officer who stuck his head up at the wrong moment.

Because of this, the First Kansas, Second Colorado, and Third Indian infantries were able to gain the far bank and begin establishing a bridgehead while suffering relatively few casualties. Ned and the men of Company G were near the center of the advanced Union line, now shaped like an inverted U, so that they were the farthest forward, and closest to the enemy earthworks. And when they closed to within a few dozen yards,

294

the Union cavalry soldiers on the far shore had to let off firing for fear of hitting their own men.

It was the moment the rebels had been waiting for; suddenly the eerie rebel yell rent the air, and hundreds of enemy infantrymen poured up over their earthworks, bayonets extended.

Ned dug in his heels and braced himself for the impact. He risked a quick glance to his right and saw Auggie standing in an oddly relaxed stance, sideways to the advancing enemy, with his saber out front, hanging casually at an angle toward the ground.

Ned had no time to wonder what Auggie's odd pose signified; a moment later, a rebel bayonet was racing straight toward his chest. He knocked the rifle aside with his own, and the reb crashed into his chest with a hard thud! The blow nearly took his breath, but he'd braced for it, so he kept his feet. He shoved the man backward and thrust his own bayonet into the man's belly, pulling it out just in time to deflect another bayonet. This time he hammered his opponent to the ground with the butt of his rifle.

All around him, a chaotic maelstrom of sweat, steel, and blood swirled. He saw Auggie facing two foemen, the lieutenant frantically deflecting their rifle thrusts with his blade. Ned stepped toward them and ran his bayonet through the nearest man's neck. It made an odd, sucking noise as he yanked it back out. Blood spurted from the wound, splattering Ned's tunic. Auggie took advantage of the respite to slam his sword into the other man's chest.

But Ned's momentary distraction nearly proved fatal. A rifle butt caught him on the side of the head and he fell to the ground, eyesight swimming. He gazed up to see a bayonet poised over his chest, and a burly, dark-bearded man leaning over him, a snarl on his lips. But the man's head suddenly leaned to one side at an unnatural angle, and blood sprayed out from his neck in a great splatter.

Ned felt a hand grab him by the front of his tunic and yank him to his feet. He stood staring straight at Auggie's face; it had been the lieutenant's saber that had nearly decapitated the rebel standing over him.

"Thanks," Ned gasped out.

Auggie grinned, "Reckon we're now even, *brother...*"

But the men of the First Kansas were hard pressed, and being forced slowly backward by sheer weight of numbers. Ned feared they'd be driven back into the river, which would likely prove fatal...

He faced another rebel, trading bayonet thrusts with him, each man determined to impale his foe without getting himself killed in the process.

But suddenly, the rebel stepped back, a look of shock and fear on his face, even as a blue-clad soldier came leaping past Ned. This unknown Union soldier slammed bodily into the rebel, knocking him to the ground. The attacker stabbed the downed man multiple times with a very large, wicked looking knife, blood spewing out after each thrust.

Ned realized the very same bloody scene was now playing out all around him, as more and more blue soldiers streamed forward, throwing themselves against the stunned rebels. Then he noticed for the first time an odd, shrill sound—somewhat reminiscent of the dreaded rebel yell, only this one was somehow more intense, and even more eerie, if possible. *The Indians*, he realized. *Praise the Lord!*

The Third Indian regiment, seeing the dire predicament the First Kansas faced, had pivoted and rushed forward, weaving through their blue-clad comrades to hit the rebels like a blow from a hammer.

Ned rested the bayonet on the ground in front of him. His arms ached, and he felt he might not be able to lift the rifle again. He leaned down, panting heavily, straining to catch his breath.

He watched in admiration as the Indians drove the rebels back to their earthworks. But there the rebels turned and gave battle, with reserves coming forward, firing rifles and forcing the Indian assault to a halt.

Ned took advantage of the slight respite to reload his rifle. Auggie looked down at him, saw what he was about, nodded, cupped his hands and shouted, "*Company G will reload and prepare to volley fire on my command!*"

A moment later, Company G rose as one, and at Auggie's command, fired a volley that drove the rebels to their front down from their wall, giving the Indians a chance to pull back to a safer position.

But the Confederates were still far from beaten, and the Union infantrymen were exposed in front of their earthworks with little cover, their advance entirely stalled. Though they returned fire as best they could, the federals were once again taking casualties, and in danger of being decimated.

Then, once again, Ned heard a noise growing behind him, *Horses galloping, or I'm a goose*, he decided. And moments later, a horse leapt over him where he lay prone behind a bush. The horse and rider thundered toward the enemy earthworks, accompanied by hundreds more. *Thank you for that, Colonel*, Ned thought. *Good time for the cavalry to show up!*

The riders approached the enemy earthworks at a gallop and launched themselves up and over. Once on the other side, they pivoted and began targeting the enemy with pistols, carbines, and sabers in a swirling flurry of hooves and gun smoke.

Ned and the other infantrymen rose to their feet and followed at a rush. But by the time Ned reached the enemy log wall and clambered over, there were only dead rebel bodies in the trench beyond, and the cavalry was pursuing the survivors as they fled the battlefield.

The battle of Cabin Creek was over, and Ned was still alive. As he stood next to Auggie and several other of the freemen, all still catching their breath, one of the Indian soldiers walked past them, but paused a moment and grinned at them, "Black men fight pretty damned good!"

Ned chuckled, and nodded, "So do Indians!"

The Indian laughed, then stepped up and placed his palm on Ned's shoulder, looking him in the eye. "We are now war brothers, black man."

Ned nodded, "*War brothers* ... yep, I reckon so, Indian." He placed his hand on the Indian's shoulder, mimicking the gesture.

The Indian gazed at him another moment, then nodded, and walked away.

Despite being in the forefront of the battle, Company G had suffered only three killed and five wounded, none seriously. Though Ned mourned the loss of the three men, it seemed to him they'd gotten off better than they might've, thanks to Auggie's battlefield leadership, Colonel William's brilliant command of the action, and the timely intervention by the Third Indian regiment.

The battle, though intense, had lasted only a few hours before the rebels were completely driven off and the ford secured. So Colonel Williams had ordered the wagons to cross the stream, and by midafternoon the column was once again on its way to Fort Gibson to deliver the desperately-needed supplies and equipment to the Union garrison there.

As they marched down the road, already dusty in the hot sun despite the recent rains, Auggie, marching out in front of the company, turned and walked backward, calling out as he did so, "Gentlemen … I was just talking with the colonel after the battle. He says we are the first colored brigade in the Union army to fight a battle alongside white soldiers … not to mention Indians. And nobody can say we didn't hold up our end! No, sir, nobody can dare say that. We fought well today, men … I'm damned proud of you." He then turned and faced forward once again, continuing to march.

And it wasn't lost on Ned that when Auggie spoke of the men of the colored regiment he said "we" and not "you."

Monday July 20, 1863 – Hedgesville, West Virginia:

The freemen from Belle Meade Farm had just passed through a small town called Hedgesville, and were halfway across the B&O Railroad bridge southeast of town when Cobb saw a large group of riders approaching the bridge from the south end, clearly intending to cross.

Cobb shaded his eyes with his hand, gazing at the riders a moment before lowering his hand and looking over at Big George, "Rebs."

"Damn the luck!" George immediately turned and headed back the direction they'd come, turning the packhorse by the lead as he did so. "Come on, men! We gotta get off'n this here bridge 'fore them damned slavers get here and run us down!"

And though they scrambled as quickly as they could, it was a near thing, with the last stragglers of the two dozen men jumping off into the shallow waters at the stream's edge just as the riders thundered past and onto the shore. Clearly, the riders would've trampled them otherwise, just as George had warned.

As Cobb and George stood, bent over with hands on knees catching their breath, Henry stepped up and wiped the sweat from under his hat, "Reckon they's just gonna pass us by?"

But Cobb and George just gazed at him a moment before Cobb shrugged and George slowly shook his head.

In a moment, Henry's question was answered, as the riders came to a halt just a few dozen yards beyond the bridge, then wheeled about, trotting up toward where the freeman gathered along the edge of the stream.

Fortunately, when they'd set out from Belle Meade Farm nearly two weeks earlier, they'd taken Miss Abbey's advice and not brought any weapons with them, though they'd dearly wanted to. She was adamant that they look as innocent as possible, blending in with the hundreds of escaped slaves fleeing north, in case they encountered any rebel soldiers. She argued that they'd have little chance of fighting their way through in any case; better to just blend in and not be noticed if they were determined to go—which they were.

Miss Abbey suddenly seemed extremely wise to Cobb. Without any guns, there was still a chance the rebs might just allow them to continue on their way. Just another group of runaway slaves; hardly worth noticing...

But then Cobb's heart sank with a sudden sickening shock as the riders closed the distance; he recognized their leader, a Confederate officer—strongly built, with a neatly trimmed beard, shiny black riding boots, and an odd, blank expression on his face. A man who was missing his left hand. *Walters.*

Nothing was said, but the three freemen exchanged the dark look of men about to mount the gallows. Suddenly, what had seemed like a grand adventure—heading off to Washington City to join up with the Colored Regiments and then fight for their country and help to free the men of their race who still languished in bondage—had just turned into a nightmare.

Walters stopped his horse in front of them and stared for a long moment without speaking. Then he turned to the man riding next to him, another officer, and said, "Roberts, we've no time to waste, nor provisions to take runaway slaves into custody. I'll lead the battalion into town and set up camp. You stay behind with some of your men and … well … recall that we are still, by some definition, in enemy territory. So it would be best not to leave any evidence. The stream being high and swift from the recent showers should serve. Am I clear, Roberts?"

Cobb didn't know exactly what Walters meant by it, but he imagined it wasn't good. The rebel officer said nothing, just saluted, then called out for one of the Confederate platoons, made up of twenty or so men, to stay with him. Walters turned his horse and led the others away without a backward glance.

The rebel officer named Roberts walked his horse up to them while his men dismounted. The officer gazed at Cobb and the others, "Who's the leader of your group?"

Cobb shrugged, "Don't really have a leader, but … I reckon I can speak for all of us as well as any. Name's Cobb."

The officer gazed into Cobb's eyes a long moment with a severe expression, "Cobb … if y'all know what's good for you, you'll do *exactly* as I say … y'hear?"

"Yes, sir."

"Good. Now … gather your men at the water's edge, and then—"

What the rebel officer said after that was such a shock, all Cobb and the others could do was stare back at him wide-eyed and nod their heads.

A few minutes later, Cobb, George, Henry and the other twenty freemen knelt at the stream's edge, with the water directly behind them. Standing in a row in front of them were twenty-some rebel soldiers, holding rifles.

The captain gazed straight at Cobb and nodded, then pulled out his own pistol before turning back toward his row of men, *"Present arms ... Aim ... Fire!"*

Elijah Walters watched through his binoculars from a small knoll nearly a quarter mile back from the river. A cloud of gun smoke rose from the line of soldiers, and a few seconds later he heard the familiar popping of muskets rolling across the hillside, followed by a few more pistol shots. When the smoke cleared, the row of runaway slaves lay face down on the grass. The soldiers moved forward and began dragging the bodies to the river's edge and heaving them in.

Walters lowered his glasses, turned his horse, and trotted back down the hill toward the town where the rest of his men were setting up camp.

Cobb floated down the stream, trying his best to keep his head above water while not thrashing about too much. He tried to understand what had just happened. For reasons he couldn't fathom, the rebel officer Roberts had informed him that Walters had ordered him to shoot them, but that he was not inclined to do so. That if they would just pretend to be killed, and allow his men to throw them into the river afterward as if they truly were dead, then they could float safely away and, God willing, live another day.

But as they knelt at the river's edge, looking down the barrels of the slavers' guns, Cobb had had serious doubts that the rebel officer had been telling it true—that he had lied to them just so they'd cooperate and not try to run away.

But true to his word, at the last moment, the officer's soldiers raised their rifles and fired just over the freemen's heads, after which Cobb and company played along, and fell forward on their faces. And they each lay limp as the soldiers dragged them to the bank and tossed them into the cold water.

Cobb was happy it was a hot day, so the cold dunking wasn't so bad. And after another minute went by, he risked a glance back upstream and saw that they'd floated around a bend and were no longer in sight of the rebel soldiers. So he started making his way to shore. The others quickly followed his lead, and a few minutes later, they all gathered together on the south bank of the stream in a sunny spot on the grass.

They'd lost their pack horse, and a good deal of their food and equipment, but they were still alive. *Alive to fight another day, as the Captain would say,* Cobb thought and grinned as he wrung the water out of his shirt. He then put it back on, cold and sticky wet.

ഇറ(ⅇⅷⅉℰ(ⅇⅷⅉℰ(ⅇⅷⅉ

Friday July 17, 1863 – Honey Springs, Indian Territory:

Ned decided that his earlier assumption that they'd rest awhile in Fort Gibson before returning north to Kansas had been sorely mistaken. Shortly after they'd arrived, greeted by the fort's commander, Colonel Phillips, another Union force arrived with several hundred men and a battery of artillery, this one accompanied by a Major General named James Blunt.

Ned and the other freemen watched the arriving force from across the camp. When Ned noticed that the new soldiers were led by a major general, he whistled softly and turned to Auggie, "Reckon they don't send a two-star out 'less they's fixin' to have a big ol' fight."

Auggie gazed at the general and slowly nodded his head, "I think you may have the right of it, Ned ... You may very well have the right of it."

Now, less than a week later, the entire force from Fort Gibson, three thousand men and officers, including all those brought from Fort Scott under Colonel Williams, stood formed up in line of battle near the Confederate supply depot at Honey Springs, some twenty miles southwest of Fort Gibson. The gathered Union troops waited expectantly while the opposing artillery batteries dueled.

Once again, Ned stood in awe watching the big guns firing, even as he had at Cabin Creek—only this time the enemy had them as well. It gave him a sinking feeling, imagining being targeted by those terrible guns.

Then just as the artillery fire died down, Ned was surprised to see Colonel Williams himself stride out in front of the line formed by the First Kansas Regiment. Williams cupped his hands and called out, "Men of the First Kansas ... we are ordered to advance against the enemy. I know you will do me proud." He then pivoted to face the enemy, drew out his sword, and called out, "*Forward ... March!*"

This time, the distance was too great for an all-out charge, so the First Kansas marched in three broad lines toward the enemy. When they got to within several hundred yards of the enemy's lines, they began to take incoming fire, which was sporadic at first, but began to increase in intensity. Colonel Williams ordered a pause in the march to fire a volley, shortly followed by another, and then a third. But the enemy stood their ground, and the First Kansas began taking casualties.

The two sides exchanged several more volleys before Ned noticed men running frantically toward the front. Soon, a stretcher carried by two men came trotting past. Ned glanced down and suffered a shock. The man in the stretcher was Colonel Williams.

"That ain't good," Ned exchanged a serious look with Auggie, who nodded his agreement.

"Lieutenant Colonel Bowles will take command ... He's a good man," Auggie shrugged as he finished loading his rifle, raised it and fired at the enemy, as the others in the regiment were doing, now being under orders to fire at will.

And though the First Kansas stood their ground exchanging rifle fire with the enemy, they could gain no ground, and finally the order came to withdraw. But even then, the freemen and their officers fell back but grudgingly, and in good order, fighting all the way.

The First Kansas Colored Regiment established a new defensive line behind a low rise after their fallback, and the battle appeared to have devolved into a stalemate when a happy "accident" changed the tide of the engagement.

Ned, watching from his position laying prone behind a small hillock looking across at the enemy position, noticed a large group of Union soldiers walking out into the field between themselves and the Confederates. "What the … What're them fellas doing? They gonna get theyselves shot by *both* sides!"

Auggie grabbed his binoculars and gazed out at the Union soldiers in the field. "It's the Third Indian Regiment … I don't think they're supposed to be there … Likely got their orders mixed up. Damn … they're gonna get themselves slaughtered out there."

They continued to watch as the Union Indian soldiers began taking fire, and hesitated as if uncertain where to go, finally going to ground and no longer advancing.

"Damn it!" Auggie jumped up and dashed out into the field toward the Indians.

Ned followed, but first turned back and shouted at the men, "Stay put … don't follow … we'll be right back!"

They raced across the open field, zig zagging to avoid enemy sharpshooters, and slid in next to the commander of the Third, Lieutenant Colonel Schaurte.

"Colonel…" Auggie sputtered between gasps for breath. "With all due respect, sir … I believe you've strayed off course. Right here you're directly in the line of fire of the First Kansas Colored, sir, and square in the middle of no-man's-land."

"Oh! Damn … I thought something didn't look right…"

"Yes, sir … but if you'll follow me, I'll lead you to our position, where you'll have better cover."

"Yes … yes, that sounds fine, please lead on, Lieutenant."

The order was quickly given, and the Third Indian Regiment was moving quickly back toward the position held by the First Kansas.

But even before Auggie and Ned reached their own lines again, they heard a great shout behind them, the unmistakable battle cry known as the rebel yell. Ned risked a quick glance back and saw thousands of rebel soldiers were now surging forward in an all-out attack. As the Third Indian retreated past the First Kansas line and turned to form up behind them, Ned and Auggie slid in next to the men of Company G.

"What just happened, Lieutenant?" Ned asked, between gasps for breath, looking back at the approaching enemy army.

"I think ... I think the enemy ... thought our forces were defeated and in retreat. They think to overrun and rout us."

"Well then ... I reckon they're in for a surprise," Ned frowned, raising his rifle.

Down the line to their left, Lieutenant Colonel Bowles stood up and called out, *"First Kansas will stand to, and prepare for volley fire..."*

Moments later, the advancing Confederates, coming on fast and expecting easy meat, were met by a devastating rifle volley that stopped them in their tracks and sent them scrambling for cover.

Then the Third Indian Regiment stepped forward and fired off their own volley with a thunderous *boom!* The rebels broke ranks and began falling back in full retreat.

Colonel Bowles immediately ordered a counterattack by the First Kansas, who were joined by the Third Indian in a steady march back across the field, which drove the enemy before them and sealed the victory.

As they marched, Ned was surprised to see that the majority of the Confederate casualties were Indians of the Five Civilized Tribes. But he was not especially surprised to see the Union Indian soldiers of the Third dispatching the rebel wounded of their fellow Indians with a ruthless efficiency that the white Union officers were helpless to prevent.

It occurred to Ned that between the black men of the First Kansas, and the Indians on both sides, this was likely the first battle in the war where white soldiers were in the minority.

That afternoon, during the march back to the fort, Auggie gave his usual backward-marching pep-talk to the company, "Men … after the battle, I overheard Major General Blunt telling Lieutenant Colonel Bowles that he'd never seen such fighting as was done by our regiment today. He said that the question of whether black men could fight had been settled once and for all, and that we were the best troops he'd ever had the honor of commanding."

The men gave a rousing cheer to this pronouncement as they marched, and began chanting out, "*First Kansas Colored, First Kansas Colored, First Kansas Colored…*" as they marched along.

Auggie turned to Ned as they marched, "I also heard that Colonel Williams is expected to recover, though likely to be out of action for a time."

"That's good to hear," Ned nodded. "The colonel is a good man."

Auggie grinned and tilted his head, "Not a good *white* man, Sergeant Turner?"

Ned chuckled and shook his head, "No, sir … just a good *man*."

ΣΟΣΧΟΣΒΟΣΟΣΧΟΣΒΟΣΟΣΧΟΣ

Monday August 17, 1863 – Camp Casey – Arlington, Virginia:

"C'mon, boys, put your backs into it. This here latrine ain't gonna dig its own self," Big George called out, even as he followed his own admonishment and hacked at the hard ground with his pick, loosening the soil so the others of his platoon could scoop it out with shovels.

After several more minutes, he paused and straightened up, rubbing the small of his back and wiping the sweat from under his blue kepi hat. Then, realizing his hands were covered in mud which he'd just smeared across his own forehead, he wiped his hands on his blue shirt tails. Then he glanced down and saw that

306

his pant legs were covered with the same sticky clay up past his knees, and his boots were no longer recognizable.

He shrugged. The dirty clothes were of little concern, but the boots would need a thorough cleaning and oiling else they'd quickly rot, crack, and fall apart. And George had no desire to march into battle bare-footed, despite the fact he'd spent most of his life in that condition. Probably because of that, he treasured his army-issued boots, and intended to preserve them for as long as he could.

He'd just got back to working the pick when a whistle blew up above them, over toward the barracks, signaling their midday meal break. George gratefully leaned the pick up against the side of the trench and led the platoon up out of the muck via a crude, hand-crafted wood ladder.

"Helluva way to fight a war, hunh Sergeant Washington?" Private Sid Willers gave George a wry grin as they walked toward the mess tent.

"Yeah ... reckon it ain't all thunder and glory, Private," George shrugged.

"Never expected it would be, only ... ain't seen any white soldiers down in that-there hole a diggin'. Why is it we's workin' the shovel, while them white soldiers across the way spend their day drillin' and shootin' guns and all?"

George looked over at Willers with a dark frown, "You know as well as I the answer to that. Look at the color o' your skin — there's your answer. The army thinks all we's good for is hard work. Even here in the North they ain't yet figured out we're *men*, same as any."

"Yeah, ain't that the truth, Sarge ... and I heard we's gettin' paid less than the white soldiers, though we work twice as hard. What we gonna do about that, Sarge?"

George stopped and turned to frown at Willers, "We gonna prove we're *men*, private; that's what. When the time comes, when the battle is hottest, and the fear is greatest, and grown men are cryin' out for their mommas ... *then* we gonna prove we're men. That's what."

Monday August 17, 1863 – Hagerstown, Maryland:

Tony stepped into Nathan's tent, came to attention, and snapped a salute, "Requesting a moment of the colonel's time, sir."

Nathan set down the requisition he was examining and frowned at Tony, "At ease, Tony. Why so formal all of a sudden when it's just us in the tent?"

But Tony had a serious look and stepped forward, setting something on the table. When he lifted his hand, Nathan saw a large wad of paper money and a pile of coins sitting on the table. He looked up at Tony, "What's this?"

"Money, sir."

Nathan scowled, "Well, yes, I can see that ... but—"

"It's the money I owe you, sir."

"You *owe* me? Tony, you don't owe me any money—"

"Yes, sir, to my mind I do."

Nathan sat back in his chair and rubbed at the whiskers of his beard, gazing at Tony, "All right ... would you be so kind as to explain your thinking on the matter, then, that I might better understand it?"

"Yes, sir. I found out just now that the black men in the colored regiments is bein' paid six dollars less a month than the white soldiers of the same rank. So I went and asked the paymaster why is it I always get the same pay as the white fellers in *this* regiment. He said I don't ... but he also said that *you*, sir, have been making up the difference outta your own pay."

"Oh, *that!* To be honest, I'd nearly forgotten about it. When I first found out about the difference in pay, I was fairly steamed, as you can well imagine. I fought with the army on it, but to no avail. I may not be able the change the whole system, but I can at least make sure you are paid the same as the other soldiers in my regiment. My little arrangement with the paymaster seems the fairest solution."

"No, sir … it ain't fair. Ain't fair that you gotta pay outta your own pocket—like you don't earn your pay more'n all the rest of us put together—and it also ain't fair me bein' paid more'n the other black men that's fightin'. Ain't sayin' it's fair we's bein' paid less, but if that's the bitter pill bein' fed us black men, then I reckon I gotta swallow it same as all the others."

Nathan gazed at Tony a long moment, then nodded, leaned forward, reached out his hand and slowly scooped the money toward him. Then he stood and gave Tony a salute, "You're a good man, Tony, as I've always believed and said; every day you make that more clear and obvious.

"And … I suppose it's good that you now know the truth about the difference in pay, as I was going to have to tell you about it anyway…" Nathan reached to the side, picked up a sheet of paper, and handed it to Tony.

"What's this, sir?"

"It's your transfer papers, Tony, and a promotion to the rank of sergeant in the colored regiments. Congratulations, you are now the newest member of the United States Twenty-Third Colored Regiment, which, as I understand it via a letter from Miss Abbey, now includes Cobb, Big George, Henry, and twenty-some others of our old Mountain Meadows freemen. She also told me that Phinney decided to stay home this time, so she has appointed him as officer in charge of guarding Belle Meade Farm.

"You leave for the east on the first train in the morning."

"Oh! Thank you, sir. Thank you very kindly for that."

"No, thank *you*, Tony, for your service to the Twelfth. And I know you and the others of our men will make me proud in the Twenty-Third."

Saturday August 22, 1863 – Camp Casey – Arlington, Virginia:

Henry, Cobb, and Big George sat around a blazing campfire in the open area in front of the Twenty-Third's barracks. And to no one's surprise who'd known him back at Mountain Meadows, Big George, now known around camp as Sergeant Washington, had recruited several other men to build various instruments and join him in banging out numerous well-known and made-up tunes on Saturday nights.

George was pounding away on a drum he'd fashioned from a nail keg with a piece of mule hide stretched across one end, while other men accompanied him on other odd handmade instruments. The rest of the men gathered round, including nearly all the freemen who'd come east from Belle Meade Farm, and belted out the songs with great enthusiasm, and some even with a good measure of skill.

As most of the songs George preferred were of a humorous bent, the end of each tune was generally filled with much laughter and raucous, good-natured ribbing.

During one such pause in the music, a black man wearing a long army overcoat and carrying a haversack weaved his way through the men and stepped up next to George, turning his back to the fire. In the darkness, with the firelight behind him and his hat pulled low, no one recognized the newcomer. An expectant silence fell over the group.

George looked up at the man, "You're welcome to share our fire, stranger. And our music, if you have a liking for such..."

The man didn't immediately answer, but slowly nodded his head, "A man I know once said, 'They got them some good drums, and some fine deep voices, I believe. But they's lacking in the higher tones. And they got no tuneful instruments to speak of.'"

George's eyes widened and he leapt to his feet, scooping the newcomer off his feet in a great bear hug, while those sitting around looked at each other in wonder, as if Big George had suddenly gone mad.

After a moment, George set the newcomer back down. In his exuberance, George had knocked the man's hat off, and all could now see his face: "*Tony!* Tony, where on God's green earth you been, boy?!" Big George grinned as he slapped him hard on the sides of both arms. Tony beamed, taking the big man's affectionate blows with good humor.

The other freemen from Mountain Meadows jumped up and surrounded Tony, shaking him and patting his back, while the other men looked on, smiling and laughing, knowing they were witnessing a most joyful reunion.

Chapter 13. Confederate Inferno

"Libby Prison was the Inferno
of the slave Confederacy.
Well might have been written over its portal,
'All hope abandon, ye who enter here.'"
- Charles Carleton Coffin

Sunday July 5, 1863 – Richmond, Virginia:

William, being a surgeon, was immediately put to work in the Libby Prison hospital, located on the ground floor of the three-story brick warehouse-turned-prison. Sadly, one of his first patients was Phillipe. Phillipe had developed a cough during the journey to the prison, which had worsened since their arrival. And then a fever had set in, accompanied by vomiting and diarrhea, such that less than a week after their arrival Phillipe had been moved to a hospital bed.

William had quickly discovered that being in the hospital was far from ideal for a sick man. Medicine was almost nonexistent, and rations entirely inadequate; men who might've made a quick recovery with proper food and medicine died within a few days, and the surgeons were nearly helpless to do anything about it.

But Phillipe was a strong and vigorous young man, so to William's thinking, he should have been one of those who fought through to a recovery, despite the deplorable conditions. But Phillipe seemed entirely despondent, and unresponsive to William's attempts to cheer or motivate him.

And when he thought about it, William realized Phillipe's downcast demeanor had started when they were first captured, well before he'd shown any signs of illness. The only thing William could figure was that the shocking murder of Sergeant Dixon by Walters had hit him unusually hard. But Phillipe was a veteran soldier, first with the French army and then lately fighting along with the rest of the Captain's men. He'd seen many men killed in battle ... so the death of the sergeant, as deplorable as that had been, didn't seem sufficient to explain his malaise.

And even as Phillipe's health continued to decline, the hospital witnessed the death of a dozen or more young men nearly every day, with no help in sight.

ᔕᕈᙢᘔᘗᙢᔕᕈᙢᘔᘗᙢᔕᕈᙢᘔᘗ

More than twelve hundred Union officers were packed into what had before the war been a warehouse for storing and processing tobacco. It had three stories, divided into three sections each, east, west, and middle.

The first level housed the prison administrative offices and guardrooms on the west end, kitchen in the middle, and hospital in the east section. The second and third floors housed the prisoners in six large rooms, with no furniture nor beds.

The building also had a cellar—dark, dank, and rat infested. This served as slave quarters on the west end, and in the center were four prison cells, used for punishing prisoners who attempted to escape or violated other prison rules. The east end had once served as a kitchen, but had been walled off and abandoned, likely due to the uncontrollable rat problem.

The prison was located at the James River's edge, so running water was piped in from the river for drinking, bathing, and flushing out the trough that served for a toilet in the water closet on each floor. The barred windows were small and open to the elements, such that the rooms were unbearably hot in summer, freezing cold in winter, and always dark, even on the sunniest days.

Prisoners were never taken outside, and were not allowed to linger at the windows; guards stationed outside were under orders to shoot any prisoners seen standing at the windows.

But for Zeke, the worst part of Libby Prison was not the overcrowding, discomfort, disease, lice, rats, or even inadequate rations; the worst part of prison for a young man used to a vigorous, outdoor lifestyle was being shut indoors, in a dark, airless room with a complete lack of anything to do. It was an unimaginably slow, painful form of torture for Zeke, who'd spent

313

his whole life either working on a farm or more recently, fighting in the war.

Every day in Libby was the same as the one before. At six a.m., the black Union soldiers, who were used as slaves by the confederates, were brought upstairs to beat reveille on drums. Men would then queue up at the faucet for a quick, cold wash in the rusty looking water. Those few lucky enough to have a toothbrush, William among them, also brushed their teeth before returning it to a pocket or buttonhole where they would zealously guard the precious instrument.

One of the prisoners might then recite the morning's headlines from a newspaper purchased from the guards for a quarter. Normally, the captives pitched in and bought two or three copies so they could be passed around.

While the Confederate-skewed news was being shared, one of the black prisoners would walk around with a bucket of burning tar to fumigate the room in a vain attempt to beat back the prison's relentless vermin. But this exercise did little more than add to the foul odor of the place. So one of the regular rituals, after breakfast and the first of two daily headcounts by the guards, was the pursuit and extermination of lice.

Zeke thought it a scene almost comical if it weren't so pathetic, and a thing he could've never imagined before coming to Libby; the entire room of several hundred men would strip naked and begin meticulously examining their clothing, skin, and hair for the tiny, relentless antagonists, and crushing them with their fingernails when captured.

William and Zeke would take turns examining each other's hair, picking out the nasty little creatures the prisoners had nicknamed "graybacks"—not coincidentally the same nickname they used for the other most hated Libby "vermin," the Confederate prison guards.

But despite this vigorous daily practice, the lice retained the upper hand in the conflict, such that at times they seemed to simply rain from the ceiling. And it was taken as a sign that a man was not long for the world once he simply lay down and gave up the fight, allowing the lice to rule uncontested.

314

Later in the day, as the hours crawled by, they'd have another meal, such as it was, another head count, and then finally "lights out" at nine o'clock, which was a euphemistic way of saying a mutually agreed time to shut up and try to get some sleep, since there were no lights in Libby Prison. Some days, Zeke wished that he could fall asleep and stay that way until this interminable nightmare was over and he could be free once again.

But the next day would be the same, as would the one after that, and the one after that … And with the prisoner exchanges halted, their bitter, helpless, hopeless existence had no end in sight, except for the grim prospect of dying of some malady or slowly starving to death.

෨෩ඓ෪ඏ෨෩ඓ෪ඏ෨෩ඓ

Sunday July 12, 1863 – Richmond, Virginia:

The day arrived that William had been dreading but knew he was helpless to avoid: the day Phillipe would die. It was a sad, ironic contrast to the unusually upbeat mood of the Union officers in Libby, as news of the great victory at Gettysburg spread like wildfire through the building, despite the guards' best efforts to suppress the reports. Groups of officers were marching about, banging on hand-made drums, belting out "The Star-Spangled Banner" and other patriotic songs to annoy their Confederate captors.

But William felt no elation as he stood next to Phillipe's bed, holding his hand. The hand felt cold and lifeless, though Phillipe's chest yet heaved up and down with a rasping, rattling, wheezing noise that to William's trained ear, meant death was imminent. William already felt exhausted, up half the night listening to the man next to him hacking out a deathly, rasping cough. A man whose condition didn't yet warrant hospitalization, in the Confederates' view.

Phillipe's face was pale and wraithlike, with sunken cheeks and dark circles under his closed eyes—a frightful shadow of the vigorous man he'd once been. William assumed that Phillipe would simply expire in his sleep, and they'd have no more words

315

together on this earth. The thought brought a deep sadness and sense of despair; a feeling that the world he knew was slowly dying from an incurable disease of madness and violence—a sickness he was helpless to heal.

He lifted Phillipe's cold right hand and gently tucked it back under the dirty, ragged blanket that would soon cover another patient. But to his surprise, Phillipe's eyes opened, and for a moment he seemed more focused than he'd been at any time in the last several days, "William…" he rasped in a voice barely above a whisper.

William leaned in closer so he could hear what would likely be the man's last words, "Yes, I'm here, Phillipe. Zeke wanted to be here too, but the guards wouldn't let him through…"

"Closer…" Phillipe, nodded his head in a sign for William to move in.

"I wish to confess…"

"Oh … yes, of course," William chided himself for not remembering until just now that Phillipe, being of French descent, was Catholic. "Shall I send for the chaplain?"

"No … you, William … I wish to confess to you…"

"But I…"

"William … I have betrayed Nathan…"

"You … what? Phillipe, you're not well, not thinking clearly. It's not your fault we were captured. You've done nothing wrong…"

"Yes … yes I have." Phillipe began coughing and couldn't seem to stop or catch his breath. William feared he might not be able to say anything more. But after a moment, the cough seemed to settle again. Phillipe took a sucking breath, "William … when Walters … put a gun to my head … I … I was afraid. A goddamned coward. I told him everything he wanted to know … where to find the colonel … the regiment … I was a coward … Should have let him shoot me instead."

"Oh, no, Phillipe. It wasn't your fault. There was nothing else you could've done with a gun to your head."

"Yes … I could've died a *man* that day … instead of a *coward* now … a damned coward…"

316

"But..."

Phillipe closed his eyes and would say nothing else. A few moments later his chest heaved violently, then stopped entirely, and he breathed no more.

Tears welled in William's eyes. He removed his glasses and wiped them off with his sleeve. He'd not been shocked that Phillipe had told Walters what he wanted to know; most men likely would've done the same under the circumstances. No, the shocking thing to William was that Phillipe had been so upset about his own betrayal that he had given up living and willed himself to die, refusing to fight back to health.

William now had the sad task of writing a letter home with the tragic news. A task made more miserable by the strict prison rules limiting each letter to six lines, and nothing at all criticizing the Confederate government or the prison for fear of being thrown into the dungeon with the rats.

One last thing William would do for Phillipe, he decided, was to take his deathbed confession to his own grave, and never tell another soul. As far as the world would ever know, Phillipe had been a courageous soldier and had died a hero's death.

ຣ໐ແຊເ໐ຮບຣ໐ແຊເ໐ຮບຣ໐ແຊເ໐

Wednesday August 5, 1863 – Wheeling, West Virginia:

Adilida sobbed unconsolably, leaning her head into Edouard's shoulder as he silently re-read the brief letter from William that had arrived in the day's post. Tears rolled down his cheeks as an emptiness and despair filled his heart such as he hadn't experienced in many long years, not since the death of Addie's parents when she was only a child. And for the first time, he felt his years. *No father should outlive his son...*

> *Dear Abbey, Margaret, et al., sorry this is terse per rules.*
> *Phillipe took ill on the march to Richmond. I did all to aid*
> *him, but today he succumbed and has passed. Zeke and I*
> *are deeply saddened, but in good health. Tell Adilida and*

317

Edouard we are sorry for their loss. He was a good man
and brave soldier who deserved a better fate. – William.

ഇ൜ര൘ഇ൜ര൘ഇ൜ര൘

Monday, September 14, 1863 – Richmond, Virginia:

"Miss Evelyn, sorry to disturb you ma'am, but there's a young gentleman at the door. An officer, and says he's a friend of yours," the young freeman maid Bess announced with an amused look.

"Oh, thank you, Bess. Did this young officer give his name?"

"No, ma'am. I asked it, but he says he wishes to tell you himself…"

"Hmm … that's odd. Very well, please see him in, if you would. Thank you, Bess."

"Certainly, ma'am."

Evelyn now felt a twinge of trepidation. *Another officer from the Signal Corps? Thought we'd put them off the track for a time at least … Have they decided to begin their investigation anew?*

She stood to greet the officer, as Bess escorted him in from the front door to where Evelyn had been seated in the sitting room of her house.

But when the officer stepped into the room, Evelyn gasped with surprise and jumped to her feet, followed by her brightest smile, *"Oh, my goodness! Jubal!* I can't believe you're here!"

The tall, handsome young lieutenant removed his hat and bowed slightly, "Yes, Evelyn, it's me." Jubal blushed as a grin lit his features. He was dressed in a neat, freshly pressed, gray officer's uniform, embroidered in gold, with butternut trim, and shiny black shoes.

"And look at you! Why, Jubal … I swear you've grown an inch since I last saw you!"

He shook his head, continuing to grin, "Oh, I don't think so … Likely I just look taller on account of being a bit … *leaner.* Sometimes rations are a bit scarce out on the march, you know."

"Oh, you poor dear. Well, we won't allow that sort of treatment in *this* house at least." She stepped past him into the hall, and called out, "Bess, would you please fetch some refreshments for Lieutenant Collins ... Tea and some of those sweet biscuits, for starters..."

"Yes, ma'am. Straightaway, ma'am," a voice could be heard to say from down the hallway.

Evelyn stepped back into the room, still beaming, "It is *so* good to see you again, Jubal, *truly*." And she meant it; to see him looking well and fit felt genuinely joyful.

She realized something about him had changed. There was now a maturity and confidence that hadn't been there before. She decided it was a good look on him.

"Please, Jubal, have a seat, and then you must tell me everything that has occurred since we last exchanged a post."

"Yes, ma'am." He moved over and took a seat opposite the one she'd been using, setting his hat aside on the end table. "Guess that'd be since just before we fought in the great battle up Pennsylvania way..."

— — —

For the next two hours, Jubal poured out his heart to Evelyn, describing his adventures and misadventures in the war since the beginning of the Gettysburg battle—sometimes in such excruciating detail that Evelyn involuntarily flinched or shuddered at the horrific narrative. And he also described the depth of his feelings during those trials, such that she was obliged to wipe her eyes with a handkerchief from time to time.

When he concluded his tale, at the point where he received his furlough and headed home to Richmond, they sat in silence for several moments.

Then Jubal looked up and said, "And now, it's your turn, Evelyn. And if you would, first ... please satisfy my curiosity about how it was you ended up in Frederick, Maryland just at the time we were marching through there on our way to the battle over at Sharpsburg. I wrote you a letter asking that question, but never received an answer ... so I suspect you never got it."

"Oh! I didn't realize *you* were there, Jubal. Did you see me, then? Truly?" Evelyn feigned surprise, knowing the question was bound to come up at some point. She'd already decided it would be necessary to lie to him about it. And she felt little guilt in doing so, as the lie wasn't intended to harm him, and might even protect him from the conflicted feelings that knowing too much might invoke in him.

"Yes, we were on parade, and I was marching directly behind General Lee and his staff officers. I was looking into the crowd and saw you, but you were turning away and never saw me. I went back after the parade and searched all over town for you, but never found you, and no one I asked knew anything about you."

"Oh, what a shame. I'm so sorry I missed seeing you there, Jubal. That would've been a most happy reunion."

"Thank you for saying so, Evelyn."

"No, truly, Jubal. I wish I would have known you were there. I was in Frederick looking after my dear Aunt Emeline who'd taken ill, and I must confess it was a dull task. Seeing you would've been a welcome respite from my nursing duties.

"I had heard a rumor that some Confederate troops were passing through town, so I went to have a look, having no notion which ones they might be. As you can imagine, I was surprised to see General Lee sitting up high on his horse, and immediately left to go tell Auntie about it, knowing how thrilled she'd be that the famous general was in her own little town."

The words flowed easily from her lips, not only because she'd planned and practiced the story for months in anticipation of this moment, but—she suddenly realized—she'd become extremely proficient at lying, even to people who trusted her implicitly. *Hmm ... not necessarily something one should feel proud of, Evelyn! I'll have to work on ridding myself of that particular nasty habit ... once this war is over.*

Jubal smiled, "I knew there was some reasonable explanation; I just couldn't quite puzzle it out. But now that you say it, it makes perfect sense. I was a bit worried about you, what with two large, belligerent armies passing right through the town."

"Oh, never fear, I was in no danger at all," she lied, a vision flashing through her mind of Joseph forced to shoot the cavalry soldier who was preparing to put a bullet hole in her head after she'd stolen General Jeb Stuart's marching orders.

"I was so busy caring for Auntie, I scarcely saw any more of the soldiers after that parade. In fact, I was surprised when I stepped out of the house one day, heading for the general store, and the soldiers out on the street who'd been wearing gray were now wearing blue!" she chuckled.

Jubal laughed and nodded, "Yes, the Union Army was following closely behind when we left that place."

Then Evelyn proceeded to tell Jubal all the news and gossip in Richmond she could think of. But after a time, she noticed he seemed to be paying but little attention, so she stopped talking and gazed at him thoughtfully.

He looked up with a serious, thoughtful expression she'd not seen on him before. He sat up straighter, and leaned forward, now staring into her eyes. "Evelyn, I … I have thought of you a lot while out in the war … in fact, nearly every hour of every day…"

Her heart began to sink … *Oh no, Jubal, no … not this … not this, I beg of you … please don't go there…*

But what she said aloud was, "Oh, I very much doubt that, Jubal, with all the marching and fighting you were doing. Surely you had little time to think of anything else."

He shook his head, "It's true, there were times when I had little time for thought. But most of a soldier's life is dull and routine, lazing about for days on end with little to do but think of home. And during those times, I found myself thinking of you. And … wondering … you know … if we might … if you and I, that is … if we ever might be able to move past being just friends…"

And suddenly the smug feeling she'd had at anticipating and smoothly handling his questions about Frederick completely melted away, leaving her feeling lost and adrift in a dark sea of mixed emotions.

"Jubal, I…" she began, intending to make up another lie. But she stopped herself. This one would hurt him. If not now, in the long term. *No, I'll not lie to him about this … not about something this personal, this important, this hurtful…*

321

She reached out and took his hands in hers, and looked into his eyes. But she was no longer smiling, and he immediately mirrored her serious look.

"Jubal … you have been a good friend, and I have thought about you, worried over you, and prayed for you almost every day since you've been out on campaign. You are a good man, brave, conscientious, capable … and, at the risk of sounding forward, you are a handsome man, and any woman would feel lucky to have your attentions…"

He slowly nodded, "But…"

"But … while you have been out fighting, I … I have become betrothed to another."

His expression sagged, "Who … who is he, if I may ask?"

"A man I've known for a long time, since before you and I met, if that makes you feel any better…"

He nodded, "Perhaps a little. I can at least tell myself I might've won the campaign if I'd but started it sooner…" He gave her a wan smile. "Does this gentleman have a name?"

She looked down at her feet. That was one piece of information she dared not give out.

"I … I'd rather not say at the moment. He is an officer, you see, and…" then an idea occurred to her. It was enough of the truth to cover the lie about why his name shouldn't be told.

"And, Jubal, you know better than anyone the type of activity I've been involved in here in Richmond … activity that's morally righteous, but not *strictly speaking*, legal?"

He nodded, "Yes, of course … the Underground Railroad. And you fear if you were to be caught it might damage this officer's reputation, perhaps even cause him to lose his commission?"

She nodded, "So we've agreed to keep our betrothal a secret and postpone our marriage until the war is over."

"I see … Then … I'm sorry I mentioned anything … *personal*…" he trailed off, no longer making eye contact.

An awkward silence followed. Evelyn could think of nothing to say that didn't sound trite and disingenuous. Nor could she think of any words to comfort him, though she dearly wished to.

Finally, he rose, replaced his hat, and said, "I think I have used up enough of your time, Miss Evelyn. I believe it would be best if I left now…"

She rose, "Jubal, I … I'm so sorry … You're a good man. You deserve every happiness…" was all she could think of, and even as she said it, she knew her words fell flat.

And then he turned and was gone.

ⅺ∎ⅺ№№ⅺ∎ⅺ№№ⅺ∎ⅺ№

As he strode away from Evelyn's house, Jubal fought back the tears that the welling pain in his heart was trying to force from his eyes. Months of hopes and dreams for what might have been after the war had been dashed in a single moment. And all he could think was, *I may as well just die in the war now…*

But that dark thought triggered another, which, though it didn't entirely mollify him, gave him a slim glimmer of hope: *But the war's not over yet, and even this mystery man of Evelyn's could yet be killed in the fighting. Many officers have been, after all.*

But is it a sin to wish for the death of another man? Especially a man who's an officer on our side? Hmm … maybe so … but I'd pay God his dues for a chance to be with Evelyn…

ⅺ∎ⅺ№№ⅺ∎ⅺ№№ⅺ∎ⅺ№

Friday November 6, 1863 – Richmond, Virginia:

As deplorable as conditions in Libby Prison were, rumors spoke of far worse conditions at Belle Isle, where Union-enlisted prisoners were incarcerated. William's heart went out to those men, whose only shelter as the frosts of winter began to set in were canvas tents, whose tops could be seen out across the water from the south and west windows of Libby.

The romantic name of the place, and its seemingly idyllic setting in the middle of the James River, were in stark contrast to the stories circulating about the conditions faced there by Union soldiers.

For months, William had been haunted by thoughts of these poor men, to the point where he'd spoken to the guards on several occasions, offering his medical services to those on the isle if there was ever an opportunity for him to go there.

Apparently, William's cordial, respectful requests had eventually paid off, for one day a guard came to him in the hospital and asked if he still wished to visit Belle Isle; that a shipment of blankets and warm clothing for the prisoners had arrived, sponsored by a Northern charity called the U.S. Christian Commission. The Confederate prison commissioner didn't want any outsiders to visit the island, but would allow one of the Union surgeons to accompany the mission on the agreement he be sworn to silence on anything he saw there, beyond bearing witness to the proper distribution of the goods. The Confederate government had become sensitive to accusations in Northern newspapers of confiscating goods sent for the benefit of the Union prisoners, and using said goods for the Confederate Army. So this time, they apparently wanted a reliable witness to attest to their good intentions in this particular case.

William quickly agreed to these conditions, and within minutes found himself aboard a steam freighter down at the water's edge. There he was introduced to a northerner, John Hussey, a civilian supervisor in charge of the mercy mission.

William watched as the bales of blankets and clothing were loaded on smaller boats for transport to the island. He himself stepped aboard one of the boats, accompanied by armed prison guards and the slaves who'd been charged with loading and unloading the goods.

When William stepped off the boat and entered the prison grounds, what he saw was so horrific he was nearly paralyzed by the vision. He stood, mouth agape, looking across an open field at hundreds of ragged, moldy-looking tents and thousands of gaunt, wraith-like figures huddled on the ground singly or in groups, shivering in the cold. Hundreds of others staggered about aimlessly, arms wrapped around their own shoulders in an attempt to keep warm. He realized in that moment that Libby Prison was a Shangri-la compared to this hellscape.

As he walked across the grounds, watching the slaves handing out the blankets, coats, and other clothing, he met blank stares from men, mostly in their early twenties, who would never again be the same, if they survived at all. As he passed what he assumed was a drainage ditch, he looked within and saw dozens of men laying in the bottom, their combined body heat keeping them warm. In other places, men lay curled up on the ground in small nests they'd fashioned by scooping a hole in the bare dirt.

He quickly realized the goods that he had accompanied would be woefully insufficient for the tremendous need. Perhaps a tenth of the prisoners would benefit, if that.

When the supply of goods was completely depleted, he asked to visit the prison hospital. When he arrived, he could see it was nothing more than a large, frigid tent where those on the very edge of death were sent to die. The men who passed for surgeons were not much better off than the patients—pale, emaciated, with hopeless, haunted eyes. William gave them the few medicines he'd brought with him, knowing it was no better than a tiny drop in a great ocean of need.

When he left the hospital tent, he saw a stack of bodies lying out back, a dozen or more, awaiting transport back to the mainland for burial. They'd been stripped of clothing, and had become blackened and stiff from the frost.

Hours later, William returned to the freighter to report the success of the mission to John Hussey. William sat at a table across from Hussey, and as agreed, testified that the goods had indeed been distributed to the prisoners, as promised.

And then he looked hard in Hussey's eyes, and told the *real* story of Belle Isle, in all its horrific, excruciating detail. By the end of his story, Hussey was wiping tears from his eyes. He thanked William and promised that this story would soon be known to the world.

๛๛๛๛๛๛๛๛

Three days later, after John Hussey had reported William's findings to the Union Army and the Lincoln Administration's angry response had been received back in the Confederate capital, the response at Libby was swift and brutal.

The warden was furious, and he sent guards to seize William from out of the hospital and toss him into one of the damp, black, rat-infested cells in the cellar of Libby. The sentence for breaking his word and telling what he'd seen to the Northern charity commissioner was two weeks in the dungeon. It was a virtual death sentence. Rations were so slight, and conditions so horrific, that prisoners rarely survived a week. No one survived two weeks.

But Zeke had other ideas. He was determined not to let William die. He made arrangements with one of the assistant surgeons, a young man named Isaac Watson Brown, of the Twenty-Second Illinois Regiment, to smuggle him into the hospital so he could locate William. Zeke feigned being deathly ill, rubbing soot under his eyes and flour on his face, and Isaac played along, hustling him into the hospital.

Isaac, who like William had been captured when he'd stayed behind to aid the wounded, had become friends with William, so he was more than willing to help, despite the risk. Zeke explained to Isaac that he figured the hospital must be directly above the "dungeon," with only old, well-worn wooden floorboards separating the two.

So they conceived a system where Zeke crawled around on the floor pulling up boards and calling down below, trying to locate his comrade, as Isaac kept watch for guards. Whenever a guard entered the hospital, Isaac called out a pre-arranged warning, any sentence that included the phrase "septic dysentery" in it. Zeke would scramble beneath the nearest bed until he heard the phrase "typhoid pneumonia," which signaled the all-clear.

Zeke spent an entire grinding day crawling around, prying up boards with a broken screwdriver he'd obtained from one of the prisoners. It had cost him one of his last remaining greenbacks, but that was a small enough price to pay. Zeke was exhausted and beginning to fear he'd been wrong about the location of the subterranean cells.

He'd finally worked his way into the far northeast corner of the hospital, had worked loose the last board in the very corner. "William ... William, are you there?" he called out. But there was

326

no response. He lifted the board, preparing to set it back in place when he heard a rustling noise below. So he called out again, "William?"

"Yes … yes, it's me. Zeke?"

"Yes, I'm here, William. How you gettin' along?"

"Well, it's … it's not as bad as Belle Isle, that's for sure. It's dark, wet, and cold. And it stinks. But the good news is, I have all these rats to keep me company. I'll live … unless they starve me to death."

"They will if we let them. But we ain't gonna let them. Not while I'm alive, they ain't. Now that I know where you are, I'll start bringing you rations. Don't you worry none, William."

"All right. Thanks, Zeke."

William's calm demeanor made Zeke realize that the Confederates really had no idea what kind of man they were dealing with. Likely they mistook William for a weak, intellectual type, him being a polite, soft-spoken surgeon. What they didn't know was that William was also a war-hardened veteran soldier, who'd spent years out in Texas in the harshest possible conditions, fighting against ruthless, relentless enemies.

Being thrown in a damp cell was not especially trying for William, as long as he had food and water. And now Zeke would make sure of that. They still had a few greenbacks Zeke could use to obtain extra outside food, and if necessary, he could shame the other prisoners into donating a small portion of their rations to save a fellow inmate. Or he'd threaten them if he had to … either way…

ഇന്ദ്രഃ

Monday November 23, 1863 – Richmond, Virginia:

When William's two-week punishment was up, the guards were not surprised to find he was still alive. After all, he had continued to eat his meager rations, and drink the foul, dirty water they provided every day.

They were shocked, however, when they stepped into the cell and shined a lamp on his face. Though the sudden light was

327

blinding after two weeks in the dark, William smiled up at them, squinting and blinking, "Good morning, gentlemen … or maybe good evening … Hard to tell down here."

Then he stood and walked out on his own, seemingly no worse for the experience. The guards exchanged a look of surprise, but shrugged and followed along.

When William arrived upstairs, he walked over and sat next to Zeke. "Sorry about the smell."

Zeke laughed, "Hell, William, we all stink in this place. What's a little more stench among friends. How was it?"

William tilted his head thoughtfully, "Well, it was a new experience, that's for certain. I don't recall the last time I had such uninterrupted time for thought and contemplation." Then he chuckled.

"What?"

William smiled, "I may have been going a little crazy down there at the end … the last few days, I took to lecturing the rats on various subjects, just to pass the time. They seemed quite curious, and would sit and listen for long spells. And at the end, I could swear there were more and more who would sit and listen. I believe if I spent a year down there, they'd start talking back in English, asking pertinent questions at critical junctures in the lecture."

Zeke laughed, and slapped William on the knee, "Good to have you back, William."

"Good to be back. And thanks again for saving my life. I'd never have made it on the scant food they provided. I would've had to resort to catching and eating the rats, if I could. Raw."

"Never mention it, William. Never mention it. As for eating rats … it may yet come to that if they keep cutting the rations."

₣Ↄ⁊⁊Ↄ₣⁊Ↄ₣Ↄ⁊Ↄ

Thursday November 26, 1863 – Richmond, Virginia:

Three days later, Isaác Brown stepped in front of Zeke and William where they sat on the floor. Isaac was smiling, and seemed out of breath, like he'd just run up the stairs from the hospital.

William looked up in surprise. It wasn't his shift, so he was surprised to see the assistant surgeon standing over him. "Hello, Isaac, am I needed at the hospital?"

"No, William … no … not anymore. We're being exchanged; they just announced it. I came to tell you we're leaving … now!"

"What? Who's leaving? Who told you that?"

"It's for the surgeons and chaplains … The guards just came in and said all the surgeons and chaplains are to gather at the office for transport to the exchange site. Apparently both sides are running so short on doctors they've decided to reinstate the prisoner exchange just for that single purpose. And apparently chaplains were never supposed to have been taken prisoner in the first place, per some sort of unwritten rule of war." He shrugged.

"*Oh!*" William sat where he was, trying to digest this sudden change of fortune. Then he looked over at Zeke, "But…"

"Never you mind about me, William. You go now … get back and help the fellas win the fight. I'll be fine, and it'll do my heart good to know you're safely back home again."

"But…"

"No, William, no arguing … C'mon," Zeke stood and extended his hand. William took it and Zeke pulled him to his feet.

Then Zeke chuckled, "Normally I'd say to collect your things, but … since we got none here…" he shrugged.

William grinned at him, "True … nothing to take but the shirt on my back … and a belt I've had to take in several inches by cutting new holes. And even those I'd burn if I had anything that was better…"

The two men then shook hands, and exchanged a long look. Then William turned to follow Isaac.

Zeke slowly sunk back down to the floor. He leaned his head back against the wall, and closed his eyes, thinking back on all he and William had been through together since leaving Winchester.

He'd been there the better part of an hour when he felt someone sit down next to him. He looked over, then sat up straight, "William! What're you doin' here?"

But William just stared ahead, "I couldn't do it, Zeke. They were loading up the wagons, and I … I just couldn't go … knowing you and the others were still stuck here. It just … didn't seem right."

"William, for such a smart fella, that weren't a very wise decision," Zeke shook his head. "I'm much obliged for the thought, but all's it'll likely buy me is a friend to sit down and die next to."

William nodded, "Then, if that's all it accomplishes, it will still have been worthwhile."

Zeke snorted a mirthless chuckle, gave William a wan smile, and patted him on the shoulder.

ﾊ)ﾆﾈﾊﾄﾊﾉﾆﾈﾊﾄﾊﾉﾆﾈ

Wednesday November 30, 1863 – Wheeling, West Virginia:

Abbey and Megs were in the kitchen kneading bread dough when Margaret came in, slammed an open newspaper down on the kitchen table, then sat and buried her head in her hands, sobbing.

The two older women set down the bread dough, wiped the flour from their hands, and came around to sit next to Margaret at the table, one on each side of her.

"What is it, Margaret?" Abbey leaned in and rested her hand on her daughter's shoulder.

Margaret pounded her finger on the table, pointing to an article in the newspaper, "Read it…" she choked out between sobs.

Abbey and Megs leaned forward and read the article:

> *Recently paroled Union Army surgeons spoke with reporters of the New York Times this day as to the deplorable, inhumane, shocking conditions they had*

personally witnessed while incarcerated in Libby military prison in Richmond.

The following is a brief summation of the horrific conditions upon which the surgeons reported in their testimony:

"We are sorry to report that the three Richmond hospitals where war prisoners receive medical care have insufficient medicine such that on average fifty patients die each day, fifteen hundred a month. Over ten percent of all prisoners held in the two military prisons, Libby and Belle Isle, are classed as sick men in need of the most urgent and skillful medical care. And yet, in addition to lack of medicines, these men, often suffering diarrhea, dysentery, and typhoid pneumonia aren't receiving even the most basic diet necessary for their recovery; instead they are given nothing but corn bread and sweet potatoes, which are entirely unsuitable for men in their condition. Meat is no longer furnished to any class of prisoner.

"As many as five hundred men per month in need of hospital treatment are refused it outright. Because many are denied treatment until near death, on one day, for example, eleven of sixteen men brought by ambulance to the hospital died within a day. On another day, ten of fourteen died.

"We are horrified when we picture the wholesale misery and death that will come with the biting frosts of winter. No prison or penitentiary ever seen by us in a Northern state can equal in cheerlessness, unhealthiness, and paucity of rations issued, in either of the military prisons of Richmond, Va."

Congress is currently meeting to consider recommendations to the Lincoln administration concerning this most urgent, dire, and distressing matter.

331

Abbey embraced Margaret, letting her cry for a long moment, "I wish there was something I could do, my dear."

But Margaret's response to this seemingly innocuous statement startled Abbey, "There *is* something you can do, Momma. Let me borrow the carriage."

"Borrow the carriage? Whatever for, dear? Where are you going?"

"I'm going to Richmond, Momma ... I'm going to get William and Zeke out of that evil place, even if it kills me!"

ഇൻരുൽഇൻരുൽഇൻരുൽ

Monday December 7, 1863 – Harpers Ferry, West Virginia:

The tent flap pushed back, and Tom's face appeared, "You wanted to see me, sir?"

"Yes, come in Tom, take a seat."

Tom did as he was bid, and Nathan pushed a newspaper across the camp table, spinning it around, and pointing to an article. "Have you read about this?"

Tom quickly scanned the article, "No ... *Oh my God!* Do you think it's true? That Libby Prison is as bad as all that?"

"Hmm ... when Phillipe passed, I was suspicious. A healthy young man like that expiring from a sudden illness is not unheard of, but one typically recovers. Unless..."

"Unless there are no medicines and no proper treatment. And a lack of nutrition."

"Yes, exactly."

The two men were quiet and thoughtful for a long moment, gazing down at the newspaper on the table between them. Then Nathan looked up, "When I think of William and Zeke rotting away in that hell hole..." He scowled and slowly shook his head.

"Yes ... it's heartbreaking ... and also frustrating," Tom agreed. "But what can we do? They've stopped the prisoner exchange cartel because of the Confederates' refusal to treat the freemen as proper soldiers." Tom shook his head.

Nathan nodded, "Yes ... Even threatened to execute white officers in charge of colored regiments, though I'm sure they'd never go through with it; Lincoln would be forced to start executing captured Confederate officers in that case, and then where would be we?"

Tom sat up straighter, "Hey, I just had a thought … With Lee falling back into Virginia for winter camp, and us doing the same here in Harpers Ferry with pretty much nothing to do … what if all us old Texas men dressed as civilians, slipped into Richmond, and busted them out?"

Nathan grinned and snorted a laugh, "I like your way of thinking, Tom. It's not a bad idea…"

"But…?"

"But you know as well as I do, that would likely be not much better than a suicide mission. Oh, we could possibly break them out, but then we'd have to make it back a hundred miles or more cross country through enemy territory in the dead of winter, all the while hunted by every rebel in Virginia." Nathan shook his head, "In the end we'd likely accomplish nothing."

Tom nodded his agreement.

"But … you have given me a thought, Tom. We do know people in Richmond who might be able to get them out."

Tom was thoughtful, then his eyes widened, "Well, yes, we do! Starting with Miss Evelyn … then there's also Joseph, of course. And don't forget the Employer."

"Exactly. I'll pen a letter to Evelyn this very moment, and then we'll need to figure a way to get it into the Confederate post…"

❧☙☙❧☙☙❧☙☙

Monday December 7, 1863 – Richmond, Virginia:

"Hey, William … William, wake up…" Zeke elbowed William, who had nodded off sitting with his back to the wall after a long shift working in the hospital.

"*What?* Uhgh … Oh, hello, Zeke … What is it?"

"It's going around like wildfire, William. There's gonna be a breakout; hundreds of men are going to rush the guards and bust outta here."

William was suddenly wide awake, and sat up straight, "What? A breakout? Who ... what ... what are they saying?"

"That Colonel Rose and Major Hamilton have a plan to get into the dungeon in the cellar, and then go out the outer door on that level. They're recruiting men to go with them."

"Hmm ... yes, I recall there was an open portal to the outside, and I thought it odd there wasn't even a door on it. I guess they assumed the prisoners down there were already locked in cells, so a door was unnecessary and just made it stuffier for the guards."

"Yep, that's what they're saying. And Major Hamilton came and talked to me a few days ago, asking questions about how I'd gotten food to you when you were down in the dungeon. So I told him about pulling up the floorboards in the hospital. I didn't think much of it at the time, figurin' he also had a friend down there who needed help. But now ... I guess he had *other* ideas for it..."

"Seems so. But that outer entry is heavily guarded, night and day. Guards are constantly patrolling it."

"That's why they need more men, to overpower and disarm the guards. C'mon, William, if we're goin', we gotta go meet with Colonel Rose. 'Cause o' all the rebel spies and informers in Libby, he's requirin' everyone who's going to swear a sacred oath not to tell the rebs about it."

"What good'll that do? Won't a spy or a turncoat just swear the oath, and then tell the guards anyway?"

"William, I know you're a *scientific* sort of fella, but most folks figure an oath sworn on the Bible is sacred ... you break that, and you go straight to hell, no ifs, ands, or buts. Don't matter the reason, nor which side you're on."

"Oh, I see. All right ... in that case, I'm in. Let's go see the colonel."

Moments later, William and Zeke were sitting cross-legged in front of Colonel Thomas Ellwood Rose, a quiet, unassuming thirty-three-year-old schoolteacher from Pittsburgh. Rose, who'd been the commanding officer of the Seventy-Seventh Pennsylvania Infantry before his capture at Chickamauga, had dark curly hair—gray-tinged—and a bushy beard. But the colonel also had hard, serious eyes, and a reputation for steely courage under fire. And more importantly, given their current circumstances, since the day of his arrival at Libby, Rose had been single-minded in his obsession to escape.

Sitting next to Rose was wiry-thin Major A.G. Hamilton of the Twelfth Kentucky Cavalry, who'd been a home builder before the war. Hamilton and Rose were co-conspirators in the current escape plan.

Zeke laid his hand on a well-worn, dog-eared Bible and swore an oath, at forfeiture of his soul, not to speak of the present operation to another soul who'd not also sworn the oath. William had already sworn the same.

Major Hamilton nodded and smiled when Zeke finished, "In your case, Captain, that oath was hardly necessary. We already know that you and Captain Jenkins have had your run-ins with the guards ... and have—inadvertently, perhaps—helped us advance our plans."

Zeke nodded, "Well, Major ... Colonel ... you can count on us; we're all in, whatever you need us to do. We've had some experience with hand-to-hand fighting, and likely can help take out the guards if it comes to it."

Rose gave him a serious look, "Be careful what you offer, Captain ... We are very likely to take you up on that. *Desperate times* ... you know."

ഓരോ ഓരോ ഓരോ

But two days later, the excitement that had been building by the hour suddenly deflated. The escape had been scrubbed. When Zeke sought out Colonel Rose and asked him why, Rose shrugged, "Major Hamilton and I had sworn in over four-hundred men, and more kept coming. We realized such a large breakout would rouse a devastating armed response from the enemy. Likely we would suffer a terrible toll in casualties, our men being unarmed beyond whatever weapons we could take from the prison guards.

"But the final blow was our inability to determine the current location of Union lines. With several hundred men wandering

335

about a hostile countryside with no idea where safety lay, it seemed unconscionable to carry through with it."

As disappointing as it was, Zeke had to agree with the Colonel's logic. He steeled his heart and returned to the monotonous drudgery of everyday life at Libby. But even as he did so, his famished, emaciated stomach growled its usual aching complaint.

❧◊☙◊❧◊☙◊❧◊☙◊❧◊◊❧◊

Monday December 21, 1863 – Richmond, Virginia:

It was the middle of the afternoon, and Evelyn was in her sitting room trying unsuccessfully to concentrate on a book she'd been reading, when there came a knock on the front door. Happy for the interruption, she rose and stepped across the foyer to answer the knock.

When she opened the door, she was met by a thin young lady of Evelyn's own age or slightly older, with straight, shoulder-length brown hair. The woman was dressed in high-quality but casual clothing, the style an upper-class lady might wear when traveling. Evelyn decided this young woman could be quite pretty if she put a little more effort into it.

"Miss Evelyn Hanson?" the lady asked.

"Yes ... How may I help you, *Miss...*?"

"My name is Miss Margaret ... Here in Richmond, you may call me Margaret *Williams*, though it isn't my actual *last* name."

"Oh! I see ... Then, do I assume correctly you've been sent by Angeline?"

"Angeline? No ... I'm not familiar with anyone of that name. I have recently come from ... from the *West*. May I come in?"

"Oh! Yes, of course! Where are my manners? I'm so sorry to keep you standing on the stoep! Please, come in and be welcome in my home."

She ushered the woman in, leading her across the foyer to the sitting room. There she offered her a seat, "May I offer you tea?"

"Oh, yes, please. That would be delightful. I've just walked here from downtown, and I am fairly out of breath."

336

"Give me but a moment to get it started. Please, make yourself at home, Miss Margaret."

"Thank you, Miss Evelyn."

Evelyn hurried down the hall toward the kitchen to give instructions to one of the new "trainees" to prepare tea. As she walked her head was spinning, *Who is this woman? From her accent and manners, she could very well be a Richmond native and is certainly of the upper class. But she said she'd come from the west ... West Virginia? But no railroads are running to or from West Virginia with the war on. Or has she come from somewhere else? She is traveling under an alias, but was not sent by Angeline ... then who sent her? And more importantly ... why is she here?*

She could not puzzle it out, so she finally shrugged her shoulders and decided she'd likely find out soon enough. Having arranged for the tea, she re-entered the sitting room and found Margaret sitting patiently, right where she'd left her.

"Tea will be served shortly; in the meantime, perhaps we can become better acquainted."

"Yes, certainly. I'm sure you're fairly bursting with curiosity about who I am and why I'm here."

"Well ... now that you mention it ... I am a bit curious ... but I wouldn't want to press you if you're unwilling."

"Perhaps it would help if I told you I have come from Wheeling ... and am well acquainted with a number of people you personally know there."

Evelyn's eyes widened, "*Wheeling?* Then ... *Nathan* has sent you?" Her heart raced; another message from Nathan!

"Well ... no. I have come of my own accord; in fact, I am certain Nathan would *not* approve, and would likely consider my mission too dangerous for a lady."

"That *does* sound like Nathan..." Evelyn nodded, recalling how Nathan had previously tried to convince her to give up her espionage activities and relocate to Wheeling to marry him there, and then stay safely home on the farm.

"So, then...?" Evelyn prompted.

337

"Why am I here? Well, to be honest, Miss Evelyn … when I set out for Richmond, I did *not* intend to visit *you* at all, despite your connection to Nathan and his people."

"Well, no blame to you for that. It is a very *dangerous business* in which I find myself, and it's best avoided, if possible," Evelyn nodded, assuming the woman had at least a general understanding of the things she was involved in from Nathan and Miss Abbey.

But Margaret didn't immediately respond, gazing steadily at Evelyn. "My hesitation wasn't because of the danger. To be blunt, Miss Evelyn, I was hesitant because of … of my feelings toward *you*."

"Toward *me*? But we've never met … Why…?" but Evelyn paused, and something seemed to be tickling the back of her mind … like she *should* know this woman, or at least know *of* her.

"*Margaret* … I *have* heard that name before from Nathan. Margaret *Walters?*"

The question made Margaret wince, as if in pain. "Yes…" she whispered. "But I beg you not to repeat it again. I am no longer known by that name, and it's best it *never* be used here in Richmond."

"Oh … yes, of course, forgive me … Now I recall … after your escape, Miss Abbey adopted you, and you are now considered Nathan's sister, and go by Chambers?"

"I *am* his sister. At least, that is how he treats me."

"Oh, yes, certainly. But … a moment ago you hinted at … *feelings* toward me that did *not* sound positive…"

Margaret gave Evelyn another hard look.

"To be blunt, Miss Evelyn … I have heard a great deal about your one visit to Mountain Meadows … and the odd circumstances surrounding your sudden departure. And then again, a similar incident seems to have occurred later at Harpers Ferry. I have come to understand that these were very hurtful episodes for Mr. Chambers, who is a man deserving of much better treatment. I have grown quite fond of him and … *protective*, one might say. And … that has made it difficult for me to entertain any pleasant feelings toward you."

Evelyn looked down at her shoes and felt heat on her face. She'd spent countless days and nights chastising herself for her actions at Mountain Meadows, and later at Harpers Ferry, though that was an entirely different circumstance, and not completely her fault. But regardless, she was unprepared to be confronted about the earlier failures in her relationship with Nathan—especially by a stranger, Nathan's sister or no. It was still, after all this time, a painful and sensitive subject.

"I ... can't blame you for that..." Evelyn spoke barely above a whisper, her voice choking up and tears welling in her eyes. "I feel much the same myself, when I think back on it. Hurting Nathan was ... one of the most despicable things I've ever done. But ... Nathan and I have since resolved our earlier ... *issues* ... I believe he would tell you the same, if he were here."

Two freeman maids, Bess and Pegg, stepped into the room with the tea and biscuits and arranged them on a side table, enforcing a short pause in the ladies' conversation.

When the maids departed, closing the doors behind them, Evelyn asked the question that had suddenly entered her mind, "Forgive me, Miss Margaret, but ... circumstances being what they are ... Well, I don't mean to be rude but, it just occurred to me that certain ... *persons* ... who might wish to incriminate me, may have intercepted letters from Mr. Chambers and might know he now has a sister named Margaret, whom I have never before met. Can you somehow prove that you are who you say you are?"

Margaret was thoughtful for a moment, gazing up at the ceiling. Finally, she looked back at Evelyn and said, "No enemy spy would know the names of Nathan's most trusted freemen, aside from possibly Megs: Tony, Cobb, Henry, Big George, and Phinney. Oh, and also Rosa, of course. I not only know their names, but I have lived with them, and know everything about them. Ask me anything; I can answer without hesitation."

Evelyn nodded, a smile touching her eyes. "Very well, then ... My next question is, if you did not come to Richmond intending to see me, why *did* you come?"

"I have come ... to break Nathan's men out of Libby Prison."

"*Oh!* Yes … William and Zeke … yes. I've been worried sick about them and their dire circumstances, especially after hearing of Phillipe's unfortunate passing. The prison has developed a horrid reputation, and with the prisoner exchanges suspended…" Evelyn shook her head sadly.

"Yes," Margaret agreed, "and you should know … William and I have developed a *special* relationship."

"Oh … I see. And I *approve,* if that means anything to you. William is a fine man—brilliant, kindly, and extremely capable in many different ways. I am quite fond of him … and of Zeke too, who is also a fine, brave young man.

"But breaking them out of Libby—that's a tall order, Miss Margaret. If it were easily done, I would've already made the attempt."

Margaret smiled; not a warm smile, but the confident smile of a person certain of her abilities. "My dear Miss Evelyn; if there's one thing I know all too well, it's how to escape a nefarious incarceration!"

Evelyn raised an eyebrow, then nodded. Margaret's very presence in Evelyn's sitting room spoke to the truth of that statement, considering her previous confinement by her own evil, murderous husband.

Evelyn smiled, "I believe, Miss Margaret, *that* is a thing we share in common. You see, I too have some experience in breaking out of a prison. And … fortunately, here in Richmond, I have many allies who can assist me in such *challenging* tasks, including—you may be surprised to hear—several very capable *women.*"

"The woman *Angeline* you mentioned at the door?"

"Yes, she has been a mentor to me in this … *business*. And there is another I work with often, who is also a great asset."

Now it was Margaret's turn to smile. "A web of female spies? Right here in Richmond, under the very noses of the slavers? How delightful! Perhaps I will enjoy my visit here more than I'd expected."

Evelyn returned her smile, "I'm happy you approve."

But then Evelyn's expression turned more serious. "But, this thing you speak of is a very serious matter; one which—if it were to go wrong—could destroy everything we've worked for, not to mention put many lives at risk."

"Yes … so I assume; but if we don't act, I fear our men will die in that horrid place. If you have decided to trust me, then perhaps you would be so kind as to tell me all you know about the present circumstances surrounding the prison and the various resources you have at your disposal."

"Margaret … I now know you are who you say you are. And if Nathan considers you his sister, and Miss Abbey her daughter, I can't imagine anything that would speak more highly to your good character and trustworthiness."

Margaret didn't immediately respond but gazed at Evelyn intently for several moments with a thoughtful expression, then smiled, "Evelyn, you are … *not* at all what I had expected."

Evelyn returned the smile with a bright one of her own, and a chuckle, "I'll take that for a compliment, Margaret."

ഇരു⊗ഇഇരു⊗ഇഇരുഇ

Tuesday December 22, 1863 – Richmond, Virginia:

"Margaret, Elizabeth is our foremost expert on Libby Prison, but I'll let her speak to that."

The four ladies—Evelyn, Angeline, Margaret, and Elizabeth Van Lew—sat at tea in the Hughes' manor house sitting room and had just finished formal introductions.

"Thank you, Evelyn dear," Elizabeth set down her tea, and gazed intently at Margaret. "I have been inside many times, and have developed an … *understanding* … with several of the guards."

"You mean you've *bribed* them," Margaret grinned as she blew on her tea.

"*Oh!* I like this one, Evelyn," Elizabeth sat up and beamed at Margaret, "Where did you say you recruited her?"

Evelyn laughed, "You recall me speaking of the gentleman now living in West Virginia and fighting for the Union side, Mr. Chambers?"

"Yes, certainly ... the man you're in love with."

Evelyn blushed, but nodded, "Margaret is Mr. Chambers' sister."

"Ah, I see. Runs in the family, then."

Margaret smiled, "You could say that."

Elizabeth continued, "I have been an uncompromising Unionist from the outset, and ever since the First Manassas battle, I've been visiting Libby, trying to provide what comfort and solace I might to the poor dears who are incarcerated there. Fortunately for me, the place is only five blocks from my house. I used to visit nearly every day.

"But no longer ... As Angeline will attest, I have fallen under the suspicion of the higher ups in the government, so I had to curtail my activities. Now I dare not even walk within sight of the building for fear they will arrest me."

Angeline nodded, "We've worked hard to develop a ruse to distract the government's agents from pursuing Elizabeth, which has involved convincing them she is ... well, not of a sound mind, I suppose one might say."

Elizabeth laughed, "They think I'm batty, is what you mean! Can't say I blame them. Sometimes I believe it myself. But I digress ... The truth is I have been forced to be more circumspect concerning the prison. But still, I expect I know more about it than anyone else on *our* side."

"Which leads us to this." Angeline placed a large, rolled up sheet of paper on a folding table she'd had the maids set up in the room for just this purpose. She unrolled the paper and laid it out on the table, placing weights on the corners. "Please, ladies," she gestured for them to gather around her.

Margaret saw that the paper held a blueprint, "Libby Prison?"

"Yes. Jonathan was able to obtain the original drawings of the warehouse facility. And we're hoping Elizabeth can provide details about what has been modified in the building to make it into a prison. After that, we can discuss any ideas for breaking our men out."

"Before I agree to this discussion," Elizabeth placed her hand over the center of the drawing, "I want an agreement among us, that this escape will be about more than just the two men Evelyn had mentioned in her message summoning me here. As much as I'm sure they are more than worthy of being rescued, the same can be said for all the other men there. I'm not going to spend a whole lot of time, energy, and risk just to rescue two men, no matter how special they may be."

Evelyn and Angeline looked at Margaret for an answer. Margaret held a frown, "But … the more men you try to break out, the more difficult, dangerous, and risky it is … and the more likely to fail."

Elizabeth nodded, "That's true. But if a thing is worth doing, it's worth doing right, and worth taking risks over."

"But surely, you're not talking about getting all … what is it, a thousand officers … out? That would require the Union Army capturing Richmond. And if that happened, they would hardly need us. Either that or a general prison uprising, which would likely get a lot of our men killed in the process."

"True," Elizabeth nodded. "I'm willing to compromise on it to some extent. Let's say our target is at least a few dozen men, to make it more worth our while."

Margaret looked at the ceiling a moment, then back at Elizabeth, "Deal." And to seal the agreement, Margaret held out her hand and Elizabeth shook it.

For the next several hours, they went over the drawings in detail, then Angeline produced maps of Richmond in general, and the waterfront warehouse district specifically. Many different ideas were discussed, from various types of ruses, to armed attacks by hired mercenaries or Jonathan's men, to prisoners rushing the door and overpowering the guards.

But no idea seemed like an obvious choice, so they continued to contemplate and discuss.

Margaret was once again gazing at the drawings of the prison building. "Elizabeth, tell me again about the cellar … what's down on this end?" She pointed to the east end of the building.

"Nothing."

"What do you mean?"

"I think it used to be a kitchen, but perhaps the rats were too thick, so they moved the kitchen upstairs and sealed that area off."

"Sealed it? Like with bricks or something?"

"Yes, I think so. As you can see, there was a staircase down to it, but that's now closed off. Though if I recall, from the one time I went to visit some poor soul down in the dungeon, there's still a single door into it from that level, though likely it's kept locked."

Margaret was quiet once again, continuing to gaze at the blueprints. She suddenly sat up and looked at Evelyn, "Do you think your people can obtain, or create from whole cloth if necessary, a very detailed and accurate map of the areas surrounding the prison, especially on the east side? Buildings, walls, fences, drainage lines, and so forth? Oh, and including slope and elevation? And ideally also what kind of soil to expect in the general area…"

Evelyn frowned, "Very likely, though it may take some time. Why? What are you thinking?"

"I'm thinking … of a *tunnel*."

☙❧☙❧☙❧☙❧☙❧

Thursday December 24, 1863 – Richmond, Virginia:

It was late in the afternoon, and Evelyn had been preparing herself for a Christmas celebration at the Confederate White House when she was interrupted by the arrival of Joseph, who stopped by to deliver a letter.

To Evelyn's surprise and joy, it was from Nathan. And though she was thrilled to receive it, and to finally hear from him after so many months without communication, she had to chuckle and shake her head at the favor he was requesting.

Dec. 2, 1863

My Dearest E.,

I am writing because of a concern I have for two individuals of whom you are familiar – longtime business associates of mine, W. and Z. As you know, these men are currently housed in Richmond in accommodations that are, it turns out, not especially to their liking, nor conducive to their continued wellbeing.

I understand you are familiar with certain persons whose employer may have the ability to help these men to relocate to more favorable lodging, perhaps even in an entirely different locale.

I would be much obliged to you if you and your acquaintances were able to do any such things as are in your power to bring about a better living arrangement for these two highly favored individuals.

Also, on a personal note—as always, I wish you all health and every happiness, and pray that we may see each other again in person in a brighter future that is not too far distant.

I am, as always, your humble servant and very most loyal friend,

N.

A little late to the party, my darling, she thought and smiled, walking straight into the sitting room to share the letter with Margaret.

Margaret looked up from the book she was reading as Evelyn entered. Evelyn grinned, but said nothing, just handing the letter to Margaret.

Margaret read it through quickly, and then returned Evelyn's smile, rolling her eyes, "Now when we pull this thing off, he'll think it was all his own idea!"

The two shared a laugh.

Evelyn then gave Margaret a more serious look, "Are you sure you won't accompany me tonight, dear? Varina puts on a lavish affair, with live music, exquisite libations, and the very finest of cognac and brandy."

"No, but I thank you. I never much cared for such functions. I am horrific at small talk and gossip; I end up feeling much like a fish out of water. Besides ... I've brought nothing appropriate to wear."

"Oh, well that is easily solved. You and I are much the same size ... though you're a bit thinner, I believe."

Margaret snorted a laugh, then looked down toward her own bosom, "Yes, you *could* say that..."

Evelyn chuckled, "Anyway, we could make some quick *minor* adjustments..."

But Margaret shook her head, then frowned, "More seriously, Evelyn ... I fear someone might recognize me and start asking questions about ... you know ... *him*. I would rather not have to speak of such matters."

"*Ah*. Yes, I understand. Well, then I shall at least ask the maids to prepare you a special treat for Christmas, so I'll not feel guilty about leaving you at home."

"Thank you, dear. That is very thoughtful of you."

ﺔﻬﺨﺘﻛﻬﺨﺘﻛﻬﺨﺘﻛ

Tuesday January 12, 1863 – Richmond, Virginia:

C.S.A. Captain Bob Hill, formerly of the Twenty-Seventh Virginia Regiment, Stonewall Brigade, strode down the street, headed toward his new assignment in Richmond. It was not a duty he was pleased with, but he had to admit he was not yet ready for the rigors of combat. And it did feel good to be back in uniform and walking normally again without assistance. It had been a long, painful recovery after his near death at the Battle of Sharpsburg, what the Yankees called Antietam.

He was going to meet his new commanding officer for the first time and receive orientation concerning his new duties. His mind was preoccupied with these thoughts, along with a certain mild anxiety at starting something new, when he saw two high-class young ladies walking in his direction along the sidewalk.

As they neared, he tipped his hat to them and smiled, glancing from one to the other. The one on the right had long blonde hair sticking out from a fashionable hat. She was an uncommonly pretty woman. And the one of the left was…

He stopped mid stride, "*Miss Margaret…?*"

The ladies stopped, and the lady on the left, thin and dark haired gazed at him a moment, "Bob…? *Bob Hill!*"

And then she was hugging his neck. And though he was still recovering the shock of seeing her, he returned the embrace gently, suffering a mild spasm of pain from the squeezing.

They separated, and he beamed at her, which she returned with a bright smile of her own, "Miss Margaret … until this moment I knew not whether you yet lived or had died back in western Virginia. It is so … so *wonderful* to see you again, alive and well!"

"Likewise, Bob. With all the fighting, I feared you'd been killed out in battle somewhere. But I have prayed for you often."

He looked down at his feet a moment, "Well, that very nearly happened … But I am well now."

"Oh! I'm sorry … Miss Evelyn Hanson, please meet Bob Hill. You recall my story of how I escaped from … from *my former husband* … it was Bob who made it possible for me to escape."

"Oh, yes of course. And now that I am reminded, I do recognize you from … a certain wedding at Mr. Chambers' farm, Captain Hill."

"Likewise, Miss Evelyn. And I pray you will accept my most earnest, heartfelt apologies for my unconscionable participation in Mr. Wal … er … *Margaret's former husband's* actions that day. I have since repented of my service to him, and have strived to make amends as much as possible."

"Very commendable of you, Captain Hill. And from all Margaret has told me, you have since more than made up for any past mistakes."

"Thank you for saying so, Miss Evelyn. That means a great deal to me, I assure you. And you would do me a great favor if you would also extend my apologies to Mr. Chambers when next you see or speak to him. I would do so in person if it were possible, but … do I understand correctly that he has ended up on the … uh … *other side* of the present divide?

"Yes, that's correct, Captain Hill. Mr. Chambers is now a colonel in the Union Army."

"Well, I for one have only the greatest respect for your Mr. Chambers, regardless of where his loyalties may lie."

"I shall certainly relay your respects when next I see him … whenever that may be," Evelyn smiled.

"Miss Margaret, I am simply burning with curiosity concerning how you made your escape, what came after, and how you've come to be back here in Richmond. But … I must apologize again … I am now running late for my duties. Please, would you be so kind as to write your present address on this card, that I might come visit you?" He handed her a slip of paper and a pencil that he drew from his pocket.

"Oh, just give it to me; I'll do it," Evelyn said. "She's staying at my house, so it's easiest for me to write the address."

"And, yes, of course, Bob," Margaret nodded. "I would love for you to come visit that we might get caught up. Perhaps after your duties are finished for the day? Where are you currently assigned, the War Department?"

"No … I've just been assigned as an officer of the guard at Libby Prison."

Evelyn's hand stopped for a nearly imperceptible single heartbeat, and then she finished writing out her address as if nothing unexpected had just been said.

❧❦❧❦❧❦❧❦❧❦

"Well, *that* was interesting," Evelyn prompted as they continued down the sidewalk after Captain Hill's departure.

"Yes … most unexpected, and … unsettling in several ways."

"Well, starting with … the man is clearly in love with you." Evelyn eyed Margaret thoughtfully.

"Oh, no … I don't think so … certainly *not*, Evelyn … Do you really think so?"

Evelyn snorted, "Do you think I can't tell? Now you're just being silly, Margaret. But as interesting as *that* is, and likely *conflicting*, given your feelings for William, the more thought-provoking news is that he works at Libby."

"Yes, I noticed that too," Margaret said with a wry smile. "So ... now what? In *your* world I suppose one would try to figure out how to use him to best advantage, somehow?"

"*My* world? As far as I can tell, we inhabit the same one."

"You know what I mean, *spying* and all. Now we know someone who's in charge of the guards. Should we try to use that to our advantage? But ... I don't know if I could lie to him, or deceive him, after everything he's done for me."

Evelyn rolled her eyes. "You get used to it."

ℰ❍ℭℛℭℬℰ❍ℰ❍ℭℛℭℬℰ❍ℰ❍ℭℛℭℬ

Saturday January 14, 1863 – Richmond, Virginia:

Margaret fidgeted nervously as she sat in Evelyn's sitting room awaiting the arrival of Captain Bob Hill.

Evelyn suppressed a smile. Clearly, Margaret was not used to entertaining men in general, and this meeting, with its conflicting emotional undertones, was likely more anxiety provoking than was typical.

Margaret looked up from her tea, "Evelyn, what's taking so long?"

Evelyn looked up at the clock on the wall, then back at Margaret, "My dear, it's still a full quarter of an hour before the time Captain Hill said he would arrive."

Margaret shook her head, "Sorry ... I didn't mean *that*. I know he's not yet late. I meant, what's taking so long to gather the information we requested concerning the prison?"

"Ah, that. Yes ... I can understand your impatience on it, but you must be realistic. I spoke with Jonathan at length just yesterday, and he tells me that no such detailed maps exist as we have requested. He has very good resources in that regard, so you can trust what he says is true.

"So, he has had to hire people to create the maps and to gather the other needed information. But, as you can imagine, most of the cartographers in Virginia are presently busily employed out in the field with the army. As I understand it, when planning campaigns and battles, accurate maps are worth their weight in gold — or rather, their weight in bullets, anyway.

"And of the cartographers that are left, you can imagine finding one who is pro-Union to begin with, and can operate discretely on top of that is quite a challenge. He also has needed to find someone who is an expert in soil types, another who is knowledgeable about sewers and drainage, and so on. And all these people will have to do their work without being obvious about it and arousing the suspicions of the prison guards."

"All right, all right … I get your point. It is a nearly impossible task, and I am being impatient about it. But … when I think of William and Zeke slowly starving in that place, and susceptible to taking ill at any moment … I can barely sit still for the frustration and fear."

Evelyn reached over and patted Margaret's hand, "Understandable, dear. I felt much the same way when I first became involved in this business. But I have learned that doing things well often takes time. And that extra time taken can make the difference between ultimate success and total disaster."

Margaret nodded, "I have a lot to learn in that regard."

Evelyn smiled, "You are doing remarkably well, Margaret. You make an excellent spy, or rather you *would*, if you wanted to keep doing it."

"No, thank you! Once William is out of that horrid place I intend to return home as quickly as can be managed. I have no desire to stay in Richmond an extra moment. Oh! No offense to *you*, Evelyn. Meeting you has been one of the most wonderful, most pleasant surprises I've ever experienced."

"Thank you for saying so, Margaret. Likewise, for sure. I'm so happy we met. I feel that we are going to be the very closest of sisters … when that happy day finally arrives. Oh … there's Captain Hill now…"

They stood and turned toward the doorway as Bess answered the knock at the door, and ushered the captain in.

After greetings were exchanged, they all three took their seats. Normally, under such circumstances, Evelyn would've made polite excuses and left the couple alone. But Margaret had begged her to stay, saying she hoped it might prevent Bob from saying anything too personal, which she wished to avoid, given her relationship with William. Evelyn had told Margaret of her own similar difficult encounter with Jubal, so she understood perfectly.

On Bob's insistence, Margaret told the entire story of her escape from Walters, meeting up with Henry, and their harrowing trek north until rescued by Captain Chambers. She also told of her delight at being adopted by the Chambers family, and gave a brief account of Nathan's confrontation with her father. Then she spoke of her new life at Belle Meade Farm, and even the frightful night when Walters showed up and she was saved by the heroic efforts of the freemen. The only thing she left off was any mention of William.

Bob listened with great interest and empathy, commenting appreciatively at several points, and asking pertinent, probing questions.

Evelyn also listened with fascination, as she'd never heard the entire tale before. And she beamed as she wiped her eyes with a handkerchief when Margaret told of Miss Abbey's offer to adopt her.

Then it was Bob's turn, and he talked about enlisting in the Army and fighting with a regiment in the famous Stonewall Brigade, which immediately piqued Evelyn's interest.

"Which regiment were you in, Captain?"

"The Twenty-Seventh Virginia, Miss Evelyn."

Evelyn gasped in surprise, "Oh my goodness, Captain! Then … *you* must be *that* Captain Hill! Why, my good sir, you won't believe it! I have already heard all about you from my dear friend Jubal Collins, who has served as a lieutenant under you!"

"Well, isn't that something, Miss Evelyn! Jubal is the finest young man I know. He and I have been very close; in fact, he saved my life at the Sharpsburg Battle."

Bob proceeded to describe his time in the army, with emphasis on his relationship with Jubal, leading up to the devastating Battle of Antietam where Bob was seriously wounded in the sunken farm road, what was now referred to as "Bloody Lane." He told how Jubal had carried him unconscious back to the field hospital where the surgeons saved him from bleeding to death.

And then, when he'd finished his narrative, he reached inside his coat and pulled out a stack of folded sheets of paper and handed them across to Margaret.

"What's this?" she asked, looking at the papers in her hand, then up at Bob with a startled expression.

"Letters … to *you*, Miss Margaret. I … wanted to write to you … to tell you all the things I was doing, and seeing, and … *feeling* … while out in the war. But I didn't know where you were, or even what name you were using in order to hide from Walters. So I have kept them all this time, never knowing if you would ever have the opportunity to read them." He chuckled, "Jubal used to chide me for writing letters that I could never send. But I found it comforting. Like I was speaking to you, even if I could never hear your replies."

"Bob … I don't know what to say … I am so … *touched*. And I certainly would've written back to you, had it been possible to do so."

Evelyn was also touched, and decided she liked Captain Bob Hill *very* much; in fact, she now felt like she knew him quite well, not just from this meeting, but from all the times Jubal had glowingly written about him in his letters. She made up her mind right then and there, that she would do nothing to try to take advantage of his position at the prison—nothing at all that might put this good man at risk.

❧◌◌◌◌❧◌◌◌◌❧◌◌◌

"Whatcha got there, William?" Zeke leaned over to look at the slip of paper William was studying. From what Zeke could see, it was mostly a jumble of meaningless letters and numbers.

"It's a cipher, I believe. It was slipped to me by a young lady who was in the hospital, supposedly on a mercy mission from one of the local charities, distributing blankets and food to the sick." William turned and met eyes with Zeke, "It appears to be a message from Miss Margaret."

"*Miss Margaret?* Holy Jesus, William! What does it say?"

William looked at Zeke and scowled, "Did you hear me say it's a *cipher…*"

"Oh … yeah, sorry. I wasn't thinking. Just excited, is all. Can you *de*-cipher it, do you think?"

"Yes, very likely. I've never done it before, but Tom Clark was explaining it to me back when Margaret wrote her cipher to the Captain back at Mountain Meadows, and the concept seems fairly simple and straightforward. He said the first part, which is in plain English, contains a riddle of sorts, which holds the key to the rest.

"Hmm … let's see … the part in English says, 'An uninvited, unwelcomed, and unpleasant neighbor tried to disrupt the class.'"

"Okay … so what's the answer to the riddle?"

"Well, clearly she's talking about the incident at Belle Meade where the Captain's disreputable neighbor came to disrupt the class Margaret and I were teaching to the freemen. Now … what *was* his name…?"

"*Ward*. Jesse Ward. Ended up getting hisself shot along with several of his friends. Only nobody ever figured out who done it, though I'm sure lots o' folks reckoned us men o' the Captain's did it. Though we didn't, much as we wanted to."

"Ward … yes, that's likely it. Now let me see…" William began counting out numbers, mumbling letters, and scratching out notes on the floorboards with a short scrap of pencil, to Zeke's total bafflement.

Zeke, realizing the process would likely take a while, leaned back against the wall, closed his eyes, and nodded off. He was awakened by William shaking his arm.

"Listen to this," William spoke in hushed tones, and to Zeke's amazement, William was now reading the baffling message as if it was clearly written out in plain English.

"It says:

> *Here in R with EH. Get you Z and 2dz others out. Dig tunnel fr E cellar. St NE corner. Hard dry soil. SE to shed aprx 50ft. When out W and Z only 2N21 3EGRACE HSE- 3STY-BRK on RT. Safe 3LT 3FLR. Lv M, EH, all BMde."*

Zeke's eyes widened. "Well, I'm getting most of it ... and I'm *liking it!* Seems to me she's hooked up with Miss Evelyn and some pro-Union friends, I'm guessing. And they want to get us out. Along with a couple dozen of our closest friends, I think it means. And they've figured out our best course is to dig a tunnel from the east cellar and come up in a shed out that way. Hmm ... fifty feet ... that'll be no easy task. But from what I know of those two clever ladies, they've probably got ahold of a map of the prison somehow and spent days studying it to figure out the best route. So, I for one, will trust them on it.

"But what's that last part mean, just before the '*Love Margaret, Evelyn, and Belle Meade*' signoff? Seems like more cipher code to me..."

William nodded appreciatively, realizing that Zeke was really quite clever for having been raised on a farm with only a minimum of schooling, "I think you have the first part correct, to your credit. I believe that odd next part contains directions to a safe house for you and I—two blocks north on Twenty-First Street, then three blocks east on Grace. Then look for a three-story brick house on the right. We will know it's the right place, and if it's safe to enter, by three lamps lit in windows on the third floor."

"*Damn*, William ... I knew you were a smart fella, but ... you never fail to amaze..."

William leaned back against the wall, closed his eyes, and smiled—a warm glow replacing his now habitual cold despair. And his mood had nothing to do with Zeke's glowing compliment, as nice as that was. Holding next to his heart a note written out by Margaret in her very own hand, right here in Richmond, gave him such a glorious feeling after all these months of horror and deprivation, he thought he might burst. *And she's right here, in Richmond at this very moment, likely less than a mile from where I sit…*

"So, what now, William? After they closed down the lower kitchen, and them fellas tried to escape out a window down there, they sealed the stairs to the east cellar. Far as I know, the only way to get to it now is from the dungeon door. And that would mean goin' down through the hospital's floorboards again. And Colonel Rose has said the rebs are onto that now, and will be watching for it."

William sat up and opened his eyes, "I think you just hit on our next move, Zeke…"

"What, try the hospital again?"

"No … it's time we had a talk with Colonel Rose."

෩ඞၽ෩ඞၽ෩ඞၽ

William and Zeke arranged to meet with Colonel Rose and Major Hamilton after lights out back in the kitchen on the east end of the large room where they were housed on the second level of the prison. Rebel informants and spies were still a serious concern, so they wished their meeting to be in private.

The four men sat cross-legged on the floor, barely visible to each other in the gloom of the dimly lit room.

"Colonel … Major," William began, "Captain Benton and I have been contacted by a certain long-time friend of ours who is currently in Richmond in company with another trusted person we know who is of the pro-Union persuasion. These friends of ours are determined to help get us out of here along with perhaps a few dozen more men. We believe they have reliable connections in the city who can assist us once we are on the outside."

Colonel Rose sat up straighter, "You have our attention, Captain Jenkins … Go on…"

"In the hospital I was handed a coded message by a visitor which, though terse, indicates our friends have studied the prison building and its environs in great detail and have concluded the best route for escape would to be via a tunnel to be dug from the east cellar. Specifically, starting in the very northeast corner, heading southeast for approximately fifty feet, then coming up inside a shed there. Looking out the window, I can see there is a shed exactly where they indicate. They also indicate that the soil is dry and compact in that area, which should be good for tunneling, I assume."

The colonel and the major turned to each other and exchanged a look, the meaning of which was lost on the two captains.

Rose turned back to William, "Interesting you should say that, Captain … A few months ago, when the kitchen in the east cellar was still functioning, the major and I hatched a plan to do that very thing. We even obtained some rudimentary tools and began sneaking down into the kitchen at night to excavate.

"We were making good progress, but then the exchange of surgeons took place, coinciding with several hundred other prisoners being transferred out. This thankfully helped alleviate some of the crowding, but the unfortunate side effect was that the extra kitchen in the cellar was no longer needed. And the thing was so noisome and rat-infested that they decided to shut it down permanently and seal off the stairway, effectively quashing our plans.

"After that, we switched our focus to the dungeon escape route via the hospital floorboards that you are already familiar with. But, as you know, we eventually abandoned that plan as well, being too dangerous."

"And there's no other way into the east cellar now?" Zeke asked.

"We'd considered various other options," the colonel answered, "down into the dungeons via the hospital being the obvious route. But the guards are now onto that, and it'd be impossible to disguise the many comings and goings that'd be required to excavate a tunnel."

The colonel was then quiet for a minute, looking down at his hands as if considering what to say next. He looked back up, met eyes with William and Zeke in turn. "Gentlemen ... you don't yet know me well, but you will. And when you do, you will realize that I am a man who does not know how to quit. I will *never* stop trying to escape ... not until I am dead and my body is stiff and cold in the ground."

Then he looked over at Major Hamilton and nodded. Hamilton rose to his feet, stepped past William and Zeke, and moved around behind one of the large cookstoves that sat in the large cooking fireplace, whose chimney rose up from the kitchen below, heading toward the roof.

Hamilton then knelt down behind the stove to where he could no longer be seen. But they heard a soft, scratching sound. So William and Zeke stood and moved around the stove to see what the major was doing. Colonel Rose followed.

They immediately noticed that Hamilton had removed several bricks from the fireplace and was working on another; bricks that'd clearly already been painstakingly removed and then replaced to appear solid.

After a few more minutes, a gaping hole appeared in the chimney, large enough to admit a man.

William looked over at Colonel Rose, "Down to the east cellar?"

Rose just smiled and nodded.

CHAPTER 14. DIGGING OUT OF HELL

"Long is the way and hard,
that out of hell leads up to light."
- John Milton

Monday February 1, 1864 – Richmond, Virginia:

Colonel Rose and Major Hamilton led William and Zeke down the secret entrance to the east cellar through the tunnel they had previously excavated down the kitchen fireplace flue. Rose explained how Hamilton had done construction work before the war, and had a skillful hand when it came to extracting the bricks and then creating a usable tunnel down through the chimney, with nothing more than a borrowed jack knife.

William and Zeke were flabbergasted when they arrived at the cellar down a rope ladder that'd been built by another prisoner. The cellar was dark, damp, and smelled of rancid grease, sewage, and accumulated years of river rat feces, the source of which scurried about everywhere. But to William and Zeke, these things were of little import compared to the excitement of learning that the first major obstacle to digging a tunnel had already been surmounted by the colonel and major.

Colonel Rose turned to them, his eyes gleaming in the dim light leaking in from the streetlamp outside the one barred window on the far southern wall. "We've been attempting to tunnel out since shortly after abandoning the mass breakout scheme back in mid-December. But each attempt has failed for one reason or another. At this point, the men we've recruited to help have mostly lost interest in the effort; I can hardly blame them. Major Hamilton and I had gone back to considering other options … until you two came to us with this new idea."

Rose then spent several minutes poking at the dirt in the very northeast corner of the cellar, feeling its texture, and even smelling it. Then he looked up and grinned, "Yes, gentlemen … I think this just might work. Fifty feet … it's much more ambitious than what we've tried before. But ... coming up inside the old tobacco shed ... that's good. It gives us a way to exit the tunnel out of sight of the guards. We'd previously planned to tunnel out to the sewer line to give us cover all the way to the river. But we discovered that the sewer was built using three-inch thick oak—impossible for us to penetrate with the meager tools at our disposal. And then the stench of sewage leaking out was suffocating. Several of our men fell ill from the fumes, so we had to give it up.

"But I have a good feeling about this new location. And knowing we have allies on the outside who have studied the prison and have come to the same conclusion ... it's most reassuring."

ᏏᏓᎦᏬᏏᏓᎦᏬᏏᏓᎦᏬ

The next evening after lights out, Rose, Hamilton, William, and Zeke climbed down the fireplace into the cellar. Rose began the excavation as Hamilton explained the process to William and Zeke in a hushed voice, "One man digs, with a rope tied to one ankle so he can be pulled out in case of a cave in or if he simply passes out for lack of oxygen. A second man stands at the tunnel entrance and waves this fan," he held up a section of gum blanket that had been stretched tight over a light wooden frame. "He does this to force air up into the tunnel so the digger doesn't suffocate."

William and Zeke nodded, then exchanged a dark look. William decided this was *not* going to be fun.

"The other men alternate keeping watch and emptying the dirt from the tunnel, which is collected in this." Hamilton held up a large spittoon with a long clothesline tied to it.

"Where are you dumping the dirt?" William asked.

"See that big pile of straw?"

William looked where Hamilton indicated, but in the darkness all he saw was what looked like a large lump on the floor. "Whenever they freshen the mattresses in the hospital, they dump the used hay in here. We've been hiding the dirt underneath the pile."

"You said someone had to keep watch?" Zeke asked. "Do you really think the guards will check this place? After all, it's sealed off, ain't it?"

"The stairs are sealed, but there's still a door that leads here from the dungeon area that they can come through. And they do check this cellar—more often than you think. And when they do, we have only a few moments to hide while their eyes adjust to the darkness, and the scurrying and squealing of the rats covers the noise of our movements."

Then Hamilton chuckled softly, "Fortunately, they like the darkness, stench, and rats even less than we do, them being less accustomed to it. They usually leave fairly quickly, figuring they've done their duty. So far, we've not been caught, but we have to be careful. We fear informants or spies may have told the guards that something is afoot."

For their first shift, the tasks were relatively simple as the fanning, performed by Major Hamilton, was only to cool the colonel from his exertions. The spittoon sat on the floor of the cellar, so it could easily be emptied and replaced by William. Zeke took the first lookout, standing to the side of the one barred window high up on the south wall, looking down toward the river.

While Zeke watched, sentries paced close enough he could've reached out and touched them. From that position, he could also hear if anyone approached the door and began to unlock it. He quickly realized the advantage of his current assignment; standing next to the open window looking out at the street lamps, he was the only one of them who had a reasonable amount of fresh air and light. The downside, he also realized, was that with the temperature dropping into the teens, his posting was terribly cold, especially considering he was still wearing the summer-issue uniform he was captured in and had no jacket. As he shivered, blowing into his hands and rubbing them against his upper arms, trying to keep his teeth from chattering, he was amused to learn that his captors were apparently not much better off. When the guards called out their usual "all is well" on the hour, this time he heard one of them call out, "Post number sixteen; it's one o'clock … and *cold as hell!*"

William and Zeke quickly learned that Colonel Rose was a prodigious digger. He started the tunnel and dug for four hours straight before stopping to switch places with the major, at which point William and Zeke also switched tasks. By that time, Rose had already excavated more than two feet of tunnel, eighteen inches high and twenty-four wide.

Major Hamilton dug for two hours, followed by William, then Zeke for an hour each, after which Colonel Rose announced it was time to head up to make sure they had time to get everything back in place before the six o'clock reveille.

In eight hours of digging, they'd excavated five feet of tunnel. And though he didn't care for the tightness of the quarters, William didn't mind the work. The exertions and cheery flickering of the candle provided a warmth that was a welcome compared to the drafty, freezing-cold upstairs of Libby.

⌘⌘⌘⌘⌘⌘⌘⌘⌘

The next two nights, the routine was nearly identical to the first, except that both nights, the guards entered the east cellar for a quick inspection: once the first night, and twice the second. Though it'd been frightening and tense, causing the tunnelers to scramble to pre-planned hiding places, the guards had quickly retreated, even as Major Hamilton had described.

But William noticed that both the colonel and the major seemed surprised by the frequency of the visits. Something had changed.

⌘⌘⌘⌘⌘⌘⌘⌘⌘

On the fourth night, Colonel Rose once again took the first shift digging, and dug for three hours before backing out of the hole and flopping down on the ground panting heavily, covered in sweat and dirt.

Major Hamilton took the next shift, but he only lasted an hour before scrambling back out, breathing heavily.

361

Zeke took the next shift, but after a half hour he backed out, turning to Colonel Rose and saying, "The candle won't stay lit, Colonel."

Rose just nodded, "Yep ... Once we get far enough in, there's not enough air for it."

"Well, sir ... if there ain't enough air for the candle, how the heck do you expect a man to breathe in there?"

Rose gave Zeke a hard look, "A man's got more courage than a candle, Captain. And more desperation..."

Zeke gazed at him a moment, mouth agape. Then nodded, turned, and scrambled back into the tunnel.

But after another half hour Zeke backed out and collapsed onto the floor, panting for breath as William waved Hamilton's makeshift fan over him. "It's all I can do, Colonel," he gasped.

"It's fine, Captain. You've done well. It takes some getting used to."

"Can't believe y'all have already tried three tunnels before this'n ... You never told us what happened on them others, Colonel."

The colonel was thoughtful for a moment, "We started our first tunnel in the southeast corner, thinking to hit the main sewer line just twenty feet out. We'd found out from talking to some of our black soldiers—who've been worked by the rebs as if they were slaves—that the sewer line here is six feet in diameter and empties right into the James. If we could reach it, we could walk right down to the river, and make a clean escape from there."

"Sounds like a fair plan ... What happened?"

Rose snorted a mirthless chuckle. "I nearly drowned is what. It was my turn to dig, and as I neared our goal, I noticed a trickle of water had started coming into the tunnel. It wasn't much, so I ignored it and kept digging. Then I poked the chisel in one last time, and a great flood poured into the tunnel. If I'd not had a rope tied to my ankle, I'd have been a dead man. But the others dragged me out, sputtering and coughing. Reckon the south end of the cellar is too close to the water and we dug into the water table."

Zeke and William nodded.

"For the second tunnel, we moved farther north, and again tried to hit the sewer line. But as I mentioned before, when we got to it, we discovered it was lined with thick, hard oak that we couldn't penetrate with our crude tools. And yet we were willing to make the attempt. But sewage began leaking into the tunnel, smothering and sickening the diggers to the point we had to abandon the effort and fill it back in. And the third tunnel, higher up, collapsed when we inadvertently dug underneath a heavy pile of bricks from a discarded oven out in the prison yard." He shrugged.

William took the next shift, but when he moved toward the hole, Colonel Rose knelt down in front of him, holding out a rope which had a looped slipknot on the end, "Time to use this now, Captain Jenkins … far enough in now that it might become necessary."

William gazed at him a moment absorbing the implications of what he was saying, then nodded and raised his foot as Rose slipped the rope on and snugged it down.

But as William reached up to scramble into the hole Zeke held out a hand, "Just hand me your glasses, William."

"What? Without them I can barely see where I'm going."

But Zeke laughed, "William … the candle won't stay lit … A blind man's now the same as an eagle in this here hole."

William thought about that a moment, swallowed a lump in his throat and nodded. He removed the glasses and handed them to Zeke who carefully placed them in his pocket.

What William did next was the bravest thing he'd ever done in his life, and far more frightening than any of the gunfights he'd been in. He'd not told any of the others, not even Zeke, that he had an irrational fear of tightly enclosed spaces, especially in darkness. The previous digging hadn't bothered him overly much; the tunnel had still been shallow, the candle provided illumination, and there had been plenty of air to breathe.

He realized he also had a fear of not being able to breathe freely, a thing that'd made him dislike swimming, boating, or any other situation where one might suffocate. And now … he was voluntarily crawling forward into a dark, airless hell.

363

William made his way down the dark hole on his stomach. The tunnel was only tall enough for one to squirm forward; it was impossible to crawl on hands and knees. Rose had explained that making it large enough to crawl would take twice as long to dig, so they'd settled on the minimum a man needed to wriggle through on his belly. William, recalling his recent time spent in the dungeon, began an internal conversation to buoy up his courage, even as he'd done on that occasion. *Come on, William ... you can do this ... You've done worse ... Zeke did it and lived ... You can do this ... You'll be fine ... You can do this ... Can't be a damned coward in front of the others ... Keep going ... keep going, William ...*

After what seemed to have been hours of crawling, his left hand bumped against something hard and cold on the floor of the tunnel. *The spittoon...*

He slid past it and reached out to touch the end of the tunnel, and feeling around on the floor he located the digging tools: two jack knives whose blades had been ground into teeth to serve as saws for when wooden posts were encountered, a chisel for harder rock and to loosen the compacted dirt, and the broken piece of a shovel with no handle for general digging and for scooping dirt into the spittoon.

William picked up the chisel and started poking at the end of the tunnel in complete darkness. But within a minute of working, he was sweating profusely and found he was already having trouble breathing. A panic took hold of him, and he dropped the chisel. *I can't breathe ... Can't see ... This is a tomb ... I'm going to die in here ... Got to get out...*

He started to squirm backward, but then an image flashed before his mind's eye unbidden ... He saw Margaret ... sitting next to him on the bench down by the Ohio River back at Belle Meade Farm. The sun was shining on her hair giving it a soft, sparkling glow ... and she was beautiful ... smiling up at him ... she closed her eyes and leaned up for a kiss...

He stopped, took a deep breath of the fetid air, wiped the tears from his eyes, and crawled back to the end of the tunnel. He picked up the shovel and began scooping up the dirt he'd loosened.

At the end of the fifth night, during which the guards once again raided the east cellar twice, Colonel Rose called a quick meeting of the diggers.

"Gentlemen ... I'm becoming concerned about our pace. Our men—good, honest Union officers—now turn on each other for the merest scraps of food even as the rebels have cut our rations again, from our previous near-starvation level to ... whatever you would call them now. Dozens of men die daily from disease. And lately the guards have increased their wariness. I fear there are traitors or spies among the prisoners who've aroused their suspicions. We four are also becoming exhausted, working all night and getting little sleep.

"I propose that we see if we can convince some of our previous diggers to rejoin the effort, given our new plan. This will not only give us a much-needed respite, but the off-duty diggers can keep an eye out the upper windows for any unusual activity by the guards. And to pick up the pace, I propose we go back to night *and* day shifts."

"Day shifts?" Zeke was surprised by this proposal. "What about the two daily head counts? Won't the diggers on the day shift be missed?"

Hamilton smiled, and nodded, "We've done it successfully before. We have developed certain ... *tricks* ... for dealing with the head count—for fooling *Little Ross*."

"You mean the civilian head clerk, Erasmus Ross?"

"Yes ... young Mr. Ross seems to be good with numbers ... but not so alert that he can't be fooled. Wait and see."

Colonel Rose proved to be every bit as persuasive as he was courageous and tireless. He was able to recruit nearly all of the original diggers to join the new effort, such that he was able to put together three five-man teams.

And then, during the first head count of the first day shift of tunneling, William watched with amusement as the Union officers fooled the head count. As the two upper floors were divided into three rooms each, with the doors between nailed shut, Erasmus Ross had to exit the room he'd finished counting, go down to the lower level, then back up the stairs of the next room. But unknown to the guards, the prisoners had cut secret flaps in the nailed-shut connecting doors so that prisoners could slip through from one room to the next. So while Ross was walking from one room to the next, prisoners would move from room to room to make the head count correct.

William was impressed.

But the next day, the guards seemed to have become suspicious and squeezed all the prisoners into one room, where they were lined up in rows as Ross walked down the rows making his count. William was sure the game was up this time, as they'd not be able to move from room to room as they'd done before.

But as he watched, prisoners in the front rows surreptitiously ducked down and slipped back to the rows farther back in the room, so that they were counted twice, again making the count come out exactly as required.

ᏚᎣᏣᎡᏟᏯᏞᏌᏚᎣᏣᎡᏟᏯᏞᏌᏚᎣᏣᎡᏟᏯ

Sunday February 7, 1864 – Richmond, Virginia:

It was again the night shift in the east cellar, and William was feeling a keyed-up excitement; Colonel Rose had just announced he believed they'd reached the requisite fifty feet in the tunnel. So he'd untied the long clothesline from the spittoon and crawled back down the tunnel to take a measurement.

He'd only been gone a minute or two when Major Hamilton gave the signal that meant guards were coming. Zeke, who'd had fanning duty, scrambled under the fender of an old kitchen stove near the tunnel entrance, while Hamilton and Lieutenant Lewis Mitchell, the newest member of their team, ducked under a broken table near the front door.

William, who'd been on spittoon-emptying duty, scrambled under the large pile of straw just as the door swung open with a squeak, and a dim beam of light streamed in through the doorway from the windows in the dungeon area.

And the usual deadly fear of being caught by the guards suddenly took on a new aspect: this time they'd brought a hound, who immediately began sniffing along the floor.

William watched in growing fear as the hound moved along the floor in a zig-zag pattern, its nose to the ground, coming generally in the direction of the straw pile. And then, as if in a living nightmare, William saw the hound pick its head up, give a quick bark, and trot directly toward his hiding place.

William held his breath as the hound crept to within a few feet of his face, sniffing vigorously. Then the animal looked up at him and began a deep growl.

At that moment, William felt an odd sensation, moving up his back and across his right shoulder. There was a sudden scrambling motion as a piercing loud squeal assaulted his right ear; a rat leapt down onto the floor, saw the hound, and bolted across the room, the dog hot on his trail, barking furiously. But before the hound could close on the rat, another rat, startled by the sudden motion, darted out of a hole and scurried in front of the hound, who changed directions, targeting this new quarry. In moments, more rats were squealing and scurrying around the room in dizzying numbers, the dog barking, growling, and chasing with great enthusiasm.

"Damn it, Toby! Heel ... heel! Get over here you damned knot-head. Damned dog. Damned rats. Get over here, you!" Two guards came in, whistling, cursing, and trying to grab the excited dog. They finally cornered it and leashed it before dragging it out of the room and closing the door.

William let out a long breath, and then couldn't help chuckling for the absurdity of it all.

Once the noise from the guards and their hound had died down, Colonel Rose re-entered the cellar. William and Zeke greeted him. William could see Rose had an excited look, "Who's turn is it to dig?"

"Mine," William answered, realizing that the prospect no longer frightened him. *Guess one can get used to anything...*

Rose gazed at him a moment before making an incongruous statement, "Captain Jenkins ... I believe you should wear your glasses this time..."

"Sir? It's still too dark in the tunnel for..."

But Colonel Rose broke into a grin, "By my measurement, we're now at fifty-three feet. Time to dig *up*, Captain. With luck, you'll be the first of us to breathe free air once again, and I suspect you'll want to have a look around. Good luck."

William had to keep his excitement in check and not overexert himself. With the tunnel now over fifty feet long, the air was so thin, one had to pace oneself to keep from passing out. Because of this, Colonel Rose had given the diggers instructions to tug once on the spittoon's clothesline every minute or so to signal they were still conscious. Three tugs indicated the spittoon needed emptying. If no tug came after two minutes, the men in the cellar would start pulling the digger out by the rope around his ankle.

William was now digging upward, which required him to work laying on his back, looking straight up toward where he was digging. He no longer feared the dark and the confinement, but the fear of dirt collapsing and smothering him was constantly on his mind. But he was determined to break through to the surface on his shift, so he concentrated on an image of Margaret in his mind, focusing on the same one he'd envisioned before, of her sitting by the river in the sunlight.

He soon discovered that digging upward had the advantage of gravity being on one's side, as the dirt fell loose rather than having to be scraped off the wall. At the end of two hours, he was able to stand in the vertical shaft he'd dug, and then he banged the chisel into the ceiling and a pile of dirt fell on his face and shoulders. For a moment he feared a cave-in. But then a flow of cool, fresh air filled his lungs. He was out!

ഈരുഇൽ ഈരുഇൽ ഈരുഇൽ

William's momentary elation turned to dismay and fear as he poked his head out for a look. The first thing he saw was a fence, the fence surrounding the area that housed the tobacco shed that'd been their goal. And he was on the wrong side of it! They'd

368

somehow come up ten feet short of their goal. And worse, he was out in the open of the prison yard. He suppressed a gasp as he looked to his left and saw a guard approaching, coming straight toward him not more than a hundred feet away. He ducked back into the hole, but he resisted the urge to retreat back into the prison cellar. For one, it would make too much noise trying to scramble back through the hole. And for another … a part of him needed to *know* … if this was the end of their escape effort.

So William gazed up out of the ground as the guard walked to within five feet of his hole and looked around. He walked over toward the fence and looked in that area. He then turned and gazed across the ground, at one point looking directly at William where he crouched within the tunnel. Then the guard turned and strode away, muttering, "Damned rats … Stinkin' things are everywhere…"

But William had an entirely different reaction to that of the guard. *Thank God for darkness … and for rats!*

When William retreated to the cellar and informed Colonel Rose of the disaster, the colonel immediately climbed in the tunnel to investigate. Two hours later, Rose returned and announced that all was well. He'd managed to re-route the tunnel back toward their destination and had used the dirt he excavated to refill the vertical shaft. He figured two more days of digging would get them into the shed.

෴෬෬෬෭෮෴෬෬෬෭෮෴෬෬෬෭

Colonel Rose's brief glimpse of freedom as he poked his head up out of the hole William Jenkins had dug had such a strong impact on him that his previous dedication to the idea of escape became an all-encompassing, driving obsession. When his usual shift was over, he refused to leave the cellar and insisted on doing the digging himself, no longer taking breaks, and no longer relinquishing the duty to any other.

For hours on end, in complete darkness, he toiled away, either on his stomach or on his back, in the increasingly thin air, moving forward one painful inch at a time. During all that time, other than the occasional visit by one of the men to return the empty spittoon, his only company was the ever-present rats, which crawled across some part of his body every few minutes.

But he no longer paid them any mind, unless they decided to bite, in which case he gave them a quick whack with the shovel.

He'd marked the place where the original vertical shaft had been so that he could easily find it in the dark with the toe of his boot. So then he could use his own height of six feet to measure the distance he'd moved forward.

At the end of ten hours, he measured and was at the required ten feet. It was time to go up once more. But now his body was nearing complete exhaustion, such that even his iron will was failing to make it obey. His arms now ached painfully, and his hands twitched and shook uncontrollably.

He began the vertical shaft, but to make sure he didn't somehow come up short again, he decided to dig it at a forty-five-degree angle. Two more hours passed with his body wracked with painful spasms, and still he'd not reached the surface. He lifted his hands once again and the chisel fell from his grip, and his head seemed to spin. With a sudden shock he realized he could no longer breathe. The shaft was now so long that with the vertical bend there was simply no air left. He knew he was going to die … and there was nothing he could do about it.

With his last remaining strength, he pounded in vain against the dirt ceiling of what had become his tomb, venting his anger and frustration at coming so close, and yet failing in the end. And then his mind went as black as the tunnel surrounding him.

ℬᑎℭℜℭℬᑎℬᑎℭℜℭℬᑎℬᑎℭℜℭℬ

Colonel Rose coughed dirt from his mouth and wiped it from his face, snorting his nose to blow it from his nostrils. Then he realized the absolute darkness he'd lived in for the last full day was no longer so absolute. And the air was fresh and cool. He gazed up and saw … thin strips of light, leaking in between what appeared to be wide boards. After a quick prayer of thanks to whichever saint or angel had preserved him when he was surely a dead man, he scrambled up to the lip of the tunnel and cautiously peered out. What he saw filled him with more joy than

370

he could ever remember in life; he'd come up exactly where he wished to be and intended, right in the middle of the tobacco shed.

And despite his exhaustion, the fresh air and sudden taste of freedom infused him with new vigor. After covering the tunnel exit with a large barrel, he crept to the door of the shed, slowly opened it, and peered out. Seeing no guards, he walked to the gate of the outer prison compound and slowly opened it, careful to make as little noise as possible. He knew the general layout from studying it out the upstairs windows of the prison, so he knew where the guards would likely be and where they wouldn't.

He looked up the street and saw a guard pacing, but headed in the opposite direction. So he slipped out, reclosed the gate, and calmly strolled down the street, as if he were just another hungry, shabby street dweller.

It occurred to him that the overcrowding, lawlessness, and poverty that'd taken hold in Richmond since the start of the war would greatly aid in their escape; the emaciated, ragged prisoners would look little different from the majority of the pedestrians out roaming the streets at night.

Feeling buoyed up by his sudden taste of freedom, Rose decided to circumnavigate the entire prison grounds, which might also serve as a reconnoiter to see exactly where the guards were positioned. An hour later, having completed a full circuit of the prison grounds, he returned to the outer gate and slipped back inside, heading to the tunnel exit. For a moment, a voice in his head argued not to return to the hell that was Libby, but to simply keep running now that he was free. But he paid it no mind and slipped back into the tunnel.

Minutes later a quietly jubilant group of four men received the good news from Colonel Rose. But after a brief meeting they all concluded it would be best to wait until nightfall again to conduct the breakout, since it was already nearing dawn. The prisoners would best be served with an entire night of darkness in which to make their escape from Richmond out toward Union lines.

Rose then announced that each of the fifteen diggers would be allowed to invite one other man, making a total of thirty for the initial escape, close to the two-dozen figure he'd originally agreed to with Captains Jenkins and Benton when they'd started the fourth tunnel. A few trustworthy men were let in on the secret and were told to wait an hour after the second set of thirty men were well away, then let the rest of the prisoners know that they could use the tunnel if they wished.

๑๐๓๓๓๓๓๐๓๓๓๓๓๓๓๓๓๓

Tuesday February 9, 1864 – Richmond, Virginia:

After serving another long, futile shift in the prison hospital, sadly watching two more men expire needlessly for lack of basic medicines and nutrition, William returned to the prison room and sat down on the floor next to Zeke.

"How goes the waiting?" he asked in low tones.

"Slow … slowest damned day of my life, I swear. I keep having this dread that some rebel informant's gonna spoil the whole show. That the guards'll come swooping in here at any moment and the whole damned thing will've been for naught. It's giving me an ache in the stomach on top of the usual one for want of food."

William reached over and patted Zeke on the knee, "Not much longer now. I have a good feeling about this."

But William chose not to share with Zeke that most of those "good feelings" he was having were due to a growing excitement at the thought of seeing Margaret for the first time in nearly a year. He kept picturing her in his mind—her smile, the warmth of her embrace, her laughter. He smiled, leaned back, and closed his eyes. *Tonight, my dear … Tonight we will finally be together again.*

๑๐๓๓๓๓๓๐๓๓๓๓๓๓๓๓๓๓

William and Zeke volunteered to be the last out of the fifteen "diggers," since they'd been the last to join and had only worked for a few weeks on the last tunnel, while the others had toiled for months, including on the three earlier failed attempts.

As they stood in the back from of the upper floor, waiting for their turn to crawl down the rope ladder through the fireplace flue

372

and into the cellar, they turned to each other and shared a grin, a firm handshake, and a quick embrace.

William waited for Zeke to enter the tunnel, and then he turned to the man behind him, who had volunteered as the gatekeeper, "Remember, the next group must wait an hour, as Colonel Rose has instructed … too many of us out at once will be more likely to raise suspicions…"

"Yes, Captain … You can count on me. And … good luck, sir!"

"You too."

After the familiar tight squeeze down through the fireplace, William stepped across to the tunnel and immediately climbed in. Zeke was already gone up the tunnel.

It was the first time William had to scramble the whole way, but in his excitement, the journey went by in a blur, and he was soon poking his head out the exit, gazing around the dark shed.

"Psst … over here, William."

William climbed out and moved over to where Zeke stood by the door. "Okay, let's go…"

They followed the route that Colonel Rose had described to the group: out the shed door, across the fenced-in area to the outer gate, then quietly out onto the street. From there, they just had to stroll away, blending in with Richmond's teeming, wretched street dwellers, still active on the streets at this early hour of the evening.

William and Zeke turned and walked casually up Twenty-First Street, trying to project a calmness that they certainly did not feel.

ᏏᏄᏒᏇᏎᏏᏄᏒᏇᏎᏏᏄᏒᏇ

Evelyn and Margaret relaxed in the sitting room at Evelyn's house when there came an urgent knocking at the door. Though the daylight had ended, it was not yet dinner time, and the two ladies had been alternating between casual conversation and reading.

Evelyn heard the maid Pegg answer the door, and then a rush of footsteps, and the twelve-year-old freeman boy Tad was at the doorway to the sitting room, all out of breath. But he remembered

373

his manners, and removed his hat, "Sorry for the intrusion, ma'am."

"It's all right, Tad … What is it that has you so out of breath this evening?"

"It's happening, Miss Eve! The prisoners … they've tunneled out, and they's escapin'. They's all over the streets, running in every direction to get away from Libby!"

Both ladies were instantly on their feet, "What of the guards?" Evelyn held Tad with her eyes.

"None yet, ma'am … seems they ain't yet noticed the breakout."

"Good, good! Margaret—"

But Margaret was already out the door into the foyer, grabbing her hat off the hook there, and tying it on.

"Wait, Margaret … Where are you going?"

"Out … to Elizabeth's house, maybe … I don't know … I can't just sit here!"

"Please, Margaret … wait a while. It may not be safe. If the guards get wind of it, there could be violence. Wait a while, and I will go with you … I need a little time to send couriers out with messages to the others … so they'll be on the lookout to assist the escapees."

"You don't need me for that, Evelyn. I'll be fine … I will head straight to Elizabeth's house and await you there."

Evelyn could see there was no talking her out of it, and she wasn't sure she could blame her. If Nathan were out there on the streets somewhere in mortal danger, she would not be able to sit still either. "All right … Just please be careful."

The two exchanged a serious look, and then Margaret broke into a grin, "It's happening, Evelyn! They're finally getting out of that horrible place."

Evelyn returned the smile and stepped up to Margaret and they embraced warmly. Then Margaret stepped back, turned, and rushed out the door and into the night.

࿇ ࿇ ࿇ ࿇ ࿇

Captain Bob Hill sat at his desk in the guardhouse, once again going through the frustrating, useless, and heart-wrenching exercise of requesting additional food, medicines, and clothing for the inmates. When he'd first taken up his duties as officer of the guard at Libby, he'd been shocked by the condition of the inmates.

Those in the hospital appeared to be dying, and when he pulled aside the Union surgeon Captain Jenkins and asked him about it, Jenkins just shrugged and said, "They *are* dying, and there's nothing I can do about it. There is no medicine, and rations are insufficient to bring them back to health on their own."

And the inmates not in hospital were not much better off. Bob could see that these unfortunate men were slowly starving to death. It was unconscionable, and it gave him a sick knot in his stomach that never seemed to go away. He'd been forced to steel his heart to it, but he was also determined to do whatever he could, as fruitless as that might be.

He shrugged and put his signature to yet another request to the war department, knowing full well it was likely worse than useless—would likely earn him a reprimand. But he no longer cared.

He looked up at a sudden noise, as one of the guards came into the room in a rush, barely remembering to stop, place the butt of his rifle on the floor, and snap a salute.

Bob returned the salute but remained sitting, "What is it, Private?"

"Sir! Me and Joe, uh … Private Joe Wilkens, I mean … was standing our watch, like we usually does … the three o'clock to midnight shift as you well know, sir … uh, at the southern post that is, sir … when a civilian comes up all of a lather. He bein' an older fella was a bit outta breath … Took him a spell to be able to tells us what'd riled him so. Don't know the man personally, sir … Never seen him before, so don't know if he's the calm, trustworthy type or not … Can't vouch for him personally, sir."

"Yes, yes … please get on with it, private. What did the fellow say?"

"Yes, sir. Well, sir, this old feller claimed to have seen several suspicious looking jaspers sneakin' along the side of the road where it's dark, headin' north from Libby, sir."

"Hmph. Likely beggars or thieves. Probably raided the prisoners' gift boxes. Crime's running rampant in Richmond these days, especially with all the food shortages. Not our duty to chase after criminals, Private," Bob returned his attention to the paperwork in front of him.

"Oh, I agree, sir. And I thought the same ... and told the old man that very thing. I'd not bother you if that were all there was to it, sir."

Bob set down his pen and looked back up, "All right ... then what else *is there* to it, Private?" He was growing exasperated with the private's inability to get to the point.

"Well, sir ... what caught my attention, so to speak, was when the old man said, 'These sneakin' fellers was wearin' ragged lookin' *blue* uniforms, with brass buttons down the front.'"

"*Oh!* Why didn't you say so in the first place, Private?"

"I was ... gettin' to it, sir..."

Bob leapt to his feet, came around the desk, grabbed his hat and gun belt from a hook on the wall, and headed out the door, "C'mon, Private!"

🙰🙰🙰🙰🙰🙰🙰🙰

Though some of the soldiers moved as quickly as possible, thinking to put as much distance between themselves and the prison as they could before daybreak—and wisely so—William and Zeke fortunately had better prospects, thanks to Margaret and Evelyn. They had explicit directions to a safe house only five blocks from the prison, so they could proceed at a more steady pace that might avoid suspicion.

They'd already made it to the corner of Twenty-First and Grace, so a right-hand turn would make their destination less than three blocks farther.

After looking both ways and seeing no one, they stepped out onto the road and strode to the street corner. But as they neared

376

it, someone stepped from behind a tall bush and turned directly toward them, blocking their way and forcing them to pause.

Though it was dark, it was clear from the person's outline that it was a woman.

Zeke—by previous agreement—was to do any talking, him being a native Virginian. He tipped his hat and said, "Good evening, miss."

He heard a slight gasp, *"Zeke? William?"*

William's heart skipped a beat in sudden recognition. "Margaret! You shouldn't be out here..."

She stepped forward into the light and he saw her face for the first time in a year. His heart leapt into his throat as he took a step closer.

And then an explosion behind him made him flinch...

William was still looking at Margaret when her expression changed from excitement and joy to shock. Her eyes widened and she gasped as she slumped forward into William's arms. He hastily laid her on the ground, his surgeon's eye quickly finding the bullet hole in the side of her abdomen.

"Hold on Margaret. Hold on!" he demanded as he shoved his hands hard over the wound to staunch the flow of blood.

☙ℭ℧☜℘☙ℭ℧☜℘☙℘ℭ℧

Prisoner escapes were not that uncommon, and the escapees rarely made it far before being recaptured, so Bob Hill wasn't overly concerned. As emaciated as the prisoners were, in a cold, hostile country where most citizens would eagerly turn them in or help capture them, they had little real chance. And yet, having seen their living conditions, he could hardly blame them for making the attempt.

He actually had a great deal of empathy for them, but it was still his duty to track them down and bring them back. He did, however, go out of his way to treat them as kindly as possible while doing so, in contrast to most of the other officers.

He'd gathered two other guards in addition to Private Reuben Bailey who'd initially reported the escape to him. They trotted up Twentieth Street, though the old man who'd reported seeing the

Union officers had described Twenty-First Street. Bob figured he and his men could outrun the poorly conditioned prisoners and cut them off at Franklin Street, a block farther uphill.

But when they reached the corner of Franklin and Twenty-First and looked back south, they saw no one. Bob lifted his binoculars, ignoring the sharp pain in his side from where he'd been wounded. *Not quite ready for all this running around*, he decided, resisting the urge to rub where it hurt. He refused to show that sort of weakness in front of other soldiers.

He gazed slowly along the hedgerow down the left side of the street to see if he could spot any tell-tale signs of men hiding there, but there was nothing.

Then Private Bailey, who'd been looking north up Twenty-First toward Grace Street, called out, "There they are!"

Bob turned to have a look, and to his horror, saw the private aiming his rifle. Before Bob could shout an order to stop, a shot rang out, and gun smoke curled up around them. "*Got one!*"

"Damn it, Private! Who told you to fire your weapon?! There are civilians about. And besides … I want them captured, not killed."

"Sorry, sir. But it don't likely make no difference. Poor devils is starvin' to death, anyway. Likely did him a favor."

Bob continued to scowl at the private, "We'll discuss your *punishment* later … the rest of you, *no more gunfire!* Is that understood?"

"Yes, sir … yes, sir!" the other two privates nodded.

Bob raised his binoculars and looked up the block. He could see a man down on all fours, but not lying on the ground. Bob prayed the injury wasn't too serious. Another man stood over the first, looking down at his wounded comrade.

"Come on…" he said and took off at a trot toward the downed man.

But when they came to within a few yards his breath caught in his throat. He took in the horrible scene in a rush. The man kneeling did not appear to have been hit after all, but appeared to be rendering first aid to a woman lying on the ground. The other man was also gazing down at the woman, not bothering to look up at the approaching guards, though clearly he knew they were there.

Bob turned to the privates and held up his hand, "Stay here." Then he turned back toward the tragic scene, and respectfully removed his hat and held it over his heart. He stepped up next to the men, who he could see were obviously Union captains from their uniform tunics.

Bob knelt down and looked at the face of the man on the ground. He recognized him immediately as one of the Union surgeons, Captain William Jenkins. Oddly, Jenkins had tears in his eyes as he gazed down at the woman, pressing his hands down onto a wound on her left side.

He glanced up at Bob, but seemed entirely disinterested, focused on caring for the woman on the ground in front of him. The woman's eyes were closed, but whether she was unconscious or dead, Bob couldn't tell. "Captain Jenkins … is she…?"

"She's been hit in the side. It's bad … but she yet lives…" he said in a rasping whisper. Bob could see Jenkins' hands were covered in blood.

"I'm very sorry; I never ordered anyone to fire … she—" he glanced down and took in the woman's face for the first time; his heart stopped.

"*Margaret!* Oh, my dear God, *no!*"

"You … *know* Margaret?" Jenkins gazed at him.

"Yes … I … *wait*, you also know her?"

Jenkins nodded.

And then Bob made the recognition, though he hadn't before back at the prison. From Walters' disastrous raid on Nathan Chambers' slave wedding. William Jenkins was one of the Mountain Meadows men!

"You were one of Captain Chambers' men!"

William was wide eyed, staring at Bob. "You're … you're *that* Bob Hill? The one who worked for Walters, but helped Margaret escape?"

Bob nodded, then glanced back at the soldiers standing where he ordered them to stay. In that moment he made a fateful decision and took immediate action on it.

"Well, don't just stand there … I've got these prisoners in custody and will help look after this wounded lady. You two go and look for any others that might've escaped. Bailey, you run back to the prison and fetch an ambulance, straightaway."

"Sir!" the three shouted and turned to trot back down the hill.

"She … she knew you would break out tonight … she was meeting you here," Bob realized.

Jenkins nodded, tears still welling in his eyes.

Bob leaned his face close to William's. "Listen, Captain … it's clear she means a great deal to you … She does to me as well. My heart aches from this senseless tragedy … But we mustn't let her die. Get her out of here. We both know it'll do no good sending her to the prison hospital. By the time competent help arrives, she'll be done for. You must take her to Miss Evelyn's house … care for her there. Later I will locate another capable surgeon and send him to assist you."

"But you—"

"Get out of here! Take her with you."

William looked over at Zeke, a puzzled expression on his face. Zeke shrugged.

Bob glanced back down the street and saw the two soldiers were now trotting in the other direction, poking into bushes and hedges as they went. He turned back, drew out his revolver, and offered it to Zeke, handle first.

"Take it," Bob insisted. "You may need it. But first, hit me with it."

"What? *Why?*" Zeke asked.

"I'm letting you men go … but it must look like you got the jump on me, took my pistol and knocked me out to make your escape…"

"I … I can't … A blow like that might kill you, captain."

"Then punch me … hard enough to bloody my nose or blacken my eye. You … do know how to throw a punch?"

Zeke gazed open-mouthed at Bob another moment, then his right fist flashed out and caught Bob just under the left eye, knocking him backward onto the street, where he lay staring up at the sky.

Bob Hill stayed where he was, continuing to gaze up at the stars, fighting against an aching pain in his chest that had nothing to do with his war wounds.

What should've been a celebratory gathering at Elizabeth Van Lew's house that night was darkened by the arrival of William and Zeke carrying a badly wounded Margaret. She was quickly rushed into a back bedroom, where William examined, stitched, and bandaged her as Evelyn held a lamp overhead, gritting her teeth at the horrific sight, but refusing to look away.

When William was satisfied that he'd done all he could for the moment, he sent Evelyn out to the sitting room to share the news of Margaret's condition. "William says the bullet passed clean through her side, and appears to have missed any major blood vessels or important organs. That's the good news. The bad news is the bullet likely carried some of the material from her clothing into the wound, where it can't be removed without doing her more harm. William says such material may cause festering, but there's little he can do about that … He says … *he says*…" then Evelyn found her throat constricting, and felt a sob building that threatened to render her incapable of speech. "He says we must now pray for her…" she managed in barely a whisper.

Elizabeth stood and came over to Evelyn, taking her by the hands and leading her to a chair. There the two sat, side by side, Elizabeth embracing Evelyn, gently patting her on the back.

Zeke felt like he'd been kicked in the chest by a mule, and could not even imagine how William was feeling. He couldn't recall ever going from such a high height at their escape to such an abysmal low at the dreadful wounding of Margaret. He did as William had bid—the only thing he could think of to do—and prayed for Margaret's swift return to health.

During the next several days, little was said as Zeke and William were treated to wholesome meals, warm, clean bedding, and new clothes for the first time since the Battle of Winchester, now nearly eight months ago. Zeke could feel the strength flowing back into his limbs.

William too looked healthier, though he no longer smiled, and rarely made eye contact during the short periods he left Margaret's side.

True to his word, on the second day after Margaret's injury, Captain Hill sent the promised medical help. But not a surgeon.

A knock on the door produced a dark-haired, fortyish, upper-class woman with keen, intense eyes, and a warm smile that reflected her general demeanor.

"My name is Phoebe Pember ... I am chief matron at Chimborazo Military Hospital," she announced to Evelyn and Elizabeth as they greeted her in the sitting room. "Captain Hill tells me you have a wounded woman, and are in need of a surgeon ... a surgeon willing to fulfill his Hippocratic Oath without regard to the ... *political persuasion* ... of the patient. The captain sent me directions to *your* house, Miss Evelyn, but your servants redirected me here ... and so, here I am."

"But..." Evelyn frowned, "Surely, Miss Phoebe, you are not a surgeon..."

"No, Miss Evelyn, I am not. But when I quizzed Captain Hill on the specifics of situation, he admitted there was already an extremely capable surgeon in residence, and what was really needed were medicines, bandages, and surgical equipment — and general assistance, that the surgeon might not have to do it all himself. So, I have come to see for myself, so that I may arrange to send such help as may be required. Unfortunately, after today I will likely not be returning, as I have a hospital to run."

"Oh, thank you, Miss Phoebe. It is a great relief to have your assistance," Evelyn answered.

"And how is our patient doing, may I ask?"

"Well, she is now conscious, but bedridden, and in a great deal of pain. Our surgeon is concerned that the wound may be festering."

"Hmm ... I see. Well, I have also taken the liberty of bringing medicines and supplies I thought the surgeon may need," she said, holding up a heavy carpet bag. "Please lead me to the patient, and introduce me to the surgeon, Miss Evelyn."

Evelyn smiled, and gestured back down the hallway, "This way, if you please, Miss Phoebe."

William and Zeke now lived in a walled off room in Elizabeth's attic behind a secret door, where they stayed whenever William wasn't tending to Margaret. It was small, dusty, and unadorned. But compared to where they'd just been, it was heavenly.

On the third day, Zeke was surprised and taken aback when he and William were led out of their hiding place and into the house's sitting room, only to find two Confederate officers sitting there sipping tea. Zeke didn't know the major, but the other he knew well: Libby Prison's civilian clerk, Erasmus Ross of the dreaded head counts. His heart sank; they'd been betrayed!

But as they entered the room, Ross stepped forward and smiled, extending his hand, "Congratulations, gentlemen, on your successful escape."

"Mr. Ross ... I ... don't understand," Zeke stood looking from Ross to the Confederate officer, then over at William, who shrugged.

Then the Confederate officer held out his hand, "I'm Major Oliver Boyd, but please call me Ollie. We're friends of Miss Evelyn and Miss Elizabeth."

"Oh!" was all Zeke could think of, then looked at Ross, "So then ... you're..."

"Yep, a pro-Union spy, recruited by Miss Elizabeth. Captain Benton, you don't really think you prisoners were so clever with your little head-count games that you would've fooled a dedicated secessionist?" He chuckled, "It was all I could do not to burst out laughing at your antics, even as I fudged the numbers to match the count I needed. Except the morning after the big breakout ... there was no disguising *that!* Even I was shocked by the result."

Zeke grinned, "How many made it out, Mr. Ross?"

"One hundred and nine, altogether. Though I understand a handful have already been recaptured."

"Gosh … more'n a hundred. Must be one o' the biggest prison breaks ever. How about *that*, William?" he turned and grinned at William. But he wasn't surprised that William didn't return the smile. But he did manage a nod. Zeke wondered if William would ever smile again. Likely not until Margaret made a full recovery. If she ever did.

Evelyn and Elizabeth soon joined them, and they had tea and biscuits as they discussed next steps.

Several different options were discussed, including staying in Elizabeth's attic for an extended time, a month or more, until the furor died down, and then quietly slipping out of town.

But Evelyn pointed out that Elizabeth was already under suspicion, and there was always the possibility of a raid, if anyone remembered her long-standing connection with the prisoners of Libby Prison. She was just too obvious a target for long-term safety.

Likewise, Evelyn too had recently been under a dark cloud of suspicion, so her house also was not necessarily safe long term.

But William ended all discussion when he announced, "I won't be leaving. I'll not leave Margaret in her present condition. You'll never convince me, so don't bother trying."

₡₧₧₧₧₧₧₧₧

Despite William's pronouncement, Evelyn put her people to work acquiring suitable clothing, boots, weapons, canteens, knapsacks, and portable food for the journey north without being too obvious about it and drawing unwanted attention.

In the meantime, William and Zeke spent their days in Elizabeth Van Lew's attic, taking advantage of the comfort, warmth, and plentiful food that implied.

With the unusually frigid weather stubbornly refusing to loosen its grip on the Virginia countryside, Evelyn knew once the men left Elizabeth's house, all such comforts would become nonexistent. At least until they reached Union lines—if they were able to.

"Good morning, Margaret," William walked into the bedroom and immediately stepped up to her bed and placed his hand on her forehead. He slowly shook his head, "Still feverish…"

But she reached up and pulled his hand from her forehead and held it in hers.

"Miss Evelyn said you wished to see me straightaway," William said. "Is something amiss, other than the fever?"

"No, William … not concerning my health. It seems much the same. It hurts … and I have chills."

He frowned, "I will fetch you water…"

"No … *stay* … That's not why I wished to see you."

"Oh?" William reached toward the wall, pulled over the simple chair that stood there, and sat down next to her bed. He leaned over toward her, continuing to hold her hand. "What is it, then?"

"William … Evelyn tells me you refuse to leave and go to the North, though she has now made all the necessary arrangements."

"Yes, that's true. I should think that would be self-evident, with you in the condition you're in."

"William, you must go."

"Oh, no Margaret. That I will never do while you remain ill."

She nodded, then said a thing unexpected, "William, you are being terribly selfish."

"*Selfish?* How do you mean?"

"Evelyn tells me the Confederate Signal Corp searches door to door for the escaped Union officers, breaking into locked rooms, arresting suspected collaborators, stopping and searching civilians in the streets. Allowing no one to come or go from Richmond without papers proving who they are…"

He shrugged, "Not surprising. Allowing over a hundred officers to escape must be a great embarrassment to them. But what has that to do with me being *selfish?*"

"William, Elizabeth is already under suspicion, and at various times, Evelyn has been as well. How long do you think it will be before the Signal Corps kicks in the front door and finds you here? And what will happen to those fine ladies when they do? And what will they do to me? Do you think they will make sure I get the very best medical care in one of their prisons?"

William's mouth dropped open, "I … I hadn't thought of that. I just fear—"

"William, if you fear I won't get adequate medical treatment, you needn't worry. You said yourself that the nurses Miss Phoebe has been sending by are excellent, and can do as much for me now as you can."

"It's not that…" he trailed off, and gazed down at the floor, no longer able to look her in the eye.

"What, then?"

"I … I fear … if I leave, I will never see you again in life." He bowed his head, removed his glasses and wiped his eyes.

"Oh, William … my dearest…" She pulled his hand to her mouth and kissed it, tears welling in her own eyes.

"I will make you a deal, my darling."

He looked up expectantly.

"I won't die of these wounds, if you won't die escaping to the North. We will meet again when this war is finally over. And then … *then* we will never be parted again."

He nodded his head and gazed into her eyes for a long time before finally answering. "You're a wonder, Margaret. A pure wonder…"

ॐଓଔ๛ॐଓଔ๛ॐଓଔ

As they prepared to depart for the North, William and Zeke received some unexpected good news: Confederate Major Boyd had agreed to accompany them as their guide. Neither William nor Zeke were familiar with this part of Virginia, so his knowledge would be invaluable.

From what Zeke had learned from Evelyn, Boyd had had some sort of falling out with the Confederate Army higher ups, including General Lee, and wished to desert and fight for the Union army instead. Zeke thought the major seemed like a highly capable and intelligent fellow, and was pleased he'd be going along.

Monday February 15, 1864 – Richmond, Virginia:

They left Elizabeth's house a few minutes after six o'clock, once the sun was fully set. They went out the back door and cut across several neighboring yards before reaching Twenty-Fourth Street where it crossed Broad Street.

Zeke knew they were in for a long, cold slog. The temperature had been in the low teens during the daylight hours, and now that the sun was gone it would only get colder. And though they had on new clothes—with no holes or patches, unlike what they'd become used to wearing—cold weather clothing was not usually needed in Virginia, so had been impossible to come by on short notice. They would just have to suffer it, he decided.

They headed up Twenty-Fourth Street, moving in a northeasterly direction, away from the James River waterfront. Zeke smiled at the sudden realization that every step he now took led him one step farther away from Libby Prison, a place he hoped never to see again.

It was about twelve blocks up Twenty-Fourth street until they reached the edge of town and could disappear into the countryside. They knew that first dozen blocks might very well be the most dangerous of the journey. Evelyn's people reported that the rebels still scoured the town for escapees, even though most who'd not been recaptured had disappeared into the countryside by this point.

To increase their chances, Miss Evelyn had decided they should adopt the aspect of common laborers going out on a job, so each carried a shovel or a pick over his shoulder, and they strode along with confidence as if they hadn't a care in the world—though Zeke decided nothing could be farther from the truth. Every time they crossed a street and looked down the intersection in both directions, he feared seeing a Confederate patrol coming toward them.

Miss Evelyn had also insisted that if they were questioned by a patrol that only Ollie and Zeke should speak, them being

Virginians. William, being a northerner, should say as little as possible. Zeke snorted a laugh as he thought about that; William hadn't said more than two words all day, so it was unlikely he'd start blabbing away now.

And though they encountered several civilians on the street, these nodded and smiled courteously, and none seemed to eye them with suspicion. Zeke breathed a sigh of relief when they finally reached a wooded area past the edge of town without encountering any enemy patrols. They tossed their tools down into a ravine and set out across country, intending to avoid all roads and towns as much as possible.

Two and a half hours into their hike, they came to their first obstacle, the Chickahominy River. Though it was narrow, and not especially deep, it flowed swiftly enough to prevent it freezing over, though ice lined the sides of the bank on both sides. Ollie had warned them this was coming, with the rebels guarding every bridge within fifty miles of Richmond, but Zeke still groaned when it came time for it.

He met eyes with Ollie, rolled them, and then started stripping off his clothes. Ollie and William did the same. In short order, all three men stood stark naked except for their hats in a temperature that was likely now in the single digits, preparing to ford a stream whose water would be frigid almost beyond endurance.

But there was nothing for it if they wished to keep their boots and clothing dry, so they quickly stuffed everything into their knapsacks, slung them over their shoulders, and plunged in. Zeke flinched at the discomfort when the water rose up his legs from the knees to just over his waist. *Brrrr ... damn, that's nasty cold! Like to freeze the old bollocks right off!*

It was over quickly, and thankfully the water had never gone higher than mid-chest, and the river bottom was smooth and firm.

Once on the far bank, they re-dressed as quickly as their frozen limbs would allow, and were grateful to be moving again, giving them at least a fighting chance of warming up their shivering bodies.

Once across the Chickahominy, they had two options: to turn right and follow the river toward the Union lines at Williamsburg,

Virginia, the shorter route at just over fifty miles, or to continue to the northeast toward the Potomac, and eventually Washington City.

The majority of the escapees had planned to head for Williamsburg. It was not only the shorter route, but once you were across the Chickahominy there were no more major rivers to cross, though there were swamps and bogs. There was also the possibility of being rescued by a far-ranging Union cavalry patrol.

The downside of that route was, the Confederates also knew it was the easiest, shortest route. So it was simply crawling with enemy patrols, all of which would be on the lookout for escapees.

The northern route was twice as long and included multiple large rivers to cross.

The advantage, of course, was the Confederates also knew this.

Since they'd had the advantage of being fed and housed for several days before setting off, the northern route made the most sense. So they continued in the direction they'd been heading, making a beeline for the Potomac River.

They hiked for the rest of the night, another fifteen miles, reaching the edge of the Pamunkey River just as the pre-dawn sky was beginning to glow in the east. The Pamunkey was much broader and deeper than the Chickahominy had been, so there was no chance they could wade it. Its waters also moved at a much more sedate pace, such that the recent long stretch of freezing temperatures had turned its surface into a slowly churning, white obstacle course of large, ragged, grinding chunks of ice.

They'd have to figure some way across it, but at the moment they were exhausted, frozen, and in need of sleep. So they crawled under a bush and lay down, their bodies as close to each other as possible to share heat. It was a thing no man would've been comfortable with doing before the war, but they'd all been soldiers long enough to think nothing of it. It was common sense, and could save their lives. And ... Zeke had to admit, it was comforting to feel your comrade right next to you as you slept, knowing he would risk his life for you without hesitation, as you would for him.

After sleeping until midday, Zeke awoke to a chopping noise. Dragging himself out from under the bush, he saw William hacking away at a large branch with his belt knife.

"Raft?"

William nodded, "Don't see much other choice. Ollie's looking for some vines or something to tie the thing together. Have a bite, and then join me."

With the rudimentary tools they had with them, it took all day and most the night to fashion a raft large enough and sturdy enough to hold all three of them and their gear, and the work had been exhausting. As dawn was only an hour away, they decided to stay put and rest until sunset, then use the raft to cross the river.

ᔕᑯᏟᏕᏕᏉᔕᑯᏟᏕᏕᏉᔕᑯᏟᏕᏕ

As the sun dipped near the western horizon, they shoved the raft into the water. Zeke decided the term "water" wasn't exactly right; it was more like wedging the raft in amongst chunks of ice, trying to force it to where it was actually floating rather than rocking unsteadily on top of ice chunks.

They'd decided to fashion long poles instead of paddles for obvious reasons, and that proved to have been a good decision, as the poles allowed them to push and prod the chunks of ice out of the way and to slowly maneuver the unwieldy, rickety craft through the ever-moving, ever-shifting obstacle course.

And after two hours of grunting, cursing, straining effort, and several near dunkings and capsizings, they bumped against the northern bank and scrambled ashore.

They started dragging the raft ashore, thinking to dismantle it and scatter the pieces to disguise the evidence of their passing, but they'd not dragged it halfway up the bank when someone shouted out, "Hey! Who goes there!"

Without a word they dropped the raft, grabbed their knapsacks, and scrambled into the thick woods that started only a few dozen yards from shore. They heard a gunshot, but by then they were well concealed under the dark eaves of the forest, with night coming on fast. And since they were already moving in the direction they intended to go, they simply continued on as if nothing untoward had just happened.

ᏚᏣᏍᏬᏚᏣᏍᏬᏚᏣᏍᏬ

Tuesday February 22, 1864 – Rappahannock River, Virginia:

After stealing a boat and using it to cross the Mattaponi River the day before, today they'd hiked another twenty miles, and reckoned they must be within a mile or so of the Rappahannock River when they began hearing an odd, roaring, rumbling sound in the distance ahead of them. They stopped to listen.

"Train yard?" Zeke asked Ollie.

"No trains at all around here," Ollie shook his head.

"What is it, then, do you think?" William tilted his head, as if that might give his ears a different perspective on the odd sound.

Ollie shrugged, "I have no idea … Never heard anything like it before. But from the sounds of it, we'll know soon enough. It can't be very far ahead … *whatever* it is."

Within a few minutes, the mystery was solved as they crested a rise and looked down into the valley of the Rappahannock: the mighty river, more than a mile across at this point, featured enormous ice floes. Like fleets of miniature icebergs, the huge chunks of ice bobbed along, jostling and bouncing into one another as they drifted. It was this rumbling, crashing sound that they'd been hearing for the last several minutes.

But though the chunks of ice were impressive and created a great cacophony, they could see there were yet large gaps between them, making it possible for a small boat to navigate through. Easier than on the much smaller but more heavily ice-bound Pamunkey River.

Now they'd just need to steal another boat. And that didn't seem like it should be too difficult, given the valley was dotted with any number of good-sized farmhouses, and sunset was not far off. Zeke figured any house this close to a major waterway was bound to have a rowboat or two laying about, just waiting to be taken for an excursion such as they had in mind.

They came to a place where the trees thinned out. In front of them was a gravel road, and then a pasture several hundred yards wide, on the far side of which was another thick stand of trees. Off to the left they saw farm buildings and what appeared to be slave cabins down near the river's edge. They crossed the road and started across the pasture, but hadn't made it halfway across when they heard a shout back to the left toward the nearest farmhouse.

Zeke's heart sank; when he looked toward the noise, he saw a dozen or more Confederate soldiers, no more than a half-mile distant, pointing at them and shouting. Several civilians quickly joined them, and Zeke groaned when he saw what they had brought with them: hounds. Three hounds, pulling hard on their leashes.

"Quick, into the trees!" Ollie shouted, and they took off at a sprint toward the distant trees across the pasture. When they reached the tree line, they forged ahead, pushing through the thick undergrowth. Ollie led them on a zig-zagging, twisty path, never pausing, but sometimes looping around in a full circle before heading off in a different direction. All the while, they could hear the baying of the hounds in the near distance.

Finally, Ollie called a halt, and they each leaned over, their hands resting on their knees, breathing steamy clouds each time they exhaled into the frosty air.

After a few moments, Zeke stood up straight, unbuttoned his gun holster, and pulled out his revolver, proceeding to check on the state of the rounds he'd loaded earlier.

He looked over at Ollie and William, who were staring at him open mouthed. Finally Ollie said, "Zeke ... you saw how many there were, and they've got rifles ... we're not going to fight our way out of this."

Zeke nodded, giving each of them a hard look, "I don't *intend* to fight my way out ... but I don't intend to go back to that rat-infested hellhole neither. I ain't lettin' 'em take me alive..."

Ollie gazed at him another moment, then reached down and unholstered his own gun, "Hell, they'll likely hang me for a traitor and a spy, so I may as well go down fighting..."

William looked from one to the other, shrugged, and pulled out his own weapon, "Nothing else to be done, I suppose. Though Margaret will never forgive me."

They waited expectantly as the sounds of the pursuit came closer for a time, then more distant, and then again closer until finally fading away altogether, just as the sun set and darkness began to settle into the valley.

But even as they started to hope they might be saved by the darkness, they heard a new sound: first bugles, and then drums. A steady drumbeat, as if for men on a timed march. Zeke holstered his pistol, set down his knapsack, and walked over to a large tree a few feet away. He reached up, grabbed the nearest branch, and swung himself up. He quickly scrambled up out of sight of his comrades below.

A few moments later, he dropped back down to the ground with a thump. He stood up straight, wiped his hands, and grimaced. "What I feared. They's likely a hundred or more of 'em now, soldiers and civilians. All armed. They's all in a row, marching in step, beating the bushes as they come. Looks like they's on both sides, so they'll meet in the middle."

He shrugged, and once again pulled out his pistol, "Reckon our race is run, boys. It's been good knowin' you."

But even as he said this, they heard a rustling sound in the underbrush behind them. All three men turned toward the sound and pointed their guns at a bush that was clearly moving.

"Don't shoot! Don't shoot, masters!" a voice said, and a moment later a middle-aged black man stepped out with his hands raised in the air.

Zeke lowered his pistol, as did the others, "What're you doin' here, mister?" he asked.

"Well, sir, we heard 'bout the big old prisoner escape over to Richmond, and then we seen all the fuss, what with guns and hounds and all, and we figured the slavers musta treed themselves a couple o' Yankees."

"Three Yankees," Ollie corrected him.

"Yessir, I can clearly see that now. Anyhow, my name's Jimmy and I come out here so's to help you fellas outta this here fix you done got yourselves into."

"That's mighty kindly of you," Zeke nodded. "But why would you be wantin' to do that, seein's how you don't know us from Adam?"

"Well, you's Yankee soldiers, ain't you? Y'all are who's gonna free my people. Who got more reason to help you than us?"

"Good point. But *how* can you help us?"

"Follow me, masters ... we's fixin' to hide y'all. Come quick now, they's closin' in fast."

Zeke scooped up his knapsack and slung it over his shoulder. Jimmy turned and headed back the way he'd come. Zeke, William, and Ollie followed close behind.

Zeke quickly figured out that Jimmy was headed toward the river. When the trees reached the water's edge, he led them right down to the water line before turning left, following the edge of the river upstream. Jimmy ran with his head ducked low so that it wouldn't be visible above the riverbank. The others wisely followed his example. After a few hundred yards, they came to a shallow ravine, not more than five feet deep out of which trickled a noisome stream that emptied into the river, though at the moment it was mostly ice. Zeke assumed the stream was used to drain off sewage from the cabins.

Jimmy turned left and followed the ravine inland a few dozen yards. There, he climbed up the bank and they followed. He hustled them into a log building and closed the door behind them.

They stood in a tiny, one room cabin, panting heavily from their long run. Zeke looked around the room and quickly noted that, despite its close quarters, the house currently contained Jimmy, a gray-haired black man, a young woman about Jimmy's age, and two toddlers, a boy and a girl.

Zeke removed his hat, and bowed slightly, "Good evenin' folks. And ... thank ye very kindly for ... well, for savin' our sorry skins, I reckon is about the size of it."

Zeke's heartfelt gratitude seemed to break the ice, and there were grins all around, as William and Ollie followed suit, thanking their hosts profusely.

But the old man waved his hand and said, "No, sirs ... y'all ain't got no call to be thankin' us. It's *us* outta be thankin' y'all for riskin' your lives out in the war in order to free our kind. Yes, sir ... we are some kinda powerful thankful for that, you can surely bet!"

Just then the door burst open, and another young black man stepped in. But this one had no time for politeness; looking at Jimmy he said, "The foreman comes ... be ready..."

Jimmy pointed toward a bed on one side of the room. "Y'all hide behind the bed, and my family will sit in front to hide you. I'll try to lead him off..."

Then he turned and was out the door, closing it behind him. Ollie and William did as they'd been instructed and moved over behind the bed, kneeling down on the floor behind it. But Zeke wanted to see what was happening outside, so he crept up to one of the windows, and peeked out from the side.

He saw a white man approach the house, hands on hips. The man walked up to Jimmy and said, "Hey, Jimmy ... y'all seen any strangers about? White men?"

"No, sir ... Friends o' yours are they, sir?"

The man laughed, "Not hardly! These fellas we're lookin' for are goddamned Yankees. Likely some o' them that busted out o' the prisoner camp over to Richmond way. We're fixin' to catch 'em and send 'em straight back, the skunks."

"Oh, well, sir ... that bein' the case, I'll round up all the fellas, and we'll go with y'all and see if we kin help catch them damned rascals."

And then Jimmy cupped his hands and started shouting for the men to come out and help in the search. In less than five minutes it was quiet again, and all the men had departed.

Zeke shook his head in wonder, a grin spreading across his face, "Well, ain't that somethin'," was all he could think of to say.

જીૹૡઉ૪ૹૹૡઉ૪ૹૹૡઉ

Two hours later, Jimmy returned, slipping quietly into the house and closing the door. He turned, and a broad grin lit his features. "They done give up the chase ... and you never seen a more downcast, sour lookin' bunch o' white folks," he chuckled, and everyone else in the room laughed with him, including the three *white folks*.

Then he gave them a more serious look, "With all the excitement, we ain't yet had our meal. Ain't much, but we'd be pleased if you'd join us."

Zeke smiled, "We'd be honored. Thank you very much, Jimmy, and all of you."

Zeke greatly appreciated the simple meal of boiled black-eyed peas, cornbread, and salted pork, as they'd had nothing but hardtack and jerky since leaving Richmond, and they'd been carefully rationing that. But even more than that, he appreciated the comradery of these folks who recognized and appreciated the sacrifice these soldiers had been making on their behalf. He found it inspiring and uplifting, and gave him new resolve to continue doing his part in the fight, as soon as he got back to the regiment.

After the meal was finished, they said their goodbyes and Jimmy led them back to the river. He took them farther upstream to where several row boats were tied with their bows up on the bank and their sterns just touching the water. Jimmy untied one of the larger ones, big enough for five or six people, then he and another slave named Fred pulled it out into the water. "Hop on in, y'all, and we'll be 'cross that ol' river in two shakes."

⊱⊰⊱⊰⊱⊰⊱⊰⊱⊰⊱⊰

Tuesday February 24, 1864 – Potomac River, Virginia:

After Jimmy dropped them off on the north side of the river, and they once again thanked him profusely, they immediately headed off into the night, continuing in their generally northeasterly direction. Their next destination was the mighty Potomac River, more than thirty-five or forty miles distant. This time, they were determined to march night and day if they had to, with only minimal stops to rest and eat.

The weather continued its reign of frigidity, forcing them to stoically endure two more days so cold that Zeke was feeling a longing for their neat little campfire back on the Mattaponi River.

But after a gut-wrenching slog of a full night and nearly a full day, the moment they'd dreamt about for months suddenly arrived. They stepped out from a thick copse of trees into an open field, and there spread out before them was what appeared to be a broad lake: the Potomac River, more than five miles across at this point, very close to where it emptied into Chesapeake Bay.

On the far side of the water in the distance they could see hills rising. Those hills were in Maryland ... in the North ... back in the United States ... Home. Zeke felt a tear building in his eye at the thought, and he swallowed a lump in his throat. The three men shook hands and beamed, though not a word was spoken.

They walked along the water's edge until they came to a set of three cabins. An older black man sat on the front porch of the first cabin, whittling on a stick with a small knife.

"Evenin' masters," he said, rising from his chair, and bowing respectfully. "How can I be helpin' y'all?"

Zeke decided to trust that this black man would be willing to help them just as the others had, so he told the simple truth, "We're escaping Union soldiers, and we need to get across the river."

"Oh! Well, then follow me, good sirs!"

The old man, who introduced himself as Tyson, led them back the way they'd come, and then a half mile farther to a small house near the edge of the water. Zeke nearly started salivating when he saw the sturdy rowboat tied out front, slowly moving with the water.

They went inside, and Tyson introduced them to a white man named Joe Horner and told Joe their story, as he knew it. Joe shook hands with them enthusiastically. "So, y'all are some o' them as busted out o' Libby and made old Jeff Davis piss in his britches!" He hooted a laugh and slapped his thigh. "Best damned thing I ever heard of! Dug a tunnel, did you? Damn, that was fine ... mighty fine. Well, as you can see, I got no use for damned secesh, nor slavers. Keep tellin' Tyson I'll take him across in my boat and he'll be free. But he won't leave without the others. He's a good man."

Tyson grinned, and said, "Well, just reckon what with Mr. Lincoln's Emancipation and all, it won't be long now. May as well just wait it out…"

"Anyhow, reckon you fella's is lookin' for a boat," Horner continued. "Just happen to have one outside, as you saw when you came in. Now, I'd take you myself, but as you can see," he held out a heavily bandaged ankle, "done twisted the damned thing and it hurts like the devil whenever I get bounced around on the water."

"But … Mr. Horner … we can't just take your good boat. We haven't any money to pay you for it…" Zeke shrugged his shoulders.

"Oh, I'm only lettin' you borrow her. I'll get her back soon enough. Listen here … This is what you do: See that lighthouse over yonder … that sits on a little island called Blackistone Island. The fella that lives there with his wife and small babe is a friend o' mine named Jerome McWilliams. You go over to see Jerome, and he'll put you up for the night in his fine house, fix you a warm meal, and tomorrow he can row you over to the north shore. He'll bring my boat back when he has the time."

So, they said their thanks and their goodbyes, then clambered into Mr. Horner's boat as Tyson untied it and shoved them off. The boat featured two good, sturdy oars, and Zeke volunteered to take the first shift.

And though he was tired from their long trek, and still weak from months of captivity and malnutrition, he pulled the oars with vigor and determination, inspired by the thought of their impending freedom, now less than five miles away.

But they'd not gone much more than a hundred yards from shore when William hissed, "Damn … Look, there by the shore…"

Zeke glanced back toward the shore, and just down the shoreline from Mr. Horner's house stood six Confederate soldiers with rifles. One appeared to be looking at them through binoculars. He lowered the binoculars, and began waving at

398

them, clearly signaling that he wished them to return to shore. The soldiers next to him all pointed their rifles threateningly as if the reinforce their officer's wish.

"He wants us to turn back," Ollie said.

"Well, he can go suck eggs," Zeke pulled harder.

A moment later he saw a puff of smoke rise suddenly from one of the rifles, which was followed almost immediately by zipping sound, a splash a few dozen yards short of the boat, and a distant *pop!*

The officer gestured again … That one had been a warning. The next…?

Zeke ignored the officer and continued to pull on the oars. His arms had started to ache, but he ignored them.

Then the remaining five rifles opened fire, and bullets impacted all around the small boat, including two hard *thuds!*

Damn it, those hit wood! Zeke willed his arms to pull harder. He now had twenty or thirty seconds before the enemy rifles would be reloaded for another round.

William and Ollie drew their revolvers and began returning fire, aiming at a high arc as they emptied all six chambers on each gun. They knew they'd never hit anything from this distance, but it might give the enemy something to worry about and slow down their reloading.

Zeke thought it was having the desired effect, as the expected second volley took nearly a full minute from the first. And when it came, all the rounds fell well short. Zeke breathed a sigh of relief … They were now out of range.

But then he felt something sloshing against his boots. He looked down and saw water oozing into the boat, quickly filling the back end up to his ankles.

"Damn it, we're taking on water. Those bullets breached the hull!"

William jumped up and scrambled past Zeke into the back of the boat, "Quick, Ollie we must bail out the water…"

"With what?" Ollie looked around frantically for a bucket, a pail, even a cup, but there was nothing.

"Use your hats," Zeke said as he continued to pull at the oars.

William and Ollie went at the water with desperate enthusiasm, but Zeke could feel the boat growing heavier and his arms growing weaker.

"Quick, one of you … take the oars, my arms are done … I'll bail instead.

It took several seconds to rearrange themselves, with Ollie now taking the oars and Zeke bailing with his hat. But Ollie, though strong, was unsteady and having a hard time finding a rhythm, never having done it before. Zeke had a sinking feeling that the studious, intellectual William would fare even worse.

And though they bailed furiously, and Ollie strove mightily and was finally getting the hang of it, Zeke realized it wasn't going to be enough. The water was filling the boat too quickly. They could not keep up with it, and soon the boat would flounder and … they were now far too distant from shore to make it back swimming. *So close…*

He glanced out longingly toward the distant island with its stately lighthouse … And then he saw something … a white speck out on the water, but growing larger. He sat up and squinted his eyes in the glaring sunlight … could it be…?

It was! A boat! A rowboat much the size of their own, heading straight toward them. When it came to within a dozen yards, a man called out, "Take the line, and tie it to the bow. Ship the oars, and all three of you bail. I will pull you!"

Being good soldiers, they immediately did as ordered, and soon the boat was moving once again, confidently striding through the water despite its extra weight in liquid. And the three men in the leaking boat bailed water like their lives depended on it, which … they did.

෨෨යෙ෪ෂ෨෨යෙ෪ෂ෨෨යෙ෪

Once Jerome McWilliams had rowed them safely in to Blackistone Island, and they pulled the punctured boat up onto the shore, the three men collapsed in the grass by the shoreline in utter exhaustion.

McWilliams came over, sat down next to them on the grass, and quizzed them on their adventures, listening to their answers with wide-eyed amazement. When they'd finished their tale, he said, "Well, gentlemen ... all I can say is, welcome to Blackistone Island ... and welcome back to the USA."

The next day, after a wonderful, warm meal cooked by Mrs. McWilliams, and a luxurious night's sleep on a real bed in a warm, dry house, Jerome hoisted the emergency semaphore that would flag down any passing Union warship. Shortly before noon, the *USS Ella*, a steam-powered gunship, anchored herself off Blackistone Island and sent her tender across to pick up the three officers.

Minutes later, the three men were welcomed aboard the Union gunship to the enthusiastic cheers of the sailors on deck. Zeke felt a welling of joy such as he'd not experienced since before their capture. They were truly free at last, and now safely on their way home.

ФѤЦӃӆФѤЦӃӆФѤЦӃ

Friday February 26, 1864 – Harpers Ferry, West Virginia:

Tom felt buoyed up by the news that was running through the camp like wildfire; that there'd been a major escape from the notorious Libby Prison in Richmond, and more than a hundred Union officers had broken out. He prayed that William and Zeke were among them. He was eager to share the good news with Nathan, not knowing if he'd already heard about it.

But when Tom flipped back the tent flap and entered Nathan's command tent his heart dropped, and his previous mood dampened. He could tell from Nathan's expression that something was amiss.

"Sir ... I ... assume you heard the news of the escape...?"

Nathan nodded, "Yes..." But he looked down at the desk, not meeting eyes with Tom. It was then Tom noticed a telegram sitting in front of Nathan on the desk.

"Has something happened to William or Zeke?" Tom stepped over and took a seat at the table on the side opposite Nathan.

"No ... In fact, they were among those who escaped and are now safely in Washington City. This telegram is from Zeke, confirming the good news. But ... something deeply concerning has also happened..." Nathan frowned as he handed the telegram across to Tom.

Washington, DC
February 26, 1864

Col. Nathaniel Chambers
Harpers Ferry, W. Va.:

William and I escaped Libby Prison and reached Potomac, there picked up by Union warship and dropped at Washington City. Will report for duty in Harpers Ferry shortly. Am bringing a new officer for the 12th. William to stay longer and report to authorities on dire state of Union prisoners in the South.

I am sorry to inform you that your sister, Margaret, was in Richmond during escape, and was shot and wounded. She is recovering in Evelyn's care, but condition unknown at this time.

Zeke Benton,
Captain, 12th W. Va. Infantry

Chapter 15. Dread of Disaster

"Dread of disaster
makes everybody act
in the very way
that increases the disaster."
- Bertrand Russell

Thursday March 10, 1864 – Harpers Ferry, West Virginia:

"Any word from William, sir?" Tom looked up and set aside the newspaper he'd just picked up as Nathan stepped into the tent.

"None. If he keeps ignoring my telegrams I may soon resort to threats, using terms like 'AWOL' and 'dereliction of duty.' But for now, I'll give him a bit more leeway."

"Hmm … Do you really think it's all about the prisoner situation, or could it be more about Margaret?"

"I think there's a lot of truth to what you're implying, Tom. I think he's having a hard time facing all of us … feeling guilty about what happened to her, and not knowing her condition. Frankly, until we hear something from Evelyn, we will all be plagued by worry for her," Nathan admitted.

"Agreed, sir. It's been good having Zeke back, though. And despite all he's been through, he seems not much worse for the wear, now that he's beginning to fatten back up a bit. There is something different about him now, though … Hardened, stronger, and more determined I think."

"Yes, I've seen that too. There's a fire in him that wasn't there before … an anger, I think … as if he's itching to strike back at those who held him captive. Not necessarily a bad thing, given the circumstances."

"And Oliver Boyd … he's been a nice addition."

"Yes, that was a pleasant surprise, above and beyond the much-appreciated letter he carried out for me from Evelyn. Do you think he's put out by only receiving a captain's bars, when he was a major for the other side? I didn't want to push my luck with the war department due to his previous ... *employment*."

"He seems quite happy, sir. From talking with him, I believe he was always a bit conflicted when he was working for Lee, always feeling like he was on the wrong side in the war. And now that his wife Belinda has made it to the North and joined the growing throng at Belle Meade, he seems quite content. Not to mention very appreciative of you, sir."

"Good, happy to hear it. He's a good man. Very intelligent and analytical. Somewhat makes up for William's absence."

They were quiet for a moment as Nathan puffed on the cigar he'd been smoking. He noticed the paper laying on the table, "Anything interesting in the newspaper today, Tom?"

Tom picked the paper back up, and flipped it to the front page, "Hmm ... Let's see ... *oh!* It says here, the president has appointed Ulysses Grant as Commanding General over all Union Armies with the rank of Lieutenant General." Tom lowered the newspaper and whistled, "When was the last time an officer had *that* position and rank?"

Nathan tilted his head in thought a moment, then looked back at Tom, "That would've been ... a fellow named *George Washington*..."

"Thought so ... Large shoes to fill..." Tom slowly shook his head. "I hope he's up to the task."

But Nathan nodded, "I think ... it may *not* be the desperate move it appears on the surface. I knew Grant during the war in Mexico. A good man. Smart, efficient, tough as nails. One of those rare men who not only doesn't rattle under fire, but seems to thrive on it." He chuckled. "I recall hearing one of the officers comment at the time, 'That fellow Grant ... he don't even know what fear is!'"

Tom grinned, "Well, that seems hopeful, anyway. But do you really think he's the man to finally beat Lee?"

Nathan gazed up at the ceiling of the tent for a long moment before looking back at Tom, "Yes ... yes, I have a good feeling about Grant ... I think he's the man to finally win this war. By sheer determination and tenacity, if nothing else. I have a feeling the man just won't quit, no matter what they throw at him."

"Well, speaking of the war … what do you think they'll do with the West Virginia department? Will we get a new commanding general, do you think?"

"Yes … from all I've heard, General Kelley will be replaced, though I'm not convinced that's the best move. Although he's not done anything spectacular, I think he's been given a thankless task, with not nearly enough resources for the territory he's responsible for."

"Well, I guess that'll be for General Grant to decide then?" Tom folded the newspaper and set it aside on the table.

"Yes, that seems clear. And I expect, from Grant's previous record, once he puts the new command in place, he'll want to launch a major offensive against the rebels. That should get us out of this endless guarding, patrolling, and skirmishing we've been stuck doing up and down the Shenandoah Valley since coming out of winter camp, and finally get us into some serious fighting."

"One can only hope," Tom agreed. "One can only hope."

කටළ-ඝ-ඝ-ඝ-ඝ-ඝ

Friday April 1, 1864 – Washington, D.C.:

It was a proud day for Cobb and the rest of the freemen of the U.S. Twenty-Third Colored Infantry Regiment. Today was the day they got to dress in clean new uniforms and march past the president of the United States for review in Washington City as part of the Fourth Division of the Union Army's IX Corps. Afterward, they, along with the rest of the corps, would depart for the war against General Lee in Virginia.

All their months of hard labor, training, and drilling were finally over, and the fighting was about to begin. As he marched in step with the other men of the Twenty-Third down the broad city avenue, Cobb felt a swelling of pride. He knew he looked dashing in his bright blue army uniform and kepi hat, with polished boots, shiny brass buttons, and a rifle slung over his shoulder. He only wished his wife Hetty could see him now. He could envision her beautiful smile in his mind, and he grinned before he remembered where he was, and that he was to maintain strict discipline and a stern look while on parade.

The Twenty-Third was a small part of the huge force of twenty-one thousand men, which made up the IX Corps, so it took the better part of an hour for their regiment to reach the review stand. As they neared the stand, Cobb felt a sudden thrill; there, standing tall, larger than life, in his iconic top hat, was President Lincoln himself. And Cobb couldn't decide if he just imagined it, or if the president seemed to take a special interest in the Twenty-Third, nodding meaningfully at the black soldiers as they passed.

The president was nearly lost from view when Cobb noticed the man wearing a blue officer's uniform standing next to Lincoln. From descriptions he'd heard, this could be none other than Major General Ambrose Burnside, their new commanding general.

And then Cobb remembered what Captain Chambers had said about General Burnside: that he'd proved himself incompetent leading men in battle, and that he'd recklessly cost the lives of thousands of Union soldiers at the Battle of Fredericksburg the year before.

Suddenly Cobb's bright moment of glory dimmed, and he suffered a sinking feeling that he and the other freemen might just be marching straight into a disaster.

℘ℭℜℭℭ℘℘℘ℭℭℭℭ℘℘℘℘ℭℭℭ℘

Monday April 18, 1864 – Washington, D.C.:

"Mr. President, thank you for seeing me." Lieutenant General Ulysses S. Grant sat down opposite the president at Lincoln's desk in the White House.

"Never mention it, General. I can't imagine having any more important business than working with you on the war. Please proceed with the matters you wish to discuss, if you would."

"Thank you, Mr. President. The first item I wish to discuss is the command of the West Virginia Department."

"Oh? I thought we'd settled that matter..."

"Yes, so we had. But you'll recall I only reluctantly agreed to your suggestion of appointing Major General Sigel to the command under the assumption he would remain at headquarters to coordinate department activities from there…"

"Yes … and I appreciated your acceding to my wishes on that rather *delicate* matter…"

Grant smirked, "You mean bowing to your need for votes from the large body of German immigrants in the upcoming election? And quite possibly while running against George McClellan, of all people, if you believe the rumors…"

Lincoln shrugged, "Well, yes … that would be a crude way of putting it, but essentially true, I'll not deny. But we agreed Sigel was a competent enough general in the capacity of managing things from headquarters."

"Yes, Mr. President … in *that* capacity … but…"

"Hmm … why am I under the strong impression you are going to give me some bad news, Mr. Grant?"

"Because I *am* going to, Mr. President. Our entire scheme was dependent upon Sigel staying back at headquarters in Cumberland, while Major General Ord took command in the field. And that if worse came to worst, I could … *unofficially, of course* … circumvent Sigel and work with Ord directly as needed."

"Yes, I recall some discussions of the kind, though likely I'd have to deny it, if it ever came to light in public."

Grant snorted a mirthless laugh. "Understood, Mr. President. In any case, we never counted on Sigel and Ord butting heads. It's gotten so bad that Ord has threatened to resign his commission if not transferred away from Sigel."

"Hmm … that *is* bad news. What shall we do, then, Mr. Grant?"

"Ord's a good officer, served under me out west at Vicksburg; he's not someone I want to lose. I saw no choice but to grant his transfer. But now I have no one to replace him, and there's not time in any case before we launch the planned offensive."

Lincoln nodded slowly, allowing Grant to continue.

"And the news gets worse … Sigel has already jumped on the chance to place himself in the field. He's on his way to

Martinsburg even as we speak, to take command of his entire division. Now I must either replace him entirely, or allow this farce to move forward and play itself out."

"I see … Hmm … perhaps if you were to just … say … keep in close communication with him … You know, prompt him to do what he needs to do every now and then … Perhaps then…"

"Perhaps then he won't mess it up too badly?" Grant scowled.

"Yes, something like that…"

Grant shrugged, "If you're determined to keep him in command…"

"I am … at least for now…"

"Well, then I'll do what I can, Mr. President. But once again, it's under protest."

"Understood, General Grant. Your protest is duly noted. And much appreciated."

❧❦❧❦❧❦❧❦❧❦❧

Monday April 25, 1864 – Martinsburg, West Virginia:

Major General Franz Sigel sat at a table in the kitchen of the house he'd commandeered for his headquarters. He was short and slightly built, with dark hair and neatly trimmed goatee. He had a stern visage, which Nathan wondered was his typical countenance, or specifically in place for his new subordinate's benefit. Nathan stepped up to within a few feet, came to attention, and saluted, "Colonel Nathaniel Chambers, Twelfth West Virginia, reporting as ordered, sir."

Sigel looked up, met eyes with Nathan for a moment without smiling, then returned the salute, "Please, Colonel … *comen sie* … have a seat, if you please." Sigel gestured to a chair opposite him.

Nathan stepped forward, pulled out the chair, and sat. He immediately noticed the seat was oddly low, as if the legs had been cut short, such that the person using it seemed almost childlike, reaching up toward the tabletop which was now uncomfortably high. General Sigel, by contrast, sat on a much higher chair, with the top of the table barely above his waist.

Nathan resisted a very strong urge to scowl at what he considered a ridiculously transparent ploy by a small man trying to assume a larger stature both literally and figuratively.

"Colonel Chambers, it has come to my ears that you are unhappy with some of my choices of senior commanders," Sigel leaned forward and frowned, in a manner Nathan could only assume was intended to intimidate a subordinate officer.

Nathan returned the general's gaze evenly, "General, with all due respect, I find that words one hears about another man — from men speaking out of turn behind his back — are rarely true."

Sigel sat back straight in his chair, "Very well, Colonel … I will admit one cannot dispute the truth of this statement you have just made … So, you will please be telling me to my face, if you are having any issues with the appointments of my senior commanding officers?"

Nathan was quiet for a moment, never breaking eye contact with the general, "General, as an officer of lesser rank under your command, it's not my place to question your appointment of commanders … unless you *specifically* ask for my opinion on some matter or other."

Sigel nodded, breaking eye contact for the first time, glancing up at the ceiling, and slowly nodding, "Chambers … please tell me what you think of my appointment of Colonel Augustus Moor to brigade command."

"I know very little of Colonel Moor, never having met him before this week. And, as I said before, I'd rather not judge a man based on what other men might say of him…"

"Ah … so, you deny that you have been heard to question his appointment to command of one of my brigades?"

Now it was Nathan's turn to break eye contact as he gazed at his hands steepled on the table in front of him. "General, the only things I *may* have said in that regard, was that Colonel Moor is not the most senior commander available for that particular command, nor the most battle experienced. In my defense, I will point out, sir, that these are indisputable facts, *not* mere opinions."

"And I suppose it also stands against him that he was not trained at West Point, as were you, but is a *foreigner*, such as myself?"

"Did I say so, General? Because if any man claims I did, he's a liar. I have nothing against competent men who received their training or battle experience via some road different from mine, nor do I have anything against immigrants, having several very close friends of that persuasion."

Sigel smiled, "I see ... Well, by contrast, I for one am not ashamed to admit that I am less than enamored of your very tightly knit society of so-called *West Pointers*, since a very large number of your classmates are now numbered among the traitorous enemies of the United States ... And several others, who are *supposedly* on our side, have *not* distinguished themselves in battle thus far..."

Nathan frowned, "It's a free country, General, at least in the North ... so I'll not argue against your right to your own opinion, no matter how strongly I might disagree with it."

"Ah, so now it is out in the open, Chambers ... You disagree with your commanding general. This is not good, sir ... not good at all. I can see this may cause problems in battle, and confirms the correctness of my appointment of Colonel Moor rather than ... *some others* ... of more seniority."

Nathan slowly nodded, holding tightly to his frown, and keeping an even tighter control on his temper, "General ... it is not my wish to be at odds with you, sir. And, whatever you may think of West Pointers, I think it would be best for all concerned if we were to cooperate and work in concert with one another for the good of the command."

"Ah, but you see, this is where you are sorely mistaken, Colonel. It is not my place to ... *cooperate* ... with you. I am the commanding general. I issue the orders, and it is your duty to obey without question. Is this understood, Colonel?"

Nathan scowled, "Yes ... I believe I now understand you *perfectly* well, General. Was there anything else you wished to discuss?"

"No, that will be all, Colonel. Dismissed."

Nathan pushed back his chair, rose, stood to attention and saluted, which Sigel returned smartly without rising. Then Nathan pivoted and marched from the room.

ℬ☧☧ℬ☧☧ℬ☧☧

Thursday May 5, 1864 – Winchester, Virginia:

"Looks like you were right about Sigel, sir," Tom took a sip of whiskey as he gazed across the camp table at Nathan, who'd been unusually quiet and thoughtful, despite any softening effect the liquor might have had.

"Yes, Tom … unfortunately he *is* everything I'd feared and more. Marching the men around day and night with no point, drills following drills with no practical purpose that I can divine. And then these ridiculous, poorly organized mock battles—here in *Winchester!* The very place we fought *real* battles against a *real* enemy force a year ago!" He shook his head in disgust. "And no inclination to actually advance toward the enemy into a more advantageous position for launching the coming campaign.

"He reminds me of that incompetent scoundrel Lieutenant Martin who was your commanding officer at Fort Davis before I arrived. An utterly arrogant, incompetent ass."

Jim nodded, and chuckled, "I'd nearly forgotten about Martin … that worthless sumbitch! I'm still amazed the varmint didn't manage to get us all killed before you ever arrived to rescue us from his nonsense, sir."

Nathan scowled, "Well, now it seems we have a commander who's just as arrogant and incompetent. Only now there's not a damned thing I can do to get us out from under him. Pray to God this one doesn't go ahead and get us all killed."

Tom nodded, "Amen to that, sir. Amen to that."

ℬ☧☧ℬ☧☧ℬ☧☧

Sunday April 17, 1864 – Camden, Arkansas:

For the first time Ned could recall, Lieutenant August Gordon, commander of Company G, First Kansas Colored Regiment, seemed out of sorts, anxious, and even what might be called *snappish*.

And not being of an especially cautious nature, Ned decided to just ask it straight out as they marched side by side at the head of their company, "Somethin' eatin' at you, Lieutenant?"

Auggie looked over at Ned and scowled, "Just everything, Sergeant. Everything about this campaign has gone wrong from the start ... First, from all reports our division commander, Major General Frederick Steele, was opposed to the entire thing, what with marching about unsupported in enemy territory with poor roads, belligerent partisans, and insufficient supplies. From what I hear, his objections fell on deaf ears; General Grant ordered him to go ahead anyway so as to meet up with General Banks at Shreveport down in Louisiana.

"Well, we've now marched all over Arkansas, looking for supplies and skirmishing with the rebels, never able to pin them down for a real fight.

"Then, we finally arrive here to Camden, which is supposed to be flush with supplies, only to find out the rebs have burned whatever they couldn't carry off.

"Now we hear that General Banks has been defeated, so he won't be meeting us at Shreveport after all. So here we sit ... doing *what*? Other than starving and wandering around looking for food, I wonder..."

Ned snorted, "Is that all?"

"No ... it's just all I can think of on the spur of the moment," Auggie answered, still scowling. "Mostly it's ... it's that all this sour news has given me a bad feeling about this little food-gathering expedition we've been sent out on ... A *very* bad feeling."

Ned frowned and nodded, "Then let's hope your feeling is wrong." But Auggie's gloomy mood was starting to rub off, and Ned started wondering whether the lieutenant might be right about this mission. He suddenly felt a growing dread that they might be marching straight into a disaster.

But then he reminded himself that in addition to the 438 officers and men of the First Kansas Colored Regiment, they also had six hundred more men, divided between the Eighteenth Iowa Infantry, an artillery company with four cannons, and troopers from several cavalry regiments. They were also supposed to meet up with another force of some five hundred men in the morning.

It seemed an impressive force to Ned, considering their mission was no more complicated than escorting 198 empty supply wagons to collect a much-needed stash of corn that the scouts had located off to the northwest of Camden. And besides, Colonel Williams was in command, now fully recovered from the wound he'd suffered at Honey Springs the previous summer. What could possibly go wrong?

But as soon as that question entered his mind, a voice inside him answered, *Only everything.*

⊱⊰⊱⊰⊱⊰⊱⊰⊱⊰⊱⊰

Thursday May 12, 1864 – Woodstock, Virginia:

For one of the few times that he could recall in his long military career, Nathan felt a growing sense of dread—an unrelenting knot in his stomach warning him that they were slowly marching into a disaster, and that there was nothing he could do to prevent or even mitigate it.

General Sigel refused to take the enemy opposing him seriously, or to demonstrate any sense of urgency, despite several of the regimental commanders urging him to do so. And to make matters worse, Sigel had insulated himself from the men who had actual field experience by surrounding himself with men he personally knew and trusted, many of whom were recent German immigrants whose English-speaking skills were only rudimentary.

Even Nathan's immediate commander, Colonel Thoburn— who although pleasant enough and, unlike Sigel, was respectful to Nathan—showed no inclination to question his commanding general, nor to even offer him reasonable suggestions.

So Nathan had taken it upon himself to approach General Sigel, urging him to consolidate his scattered forces and move quickly against the enemy as General Grant had ordered, and as prudence would suggest.

But as Nathan had expected, his suggestions and entreaties were met with scorn, and he was publicly chastised for questioning the commanding general, and for going over the head of his brigade commander, Colonel Thoburn. Sigel even promised to mete out the proper punishment for these offenses once the campaign was concluded. He stated that if any such transgression were to recur, he would be forced to make a change in the command of the Twelfth.

Nathan could only bite his tongue and pray that the enemy commander was equally incompetent.

And then, as they set up camp at Woodstock, once again wasting much of a day that, in Nathan's view, should have been spent on the march, he received news that increased his growing dread of looming disaster to almost the level of premonition.

Jim Wiggins entered Nathan's tent, snapping back the flap and striding in without bothering to salute. Nathan thought Jim was as steamed as he'd ever seen him. And even Tom, who'd known Jim longer, seemed startled, sitting up to stare wide-eyed. Even Harry sat up and gazed at Jim curiously.

"Of all the goddamned, chicken shit, underhanded nonsense ... this beats all, sir!"

"*What* beats all, Mr. Wiggins?"

"That sumbitch Sigel. Now he's gone too far, sir ... This time it's gonna cost us lives, mark my words!"

"Please, Mr. Wiggins ... sit ... calm yourself if possible, and tell us what he's done that's riled you so," Nathan gestured to the chair next to Tom.

Jim removed his hat and sat in the chair next to the camp table.

"You remember a couple weeks ago you signed that requisition for more ammunition for our repeating rifles?"

The knot in Nathan's stomach made another tight twist, "Yes ... I had the quartermaster take it out of my pay so there'd be no possible issues with the order..."

"Well, apparently that wasn't good enough, sir. The quartermaster now tells me that Sigel personally canceled the

414

requisition, saying that the cartridges and rifles weren't regulation, and therefore couldn't take up valuable room in government transport. Which is a lie, since officers are commonly allowed to order personal items as long as they pay for them … And then, to make sure you couldn't make other arrangements, *herr Sigel* ordered the quartermaster not to inform you of the cancelation until we were already well on the march and it was too late to make other arrangements."

"*Damn it! Damn him…*" Nathan stared down at the table, slowly pulling out a cigar and chewing on it without lighting up. "Gentlemen … apparently my punishment has begun. And I fear you're right, Jim … this is going to cost us lives."

ℰℭℛℭℱℛℰℰℭℛℭℱℛℰℰℭℛℭℱ

Monday May 9, 1864 – Spotsylvania Courthouse, Virginia:

"Man, I do like this new commander, General Grant, sir," Sergeant Albert Wallace beamed as they gazed out at the distant ridgeline just peeking out above the thick forest that lay in the valley where the Seventh West Virginia was making camp. "Everyone expected Grant to turn tail and head back north after the tough go of it we had this past week. I heard the newspapers were calling it a Confederate victory…"

Captain James Hawkins snorted a humorless laugh. "Apparently General Grant doesn't read the newspapers, so he has his own opinions on the matter."

Wallace chuckled, "Amen to that, sir. Tough as the going's been, I say we keep hammerin' at 'em, elsewise this war's never gonna end."

"Agreed, Sergeant," Hawkins raised his binoculars and gazed at the distant ridgeline, slowly panning across. All along the ridgeline were rebel earthworks, stacks of large, heavily reinforced logs, behind which would be trenches dug deep into the hard earth. It would be a tough position to assail.

And as much as he agreed with Wallace about General Grant's aggressiveness, he had a bad feeling about attacking that ridgeline; it was like Gettysburg, only in reverse. This time it'd be

415

the Union army fighting uphill against a well-defended enemy position.

He shuddered at the thought of the carnage that would likely ensue when they were called upon to charge up that hill.

But given all he'd seen and heard, he knew with a cold certainty that was *exactly* what General Grant was going to order them to do.

ﬆﬔﬕﬖﬗﬆﬔﬕﬖﬗﬆﬔﬕ

Monday May 9, 1864 – Spotsylvania Courthouse, Virginia:

"C'mon, lieutenant … cheer up! At least we're on the high ground for once up here. And we've had plenty of time to dig in this time. Besides … after the whuppin' we gave them Yanks in the Wilderness this past week, I reckon they'll pull back and lick their wounds for a spell," Sergeant Rollins grinned, with a face so covered in grime it was hard for Jubal to remember what he'd looked like before.

Jubal frowned, "I'd like to believe you have the right of it, Rollins…"

"But you ain't believin' it, are you sir? Why not?"

"For one … from what the scouts are telling me, the Yanks aren't pullin' back this time. Seems like this new general, *Grant*, isn't the quittin' type."

"And for another … this high ground you're so keen on is a long, narrow salient…"

"A *what?*"

"A *salient* … It means it's a bulge in our line sticking way out toward the enemy. It exposes our flanks to attack, making us more vulnerable."

"Ah … I see what you mean … Bad place to be in a battle?"

"Yes … it's bad. But I suppose General Lee thought it was worth the risk in order to control the high ground … Sure hope he's right."

Rollins frowned, "And what if he ain't?"

"Well, it won't be a fun little snowball fight like the one we had at winter camp, that's certain. Likely we're in for a *very* hot time

416

of it, Sergeant," and even as he said it, Jubal had a sudden dark premonition of blood pouring down from above, filling their entrenchments, and them unable to climb out from the slick mud—drowning in their own blood. He shuddered and shook his head to dispel the evil vision.

Chapter 16. Death's Feast

"War is death's feast."
- **George Herbert**

Monday April 18, 1864 – Poison Spring, Arkansas:

"Here they come from the west, men ... Present ... Aim ... Fire!" Five hundred Union rifles fired toward the west from behind the circled wagons of Colonel Williams' command, consisting of some 1,500 men in total, including the First Kansas Colored. The effect of the volley was immediate and devastating, halting the rebel advance in its tracks.

"Reload ... They'll come again..." the colonel called out. *"Artillery ... be prepared to fire, as targets present..."* He turned and took a quick look at his four artillery pieces and slowly shook his head. Because they were cut off and surrounded, the enemy could attack from any direction ... or from all at once. So he'd been forced to spread his artillery out, pointing outward in four different directions. And his riflemen likewise had to be disbursed in a wide circle, in case the enemy attacked from multiple points at once. When an attack came, the soldiers had to scramble to get into position to target the advancing enemy.

Williams also kept a reserve force of two hundred rifles to plug any gaps as needed. Ned's company was among these emergency reserves, stationed in the center of the circle, ready to move in any direction as needed.

Adding to the colonel's problems, the woods surrounding their present position allowed the enemy to approach unseen to within just a few hundred yards before launching an assault, giving little time to re-position their big guns. During this first attack, the nearest gun had been unable to target the enemy in time to fire.

Ned and Auggie exchanged a dark look as they gazed out from their position near the center of the circle of wagons. Auggie slowly shook his head as if to say, *"Told you so..."*

Ned nodded in acknowledgment.

After a promising and uneventful start, in which they were able to completely fill their 198 wagons with desperately needed corn, Auggie's premonition of evil on their present foraging expedition had finally come true, and in spades. The 1,500 men of Colonel Williams' expedition, including the 438 men of the First Kansas Colored Regiment, were now facing an enemy force two or three times their size at a place called Poison Spring with no hope of rescue or reinforcement.

A few minutes later, a shout rang out, *"They come ... from southwest this time!"*

Men scrambled to reposition themselves so they could fire at the advancing rebels. Another tremendous rifle volley roared out, filing the circle with gun smoke. This time the rifles were accompanied by the *boom* of the big gun on that side, firing cannister shot. After the volley, the order was given to fire at will, and a steady stream of rifle fire rang out for several minutes, until once again the rebel advance was stymied, this time just short of the wagons.

Colonel Williams strode over to Ned's position. "Gentlemen ... be prepared to advance and plug a gap at my order ... I have a feeling the first two attacks were just to count our guns. This next assault..." he trailed off, and slowly walked away, shaking his head.

Ned unholstered his revolver, checking to make sure all the percussion caps were still tight and none of the grease plugs on the cylinders had been compromised. He then spun the cylinder to make sure it hadn't acquired any grit or grime that might impede its movement. Satisfied, he re-holstered it, but left the flap unbuttoned.

His bayonet was already mounted, else he would've fixed it now. He took a deep breath and waited. There was nothing else he could do.

Ten minutes went by, and then another ten, with no sign of the enemy. Ned looked over at Auggie, raising a questioning eyebrow. But Auggie shook his head. "They'll come, Sergeant ... Mark my words ... they'll come."

Ned nodded, then turned and continued gazing out past the wagons.

It had been a little more than an hour since they'd seen anything of the enemy, and Auggie was just pulling his pocket watch out for a look when a shout rang out, *"They come from the north!"*

This was almost immediately followed by a second shout, *"They come from the south!"* and then, *"Enemy to the west, coming fast!"* and finally, *"They're coming from the east!"*

⊱✽⊰⊱✽⊰⊱✽⊰

Though the Union men of the expedition fought with skill, determination, and the desperation of men whose lives hung in the balance, the odds were simply too great. Before Auggie and Ned could decide in which direction they were most needed, rebels began pouring into the circle from many different points at once. The Union men on the edges of the circle either fell back toward the center, were killed, or were cut off from retreat and forced to surrender.

Suddenly Colonel Williams stood in front of them, *"We must withdraw ... quickly ... move to the northeast; they seem weakest there!"*

With a shout, the reserve force charged to the northeast with fixed bayonets, led by Colonel Williams holding his saber aloft. Every man who could joined in the breakout, and the resulting counterattack was too much for the rebels to resist. The breakout force was soon outside the wagons, moving into the woods in a northeasterly direction, following Poison Spring Creek, a small stream that flowed from the swamps that lay in that direction.

But Auggie and Ned ordered their rifle companies to turn and serve as rearguard for the escaping force; hiding behind tree trunks, they targeted any rebels attacking the rear of the escaping force. And it was from this rearmost point that they witnessed a sight they would never forget. They could see back within the circle of wagons, black Union soldiers with their hands in the air being bayonetted or shot. And Indians who were fighting for the confederates took out knives and mutilated the black men's bodies as they lay on the ground.

The men of the First Kansas, along with the other remnants of Colonel Williams' command, fell back slowly from the lost wagons into an area of ever denser, ever damper and more swampy forest, until the enemy finally gave up the pursuit.

The next day, Colonel Williams' men remained hidden in the swamp. The day after, scouts were sent out, who reported the enemy was gone, and so were the wagons. The mutilated bodies of the Union soldiers, most of whom were black, had been left upon the ground.

Williams ordered a quick burial detail, during which tears streamed unashamed down Ned's cheeks as he shoveled dirt over the mutilated bodies of two of his oldest friends, among those who'd come west with him from Virginia, Jack and Sid. Though most of the dead were buried in a mass grave, Ned had dug a separate hole for his two friends.

As Ned scooped another shovel full of dirt with his short-handled trenching spade, he wished for a full-sized shovel for the sake of his aching back. But all the regular shovels had disappeared along with the precious corn when the rebs had taken the wagons. As he bent low to scoop more dirt, he saw a black soldier step up next to him on his left. The soldier also began shoveling dirt into the grave. Ned glanced over and was surprised to see the soldier was Captain Mathews. Mathews met eyes with Ned and nodded, but no words were spoken as they continued to work their shovels.

And then another soldier stepped up on Ned's right side. This soldier also began shoveling. Ned glanced over and wasn't surprised to see it was Lieutenant Auggie Gordon. Auggie didn't look at Ned, and he held a dark expression such as Ned hadn't seen on him before.

When they were done filling in the hole, they stood back, gazing down at the dirt. Captain Mathews removed his hat and held it over his heart. "If you please, gentlemen…" he looked at Ned and Auggie, who took his meaning and also removed their hats.

Captain Mathews turned back toward the grave and said, "I have fought the good fight, I have finished my course ... I have kept the faith. Amen." He replaced his hat.

Ned looked at him and said, "Thank you for that, Captain. It sounds like something the Captain ... uh, that is, *Captain Chambers* once said when we was buryin' some o' our folk back east."

Mathews nodded, "Your old captain sounds like a good man, as I've said before. Those words always struck me as the proper ones to say over a soldier killed in battle. And these two, Jack and Sid, were good men ... and good soldiers."

"Thank you, sir."

Mathews tipped his hat, then turned away.

Auggie stepped up to Ned, patted him on the shoulder, then strode away.

Once the burials were completed, the remnants of Colonel Williams' shattered command, now half what it had been, began the sad, twelve-mile slog from Poison Spring back to Camden.

But as he strode along, a fire burned inside Ned such as he hadn't felt since the time he'd been beaten by the old master back at Mountain Meadows. And he feared no amount of blood would quench these new flames.

℘℘℘℘℘℘℘℘℘℘℘℘

Thursday May 12, 1864 – Spotsylvania Courthouse, Virginia:

Though they'd successfully fought off the Yankees for two days—with the Stonewall Brigade doing good service out at the point of the salient, driving off several Union attacks—Lieutenant Jubal Collins was feeling no better about their position. This despite the fact they'd been drawn back to the right flank of the salient, supposedly to give them a break from the hardest fighting.

He had a sinking feeling that Union General Grant had not yet hit them with his knockout punch ... that everything up to now had only been to test their defenses. But the sledgehammer blow was coming.

But to his surprise, Jubal was almost alone in his belief that they'd not yet seen the worst the Yankees had to dish out. Several of the senior officers were talking about a Union withdrawal, and preparations were underway for a Confederate counterattack to catch the federals vulnerable during their expected retreat. Jubal had even heard that General Lee had withdrawn the artillery support for the salient in preparation for an advance down off the hill.

Jubal could only shake his head in disbelief. *The Yankees aren't done with us yet, or I'm a snake. Our guys are still thinking it's McClellan out there ... or Burnside, or even Hooker. But this Grant fellow ... he's a whole other kind of general. I have a bad feeling about this.*

But despite the growing knot in his gut, Jubal had to agree that there was now no sign of the Yankees. And he had to admit the possibility that he could be wrong. Finally tired of the waiting, he climbed up the log wall above their trench, pulled out his binoculars and gazed down at the tree line, several hundred yards below.

He slowly panned across the front. *Hmm ... trees ... trees ... more trees. But no Yank—what was that?!* A bright flash in the right corner of his view caught his eye.

The log next to him exploded in splinters, knocking him back into the trench, where he landed hard on his back. He gazed up at Sergeant Rollins looking down on him.

"You okay, Lieutenant?"

"No ... apparently, I'm too stupid for this job! *To arms, we're under attack!*" Jubal sat up and brushed the wood splinters from his tunic, noting a splatter of blood with a groan, *the surgeons will enjoy digging out those splinters ... if I live that long!*

He looked out again, this time through a loophole cut in the logs. Union riflemen poured up the hillside in long lines, uncountable thousands. Confederate units down the line opened fire, but the Yankees came on in a rush.

"*Fire at will, men!*" Jubal turned and shouted down the line, "And reload like you never did before ... here they come!"

And though his men responded with great determination, and the skill gained from hard experience, without their artillery it was clear to Jubal they would never stop the Yankees this time.

But he cleared his mind of such thoughts and fired his rifle, reloaded, fired, reloaded, fired, reloaded, and fired until he'd lost all track of time and all conscious thought of what was happening in front of him.

And then a movement off to his right caught his eye. He looked that way, and not fifty yards away he saw blue-clad soldiers pouring up over the earthworks and leaping down onto the ground on the other side, turning to target the Confederates down in their trenches with rifle shots and bayonets.

"We are breached! Every other man turn and face rear!" Jubal called out, and though those who could hear him above the tumult obeyed, it was of little use. The Union troops continued to pour over the wall, and were now targeting his own company, bullets skipping off the mud, ricocheting off the logs, and ripping into their exposed bodies.

"Get down, get down!" Jubal hunkered down in the muddy ditch, leaning up only to fire his rifle when loaded. But his men were taking a terrible beating—men falling, screaming, and shouting in the growing carnage.

We have to get out of here, or we're all dead, he thought. But he looked around and noticed that most of the men in his company were already gone, either dead or so badly wounded they could no longer move. Only Sergeant Rollins, laying up against the side of the trench next to him, was still unscathed.

Jubal reached down, grabbed Rollins by the front of his tunic and yelled in his face, "C'mon, Sergeant, we gotta get outta this ditch or we're dead men!"

Rollins nodded, and they both scrambled up out of the ditch. But the Yankee soldiers saw them coming, and a dozen or more fired at them from a distance where they could hardly expect to miss. Jubal's feet went out from under him in the slick mud, and the last thing he saw was the muddy earth rushing up toward his face.

And then, as consciousness slipped away, he had a clear vision of Evelyn, fair and lovely, with a beautiful smile just for him. *Guess that dream is dead too.*

Thursday May 12, 1864 – Spotsylvania Courthouse, Virginia:

Captain James Hawkins slogged through the mud of what had been the scene of a horrific, bloody battle only a few hours earlier. This day had been one of the hardest fought battles he'd yet endured, and that was saying a lot. After two days of probing attacks, attempting to gauge the mettle of the salient's defenders, General Hancock had finally ordered an all-out assault by his 15,000-man Second Corps, left, right, and center. It had proved too much for the ridgeline's stubborn defenders, and Hawkins and his men of the Seventh West Virginia had experienced the thrill of breaching the enemy's lines and vaulting up over their earthworks to pour into the breach behind their lines, effectively cutting them off from the rest of the Confederate Army.

But even so, the rebels had refused to surrender and had fought on. Now surrounded, they hunkered down in the mud of their trenches, facing away from their strong log barrier, with nothing but the dirt for cover, and running low on ammunition. It was a bloodbath.

When the fighting was over, nearly all the Confederate soldiers within the salient were dead, with surprisingly few prisoners. Hawkins could only shake his head in disbelief—that so many men would fight to the death for a cause that he … just couldn't understand for the life of him.

Since most of the rebels had died in their earthworks, mangled bodies piled upon bodies, the Union officers ordered that the trenches be filled in to bury the dead, once any wounded had been extracted. Hawkins felt sick to his stomach as he watched the burial, realizing that these men had unwittingly dug their own graves before ever the battle had begun.

And though the battle had been a Union victory, still the Seventh had taken a terrible beating in the process, with a growing list of casualties. Hawkins slowly walked away from the burial detail, head hung, feeling as tired, sick, and low as he could ever remember.

As he trudged along, something bright colored caught his eye—a corner of bright red and blue cloth sticking out from the mud under a bush. He stopped and picked it up. The cloth came up with a two-foot section of broken pole attached—a regimental battle flag, clearly Confederate, the blue X with white stars on a field of red easily recognizable, even covered in mud. The names of various battles the regiment had fought were sewed into the red field, most prominently, "Gettysburg," at the very bottom. He wondered which regiment it might have been. Then he noticed writing along the white trim at the bottom, and rubbing off the grime he read, *"27 Va. Regt. – Stonewall Brigade."*

Well, I'll be damned … the Bloody Twenty-Seventh again, good old Stonewall Brigade. We always seem to go nose to nose against those guys. Only … maybe no more after this horrific day.

And then he recalled his odd meeting with the young Confederate soldier from the Twenty-Seventh Virginia down in the bloody lane during the Battle of Antietam. *A young officer … what was his name…? Collins … yes, that was it, Lieutenant Collins. Seemed like a nice enough fella.*

Then he gazed back in the direction of the rebel trenches, now a mass grave, and sighed. *Rest in peace my friend.*

He detached the flag from its broken pole, carefully folded it, and stuck it inside his shirt. Then he turned and continued on his way.

ℬᗅᏸᗂᏸℬᗅᏸᗂᏸℬᗅᏸᗂ

Sunday May 15, 1864 – Chancellorsville, Virginia:

Henry leaned hard on his rifle, a scowl on his dark face. He just couldn't shake a sour mood he'd held since first light in the morning.

Cobb strode up to him and smirked, "Look like you done swallowed a rotten tater, Henry. What's eatin' you?"

Henry snorted, but held tight onto his sour mood, determined not to let the annoyingly cheery Cobb talk him out of it. "Tired o' this endless guard duty they got us on, is all…"

"Oh, is that all it is? What'd you expect, Henry? That they's gonna make you general 'stead o' old Grant, and let you lead the charge?" Cobb grinned.

Henry looked away so as not to be infected by Cobb's good humor. He gazed out at a burned-out farmhouse, next to which were parked hundreds of supply wagons across the pasture. Ever since coming to Virginia, the Twenty-Third had done nothing other than guard wagons, trains, or the commanding general's headquarters, well back from the fighting. Henry found it tiresome, and frustrating.

The colonel had told them this place where they now camped was called Chancellorsville, and that the burned-out buildings were the remains of a great battle they'd fought here the previous year. And it didn't help Henry's mood to know that the Union had lost that battle at the cost of thousands of men. In several places, they'd found bones sticking up out of the ground, where shallow graves had been washed by the weather—all in all, a sad, dreary place to be.

"Just ready to show what we can do, is all," Henry looked back at Cobb. "Reckon' I'm ready to fight again, like we done when we was down on the Kanawha with the Capt—"

But their conversation was cut short by a sudden noise out along the road. They looked up and saw a white cavalry soldier coming up the road from the southeast at the gallop.

The man had a fearful look on his face, and his horse was lathered from a hard run. The trooper continued on, headed toward the colonel's command tent.

Henry and Cobb met eyes with a serious look, "Careful what you wish for, Henry…"

Henry nodded and turned to gaze back toward where the cavalryman had headed.

For several minutes, nothing happened. Henry turned back toward Cobb and shrugged. *One more false hope*, Henry decided.

But then a sudden noise jolted him from his reverie—a bugle, sounding loud and clear: *the call to arms!*

Men scrambled to grab stacked rifles, and rushed to form up into rows as they'd practiced hundreds of times before but had never before had to do in earnest.

Cobb and Henry separated, each to his own company. Since the old Mountain Meadows freemen had come to the Twenty-Third's training camp already trained up by the Captain, they had each been given the rank of sergeant or corporal, and had been spread throughout the various rifle companies to make better use of their previous training and experience.

Henry stood to attention, his rifle by his side, in the front row of his company next to his lieutenant, a white man named Pickens.

Colonel Cleaveland John Campbell, commander of the Twenty-Third, a short, slight, unimposing man, strode out in front the gathered men leading his horse, which he mounted and then faced the gathered regiment.

"Men … I know many of you have been itching to get into the fight. Well, now the time has come, the time to show what you're made of. I know you men will do me proud.

"There's a fight a few miles down the road, and our men of the Second Ohio Cavalry are sorely beset by an entire brigade of rebel cavalry. They beg of our succor in their most desperate hour of need, to which I have agreed with alacrity.

"Right face! At the double-quick … march!"

ℰᴂℛℭℬℰ℧ℰᴂℛℭℬℰ℧ℰᴂℛℭℬ

Three quarters of an hour later, Henry and the men of the Twenty-Third caught sight of the battlefield, the sounds from which they'd been hearing for the past several minutes. They approached the battle from the northwest, still double-quicking down the road in two long columns of over four hundred men each, led by Colonel Campbell on his horse.

Henry could now see the truth of what the colonel had told them: the Union cavalry were fighting dismounted off to the left side of the road, hunkered down behind whatever cover they could find, as Confederate cavalry a hundred yards or so to the right, down a side road heading in that direction, pounded them with rifle fire. Clearly the Union boys were greatly outnumbered

428

and in imminent jeopardy of being overwhelmed and slaughtered.

Without pause, Colonel Campbell led the two marching columns of infantry straight across the battlefield along the road, right between the two opposing forces. Once they'd straddled the side road, the colonel turned his horse and shouted, *"Right face ... Present arms ... Aim ... Fire!"*

A thunderous volley belched forth from the Twenty-Third, sending the Confederate cavalry scrambling for cover.

And before the smoke had cleared, Colonel Campbell drew his saber, and shouted, *"Reload ... Forward ... March!"*

After quickly reloading his rifle, Henry strode forth with the rest of his company. And though the enemy began returning fire, it seemed desperate and erratic, with very few shots finding their mark. When they'd marched another fifty yards, the colonel called out, *"Form up ... Present arms ... Aim ... Fire!"* sending another deadly rifle volley screaming out at their enemies.

And then the colonel gave the command that sent a thrill through Henry's frame, *"Regiment will reload, then fix bayonets and prepare to charge on my command ... Reload ... Fix Bayonets ... Charge!"*

With a great yell, the freemen of the Twenty-Third Colored Infantry Regiment rushed forward toward hand-to-hand combat against the Confederate forces of General Robert E. Lee, the first black men to ever do so.

Remembering his bayonet charge training, Henry picked out one specific foe and focused on him, lest the view of a whole row of enemies become too overwhelming. The rider was burly looking, with a full dark beard, and held a scowl that Henry decided to take personally. And though Henry's legs were moving as fast as he could move them, he had a sudden sinking feeling it wasn't nearly fast enough, as the man slowly unholstered a revolver, aimed it straight at Henry, and pulled back the hammer.

But even as Henry expected to feel the impact of a bullet aimed right at his chest the man's eyes widened in surprise; the gun hadn't fired, either a misfire, or the man had already fired all six.

And then as the man raised the pistol to look at what might be wrong, Henry hit him at full sprint with the bayonet.

The shock of the impact sent a jolt through Henry's right shoulder and nearly knocked the breath out of him. But he looked up and saw the man had dropped his weapon and now grasped at the rifle barrel with hands that would no longer obey.

Henry yanked the bayonet free, and the man toppled from his saddle. The horse shied back with the man's foot tangled in the stirrups and his face dragging along the road.

Henry turned his attention to what was going on around him and was gratified to see that the brief, intense battle was already over; the decimated Confederate cavalry had turned their mounts and were actively fleeing from the field. In moments, Colonel Campbell called a halt to the attack.

Five minutes later, the Second Ohio Cavalry remounted after their near destruction, and now, itching to turn the tables on their aggressors, trotted up the road, ready to pursue the beaten enemy and exact a measure of revenge if they could.

The Twenty-Third parted to allow the Union cavalry regiment to pass. But as they reached the front of the column, their major called a halt and ordered his cavalry troopers to face the Twenty-Third.

The major saluted Colonel Campbell, then turned toward the men of the Twenty-Third, stood in his stirrups, removed his hat, and waved it in the air, shouting, *"Three cheers for the Twenty-Third!"*

And all the men of the Second Ohio Cavalry, white soldiers all, removed their hats, waved them above their heads and shouted, *"Huzzah! Huzzah! Huzzah!"*

The major replaced his hat and tipped it at the black infantrymen with a broad grin. Then he and the rest of the cavalry troopers turned and thundered off in pursuit of the enemy.

Henry stood where he was, slowly shaking his head, finding he had suddenly suffered some dust blown into his eyes. And he realized his ill humor from earlier in the day was now entirely gone.

Sunday May 15, 1864 – New Market, Virginia:

Nathan paced restlessly back and forth in front of the formed-up line of the Twelfth West Virginia, smoking a cigar, a dark scowl etched upon his brow. Every few paces, a bullet would zip overhead, or hit in the dirt near where he walked, but he—and his ever-present hound—seemed to pay it little mind.

Finally, Tom Clark, who stood a few yards back behind a hastily erected breastwork of logs, called out, "Please, sir. You are in mortal danger out there ... The snipers..."

Nathan looked up at Tom and nodded, turning to pace back in his direction. He stopped in front of Tom's position and hopped back over the hastily constructed log breastwork, followed closely by Harry the Dog.

Nathan removed the cigar from his mouth, "Tom ... it's as I feared ... Sigel has entirely bungled the battle by scattering his forces and using them in piecemeal fashion. Half our army is straggling behind some twenty miles or more, still on the far side of the North Fork, and Colonel Moor's brigade positioned out front at New Market has been left too long unsupported. He's now been decimated and is forced to fall back in disarray.

"And the ridiculous cavalry charge Sigel ordered after we'd finally stopped the rebel advance ... it was nothing but a slaughter. *Damn it!* Why not move the infantry forward instead with good flanking support? He could've won the battle right then and there, despite all his earlier mistakes. What on God's earth was he thinking?"

"He wasn't, I expect..." Tom scowled.

Nathan nodded, "You're right there, Tom. And to beat all ... here we sit, behind the rest of the brigade as a reserve ... *a reserve, Tom!* We, who have more battle experience than the majority of the regiments out here. All we can do is sit here like fat toads, dodging sniper fire, with no means of aiding in the battle until it'll likely be too late. It's infuriating!"

"Yes, sir. More *punishment* from Sigel, I presume. Likely thinks it'll teach you a lesson by depriving you of any possible glory in winning the battle."

"*Glory in winning?!* I fear there'll be no winning today, Tom. Which is a damned shame and should never have happened, considering the force Sigel had at his disposal. If he'd consolidated his forces and moved swiftly, as I and several other officers recommended, we would've rolled over these rebels as if they were a mere skirmish line. Instead..." he shook his head, then once again turned to face out toward the battle, raising his spyglass to his eye.

"Any word from Zeke and Ollie? Were they able to extract Captain Carlin and his guns from that ridge to our right?"

"Yes, sir ... though they took casualties when the position was overrun. Carlin was able to pull back, but has lost several of his guns and is now out of the fight ... Companies A and B have since taken up positions on our right flank. And with Jamie and Georgie's companies manning our left flank, I'm feeling fairly confident we'll not be easily turned at least."

"Good ... and none too soon ... it appears ... Yes, I believe Sigel has now ordered a general retreat ... I can see other units beginning to pull back.

"Damn it ... this has the makings of a rout, Tom. Pass the word down the line, nobody retreats without explicit orders from me ... We'll hold this position at least until all the other units have passed."

Moments later, as the seven hundred rifles of the Twelfth West Virginia held their position, the remainder of Sigel's force began pouring by on their left, heading north.

And then, to Nathan's complete surprise and shock, General Sigel himself came galloping up on his horse. Sigel reigned to a stop in front of Nathan and Tom, who immediately saluted, though Harry bristled, emitting a low growl.

The general appeared highly agitated, and never saluted in return. Instead, he shouted out what Nathan and Tom assumed were orders for the Twelfth, before he spurred his horse and lurched forward, swiftly galloping out of sight.

Nathan and Tom looked at each other and exchanged a shrug, "German?" Tom asked.

Nathan nodded, "Yes, and though I can speak a few words in it, I didn't understand a word of *that*, he was in such a lather ..."

"So, what now, sir?"

Nathan jumped up on the log breastwork, and gazed across the battlefield, which was quickly devolving into an uncoordinated Union retreat.

He jumped back down, "We must do what we can to prevent a rout ... If the rebels come up fast behind, there will be a complete slaughter. We must hold them off until the other units have crossed the bridge and are safely back across the North Fork of the Shenandoah."

Then the two men exchanged a dark look, "But sir ... we are too few..."

"Yes, Tom ... I know..."

⁂

The Twelfth West Virginia fell back in a fighting, leap-frog fashion, trailing behind the last of Sigel's army. Finally, the Twelfth reached the crest of a hill behind which was the slope leading to the bridge across the Shenandoah. Here Nathan called a halt and ordered his men to dig in behind a low rock wall running along the top of a hump that had a commanding view on all sides. Then he called for Billy Creek.

"Billy ... I want you to take your skirmishers across the saddle on our left and up into that grove of trees on the far side. From there you can help guard our left flank, and decimate anyone who tries to push through that draw, trying to either flank us or pursue the retreating army."

Billy gave Nathan a dark look, "And ... what will *you* be doing while I'm guarding the left flank, Captain?"

Nathan returned the look for a long moment, before reaching out and grasping Billy's shoulder with his right hand, "I'll be right here, Billy ... holding this position."

"But..." then Billy just slowly shook his head, turned and trotted off to do as ordered.

Moments later, Major Jim Wiggins stepped up to where Nathan and Tom stood, surveying the retreating Union army behind them, and the approaching rebels out front.

"Sirs ... what's the plan? We gonna give 'em a good volley, then fall back?"

But Nathan met eyes with Jim, a hard, serious look, "No, Mr. Wiggins ... you know as well as I do that'll not buy enough time for the retreat. We'll be quickly overrun and routed. We must stop them here ... at least for a time."

Jim turned and gazed out at the advancing rebel army. They could now see large groups of soldiers gathering within the tree line off to their left, and others moving up along the valley to their right. And up the center marched the main force, several thousand strong. All three forces were now within a quarter mile of the Twelfth's position. The good news was they now held a narrow pinch point with steep ground in front, which would force the Confederates to attack uphill and in a piecemeal fashion rather than in an all-out assault.

"Sir ... how long you reckon we can do *that*...?"

"As long as it takes, Mr. Wiggins."

Jim whistled, "All right ... you're the boss. But I came here to tell you, we're now down to only five hundred or so men."

"What? How'd that happen?"

"Well ... I'd not go so far as to call them deserters ... or *cowards*, but ... when all the other regiments was fallin' back, a number of our less experienced men decided it would behoove them to join the party..."

"Ah ... I see. Well, nothing for it now. Five hundred or seven ... it'll make little difference."

"I agree with you there, sir," Jim reached into his ammo pouch and pulled out a handful of repeating rifle cartridges and began counting, "Hmm ... down to just eight rounds for the Henry ... What about you, Tom?"

"Six." Tom already knew the answer as he'd already loaded his rifle with the last of what he had.

"And I'm at five," Nathan offered.

"Damned Sigel..." Jim turned his head and spat.

434

Nathan nodded but said nothing. And though it wasn't strictly speaking where he ought to be during a battle, Nathan also said nothing when Jim Wiggins settled in behind the rock wall, clearly intending to have his fight right here next to Nathan, Tom, and Harry the Dog.

And they weren't surprised when Stan also stepped up and joined them, reaching down to give Harry a pat as he did.

"So … Colonel … is going to be some fight, eh? Where's Billy?"

"I sent him across the way to guard that draw and watch our left flank," Nathan nodded toward where Billy had been sent. "He'll be on the opposite side from where Georgie and Jamie are positioned. Anyone who tries to pursue the retreating army through that gap will be caught in the crossfire."

"Ah … is good. They can hold them off long time from there."

Nathan nodded, and wondered if Stan left unsaid that Billy could likely escape back down toward the river from his position in the woods if he had to. Unlike the rest of them, who had nowhere to run if they were overwhelmed.

Nathan took one last look at the gathering storm below them, and then turned back to the three men standing next to him, "Gentlemen … whatever happens, I wish to say … it has been an honor and a privilege serving with you. And I'd not trade it for anything."

And then he removed his hat and held it over his heart. The others did the same as he recited, *They shall fight against thee; but they shall not prevail against thee; for I am with thee, saith the LORD, to deliver thee.*

They replaced their hats and the four of them shook hands, then unslung their rifles and prepared for battle.

But Nathan had a thought and turned to Stan, "Captain Volkov … I want you to gather your men and form a flying reserve force … fix bayonets and use your discretion to fill any gaps in our line that may form."

Stan grinned, "Yes, Colonel … this I can do." Then he turned and trotted off to carry out his orders.

The rebels had already advanced on the Twelfth's position three times, but each time had been stymied by devastating volley fire from its five hundred rifles, a stubborn resistance the enemy had clearly not expected at this late stage in a battle they assumed was already won.

After the third failed assault, there was a pause. Nathan wondered if the Confederates intended to bring up artillery and just pound them into submission, or if they were simply regrouping for one last, devastating charge. With ammunition running low, and the rebels bringing up more men every moment, he had a growing feeling that his desire to offset General Sigel's incompetence and avert a disaster had doomed his command, including all the men he held most dear.

And then he thought of Evelyn, and his heart sank. If he died now, he would never see her again, would never marry her, would never raise a family with her.

For the first time in his long, dangerous career, Nathan Chambers felt the chill fear of death, but not for his own sake, for his love of Evelyn.

ഇ൜ൠ഑ൠഇ൜ൠ഑ൠഇ൜ൠ഑

Since the beginning of the battle, Georgie and Jamie had held down the Twelfth's left flank with their two rifle companies, now with the help of Billy's team of skirmishers positioned across a narrow draw back in the tree line there. On the first assault of the Twelfth's redoubt, the enemy had been taken by surprise by the stiffness of the resistance, and they'd been driven back from the gap with high casualties.

On the next two assaults, the enemy had switched tactics, apparently determined to take out the center of the Twelfth's position with a frontal attack. The second time they'd tried it, Jamie, on the far left, had ordered his men to advance several dozen yards beyond the protection of their stone wall, then pivot and hit the approaching enemy from the side with a volley of enfilading fire, before pulling back at the double-quick.

Now, during a long pause in which Georgie assumed the rebels were regrouping for another push, he wasn't surprised to see Jamie striding toward him from his position down the line to the left.

Jamie stepped up to Georgie and the two men met eyes but said nothing, instead shaking hands with vigor. Jamie looked down at where Georgie's Henry rifle leaned against the rock wall, "Out of ammo?"

"Yep. You?"

"Aye. Left mine over yonder with Sergeant Miller. No use carrying the thing now."

"Nope." Georgie leaned out over the wall and gazed down the hillside, where he could see the rebel army gathering just out of rifle range. This time there seemed to be thousands more than on the previous assaults, "Reckon they'll keep on coming?"

"Aye ... I believe we've now gone and made them *mad*," Jamie looked at Georgie with a smirk.

Georgie snorted a chuckle, "Seems so." He reached down and pulled out the Colt revolver from the holster at his right hip, checking to make sure it was fully loaded and that all the percussion caps were well seated. Satisfied, he replaced it, and then did the same with the pistol on his left hip.

Jamie did likewise, though he had to reload several cylinders on his lefthand gun. Though it was unusual for officers to carry more than one pistol, all of Colonel Chambers' officers did so. The men of the Twelfth shrugged it off, assuming it was a holdover from their days out west fighting Indians.

Then, by habit, Jamie reached back behind the lefthand holster and pulled his infantry officer's sword a few inches from its scabbard, to make sure it moved smoothly.

Georgie noticed his friend's act and did the same. Then he looked back down the line to the right at his rifle company to make sure all were prepared. He was pleased to see men at the ready, leaning up onto the rock wall with grim, determined looks, hammers at the half-cock and bayonets fixed. He turned and spoke to Sergeant Adams, standing a few feet off to the right along the wall. "Sergeant, reckon we'll have time for one volley; after that it'll be fire at will as we can. Then ... reckon we'll greet the enemy with the bayonet. Please pass the word..."

"Sir!" the sergeant snapped a salute, then moved off down the line repeating the order to the seventy-three men of Captain Thompson's company.

Jamie nodded, turned, and gave the same order to the sixty-seven men of his company. He then leaned across and patted Georgie on the back. All was now ready, and there was nothing more they could do but wait.

ಬಿಂಶಂಬಿಶಂಬಿಶಂ

On they came, screaming out the rebel yell—a great wave of soldiers, many times larger than any before.

"*Fire!*" Nathan shouted, and a thunderous rifle volley rolled out from the Twelfth. But the volley didn't stop them this time, and only slowed them momentarily as they closed ranks and kept coming.

Without the repeating rifles, now depleted of ammunition, Nathan's men had no way to fend off the rebels while the old-style musket rifles were being reloaded. And there wasn't time to reload, as the enemy came on in a rush.

Then the rebels were leaping over the stone wall and engaging Nathan and his men in hand-to-hand combat.

Nathan slashed with his saber in his right hand and fired his revolver in his left. Tom had picked up a rifle and slashed the rebels with the bayonet.

Nathan risked a glance down the line to his left and saw that the men of the Twelfth were fighting back with stubborn determination and ferocity. Many had managed to reload and were now firing back at the rebels from point-blank range, inflicting devastating casualties.

But they were badly outnumbered, and in dire risk of being overwhelmed. His momentary lapse in concentration nearly cost Nathan his life, as he looked up just in time to dodge a bayonet thrust from a rebel soldier who'd leapt over the stone wall. But in his haste, Nathan tripped and fell flat on his back, even as the rebel thrust at him with the bayonet.

In a swift blur of motion, Harry the Dog was between them even as the bayonet descended. With a heartbreaking squeal the great dog was impaled and collapsed to the ground at his master's feet, just as Nathan raised his pistol and fired, hitting the rebel in the face, crumpling him to the ground.

Confederate soldiers poured up over the wall all along the line, even as the men of Jamie and Georgie's companies fought them hand-to-hand with their bayonets.

Jamie and Georgie stood side by side, a pistol in each hand, shooting down rebels as they leapt atop the wall. But in a few moments their Colts were clicking ineffectually on empty cylinders.

Without a word, they each tossed down their pistols and swept out their infantry officer's swords, slashing and stabbing at the rebels who now came over the wall in front of them and to both sides, menacing the Union officers with bayonets. But the Confederates were too many, and quickly surrounded Georgie and Jamie. The rebels slowly circled them, wary of the deadly blades, as Georgie and Jamie faced outward, back-to-back.

"I'll not be taken prisoner … not after what they did to William and Zeke," Georgie growled. "Better to go down fighting…"

"Aye," Jamie answered, for once with a serious tone, "But let's take some o' these here rebel bastards with us … what say you, brother?"

"I say amen to that, brother. Together always!"

"Together!" Jamie echoed.

Then Georgie and Jamie let loose a battle cry to rival the rebel yell, and attacked the surrounding enemy.

Georgie ducked under a bayonet thrust, and plunged his sword into the chest of a rebel to his left. But at that same moment he felt a sharp pain in his right side. He glanced down and saw a bayonet embedded in his belly, and instinctively lashed out, striking the rebel just beneath the chin, nearly decapitating him. The bayonet came out with a sucking noise, and Georgie gasped at the sudden sting of it, but looked back to his front and knocked aside another bayonet thrust, stabbing back at the man's shoulder, knocking him backward. He deflected another thrust, but the blade caught him in the left arm, punching into flesh and bone just below the shoulder. He slashed at the arms holding the rifle and took both off just above the wrists. The rebel collapsed, spurting blood from his wounds. But Georgie had to drop the sword to pull the bayonet free, and at that moment felt a hit that dropped him to his knees and robbed him of his breath. "*Give 'em hell, Jamie...*" he whispered as the world turned black.

Jamie was yet unharmed, fending off three rebels in front of him with the saber, after having already downed two others. But when he heard Georgie fall, he turned his head on instinct. The distraction cost him, and Jamie felt rather than heard the shot that hit him in the chest like a hammer. Even as he caught site of Georgie's lifeless body, his own knees buckled under him. "*Together...*" he muttered, and joined his best friend in eternity.

ℬↄℭℛↃℬↄℬↄℭℛↃℬↄℬↄℭℛↃ

Even as Nathan believed the end had come, a great rush of bodies moved past him, driving through the rebels, and continuing up over the wall; Stan and his reserves dashed past with a great shout, firing their rifles and leading with their bayonets.

Nathan gently pulled is left leg out from under Harry, who whimpered, but did not attempt to rise. "Stay put, my old friend ... I'll be back for you shortly."

Then he jumped up, raised his sword, and yelled, "*Charge...*" leaping up over the wall following in Stan's wake. Taking the cue from their leader, all five hundred men of the Twelfth poured up over the wall and crashed into their attackers, driving them back down the hill in a rush. Nathan slashed and hacked at any rebel who tried to stand his ground, and soon Tom joined him, stabbing furiously with a bayonet.

The Twelfth's unexpected counterattack drove the rebels back down the hill a hundred yards or so, until the charge began to run out of momentum. Nathan stood panting and called out for the regiment to fall back. Then he noticed a large man standing out front of the others, hands on knees: Stan.

440

Nathan ran to Stan but saw he'd been wounded in many places. Gunshots or bayonets, he couldn't tell, as Stan's tunic was splattered with blood, both his and his enemies. Nathan noticed then that Stan still gripped a rifle, but the bayonet had snapped off near the hilt. Nathan marveled at the force of a blow that could shatter the tempered, half-inch-thick steel blade.

Stan seemed to notice the damaged rifle for the first time, gazing down at it a moment before letting it lose. It slipped from his grasp to the ground with a sticky, sucking sound as a thick red liquid dripped down from where he'd gripped it.

Then Stan collapsed to his knees, even as Nathan and Tom moved up to grab him and hold him up. The other soldiers of Stan's rifle company were already falling back as ordered.

ෂාශාශශ්‍යෂාශාශශ්‍යෂාශාශ

Nathan was desperate to get Stan up and away, as the rebels were beginning to regroup below and had begun firing at them. Then, remembering an incident when he'd caught Stan napping back when Nathan had first arrived at Fort Davis out in Texas, he bent down, looked in Stan's eyes and said, "Volkov ... I'll tolerate no shirking on duty in my command. On your feet, mister!"

Stan's eyes widened, and he answered in a faraway, rasping voice, "Sorry, Captain ... I was ... I ... I was only ... *shirking*. Is true ... won't happen again, sir..."

And with a great heave Stan was back on his feet. Tom and Nathan grabbed his arms over their shoulders and started him moving up the hill, even as bullets began striking the dirt around them.

ෂාශාශශ්‍යෂාශාශශ්‍යෂාශාශ

They returned to a scene of utter devastation. The last rebel attack had been overwhelming. The Twelfth had suffered many dead and wounded.

Stan clambered back over the wall and sat heavily on the ground, bleeding from many wounds. He bowed his head and quietly muttered, "Death ... death ... all death..." and they could

441

get nothing more out of him, even as an assistant surgeon scrambled over to bind up his wounds.

Jim Wiggins had not participated in the bayonet charge, which would've concerned Nathan if he would've had time to consider it. But when they returned, they saw him lying on the ground with a tourniquet around his right leg below the knee. Tom immediately went to assist him, making sure the tourniquet was secured, and giving Jim a long drink from his canteen. Then he lay Jim back on the ground to await transport back to the field hospital.

Tom came to Nathan and spoke in quiet tones, "Shot in the ankle ... It's bad. I fear he'll lose the foot..."

Nathan grimaced, but knew he had no time to comfort Jim, as the rebels were already regrouping for another charge. He did take time to tend the fallen dog, wrapping a bandage around the oozing hole where the bayonet had pierced him. He wasn't sure whether or not to be surprised that Harry still lived. "Hang in there, old fellow..."

Stan heard Nathan speaking with Harry and sat up straight, bending over to examine the dog. "He is wounded ... but not dead ... not yet. He needs hospital..."

And then, before anyone could intervene, Stan leaned down, scooped up the great animal in his arms, stood and trotted off down the hill.

Tom started to go after him, but Nathan grabbed his arm, "Let him go. He needs the surgeons now, and he's at least headed in the right direction. We've got bigger concerns, Tom ... look..."

Tom looked back down the hill and groaned. The rebels were coming in force once again, and this time there'd be no way to stop them.

But as the rebel assault came to within two hundred yards, a thunderous *booming* of an artillery barrage roared out, emanating from the next rise above and behind the Twelfth's position. The rebel charge was suddenly shattered in mid-stride as great, gory swaths of men were cut down by deadly cannister fire belching out from the Union guns.

Nathan shouted the order to gather their dead and wounded and fall back to the position of the artillery.

He and Tom trotted down the line toward the gap that'd been guarded by Jamie and Georgie, intending to lead the regiment in that direction. But when they reached the position where their left flank had been, they came to a horrified halt.

There they found Jamie and Georgie, lying side by side. Their eyes were closed, and one might have imagined they were just resting, if not for all the blood covering their bodies. There were also eight dead rebel soldiers heaped around them, mute testament to their fighting prowess.

"Dear God," Nathan whispered as he knelt down in front of them. He reached out and touched first Jamie and then Georgie on the shoulder, saying a quick, silent prayer as he did so.

He stood and addressed Tom, "Bring them ... and all the others who've died. We've no time to grieve now ... We must leave immediately or there will be many more to bury."

When they reached the artillery position, Nathan was met by Captain Henry DuPont of the Fifth U.S. Artillery, a handsome young man with a neatly trimmed goatee beard. "Sorry we were late to the show, Colonel," DuPont saluted, which Nathan returned.

"Not *late*, DuPont ... *timely* ... you have saved us from utter destruction ... Now, please tell me how you intend to get us down off this hill."

"We've already positioned our guns in depth, Colonel. Five hundred yards apart until we are well away and can reach the bridge. As we fall back, we shall continue to be covered by our artillery farther back. Not to tell you your business, Colonel, but ... if you wish, I would recommend we now bid our rebel friends *adieu*."

"Agreed, Captain DuPont. We are beyond ready. And thank you again for saving our lives ... at least what's left of them."

"My pleasure, sir!"

ಬಿಜ಼ುಜ಼ಯಿಜ಼ುಜ಼ಯಿಜ಼ುಜ಼

The surgeons of General Sigel's army toiled feverishly to establish a workable hospital to treat the sudden flood of wounded, setting up a large tent in a field across the river from where the battle had been fought, and well back out of artillery range.

They were already overwhelmed with patients when a gigantic man came in carrying an equally gigantic dog. Both were covered in blood from head to foot. And though the man had been crudely bandaged in the field, he was clearly in desperate need of medical attention, as the white cloth was already almost entirely soaked red.

"Fix dog first..." the huge man, who wore captain's bars on his shoulders, demanded.

But the surgeons stubbornly resisted, insisting the animal be placed outside, despite the great man's increasingly belligerent attitude. The big man refused to remove the dog from the hospital, finally setting the animal down on a table, and scowling fiercely at the doctors, "You will be working on hound now, or ... I will *kill* you," he snarled, shaking a huge fist at them. The dog raised his head heavily, bared his teeth, and growled, though he could no longer stand.

But the head surgeon was equally stubborn, and not easily intimidated, folding his arms across his chest and refusing to budge. The doctor also noted the soldier was badly wounded, swaying on his feet, and would likely pass out soon, ending the dispute.

But then a second man entered the room, also wearing captain's bars, "Peace ... all of you. Stan, calm yourself! There'll be no violence in this hospital. And you surgeons, back away. These are my men; I will tend to them."

The head surgeon was still not convinced, "*Men?* One is just a hound. I'm sorry, Captain, by I am the head surgeon here and —"

But the captain turned to the surgeon, and despite his mild-mannered appearance, medium height, thin build, and thick spectacles, he spoke with authority, "I am Captain Jenkins, head surgeon of the Twelfth West Virginia. And these are *men* of the

Twelfth. *I* will see to them, and no other. You may return to your duties, doctor."

The surgeon stared at him another moment, shrugged, and then turned away to tend to other patients.

"William! You're back. Thank God. See to Harry," Stan unclenched and lowered his fist, then sank heavily down on an empty cot with a groan.

"You first, Stan ... and I'll brook no arguments. Once I've made sure you're not bleeding to death, then I'll see to Harry ... I promise."

Chapter 17. Reckoning

"For the Lord of hosts
will have a day of reckoning
against everyone who is
proud and lofty ...
that he may be abased."
- Isaiah 2:12

Saturday April 30, 1864 – Jenkins' Ferry, Arkansas:

After the disaster at Poison Spring, and with supplies running dangerously low, Union Major General Steele finally ordered the withdrawal of his forces back to the north toward Little Rock, including the remnants of the First Kansas Colored Regiment, which had lost forty percent of its men in the campaign.

But Confederate forces were determined to annihilate Steele's force before they could make good their escape, and launched their attack as Union forces prepared to ford the rain-swollen Saline River at a place called Jenkins' Ferry.

Steele's Union infantry were prepared for the attack, well-dug-in south of the river, building sturdy earthworks to repel the rebel attack as Union cavalry crossed the river and engineers built a pontoon bridge for the wagons, artillery, and infantry to cross.

Once again, Sergeant Ned Turner and Lieutenant Auggie Gordon of the First Kansas Colored Regiment fought side by side, this time behind a wall of laid timbers, sharpened abatis, and rifle pits placed in a broad curve two miles south of the Saline River.

They'd already fended off several Confederate attacks when Ned grabbed Auggie's sleeve and shook him to get his attention, "Look, Lieutenant..."

Auggie looked out his loophole, trying to figure out what Ned had seen. The ground in front of their position was damp and mucky, and a thick fog had merged with the gun smoke of the battle to make visibility almost zero, despite it being midday. But then he saw it … Artillery! The rebels were trying to move several big guns up to batter the Union earthworks. That was a serious concern, but as he was wondering what he ought to do about that, Auggie noticed something else … The rebel gunners were having trouble moving their guns. The wheels of the heavy guns were sinking in the mud, and gunners were straining to extract them.

Auggie turned to Ned and said, "Quick, send the word down the line—quietly—tell the men to fix bayonets and gather here…"

"Why? What you got in mind, Lieutenant?"

"I have in mind taking out those guns!"

Ned's eyes widened, then he nodded and scrambled down the line to their left, spreading the word. Auggie turned and did the same to their right.

Five minutes later, the fifty-four remaining men of their rifle company gathered behind the log wall, and Auggie motioned them to follow him as he climbed up and over the wall.

After a quick trot under cover of the thick fog, they surrounded the struggling artillery gunners. The rebels, taken completely by surprise, held their hands up in surrender.

Ned gazed at the rebel in front of him, a big man with a thick, dark beard, and caught his eye, "You boys fought hard at Poison Spring."

The man shrugged, "Just another fight to us."

Ned nodded, then took one long stride forward and drove his bayonet to the hilt in the center of the man's chest. "Not to us." The man gasped, gripped the rifle barrel, then slumped to the ground. Ned yanked the blade free.

For a moment, nobody spoke or moved. Ned turned and met eyes with Auggie, half expecting his lieutenant to place him under arrest.

But Auggie just stared at Ned for a moment, then turned, raised his pistol, pointed it at another rebel's face, and pulled the trigger, *boom!* The rebel collapsed to the ground.

"The reckoning for Poison Spring…" Auggie nodded, as he gazed down at the dead man, a pool of blood spreading out around his head in the dampness.

Then Ned pointed his rifle at another of the rebels, "For Poison Spring!" He pulled the trigger, and the man went down in a swirl of gun smoke.

"*For Poison Spring! For Poison Spring! For Poison Spring!*" The other freemen of the company followed their officers' lead, with rifle bullet and bayonet, and soon more than a dozen rebel soldiers lay dead on the ground.

ℰ⊃⊂ℛ⊂ℬ⊃ℰ⊃⊂ℛ⊂ℬ⊃ℰ⊃⊂ℛ⊂ℬ

Sunday May 15, 1864 – North Anna River, Virginia:

Jubal wondered how it was he was still alive after the devastating battle at the salient near the town of Spotsylvania Courthouse. Some of it was still a fog in his mind, but from the best he could recall and puzzle out, as he and Sergeant Rollins scrambled out of the deadly trench, he'd slipped in the mud and fallen hard on his face, even as Union bullets zipped over him, leaving him muddled, but otherwise unharmed. He still didn't know if Rollins had been killed or captured, but apparently their charge up out of the trench had inspired others of the brigade to follow, and the sudden charge had been forceful enough and sufficiently unexpected to punch a gap in the surrounding Union forces, allowing several hundred of the Stonewall Brigade to escape the encirclement. And during the rush to escape, from what he could figure, someone had reached down, pulled him back onto his feet by his belt, and started him moving again. So, though his head had been totally befuddled, his legs still knew what to do, and he'd followed the rest of the brigade out of the battle and back to Confederate lines beyond.

Though the war slogged on, the Stonewall Brigade was now only a skeleton of the once formidable fighting force. Once they'd pulled back and regrouped after the battle at the salient, which people were now calling the "mule shoe" because of its distinctive shape on a map, Jubal realized with a shock that the mighty Stonewall Brigade was now down to fewer than two hundred effectives. He'd heard serious talk of disbanding the brigade altogether and dispersing its men to other regiments and brigades.

And the end of the war was still nowhere in sight. He now found himself thinking more and more everyday of an end to the fighting, and of having a normal, peaceful life again, and ... of somehow reconnecting with Evelyn ... So, against his better judgement, he borrowed a pen, inkwell, and a sheet of paper, and for the first time since he'd seen her in Richmond, he penned Evelyn a letter, though he had no idea if it would ever reach her.

ↈↃ∝Ↄ℧∝ↄↂↈↃ∝Ↄ℧∝ↄↂↈↃ∝Ↄ℧

Thursday May 19, 1864 – Richmond, Virginia:

> *May 15, 1864*
> *In camp near North Anna River in Va.*
>
> *My Dear Evelyn,*
>
> *I first want to apologize for such a long spell without writing you. I would like to excuse myself by saying the war has kept me too busy to do so. But though there is some truth in that, it would not be the whole truth. I must confess to leaving our last meeting with a heavy heart, and of not handling the news of your betrothal in a manner befitting a proper gentleman.*
>
> *If I acted or spoke in a hurtful manner toward you on that occasion, I again apologize. You did nothing wrong, as there was no agreement of any kind, beyond simple friendship and letter writing, between us. The fault was all mine for letting my imagination get the best of me concerning our relationship while out on campaign.*
>
> *As for news of the war, I don't wish to shock or worry you, but the last battle we fought was the worst yet, and that's saying a lot. Near a place with the odd name of Spotsylvania, we were overrun and cutoff by the federals, and the Stonewall Brigade lost nearly half our men either*

449

killed, wounded, or captured. They now talk of disbanding the brigade altogether, though I hope they don't.

And I am still not sure how it was I escaped alive, for there was a moment during the battle I believed I was a dead man. But in the end I escaped, suffering only minor injuries from when a bullet hit a log near me and sprayed my face and neck with wood splinters. A surgeon pulled them all out, and now I look almost myself again!

I pray this letter finds you well, and—selfishly, I suppose—that I should live long enough to see you once again and, hopefully, rekindle our friendship, come what may.

Your loyal, forever friend,

Jubal Collins
1st Lieutenant, 27th Virginia

Evelyn finished reading Jubal's letter for the second time and put it down on the side table with a sigh. Her heart ached for the courageous young man, who was so good and admirable in so many ways, but whose affections she would never be able to return.

She picked up her cup of hot tea and blew on it just as Angeline and Jonathan stepped into the sitting room of their manor house.

After greetings were exchanged, Angeline glanced at the letter sitting next to Evelyn, "Something interesting, dear?"

"Yes, actually … I have finally received another letter from Lieutenant Collins. Most of it is of a *personal* nature … so I would prefer not to share it. But as far as news of the war, our side may be interested in knowing that the Stonewall Brigade was fairly decimated in the recent battle at Spotsylvania Courthouse. Lieutenant Collins says they are now talking of disbanding it altogether and, I assume, disbursing its members to other units."

"Oh, yes, that *is* good news," Jonathan smiled. "The Stonewall Brigade has been a serious thorn in the side of the Union Army since the very beginnings of the conflict."

But Angeline was more reticent, slowly shaking her head, "But devastating news for that brave young man, no doubt…"

Evelyn nodded, "Yes … very much so. He took a lot of pride in their fighting prowess, and … I expect the comradery that men share in such a group."

"No doubt … no doubt," Jonathan nodded, adopting a more serious expression as he took a seat opposite Evelyn. Angeline sat in the chair between them.

Then, Evelyn turned to Jonathan and asked the question that was foremost on her mind, the real reason for today's meeting: "Jonathan … is there not yet any word on the fate of the Twelfth West Virginia? We know they were in the Battle of New Market, and that the Union Army under General Sigel was defeated and driven off. But … there has been maddeningly little news beyond that."

Jonathan slowly shook his head, "I'm sorry, Evelyn … I have only dry facts at this point. I know they took casualties, the last numbers I saw were nine killed, twenty-six wounded, though I don't know how accurate those numbers are. The one thing you can take solace in is that Nathan Chambers clearly survived the battle unscathed, as he is still listed as the commanding officer of the Twelfth on all the reports I've seen, both Confederate and Union."

Evelyn frowned, "Well … that's something, anyway. But I personally know a number of his men … it is frightening to have no news of them."

Angeline reached out and patted her arm, "Sorry, my dear. We will keep inquiring, but with General Grant exerting such pressure on the Confederate Army here in the east, there is little attention being paid to the action farther west."

Evelyn nodded, but continued to frown. "And … what news of the Signal Corps? Do we know what our old *friend* Major White is up to? I realize we put him off the scent for a time with the Alice Spencer ruse, but…"

"He's still out there, poking around, to be sure," Jonathan scowled. "The word is he's teamed up with a Colonel Grayson, and that they are seeking some notorious scoundrel who goes by the pseudonym 'The Employer.' Sounds like a nasty sort of rascal to me," he grinned.

Angeline slapped him on the arm, "It's no laughing matter, Jonathan. We must be extra cautious now. I am starting to fear they may become more aggressive in their pursuit."

"More aggressive?" Evelyn asked, "What do you mean?"

"Well, up to now, they've been *reactive*, waiting for us to make a move, and then trying to catch us while we're doing it. I've been thinking about that, and it has occurred to me they may start taking action on their own, such as dangling tempting bait of some sort, setting traps for our people, and so on. I ... don't know of anything specific, but ... I think we should start being extra watchful."

But Jonathan smiled, and patted her on the shoulder, "Sometimes you worry too much, dear. And ... I think you give Major White and his cronies too much credit. We've outmaneuvered them so far, and there's no reason to think we can't continue to do so indefinitely."

But Angeline seemed unconvinced, a worried look upon her face, "I sure hope so, Jonathan ... I sure do hope so."

ᔐᄋᏜᏻᏰᏜᔐᄋᏜᏻᏰᏜᔐᄋᏜᏻᏰᏜ

Thursday May 19, 1864 – Strasburg, Virginia:

Nathan and Tom started the day visiting the hospital, which was thankfully no longer just an oversized tent pitched in a field. Now that the army was camped just outside the town of Strasburg, the hospital had been established inside a small warehouse in town.

They began by visiting all the wounded enlisted men of the Twelfth, surprisingly few considering the intensity of the battle toward the end. Tom guessed they actually had Sigel to thank for that, keeping the Twelfth in reserve for most of the battle, though he'd not done it for any altruistic purpose.

They moved into a smaller room reserved for officers, and there they found Stan. And, of course, Harry laying on a mat on the floor next to him. The dog's tail thumped against the floor in greeting, but he didn't attempt to rise. Billy also sat on the floor, cross-legged, next to the dog. He looked up, but said nothing, only smiled and nodded as Nathan and Tom approached.

When Stan saw them, he started to sit up, but winced with pain, a thing Tom had never seen him do before, regardless of how badly he'd been injured.

"At ease, soldier," Nathan held out a hand and gave Stan a severe look, "...that's an order. You'll stay flat on your back until William says different."

Stan lay back with a grunt, gave a quick grin, and nodded, "Yes, Colonel."

Tom slowly shook his head. *Never thought I'd see Stan like this.*

They next visited Jim. He greeted them with good cheer, despite having lost his right foot, "I wasn't going to let them surgeons take it off ... pulled out my sidearm and threatened to shoot 'em if they tried it. Then William showed up, took a look and said, 'Jim, it's got to come off.' So, I holstered my pistol, and told him, 'As long as *you* do it, William, it'll be okay.'"

Though he spoke to his men in a kindly tone, Tom noticed that Nathan never smiled the entire visit, despite Jim and Stan's best efforts to inject levity into the situation. When Tom thought about it, he'd not seen Nathan smile at all since well before the battle. *Understandable after what happened, but ... not good.*

As they turned to leave, Harry lifted himself heavily off the mat next to Stan, intending to follow. Clearly the dog was in even greater pain than the men. Nathan leaned down toward him, pointed a finger at his nose, and commanded, "Lay down, Harry ... and stay!" Harry immediately obeyed, flopping back down with a whine.

"Don't be worrying, Colonel," Stan smiled, "Harry and I will be watching over each other. And Major Wiggins."

Nathan looked at him and nodded, but said nothing, just turned and walked out the door.

Outside they found William sitting in a chair, absorbing the morning sun. He rose from his feet when Nathan and Tom approached, "Morning, sirs."

"Morning, William," Nathan answered, and Tom did likewise.

But then Nathan and William stood gazing at each other for a long moment, not speaking. Tom was perplexed, looking from one to the other … It seemed to him as if something were being said without any words.

Finally, Nathan broke the silence, "It's good to have you back, William."

William continued to gaze at Nathan without speaking, then removed his glasses, wiped his eyes, and smiled, "She's going to be all right, sir; Margaret has recovered. I was walking down the street in Washington when a gentleman stopped me and asked if I was Captain William Jenkins of the Twelfth West Virginia. When I said yes, he handed me a telegram, then tipped his hat and strode away without another word."

William reached out and handed a folded slip of paper to Nathan.

Nathan read:

William,

I am well and send all my love. Remember our deal. - M.

Nathan handed the note to Tom, then stepped forward, patted William on the shoulder, turned, and strode away.

Tom read the note, then handed it back to William with a smile. Then he followed after Nathan.

Despite the good news about Margaret, as the morning wore on, Nathan's mood only darkened, to the point he told Tom he wished to have no visitors. After that, he sat in his command tent, smoking one cigar after another without pause, a dark look in his eyes.

Tom was becoming more concerned with every moment, sitting across the table from Nathan, pretending to do paperwork. At home, in such a mood Nathan would be deep into the whiskey by now. But Nathan never drank on duty, even in such a foul humor. Tom wasn't sure if that was good or bad. *Maybe the whiskey might dull some of the anger and pain he's feeling.* But he knew he dared not suggest such a thing.

For the first several minutes Tom tried to engage Nathan in conversation, attempting to draw him out of his dark reverie. But his snappish, one-word responses made it clear he had no desire to converse. So Tom left him to his dark thoughts, and prayed this too would pass without ... *what? What is he contemplating?*

Tom felt a knot of fear forming in his chest. He had seen Nathan this justifiably upset in the past and knew his righteous wrath could become uncontrollable. He'd witnessed Nathan commit murder under such circumstances—on more than one occasion.

An hour went by, and then another. If anything, Nathan's humor worsened to the point where he no longer looked up and seemed to be breathing heavily.

Finally, Tom could take it no more, "What are you thinking, sir?"

"Thinking? Thinking..." he was quiet for a long moment so that Tom thought he had either decided not to answer or had forgotten there'd been a question. But then he spat the stub of his cigar onto the ground, stomped it out, and looked back up at Tom, "I'm thinking ... there needs to be a reckoning. A *hard* reckoning. I'm going to kill him..."

Nathan stood, stepped over to the side of the tent where his hat and gun belt hung on a hook. He grabbed the hat, slammed it onto his head, then reached for the gun belt. He started to lift the pistol, then seemed to think better of it, replacing it on its hook, to Tom's relief.

But then Nathan turned, stepped over to the small trunk next to his cot, and reached inside. He pulled out a belt that held his great Bowie knife in a sheath. He stood and strapped the belt around his waist, with the knife sheath hanging down in back.

He turned toward the door, but Tom jumped in front of him, holding up his hands, "Where are you going?"

"To Sigel's headquarters ... His arrogance and pettiness killed Jamie and Georgie. And nearly killed Jim, Stan, and Harry. I'm going to *kill* him, Tom!"

"No, sir! *No!* Don't do it! He's not worth it. Don't throw away your life for him!"

"I no longer care, Tom. What kind of man would I be if I didn't answer this crime? He killed my friends—I'd rather be dead than sit here and do nothing."

"No ... *Nathan* ... I can't let you do this!" Tom grabbed the front of Nathan's tunic with both hands and planted his feet.

"Get out of my way, Tom..." Nathan growled, a deadly look on his face.

"No, sir. I won't."

Nathan grabbed Tom's wrists and tried to pry them free, but he stubbornly resisted. They grappled for a moment, then Nathan's right fist lashed out and caught Tom square in the face, knocking him backward. He tripped over a chair and fell hard on his back on the ground.

Nathan stood over him, still scowling, "Don't get up ... and don't try to stop me."

He turned and left the tent.

Tom rubbed at his sore face. The room seemed to be spinning, and he didn't trust himself to stand. He felt like he was going to vomit.

ℰᴑᏣᏒᏣᏸ℔ᏒᏣᏸᏒ℩ᏸᏒ℩Ꮳ℩Ꮳ

Nathan rode Millie at a full gallop the two miles from the field where the Twelfth was camped to the grand manor house, called Belle Grove, where Sigel had made his headquarters.

He pulled up at the hitching post outside the house, and a soldier trotted over to take the horse, saluting as he did so. But for once, Nathan neither looked at the soldier, nor acknowledged his salute.

He leapt up the stairs to the porch of the grand house, and passed in the front door to the foyer, ignoring the salutes from other soldiers standing there, "Where's the general's office?"

"Second room on the left, sir," one of the soldiers answered, still holding a salute.

Nathan strode down the hall, approaching the door to the second room. But the door was closed, and a sergeant stood outside it holding a rifle at his side. When he saw Nathan approaching, he came to attention, saluted, and said, "Sorry, sir. The general has given strict orders not to be disturbed."

Nathan stopped and glared at the soldier, "Open the door, Sergeant. That's an order."

"Sorry, sir. With all due respect, General's orders outrank yours, sir. And he's said he's not to be disturbed."

"Well, he's going to be disturbed, whether he likes it or not," Nathan growled.

The sergeant seemed to finally understand that he was not dealing with a man who was going to listen to reason. He dropped the salute and lifted the rifle, now holding it across his chest in a more defensive posture. "Sorry, sir, I—"

Nathan reached out, grabbed the rifle with both hands, and shoved. The sergeant slammed back against the door, losing his balance and stumbling to the floor, no longer holding the rifle.

Nathan half-cocked the hammer, reached down and pulled off the percussion cap, then tossed the gun down the hall, where it fell with a great clatter on the hardwood floor.

He stepped over the prone sergeant, opened the office door, then stepped inside, slamming the door behind him.

Major General Franz Sigel sat behind a great oak desk, fancifully carved. He looked up at Nathan, and though he appeared startled, he showed neither anger nor fear. And he had an odd watery look to his eyes as if he'd been crying.

Nathan stepped up to the desk, "Your petty, stubborn pride and arrogance have cost me two of my dearest friends. Men who've survived battles that would've frozen the heart of a coward like you. Now they've died in a battle we should've won with ease if you would've just taken the reasonable advice of those who knew what they were doing."

Sigel just sat where he was, gazing up at Nathan, a blank expression on his face.

Nathan reached behind his back and drew out the great Bowie knife from its sheath, holding it out in front of him. "It's time for a reckoning … time for atonement … Now, I'm going to kill you."

But Sigel simply shrugged, "Go ahead … you will be doing me a favor. I wish to God I had been killed in the battle, instead of all those good men."

"I wish you had too," Nathan growled.

But Sigel picked up a piece of paper from his desk and flipped it across the desk at Nathan.

"Go ahead, Chambers … finish the business; I am shamed, my career is ruined, and my reputation is destroyed. I am dead already…" he waved his hand at the folded sheet of paper.

Nathan snatched the paper off the desk and read the telegram it contained:

> *Washington, DC*
> *May 19, 1864*
>
> *Major Gen. Franz Sigel*
> *Strasburg, Va.:*
>
> *General, you are hereby relieved of command of the Department of Western Virginia and the Army of the Shenandoah, effective this date. Major General David Hunter will arrive tomorrow to take command of the army. You are to report to the War Department in Washington at the earliest possible date to receive your new orders.*
>
> *U.S. Grant,*
> *Lt. General*
> *Commanding, Union Armies*

Sigel put his head in his hands, "Go ahead Chambers … finish it."

Nathan glared at him for a long moment, then shouted, "*Augh!*" raised the great knife high in the air above his head, and brought it down with all his strength.

Major General Franz Sigel looked up with a start. The heavy blade stood embedded several inches into the desktop, pinning the telegram to its surface.

Nathan pivoted and walked from the office. He stepped out into the hallway, his anger now spent. He saw that several soldiers had gathered near the general's office door, likely drawn by the commotion. The sergeant he'd knocked down took a quick look into Sigel's office, then looked back up at Nathan cautiously.

Nathan stepped up in front of him, "Sergeant, I owe you an apology. My behavior was inappropriate and unacceptable. If you should choose to bring me up on charges, I will neither fight it, nor deny it."

The sergeant looked him in the eye, nodded, and said, "Colonel … I have no idea what you're talking about, sir. My Momma always said I was clumsy; like the Lord gave me two left feet, she used to say. Seems I … stumbled and fell just now, dropping my rifle in the process. But … no harm done, seems to me. Sir!" The sergeant clicked his heels together and snapped a salute.

Nathan returned the salute as he continued to look the sergeant in the eye. He nodded, "Thank you, Sergeant. You're a good man."

ॐक्षॐक्षॐक्षॐक्ष

Nathan pulled back the tent flap and stepped inside. Tom was seated at the table, a haunted expression on his face. He slowly rose from his seat as Nathan entered, "Did you…"

"No," Nathan shook his head and sighed. "In the end, I just couldn't do it."

"*Oh, thank God!*" Tom placed his hand over his heart, and for a moment closed his eyes.

Nathan waited for Tom to look back up again, "But thankfully, Sigel will no longer be our concern. Grant has sacked him. General Hunter arrives tomorrow to take command of the department."

Tom nodded but said nothing. Then the two locked eyes for a long moment.

"Tom … firstly, before I apologize to you in the humblest and most repentant manner I can muster … would you please do me the great favor of punching me, as hard as you can, square in the face?"

459

"*What?!*" Tom stared open-mouthed for a moment, before shaking his head. "Oh … no … I don't think I could do *that,* sir."

"*Please,* Tom. It would help to alleviate a good deal of the guilt I'm presently feeling for striking you earlier. As I said, you would be doing me a great favor … *truly.*"

Tom continued to gaze at Nathan, and then looked down at his feet, as if struggling with indecision. He looked back up, sighed, then lashed out with his right fist, catching Nathan hard under his right eye.

Nathan staggered back a step, and doubled over with his hands on his knees and his eyes closed.

Tom slowly massaged the knuckles of his right hand as he gazed down at Nathan.

Then Nathan stood, rubbing the side of his face with his hand, a wan smile on his lips, "*Damn,* Tom … where'd you learn to hit like that?"

Tom grinned, "*You* taught me, sir…"

Nathan nodded, "Another one of my bad decisions, apparently."

Tom snorted a short chuckle.

Nathan then stepped up to Tom, his face again holding a serious expression, "Tom … words can't adequately express how sorry I feel for hitting you earlier, but mostly … for ignoring your good counsel. I … I let the rage consume me. I was willing to give up everything I hold dear … you, Momma, even Evelyn … just to fulfill the bloodlust. For that I am deeply ashamed, and sorry. I humbly beg your forgiveness, though likely I don't deserve it."

"Please, sir … never mention it again. It is already forgiven, and forgotten."

Nathan nodded, "Thank you for that, Tom. Now I feel like I can breathe again. But there's one more thing I would ask of you…"

"Yes?"

"Riding back here just now, I came to a decision … I no longer wish to be your commanding officer."

"You … *what?* I … don't understand, sir … You want me to leave?"

460

"No, no … not *that! Heavens* no … I'm not talking about from the *military's* perspective. What I mean is … it suddenly struck me that we've long since moved on from the days when you were just my aide de camp.

"Tom, you've become by far the best friend I've ever had in life. The most loyal, trustworthy, intelligent … someone I lean on for advice and for strength … someone I admire.

"I can't imagine not having you around. I feel unworthy — especially considering everything that's just happened — to be giving you orders, as if you were some sort of servant. The very idea of that now seems so … presumptuous, so … *ridiculous,* even."

Tom said nothing, just continued to stare into Nathan's eyes. But Nathan thought he detected a wateriness there.

"Tom, you would be doing me a great honor if from now on you would *only* address me by my given name when we are alone, and whenever military protocol doesn't demand otherwise … no longer address me as 'colonel,' or 'sir.'"

Tom gazed at him another moment, then grinned, "All right, I can do that … *Nathan.*"

Nathan smiled, and reached out to pat Tom on the shoulder, "Thank you for that." He stepped over and sat down heavily in a chair next to where Tom had been sitting. Tom sat next to him.

They were silent for a long moment, then Nathan looked over again, "Tom … I find I no longer care about my 'destiny,' of being the hero … of leading the armies that ultimately win the war. My pride has caused the death of men I truly cared about … truly *loved.*"

"Oh, that's not true, sir … uh … *Nathan.* If Sigel hadn't — "

"Sigel has the excuse of being an arrogant fool, of not fully understanding the consequences of his actions until it was too late. What's my excuse? I knew full well that placing my men where I did, tasking them with holding back an overwhelming force of the enemy would put them at great risk, would likely cost lives. Yet I did it anyway … my pride wouldn't allow me to admit I might fail, that things might go very badly. That I might … *lose…*"

461

Tom nodded, but could think of nothing to say.

Nathan slowly shook his head, "Tom, I feel more tired than I can ever recall … All I want now is for this war to be over so I can marry Evelyn, reclaim my family home in the West Virginia hills, and start raising a whole troop of ornery children. With you and Addie there as well, I hope!" He reached over and patted Tom on the knee.

"That sounds about as good as anything I can imagine, Nathan. It surely does. But … the war's not over. What now?"

Nathan turned and once again gave Tom a serious look, "Now … we must *finish* this thing."

∞⊙◈⊙∞⊙◈⊙∞⊙◈⊙∞

Wednesday May 25, 1864 – Strasburg, Virginia:

Tom poked his head in at the tent flap, "Nathan … it's *the general…*"

"*Oh!* All right, I'm coming…" Nathan stood and began buttoning up his tunic as he stepped over and grabbed his hat off the hook at the side of the tent. He held a lit cigar in his mouth, and debated stubbing it out on the floor. But he'd just lit it and didn't wish to waste it or ruin the taste with dirt. So he decided to just hold it still lit in his left hand; after all, the general had not given any warning of his first visit since taking command, so one couldn't expect perfect decorum.

Nathan pushed back the tent flap and stepped outside. Major General David Hunter sat upon his horse, a shiny, dark, picturesque Morgan, a dozen yards away. Four staff officers accompanied the general, but discreetly held back a few dozen yards to allow their commander to converse with his subordinate in private. Tom also stayed back by the command tent.

General Hunter's dark hair and mustache, and his trim, fit appearance belied his sixty years of age. And his stern visage marked him as a man not to be trifled with.

Nathan approached to within ten feet, then stopped and saluted. The general returned the salute smartly.

462

"General, welcome to the Army of the Shenandoah, sir, and to the camp of the Twelfth West Virginia."

"Thank you, Colonel. Please ... be at your ease. And ... do just go ahead and smoke that cigar you're holding, if you wish. It'd be a shame to waste it."

"Yes, sir. Thank you, sir," Nathan stuck the cigar back in his mouth and took a puff. "May I offer you one, sir? They are quite good. *Virginian*. We *liberated* them from an enemy officer, a fellow Virginian whom we captured down in the valley a few weeks back."

"Thank you, but no. Perhaps another time. Colonel, is your regiment ready to march?"

"Yes, sir. Though we suffered casualties at New Market, those of us who survived it were not overly taxed. And we have already re-equipped and re-supplied, so we are ready to fight at a moment's notice. When did you intend to march, sir?"

"Tomorrow, first light, if all the other regiments are as prepared as you are, Colonel."

"Very good, sir. We'll be ready. And may I ask, sir, the objective of the new campaign?"

Hunter nodded, then grinned, a wicked looking leer, "To paraphrase Genghis Khan, Colonel, our goal shall be, 'To vanquish our enemies, to drive them from the field, and to deprive them of their treasure. Afterward ... we shall savor the weeping of their women.'"

Nathan thought for a moment, then grinned, and nodded, "That works for me, General. I believe we see eye to eye on the matter."

Hunter snorted a laugh. "Good to hear. And to answer your question more specifically; I mean to drive the slavers completely out of western Virginia, and then take the battle to the east toward Richmond. That should serve to take pressure off General Grant and the Army of the Potomac, and make their southward march against Richmond more viable as we press the enemy from the west.

"Chambers, unless you hear otherwise, we march at sunup. And, I have just decided that the Twelfth West Virginia shall have the honor of being in the van."

"Very good, sir. Thank you, sir."

"Good day, Colonel," the general saluted, and Nathan returned it.

Hunter turned his horse, but had only gone a step when he paused and pivoted back toward Nathan. "Oh ... Chambers ... I nearly forgot." He reached behind his back and pulled out something metallic that flashed in the sunlight. He flipped it to the ground in front of Nathan, where it stuck in the grass.

Nathan glanced down and immediately recognized his own Bowie knife, last seen embedded in General Sigel's oak desk back at the manor house which served as the army's headquarters.

"Thought you might want that back, though it did make an interesting ornament on my desk," Hunter grinned. "And in future I would suggest you reserve its use for those wearing gray."

Nathan returned the grin and nodded, "Seems like sage advice, General. I believe I would be well served to heed it."

Hunter chuckled, then tipped his hat, once again turned the horse's reins and trotted off.

Tom held an amused look as Nathan bent down to retrieve the knife.

Nathan stood and gazed at the departing general, "Yes ... I do believe we'll get along *just* fine, General..."

<Enꝺ ᴏꜰ Bᴏᴏᴋ 8>

If you enjoyed *War*
please post a review
and enjoy Nathan Chambers'
continuing adventures in
Inferno.

War — Facts vs. Fiction

I get asked all the time whether this or that person or event in one of my books was factual, or invented for dramatic effect. This volume, like the others in the series, contains a good number of interesting historical facts and circumstances that may, at first, seem made up. I thought you might enjoy the following enumeration and explanation of these details. – *Chris Bennett*

First Kansas Colored Regiment battles – This regiment participated in a number of firsts during the Civil War, despite other regiments—such as the Fifty-Fourth Massachusetts, depicted in the excellent movie *Glory*—getting much more publicity: first colored regiment to be organized, first to fight in a battle (and first to win one!), first to fight alongside Union white soldiers, and first to fight in a battle where white men were in the minority on both sides. The battles depicted in this book were real, and played out very much as described:

- **Battle of Rader's Farm** – on a foraging mission, several companies of the First Kansas were ambushed by local rebel militia led by a Confederate Major. Fifteen black soldiers who were surrounded inside the Rader farmhouse eventually ran out of ammunition, surrendered, and were brutally massacred by the Confederates. First Kansas commanding officer, Colonel James Williams, a white man, ordered the nearby town of Sherwood burned to the ground in retaliation. The name "Sherwood" was stitched into the regimental flag to honor the fallen.
- **Battle of Cabin Creek** – Colonel Williams led a Union brigade on a relief mission bringing desperately needed supplies to Union troops in Indian Territory. Rebels tried to intercept the wagon train, but were defeated in a battle at the creek crossing.
- **Battle of Honey Springs** – another fight out in Indian Territory, this was the first (and likely only) battle of the war in which white soldiers were in the minority

on both sides, due to the presence of the First Kansas, and regiments from the Civilized Indian Tribes fighting on both sides.

- **Battle of Poison Spring** – Colonel Williams and the First Kansas were once again called upon for a relief mission to acquire desperately needed food for the Union army on campaign in Arkansas. Their wagon train was cutoff and surrounded by a much larger confederate force. After a desperate firefight most of the Union soldiers retreated into a nearby swamp, but of those who were cutoff and forced to surrender, the Confederates murdered all of the black men. The First Kansas suffered nearly fifty percent casualties in the engagement.

- **Battle of Jenkins' Ferry** – as the Union Army retreated from Arkansas, the First Kansas and other colored regiments were part of a rear-guard action to buy time for the army to cross the Saline River. During that battle, black soldiers captured a battery of Confederate artillerymen, but took no prisoners in retaliation for what had recently happened at Poison Spring. It is not clear, however, if the First Kansas was actually involved in the retaliation, or if this was done by another colored regiment. This specific act of retaliation is described by black troopers speaking to President Lincoln in the recent movie *Lincoln*, starring Daniel Day-Lewis.

Following the Battle of Honey Springs in Indian Territory (now Oklahoma), on July 17, 1863, Union Major General James G. Blunt, commanding, in his official report stated:

> *The First Kansas (colored) particularly distinguished itself; they fought like veterans, and preserved their line unbroken throughout the engagement. Their coolness and bravery I have never seen surpassed; they were in the hottest of the fight, and opposed to Texas troops twice their*

number, whom they completely routed. One Texas regiment (the Twentieth Cavalry) that fought against them went into the fight with 300 men and came out with only sixty.

Second Battle of Winchester – this is generally considered to be the opening engagement in Lee's Gettysburg campaign. Lee thought it vital to secure control of the Shenandoah Valley to protect his line of supply as he marched north, and the 7,000-man garrison at Winchester represented a potential threat he was not willing to leave in place. So, Lee dispatched the 25,000-man corps of General Richard Ewell to eliminate the thorn in his side, which Ewell did, as described in this book. Union General Milroy's actions are still controversial, as there is disagreement whether his stubborn defense of Winchester delayed Lee's northward advance, allowing the Army of the Potomac to cut him off at Gettysburg, or whether it was just foolhardy and he should have simply retreated to a more defensible position, such as Harpers Ferry, from which he could have threatened Lee's flank.

Colonel Joseph Warren Keifer, Commander 110th Ohio Volunteer Infantry Regiment at the Battle of Winchester – Keifer was a real-life American hero who impressed more than just Nathan Chambers and General Milroy with his extreme courage, unwavering competence under fire, and personal moral fortitude. Throughout the war, he showed his abilities by steadily advancing in rank, despite being seriously wounded in the Battle of the Wilderness, ending the war as a major general. After the war, he was elected to the U.S. House of Representatives from Ohio, and served a stint as Speaker of the House, the first ever from Ohio. During his time in Congress, he introduced a bill calling for reduced representation in Southern states as punishment for disenfranchising black voters. He also advocated posting federal troops at the polls during federal elections to protect black voters. During the Spanish–American War, President William McKinley appointed Keifer major general of volunteers on June 9, 1898. He commanded the Seventh Army Corps and the American forces that marched into Havana after Spanish forces withdrew on January 1, 1899. Keifer then returned to congress and served until 1911. He died in 1932 at the age of ninety-six.

Lieutenant James Durham's charge – James R. Durham, commanding Company E, Twelfth West Virginia Volunteer Infantry Regiment, lead a bayonet charge against the enemy during the Second Battle of Winchester, driving the enemy from their position and resulting in a serious wound to his arm—as described in chapter 3 of this book. For his actions, Durham received the nation's highest honor, the Congressional Medal of Honor, with the citation: *"The President of the United States of America, in the name of Congress, takes pleasure in presenting the Medal of Honor to Second Lieutenant James R. Durham, United States Army, for extraordinary heroism on 14 June 1863, while serving with Company E, 12th West Virginia Infantry, in action at Winchester, Virginia. Second Lieutenant Durham led his command over the stone wall, where he was wounded."*

C.S.A. Lieutenant Charles Contee's heroic defense of the bridge – as described in the book, the young lieutenant, in charge of a brace of artillery guns, was charged by Lieutenant Colonel Snowden Andrews with holding a bridge to prevent Union forces under Major General Milroy from breaking out of the siege of Winchester. Contee was commanded to fight to the last man, which he did, suffering a horrific leg wound in the process, but ultimately surviving the battle.

Twelfth West Virginia's encounter with the mysterious girl on the mountain – in his biographical account of the regiment's actions (see recommended reading below), William Hewitt describes a meeting with an unnamed young girl at the top of a mountain pass as the regiment attempted to extricate itself from the defeat at Winchester. The girl guided them to a safe path down from the mountain that would avoid rebels known to be operating in the area. Union troops did reward her with cash and other items of value in thanks for her timely assistance, as depicted in this book.

The Hodgepodge Brigade – as depicted in this book, this was an actual—though, unofficial—unit that was formed by various parts and pieces of Union formations that survived the breakout from Winchester. They banded together for mutual strength and support, which allowed them to eventually fight their way out to safety in the North. And the soldiers in the new formation did dub themselves the "Hodgepodge Brigade."

The formation was led by Colonel James Washburn (116th Ohio) in overall command (in this book I have depicted him as second in command under Nathan Chambers.) Major Alonzo Adams (First New York Cavalry) was in command of cavalry (as depicted in this book.) The makeup of the brigade was officially recorded as:

- 80 troopers – Thirteenth Pennsylvania Cavalry
- 275 troopers – Twelfth Pennsylvania Cavalry
- 8 officers, 350 men – First New York Cavalry
- 50 men – First West Virginia Light Artillery (a.k.a. Captain Carlin's Wheeling Battery)
- 650 officers and men – Twelfth West Virginia
- 500 officers and men – 116th Ohio
- 80 officers and men – 123rd Ohio (with 35 rebel POWs)
- 30 officers and men – engineering detachment
- A few men – Eighty-Seventh Pennsylvania
- 200 teamsters
- 100 civilian evacuees

Arthur Boreman, First Governor of West Virginia – took office on June 20, 1863, and gave a rousing inaugural address that seemed to speak not only for the citizens of the new state, but for all the states that continued to support the Union. The speech is reprinted in its entirety below; it's a great read.

Union Major General Winfield Scott Hancock and **Confederate Brigadier General Lewis Armistead** – the two opposing generals were in fact best friends before the war, and had the unfortunate circumstance of directly opposing each other during Pickett's Charge at the Battle of Gettysburg. Hancock was severely wounded, while his best friend Armistead was mortally wounded shortly after breaching the Union lines, in what is now commonly referred to as the "high water mark of the Confederacy." In reality, Armistead did not immediately die of his wounds, but succumbed two days later in a Union hospital.

Twenty-Third Colored Regiment – One of many units formed of freemen and escaped slaves, the Twenty-Third was the first colored regiment to fight against General Lee's Army of Northern Virginia (and they won!), as depicted in this book. They, like all colored units, faced disparity in pay and deployments at the beginning of the war, when it was generally assumed by the army that their main purpose would be in a support role. That attitude quickly changed, however, as they consistently proved themselves in battle.

Assistant Surgeon Isaac Watson Brown – he was enlisted in the Twenty-Second Illinois Volunteer Infantry Regiment in June 1861 at Belleville, Illinois. He happens to be the author's great, great grandfather (the father of my great grandmother Grace Brown Ritchie, on my father's mother's side) and first of a long line of doctors in the family, which included my father, Craig A. Bennett, MD. Though I could find no record of Isaac being in Libby Prison (which is to be expected, given the shoddy state of the prison's management), family legend says that he was taken prisoner when he volunteered to stay behind with the wounded when the regiment's position was overrun by the enemy. So, if the story is true, it's likely he would've been sent there, and I'd like to think he would've aided William and Zeke in their hour of need as described in this book.

Chief Hospital Matron Phoebe Yates Pember – she is another relative of the author, this time by marriage, having married Thomas Pember in Boston in 1856 (my mother, Marilyn Bennett's maiden name is Pember). Thomas died shortly before the war, which led to Phoebe's involvement with the hospital, having nursed her husband during his long illness. On December 1, 1862, thirty-nine-year-old Phoebe became the chief matron of the Second Division at Chimborazo Military Hospital, outside Richmond, considered to be the largest in the world at that time. Phoebe supervised 150 wards, and an estimated 15,000 soldiers were under her care during the Civil War.

Libby Prison and the Great Escape – On February 9, 1864, 109 Union officers escaped from Libby Prison in Richmond via a fifty-foot tunnel they'd dug, exactly as described in this book, making it the largest wartime escape in U.S. military history. Even the southern newspapers were impressed with the ingenuity of the Union soldiers. Colonel Thomas Ellwood Rose (Seventy-Seventh Pennsylvania Infantry), and Major A.G. Hamilton (Twelfth Kentucky Cavalry) were the masterminds of the escape, with Rose particularly distinguishing himself with his relentlessness and steely courage throughout. Unfortunately, only fifty-nine of the escapees made it safely back to Union lines: two died in the attempt (from drowning), and the remainder were recaptured, including Colonel Rose who was caught by a Confederate patrol within a hundred yards of safety. Though he was mercilessly thrown into the "dungeon" for thirty-eight days as punishment for leading the escape effort, Rose survived and was eventually exchanged, finishing the war as a brigadier general.

The epic escape odyssey of William, Zeke, and Ollie from Richmond to the Potomac, as depicted herein, is based on the actual experience of one of the most noteworthy of the escapees, Colonel Abel Streight of the Fifty-First Indiana and several of his companions. Streight was especially hated by the Confederates as they accused him of attempting to stir up a slave revolt within Confederate lines. Streight was nonchalant concerning the enemy's particular venom toward him; when asked after his escape if he'd attempted to incite a slave uprising in the South, he answered, "I did not, but would have had no objection."

Battle of New Market – the battle happened almost exactly as described, including General Sigel's bungling of the action by bringing up his superior Union force in piecemeal fashion, giving the outnumbered Confederates under General Breckinridge the ability to gain the upper hand. If you read most accounts of the battle, you will notice the cadets from the Virginia Military Institute (VMI) are featured prominently for their unexpected heroics (and their youth). In fact, for years after the battle that was about the only thing that was mentioned about the engagement in most accounts. I chose not to highlight the VMI cadets because from Nathan's perspective, they were just another Confederate formation and nothing of particular note. He wouldn't have even known they were there at the time and only would've learned about it after the fact from newspaper accounts. The main deviation from the historical facts was my placing the Twelfth West Virginia in harm's way to cover the retreat. Though they were in the reserve position as described, and General Sigel did show up during the retreat and shout unintelligible orders to them in German, Captain DuPont and his battery served as the major factor preventing a rout of Sigel's command. The Twelfth in reality suffered relatively few casualties in the battle. So, a little fiction interjected there on my part for dramatic effect.

Inaugural Address – First Governor of West Virginia

June 20, 1863, by Arthur I. Boreman - Wheeling, West Virginia

Fellow Citizens:

To be permitted to participate in the most humble capacity in the organization of the State of West Virginia would be an honor; but, to be called by the unanimous voice of her people to accept the highest office in their gift, and to the performance of its duties, at a time of so much difficulty and danger as the present, excites in my heart the profoundest gratitude toward them for the confidence thus reposed in me. And if I shall be permitted to live, I hope in after years to recur to the ceremonies of this day with pride and pleasure, not only for the part that I have taken in them, but as celebrating the most auspicious event in the history of this people.

Yet, I trust, that, in taking upon myself the solemn obligation which I am about to do, I am not unaware of the great responsibility that it imposes on me. In time of peace, and under the most favorable circumstances, the organization of a new State and its introduction into the family of the Union, is a matter of no ordinary moment; but, when fierce civil war rages all around us and in our very midst, one whose experience is as limited as that of him who now addresses you, may well claim, in advance, the indulgence of a generous constituency.

West Virginia should long since have had a separate State existence. The East has always looked upon that portion of the State west of the mountains, as a sort of outside appendage - a territory in a state of pupilage. The unfairness and inequality of legislation is manifest on every page of the statute book; they had an unjust majority in the Legislature by the original Constitution of the State, and have clung to it with the utmost tenacity ever since; they have collected heavy taxes from us, and have spent large sums in the construction of railroads and canals in the East, but have withheld appropriations from the West; they have refused to make any of the modern improvements by which trade and travel could be carried on from the one section to the other, thus treating us as strangers; our people could not get to the Capital of their State by any of the usual modes of traveling, without going through the State of Maryland and the District of Columbia. The East and the West have always been two peoples. There has been little intercourse between them, either social or commercial. Our people seldom visit the East for pleasure. The farmers do not take their stock, grain, wool and other agricultural products there to sell; the merchants do not go there to sell or buy; the manufacturers have no market there; indeed, we have had nothing to do with the Eastern people, except that our Senators and Delegates have gone to Richmond to sit in the Legislature and our Sheriffs have gone there to pay in the revenue as an annual tribute from this section of the State for the inequality and unfairness with which we have always been treated by them. Our markets, our trade and our travel are North and West of Virginia, through natural channels, or those constructed through the enterprise of our own people, or such means as they could procure. The mountains intervene between us, the rivers rise in the mountains and run towards the Northwest; and, as if to make the separation more complete, Eastern Virginia adopted the fatal doctrine of secession, while the West spurned and rejected it as false and dangerous in the extreme. Thus nature, our commerce, travel, habits, associations, and interests, all - all say that West Virginia should be severed from the East. And now, to-day after many long and weary years of insult and injustice, culminating on the part of the East, in an attempt to destroy the Government, we have the proud satisfaction of proclaiming to those around us that we are a separate State in the Union.

Our State is the child of the rebellion; yet our peace, prosperity and happiness, and, not only ours, but that of the whole country, depends on the speedy suppression of this attempt to overthrow the Government of our fathers; and it is my duty, as soon as these ceremonies are closed, to proceed at once to aid the Federal authorities in their efforts to stay its destructive hand. I do not intend to insult your loyalty or intelligence by discussing before you to-day the dogma of secession. Its bitter fruits are to be seen all around us. It is like the poisonous Upas tree that blights and withers everything that comes within its influence. We have seen and felt enough of it to know that it is fraught with evil, and that continually. The politicians of many of the Southern States, having an inordinate desire for place and power, and it becoming apparent that the great North-West was improving and increasing in population so rapidly that the controlling influence of the Government was soon surely to be with the free States, and that the South must surrender power which they had so long exerted to a majority of the people according to the principles of our Government, they became desperate, and determined if they could no longer control, they would destroy the Government. By fraud and falsehood, and by incendiary speeches, they influenced the public mind in the South and induced them to believe that they were suffering great injury from the General Government; that the rights of the South were not only disregarded, but trampled under foot; that Mr. Lincoln was a sectional President, and that his election was the crowning act of insult and injustice; that if they submitted to it they were reduced to a state of degradation worse than slavery itself; and, fearing that the people still had some reverence and respect for the constitution, they insidiously taught the faithless doctrine that peaceable secession was in consonance with the Constitution, and absolved them from all their obligations to support the Government. All this and much more of a like character they taught until they succeeded in prevailing on the authorities in many of the States to embrace their doctrine and attempt to carry it into execution, and thus they inaugurated a war of rebellion, and have prosecuted it for over two years with a zeal and energy worthy of a better cause. It has assumed fearful proportions, and it demands all the energies of the Government authorities and of the loyal people to defeat its ruinous purposes.

Under these circumstances what course should the loyal people of West Virginia pursue? But before I state what we should do, I will state that it seems to me that the position of our people in the beginning of the troubles, and their condition since, have not been understood by our friends around us. In the commencement of these difficulties we were part of a Southern State, whose convention passed an ordinance of secession, and this fact inclined many to sympathize with the South without reflecting whether it was right or wrong. We were situated between the South and the North, and in case of a collision it must necessarily result that ours would be contested territory; that if we adhered to the Union the South would deal with us much more severely than if we were a part of a Northern State, or of one that had not attempted to secede; and that we would be, what we have since been so truthfully called by many, the great "breakwater" between the North and those in rebellion in the South. All these matters were weighed and considered by us, but we determined, with a full belief of what would occur, and what has since occurred, that the Government was too good to be lost, and that the rights and immunities which we knew we were enjoying were too precious to be surrendered on the uncertainty of the results of experiments in the future. We thus took our position with our eyes open; knowing what civil war had been, and what it could only be again if once commenced; and we have not been deceived. Our State has been invaded by traitors in arms against the best government that a kind and beneficent God ever inspired man to make; they have applied the torch to public and private property; they have murdered our friends; they have robbed and plundered our people; our country is laid waste, and, to-day, gaunt hunger stares many families of helpless women and children in the face. This picture is not overdrawn. It is a simple statement of facts. Yet, notwithstanding all this, the Union men of West Virginia have not looked to the right or the left, but through all these difficulties and dangers they have stood by the Government. And I now repeat the question which I asked awhile ago: Under these circumstances what course should the loyal people of West Virginia now pursue? Shall we coincide with those who carp and cavil at everything that is done by the administration at Washington to put down this rebellion? Shall we object to the suspension of the habeas corpus and thereby attempt to prevent some traitor from receiving his just deserts? Shall we object that slavery is destroyed as the result of the acts of those in rebellion, if the Union is thereby saved? But there are those who say that we should stop the war and make peace. If we stop the war on our part will that make peace, unless we submit to be ruled by the rebels, or to a separation of the Union? If we could not

475

consent to give up our Government in the beginning and thus save ourselves the war, but determined to fight it out to the bitter end, shall we now submit to the humiliation and disgrace of permitting the success of the rebellion and the loss of our Government? In behalf of the loyal people of West Virginia I respond to all these interrogatories with an emphatic no - no - never! We want no compromise: we want no peace, except upon the terms that those in rebellion will lay down their arms and submit to the regularly constituted authorities of the Government of the United States. Then, and not till then, will the people of West Virginia agree to peace. We have done much and suffered much already, but we will do more, and suffer on for years, if need be, rather than consent to a dissolution of the Union, which would be nothing less than a surrender of the last hope of human liberty on the face of the earth.

Fellow-citizens, I now come to what is more particularly the purpose of this address: and that is, to state to you those rules of action by which I shall be governed during my term of office:

I shall co-operate with the Federal authorities in all those measures deemed necessary for the suppression of the rebellion. While the war continues I must necessarily be engaged in attending to military matters, and to the defence of the State, and it may not, therefore, be expected that I shall give much time at present to the internal civil policy of the State; but even amidst surrounding difficulties and dangers they shall not be entirely forgotten.

I shall do whatever may be in my power during my term of office to advance the agricultural, mining, manufacturing and commercial interests of the State. And it shall be my especial pride and pleasure to assist in the establishment of a system of education throughout the State that may give to every child among us, whether rich or poor, an education that may fit them for respectable positions in society. And to you gentlemen of the Senate and House of Delegates, I shall look for aid and assistance and for the exercise of a liberal policy in these times of trial; and I feel assured from your known intelligence and patriotism, that I shall receive your cordial co-operation and support in the discharge of the duties of my office.

Fellow-Citizens, we are about to part with him, who has for two years exercised the office of Governor of Virginia in our midst. And I here express how highly are appreciated, not only by myself, but by the whole loyal population of the State, his purity and fidelity, and the ability with which he has discharged the arduous and responsible duties of his office. We regret that he is to leave us, but we have the satisfaction of knowing that he is going to a new and important field where his ability and patriotism are still to be devoted to the good of his country.

If I shall only be able to discharge the duties of my office with as much satisfaction to the people and honor to myself as my predecessor, I shall expect *the approbation of a generous public. I shall, no doubt, often do wrong, this is the lot of man; and while I shall always do that which honesty of purpose and my opinion of the good of the country dictates, I shall expect you to exercise that indulgence which is due to a public officer under the surrounding circumstances.*

See the Ohio County, West Virginia Public Library website (https://www.ohiocountylibrary.org/history) for more historical information on the city of Wheeling, and the founding of the state of West Virginia.

Nathan Chambers and his men take the fight to the enemy. But their commanding general wages a new kind of war, ravaging the Virginia countryside in a scorched earth campaign that threatens to destroy the very country they are fighting to reunite. Don't miss Nathan's further adventures in:

INFERNO
ROAD TO THE BREAKING BOOK 9

Coming in late 2023.

Whenever a book of the size and complexity of *War: Road to the Breaking Book 8* is submitted for editing, changes are inevitable, including sometimes cutting entire scenes, even those the editor thinks are well written and interesting. This is done because the scene either doesn't advance the plot, doesn't help develop one or more characters, or slows down the overall pacing of the story.

Such was the case for the scene that became the short story I am making available as a free download to show my appreciation to my loyal readers. I hope you enjoy it:

SNOWBOUND
A ROAD TO THE BREAKING
SHORT STORY

To download your free copy of SNOWBOUND please use the web address below:

https://www.chrisabennett.com/snowbound

Acknowledgments

Special thanks as always to my editor, Ericka McIntyre, who keeps me honest and on track, and my proofreader and fellow Tolkien fanatic Travis Tynan, who makes sure everything is done correctly!

And, as always, I can't thank her enough for all she does for the Road to the Breaking team—our "head coach" and my most excellent partner in crime, Keri-Rae Barnum. *You are the best!*

Recommended Reading

For excellent nonfiction accounts of the events in this book, whose titles speak for themselves, please see:

- *History of the Twelfth West Virginia Volunteer Infantry: The Part It Took in the War of the Rebellion, 1861 – 1865,* by William Hewitt

- *Libby Prison Breakout: The Daring Escape from the Notorious Civil War Prison,* by Joseph Wheelan

- *The Second Battle of Winchester: The Confederate Victory that Opened the Door to Gettysburg,* by Eric J. Wittenberg and Scott L. Mingus, Sr.

- *Spies, Scouts, and Secrets in the Gettysburg Campaign: How the Critical Role of Intelligence Impacted the Outcome of Lee's Invasion of the North, June – July 1863,* by Thomas J. Ryan

GET EXCLUSIVE FREE CONTENT

The most enjoyable part of writing books is talking about them with readers like you. In my case that means all things related to *Road to the Breaking*—the story and characters, themes, and concepts. And of course, Civil War history in general, and West Virginia history in particular.

If you sign up for my mailing list, you'll receive some free bonus material I think you'll enjoy:

- A fully illustrated *Road to the Breaking* **Fact vs. Fiction Quiz.** Test your knowledge of history with this short quiz on the people, places, and things in the book (did they really exist in 1860, or are they purely fictional?)

- **Cut scenes from *Road to the Breaking*.** One of the hazards of writing a novel is word and page count. At some point you realize you need to trim it back to give the reader a faster-paced, more engaging experience. However, now you've finished reading the book, wouldn't you like to know a little more detail about some of your favorite characters? Here's your chance to take a peek behind the curtain!

- I'll occasionally put out a **newsletter with information about the Road to the Breaking series**—new book releases, news and information about the author, etc. I promise not to inundate you with spam (it's one of my personal pet peeves, so why would I propagate it?)

To sign up, visit my website:
http://www.ChrisABennett.com

ROAD TO THE BREAKING SERIES:

Road to the Breaking (Book 1)

Enigma (Road to the Breaking Book 2)

Sedition (Road to the Breaking Book 3)

Breakout (Road to the Breaking Book 4)

Insurrection (Road to the Breaking Book 5)

Invasion (Road to the Breaking Book 6)

Emancipation (Road to the Breaking Book 7)

War (Road to the Breaking Book 8)

Inferno (Road to the Breaking Book 9) – coming in 2023

Made in the USA
Coppell, TX
12 March 2024

30041375R00288